THE ENEMY WITHIN

SOVEREIGN STARS
BOOK 4

BLAIR C. HOWARD

Printed Cleveland, TN, USA
Library of Congress Control Number: 2023906498
ISBN: 979-8-9876042-5-0

PROLOGUE

WAIT NO LONGER

Orso Space
    Planet Caerus Exosphere
    Regis Magnum Shipyards
    Ninth Arm, Level Theta
    Research Division, Military (Classified)

"Marshal Hyde," Devin called as the needle spiked. "The temperature is approaching plasma levels. We should step it down."

"We're not backing down again," came the voice over the speakers. "We are on the cusp of redirecting this war, and I won't pussyfoot around while more people die."

Devin ignored the power readings for a moment and instead checked on the materials chamber readings. The distribution of the elements inside—silicon, osmium, carbon—had reached peak, and the plasmic lightning raining through the gaseous mixture would fuse them into unusable glass if they shut down too quickly. *And if we don't shut down,* he thought, *I don't know if the containment can hold.*

As he watched the incoming vid, the chamber walls began to deform. The last time this had happened, Director Crowe had cut the power to avoid a catastrophe, and she'd been reassigned immediately after.

This time, it looked as if Marshal Hyde would create a disaster.

Devin looked at the other techs in the room. Only three of them had been "trusted" enough to take this position. Now he knew why.

The power readings ticked higher. The chamber walls began to slough, and its color became so white it burned out the screen.

Which was why he didn't see when containment failed.

The heat of the sun's surface flashed through the control room. His last memory was just a white light.

Marshal Secerna Hyde screamed. She swept everything off her desk in a rage, and when that failed to assuage a fraction of her anger, she gripped the edge and flipped it over. The resounding crash and the extreme motions helped her to find some grip on calm.

"Those idiots. Those infected pus sacks of variolated excrement," she snarled in a calm and controlled manner. "How the effervescent fractures of *absolute preconcepted flatulence* am I supposed to do this when they keep sending me these salvaged carcasses."

She took a deep breath. *Studies have shown that expressing anger in a verbal manner offers more stress relief than withholding,* she remembered hearing. Alongside that came her mother's voice. *The use of gutter language is a sign of an uncreative and unintelligent mind.*

She hoped her mother was proud.

After stepping around the upended desk, she stormed out of her office. Situated two hundred meters away from the lab in question, she'd felt the explosion but not the heat. As the containment had failed, it likely had burned out the emitter contacts as well, cutting the destructive blast short.

She arrived on the scene to find the labs destroyed, walls burned through, eleven of her technicians dead and another two dozen injured. Station Medical had already scrambled from North Plate and were arriving even as she did. She wished, not for the first time, she could have her own dedicated medical corps on hand, sworn to secrecy about anything they might encounter. *But no one would want to be posted to a research lab that keeps exploding.* She wanted to complain to someone, but of course she didn't have anyone. And Sasha Crowe hadn't been nearly as much help as Hyde had hoped. Easy enough to just shift the woman—smart, capable and annoyingly principled—over to Project Vindication. At least there, her principles could complain about everything going wrong.

The explosion would initiate an investigation by the station architectural corps, but from a glance none of the damage was actually structural, only superficial. She made her way to the containment lab. She'd been assured by her suppliers on Caerus that the dutrinium for her test chamber was of the highest grade and would operate flawlessly.

Unable to contain her rage anymore, she punched up the contact for her supplier on her wristpad. Almost instantly she had a vid of a skinny young man. "Thank you for contacting Metaglione Industries. How may I—"

"Give me Crenhauser," she demanded.

"Um, I'm just the operator. I can't—"

"Give. Me. Crenhauser." She bit off each word like pieces of dried steak.

"I don't have the—"

"Put him on, or I'll have you fired and posted to the southern reaches to study fish-mating."

Not surprisingly, it took only three minutes for the lowly receptionist to contact the unreachable Arbo Crenhauser.

"Ah, Marshal Hyde," his image said with a disarming smile. "How may I help you on this fine—"

His sickeningly sweet manner was already grating. She turned the vidcapture around. "Is this what I get for ordering capital ship armor from you? I'm on a space station, you arrogant twit. We could have had a Stage Five hull breach. How dare you sell me faulty merchandise, you asinine, imbecilic traitor?"

"E-e-excuse me," he sputtered. "I sold you the very best we have to offer. And where do you get off calling me a trai—"

"Profiteering was, under normal circumstances," Hyde snapped, "ten years in prison and a fine not to exceed a hundred-fifty percent of what you were paid. Wartime profiteering, however, went from being a crime against the crown to being a Sovereign capital offense. Punishment is forfeiture of all assets, known or unknown, to the military, and execution, but..." She turned the vid back to her face so he could see her disarming smile. "I would stay the execution in order to put you right in front of the viewpane of your next chamber so you can watch it *melt*."

"Marshal," someone called out behind her. She ignored them.

Crenhauser was visibly sweating, even on vid. "I a-a-a-assure you that th-th-there was no—"

"Marshal." Now someone was touching her shoulder—no, grabbing it. She spun around to berate whoever had the temerity to lay hands on a marshal.

It was Vice Admiral Neboda, who did, technically, have the rank to lay hands on her.

"I'll deal with you later, Crenhauser," she muttered, "you sniveling mound of industrial refuse." She ended the call.

"Care to explain what happened here, Marshal?" Neboda

demanded, his elaborate and finely groomed mustache covering his upper lip entirely from view.

No, I really do not. But even if she was the current administrator over the Military Research Division, he was still the commandant of the Regis Magnum Shipyards. She took a deep breath and began to relay the details of the incident while clearly pointing out exactly how the debacle wasn't her fault.

Because it wasn't.

———

Kasa de Cevoir picked herself out of the wreckage of her monitoring station. *Five years and two double majors for an advanced degree in materials composition... and I'm stuck here in this hell hole, once again monitoring other people working because I'm **only** thirty-three. But someone from a rimward planet like Citrom—oops, I meant Tor—doesn't matter much compared to the exalted and experienced minds of a Core world.*

She was a tall young woman who wore her black hair short, bobbed just below her ears. Her eyes were the color of pale green jade.

She looked around; there was little to concern her right now. *And I'm sure not going to wait for these idiots to decide to tell us anything.* Silently, she made her way out of the room, glad to leave the wails and whines of the other technicians behind. Away from everyone, she blinked twice, and her nanomod eye came to life, showing the shipyard schematic relative to her position. She followed the datalines along the schematic until she found what she was looking for. *This office should have terminal access.*

Suddenly, her eye flashed a warning. Someone was coming —Admiral Neboda. She ducked into the office and closed the door quietly before he could spot her. Once he passed, she went to work.

She logged into the hardwired terminal as a guest, did a

quick hack to disable keystroke logging, erased that evidence, then brought up the sign-in box again. She entered the 128-digit security hash code that governed the login database into the password section, and the box reset to admin mode. *How is this place a major military research lab and they let someone this dumb create their system? I know more digits of pi than that.* She created a temporary full-access username and password (*ally-ourstarbase, $h188oL37h*) and pulled down the relevant video footage from the incident. She made sure her ocular implant was recording, then started playing the vid, without audio—she didn't want to risk any strange noises. She watched Devin disappear into a bright smear just before the vid cut off. *He was annoying, but he was kinda my friend,* she thought as she tapped other vids to life, trying to see what had caused the problem. *I mean, it's not like I could tell him anything. But he was the first Sovereign person I met who wasn't a bastard.* It was frustrating work, and she had to make certain she covered her trail before she left. But all she could tell was that the chamber grew too hot and then melted.

This is somebody's fault. She thought of the rude and egocentric marshal who constantly stomped around the shipyard, barking orders and acting like she knew best. Half the time, the things she said were rudimentary or already done. *Best not to jump to conclusions, though,* she added to herself. Just because she wanted the miserable quinsy to fall out of the airlock didn't mean she was the immediate problem.

The immediate problem being that I already have plans to live. And if the station isn't here...

If someone blew up the station, it would mean all her work to get there was for nothing. And also, she'd be dead.

With no evidence coming to the fore, she closed all the video copies and prepared to scrub any evidence of *allyourstarbase* from the records. But then she saw the live feed from control room five.

On the wall monitor was a group of hazmat-suited technicians rushing into the control room. *This must be from a body cam,* she realized. *They're monitoring the recovery.*

In the center of the room, she could see the twisted and cracked remains of the containment vessel. As the hazmat crew started pulling pieces of it away, she could see inside. What remained of its contents looked like a piece of translucent art glass, twisted and wavy, looking a little like a caramelized sugar mold. As they pulled away more pieces, the top of the chamber broke loose and fell, narrowly missing one of the techs. But behind it came a thick power cable, somehow protected from the blast and still sparking madly.

"Watch out, you idiots," she yelled at the screen.

It didn't touch anyone, but the sparking end contacted the brown glass-like substance. Instantly, it lit up like a ten-thousand-watt bulb just before the wall behind it was showered with spears of light. Then the wall was gone.

She had no idea what she'd just seen. And she wasn't willing to bet that her implant was up to the kind of video editing she could manage with a few clicks on the terminal.

She copied the recent video and ran it back at half-speed. This time, the cable touched the glass and she saw the change between moments—brown, then white, then spears of light burning through the wall.

She ran it back at tenth-speed. This time she saw the cable touch the glass and, for the briefest moment, the spot where the cable touched turned blinding white and then faded as the other side of the strange, glassine sculpture brightened. Then tendrils of pure light shot away from the glass. It was like watching lightning made of spidersilk arc away from the glass. A thousand hairlines of energy exited the glass to strike the containment wall, scorching through it with the force of a hadronic bomb.

What she'd just witnessed was unbelievable, phenomenal. It was unlike anything—

The door to the office burst open. She looked up and found

herself staring into the spotlights of a half-dozen military assault rifles.

"Get up. Get up," a voice shouted as the room filled with the sound of safeties being thrown.

Oh, pokker-guon-quinsy. She carefully stood up. "What seems to be the—"

"You are in a restricted area. Under Sovereign Code 415, you—"

"What are you talking about?" she snapped, hoping she could bluff her way out of it. "I'm Kasa de Cevoir. I have level six clearance, control room five. I just came in here to sit down."

She hoped they'd just scan her ID badge and leave her alone... *but if anyone looks at the screen...*

"Show me your badge," the voice shouted.

She made sure to fumble it a little; it wasn't hard. She really was shaking. The lead soldier snatched it away and handed it to another, who pulled out a scanner.

Check it all you want, bullyboys. It's the real thing.

"Sergeant, what's she doing in here?" The voice came from behind the soldiers. A voice she knew all too well.

Lieutenant Anjan Tarch. Tarch wasn't an idiot. Kasa blinked twice to shut off her implant. *If they see the images in my eye, they'll rip it out of my head.*

Tarch pushed her way through the soldiers, cutting a dashing silhouette against the light of the hallway.

"de Cevoir, you're away from your station," she stated.

"I just—" She forced the quaver. She had to hide the real fear to show the fake fear because she couldn't be sure she wouldn't freak the heck out. "Everything blew up," she wailed. "And Devin died. He was my friend, and I didn't know what to do. And I just wanted to go to the bathroom, and then I saw the Admiral and ducked in here, and I... and I..."

"And-and you just decided to log into this terminal?" Tarch said, her voice dripping with sarcasm. "And just logged into the security feeds? How could none of you see she'd accessed the security feeds?"

The soldiers said nothing.

"Well, you're under arrest," Tarch said. "Sergeant?"

The sergeant pulled a binder strip from his belt and zipped Kasa's wrists together tightly.

"Until we determine you didn't sabotage the test and kill eleven people," Tarch said, "you're going to be very uncomfortable. And then they're going to interrogate you as a possible terrorist in the act of committing sabotage. Take her away, Sergeant."

As the sergeant ushered her out of the room, Tarch added, "And you can kiss your career goodbye."

Nope, Kasa Su-Mei thought as she was marched to the detention area. *I already did my part of the job. Once the Tupeti get on board, I'll be going home. And my family is going to have a very nice retirement when I get there.*

Hirana Ligarch rewarded those who accomplished their tasks.

Esse, Monere District
Planet Caerus
Orso Planetary System

Meera Seluere woke up. Again.

She tried not to think about it.

Dragging herself out of bed, she staggered to the bathroom, then returned and pulled on her old running clothes. A year ago, she would never have let her clothes get this faded or worn. They were pale and dingy and... *Well... a lot can happen in a year.*

She reached out a hand for her shoes. They wriggled

closer. She grabbed them, slipped her feet into them and wriggled her toes. She really would have to buy new ones soon—the soles were worn. But having to make that choice seemed so difficult alongside all the other choices she had to make every day.

Like waking up.

Like pretending her shoes didn't wiggle.

Her therapist had said that finding a routine would help. That part of accepting that the world had changed was finding things that had stayed the same. Hence the running.

Her therapist had also said the same about her sudden divorce from Graben. Graben was dead now. Her therapist was dead now. Both of them collateral damage during the battle for Caerus. The Battle for the Slipgates, they called it.

But Sorge wasn't killed. He wasn't collateral damage.

She pushed the thoughts away and left the house before she could think on it more. Lifian would have to fix her own breakfast.

Meera was almost forty-eight, a slight woman of one-hundred-seventy-two centimeters, athletic, with white hair, brown eyes and a pointed chin. She was also the victim of the loss of her eldest son—something she knew, no matter what her therapist said, she'd never get over. For her, every day was a trial. And so she ran, and she ran, and she...

Her feet pounded the pavement as she ran. Once upon a time she had been a regular jogger, content to view the world from her place on the sidewalks, to contemplate all that life had given her.

Now, instead of jogging, she ran, her pulse pounding as she tried to keep ahead of the crushing depression that threatened her daily life. While she ran, she could almost forget the death of her son.

But she couldn't forget Gesc. No, not her second bouncy boy. He was still here. He was married, and her grandbaby was coming soon. And Lifia, her shining daughter, her beautiful jewel of a mind, was still here, too. She'd moved out of her dorm when... after the battle... and she...

Her children were interlinked with all her best memories. And all the memories of her children were linked together. Which was why it was increasingly impossible to even see them without risking the crushing depths.

Everywhere she looked now, there were reminders. Red banners with the Orso crest and the words "We Will Not Vanish Without a Fight" were the most popular, though others hung along the sidewalks or in front of houses. "Live On and Survive" was common. "Oh, Blue, Die. Oh, Blue, Die," mimicked a popular song, and one caught her eye several times —the angled shapes of red starships on a black background, pursuing a thin stripe of blue into frayed tatters at the end. She might have thought it clever if not for the feelings it dredged up.

How do other people cope with this? she wanted to wail. *How can they live with all this shoved in their faces, reminding them constantly of everything they've lost?*

And then she saw the signs she dreaded most: one had saluting silhouettes and the words, "Do you love your planet? Join the new Defense Corps." It was a call to all civilians to enlist in a new local militia. They would be tasked with keeping order to free up the military. And the other, showing three silhouettes with stars upon their foreheads... "Do you have what it takes to join the PCU? Accepting all candidates for testing."

They want people with TK and Psy.

The pounding memory hounded her, and she couldn't outrun it anymore. She took a right and started to circle back to the house. She had to see him.

———

MEERA STRIPPED OFF HER SHIRT, dripping with sweat. *Obviously, I need to clean up first,* she argued with herself. She stepped into the scrubber and set it for hot and vigorous. She tried to let the scrub distract her, but after four of the ten minutes allotted, she slapped the switch and turned it off. A final spurt of rinsing, and she was blown dry by the vents.

She was barely half-dressed before the need to see him forced her to the vanity. There she removed her old data pad from a small box layered in velvety cloth. She couldn't stand looking at it after the battle, and now she wore a new one instead. But now, she placed it on her arm and watched it light up.

<<*One old message*>>, it informed her. She tapped it open.

And there was her son. Her firstborn son.

His hair was always shorter than she expected—why had he let them cut it off? And his uniform looked a little rumpled. She remembered wanting to reach out and straighten it for him. He was looking over his shoulder, then he turned back to his screen.

"Hey-ey-ey, Mom," Sorge said, as he always did.

She sobbed so hard that it muffled the next words.

"...much time left, but I grabbed a sec to say hey. We, uh— we're about to hit it here. I mean, they're six minutes out and closing, but we're gonna give the—"

Just like every other time, a burst of static interrupted his transmission.

"...and when we're done, they're gonna crawl home with their blue tails dragging." There were cheers from the background. "Anyway, I just wanted to say—"

"Oooooh," came from the background. "Say it, Seluere, say it. Tell your momma."

"Mom, I love you..." he began, but some other face tried to push into view, and he shoved it away.

When did he become so strong? It's only been a few years since he was in college.

"...I love you, and I want you to know that you were the best mom. Thank you, for everything."

"You gonna blow a kiss—" and it cut off.

My son is dead.

*You **were** the best mom.*

He thought he was... he knew he was going to die.

She stood up, tears streaming down her face.

"*WHY?*" she screamed. "Why did he have to die?"

She kicked the vanity bench. It splintered under a blow that, had she been paying attention, should only have tumbled it over. "He was kind and wonderful," she sobbed. "He was the best son. He didn't deserve this. None of us did."

She tore the data pad from her arm, barely remembering not to hurl it across the room in a rage. "Why did my son—have—to—DIE!"

Something exploded from within her. All her rage and grief and hurt radiated out for the first time since she heard the news. All her tightly controlled emotions pushed blessedly outward, and when she stopped screaming, a calm fell over her. She felt... at peace.

Then she opened her eyes and beheld the terrible wrath of her long-held rage. The wall was smashed, the studs bent, crushed. Her bed was destroyed, the frame shattered, her mattress shredded. Her dressers were turned upside down and resting in positions that might have seemed comical if not for the pulse pounding like a hammer in her head. She glared around her room, at her old datapad—

"Mom, what are you... What happened?" Lifia gasped from the doorway.

She smiled at her daughter, her youngest and—possibly—brightest child. "Good morning, honey. Did you eat breakfast yet? You don't want to be late for Poli-Sci." Meera stepped calmly around her and walked to the kitchen.

"Mom, seriously. How did you wreck your room like that?" Lifia demanded as she followed her. "I was right here. I didn't hear a thing until you screamed."

"It's nothing, dear." *But it might be everything. And I need to understand.* She was done with refusing to see the obvious.

Meera found a pelum fruit in the basket. She focused on it. She willed it to float away.

Nothing happened.

Fly, you little bastard, she thought angrily. *Lift up. Levitate.*

Again, nothing happened, and her rage intensified again.

Fly, or I'll crush you.

Nothing.

She felt the old despair begin to flood in around the edges of her rage. But she pushed it away, refusing to drown in her misery anymore.

Where are you, Sorge? She imagined herself showing him that she could lift the pelum. The soft, fuzzy, firm pelum, hovering above...

I'm here, Mom.

And it drifted lazily out of her hand, floating as if on a string.

"Mom... how are you...?" Lifia was dumbstruck.

The pelum fell with a splat despite her effort, but it didn't matter.

"Lifia, did you say you wanted a newer data pad?"

"What? No, Mom, I didn't."

"You want one? I have a spare." She walked back to her bedroom and grabbed her old data pad... with a hundred messages saved, a thousand pictures of her children... of Sorge. She reactivated her primary biometric access. Then she placed the new data pad on her wrist long enough to wipe the memory and delete secondary access. "Boot it up, transfer whatever you want. It's yours."

"Um, okay, Mom." Lifia looked confused, and Meera almost laughed. "But are we going to talk about it?"

Meera let the rest of her daughter's litany wash past her as she searched for the access code she wanted. She punched the contact button, and in moments a crisply uniformed lieutenant said, "Thank you for contacting the Perceptual Expansion Unit. How may I help you?"

"You can connect me to whoever accepts new recruits," she stated.

"One moment," he said, and the call turned into a loading screen.

"Mom, really? You're going to join the PE unit?"

She looked at her daughter. "Lifia, dear, I know this is hard for you to accept, but your brother's death hurt me a lot. I'm not a good mom anymore. You've taken care of me for months."

"Well, you took care of me for-ever."

"And I love you for helping, but now I have to do what needs to be done."

The screen lit up to show a female officer, this one a captain. She was so glad Sorge had taught her the different ranks.

"This is Squire-Captain Lensig. To whom am I speaking?"

"My name is Meera Seluere. I want to join your unit and kill Blues."

"We have strict requirements for entry," she replied. "Can you show any evidence of ability?"

Meera twisted her arm so the lens faced the wreckage of her room.

"Is this good enough?" she asked.

"Hmm. Yes," the captain replied. "I think we can work with that."

CHAPTER
ONE

TRUST FALLING

RESDON MILITARY COMPLEX
Som Orsi City
Planet Caerus
Orso System

COMMODORE RICHARD MORIAN was seated in the most uncomfortable chair in the military base apartment he shared with his twin sister Danis.

"Armor has been replaced port and starboard," Richard muttered to himself as he scrolled through the reports on the repairs and upgrades to the *Avenger*. "Railgun ammunition is restocked, dutrinium and depleted uranium... interesting. They can replace the ammo feeds with osmium steel? I didn't know they made ammo feeders in Osfec. They must be expensive, but a ten percent improvement in cool-down? That's going to increase our rate of fire."

The war had dragged on for three long years, and it seemed like every day there was some new tragedy or problem to cope with. It helped to cling to whatever bit of good news he could get. After nine months commanding the *Intrepid* on routine patrol—a modern, top-of-the-line heavy cruiser, the kind of ship most commanders dream of being promoted to—he'd finally done what he'd longed to do and passed her off to the newly minted captain Commander Hodos Pilaza.

He sat back in his chair, bored. He closed his eyes and, as they always seemed to do, his thoughts turned to Danis. She, too, was bored, though she never said anything about it. As they could read each other's thoughts, there were few secrets between them, at least on his side; she was better at blocking her thoughts than he was. At that moment she was, as she almost always was, thinking of Prince Elio. Ever since the first time she'd rescued him—*And how many times since? The man is a regular damsel in distress. It's too much.*

While he was away on the *Intrepid*, he hadn't been able to feel her thoughts the way he had on the *Avenger*. But when he returned to Orso and found the once cute, flirty thoughts had given way to more amorous ones, he'd put his proverbial foot down. He didn't need images of Elio in his brain—and especially not those his sister was conjuring; he felt as if he was invading her privacy.

It was a difficult problem, especially so since he wasn't the one causing it. As their telepathic link grew stronger, they began to experience more and more... seepage between them. Since he'd come home, he occasionally found himself staring into her mouth as she leaned into the mirror to check her teeth. *Most uncomfortable* was the only way he could describe the situation.

His datapad chirped: a priority signal. He glanced at it. Surely there were no emergencies at the shipyard? He raised his wrist and activated the vid.

"This is Commodore Richard Morian," he said, surprised to see a familiar but almost forgotten face.

"This is Launch Coordinator Teyn Grig at the Resdon Launch Facility." The voice was stern, officious, from a stern and hardened man. "I have been receiving complaints from some of my civilian instructors that a member of your crew, Lieutenant Commander Danis *Morian,* is flouting our safety regulations. They have tried to resolve this matter... privately, to no avail. And now she appears on our training manifest again. May I ask why a squadron commander feels the need to harass civilian instructors?"

Richard hid a grimace. "I'm certain she isn't doing anything to harass your instructors, Launch Coordinator."

She's doing it to harass me, Morian thought grimly.

"You obviously recognize me, Commodore," Grig said. It wasn't a question.

"Yes, sir... of course I do," Morian replied.

"Good. Commander Morian is your sister, and as her commanding officer, I'm sure you understand that you can and will be held responsible for her wayward actions?"

"I do, sir." *Ever since the day she enlisted.*

"So, then, rather than issue a formal complaint, I need you to do something for me. I need you to make her understand the gravity of her actions and that she has to stop. If not, the consequences could be severe."

And all I wanted to do was sit here quietly and catch up on my reports.

"Of course, sir. I'll have something on your datapad in fifteen minutes."

"Make it ten." Teyn Grig said and disappeared.

Great. Now she's gotten the attention of a retired air marshal.

He tapped out a letter, using the weakest language he could. "*If* Commander Morian commits... use the *minimum force* necessary... disciplinary action will be taken *if needed.*" He signed it and sent it to Teyn Grig.

Danis, please don't do anything stupid.

———

Jump Bay, *Zephaura*, Class-3 Troop Transport
10,000 meters above Som Orsi

DANIS MORIAN LISTENED to the wind whistle by the aircraft's skin. It was so different than being in a fighter; she had no control here, no purpose. The only reason she was here was to forget, even if only for a little while. Well that, and to annoy her brother. He was always annoyed anyway, so she figured she might as well give him something to be really annoyed about and distract him from his thousand other worries.

"Now listen carefully," the jump chief shouted over the noise. "Each of you has a comm connection to your instructor. They will tell you when you reach the correct height to activate. Please follow their instructions. We don't want any accidents."

"What happens if we mess up?" someone asked.

"If your pack doesn't activate in time, your instructor will activate it for you. We need you to survive, without injuries. Death and injury raise our insurance, and the brass doesn't like that."

The jumpers laughed.

Danis rolled her eyes at the chuckling. Many of these people were dilettantes, rich thrill-seekers, and executives who preferred to ignore the realities of the universe in favor of chasing their next high. At least she could respect their choice of thrill—reports showed many such people turned to chemically induced methods of escaping the reality and memories of the Swarm-wracked worlds.

Danis, please don't do anything stupid. The thought entered her brain like an arrow. Unlike his boring paperwork buzzing in her head, she received that one loud and clear. She ignored him and the rest of the dive instructor's warnings. She'd already jumped twelve times this month, and it was beginning to get a little stale.

She thought back to her thirty-minute freefall through

Tor's atmosphere, crashing into the surface. And meeting Elio for the first time. And her heart swelled.

Why do you... she felt from her brother, and she shut him down immediately.

Finally, the chief pulled open the jump door and started calling out pairs to jump. *Instructor, client. Instructor, client.*

"This is so exciting," squealed an older woman next to Danis. "This is my third time. How many times have you jumped?"

Instructor, client. Instructor, client.

She made a quick count. "Um, forty-seven, I think."

Instructor, client.

"Oh, my. Are you one of the instructors?"

Instructor, client.

"Nope. I just do this for fun."

And the woman dropped out of the aircraft with a shriek of what Danis hoped was joy.

The jump chief looked at Danis. "Aren't you going to jump?"

"Yes," she called back with a wicked smile. "I'm going to jump."

She saw the grav field light up in the atmosphere below and threw herself out into the blue.

The feel of the air whooshing past her was exhilarating. Danis' first jump had been almost a year ago now—a high-altitude combat drop from the stratosphere to rescue Kyne Minnah and his people from a Swarm invasion. The terror of the uncertainty, the unfamiliar equipment, the surprise Blue ambush—it had been horrific, but they'd survived. She'd survived when others hadn't. Just like she'd survived falling out of her F-32A fighter when the ejection system failed.

She pushed that from her mind and focused on the sensation of falling.

She was falling at the rate of ten meters per second squared until she reached terminal velocity close to two-hundred-twenty kilometers per hour.

For the first few seconds, she felt as if she was floating along on the wind. Then she felt the tug of gravity begin to work upon her, and then she was falling faster and faster, the wind tearing at her body. After ten seconds she was falling as fast as a speeding gravcar and her body tensed.

A few seconds more and she'd ceased to accelerate.

Sixty-five meters per second. And I feel fine.

Below her, she saw the other jumpers, already wafting down like large feathers on the resistance of their gravpacks.

Danis. Stop it. It was as if Richard was right over her shoulder, but again she ignored him.

She shifted into a dive position and shot through the other divers' formation like a bullet.

She could feel Richard panicking, shouting, *Stop this foolishness* **NOW.**

She held her position for one—two—three seconds more. And then, with a grin, she activated her gravpack.

The hum surrounded her as the orange-tinted field sprang into life. The ground details became clear, approaching fast, faster, and faster, and faster.

"Yea—hooooo." she screamed as the gravpack sensed the danger and went into emergency mode. The backup engaged, and her body jerked as she came almost to a complete stop, less than fifty meters above the ground.

As she floated down the last few meters, she saw someone in a suit walking briskly toward her, followed closely by two mechanics and a uniform.

Uh-oh, she thought.

Uh-oh is right. Do you realize who that is?

Richard? What are you do—

What am I doing? I'm doing what's become necessary.

As she touched down, the suit reached her. He looked

wizened but hard as stone. Oddly, on the breast of his jacket he wore a military decoration.

"Miss Morian—"

"That's *Lieutenant Commander* Morian," she snapped.

"You're in violation of this airfield's safety and security guidelines and—"

"And you are?"

He stiffened even more. "I am Air Marshal Teyn Grig, retired."

Uh-oh...

Uh-oh is right. She could hear Richard before she could begin to deflate.

"In accordance with our policies and the waivers you signed, I'm afraid I must dismiss you from further service here at Resdon Launch Facilities."

Danis tried to maintain her self-assurance. "And what will you do if—"

"I have retained an officer of the city of Resdon. He will escort you off the premises."

Danis tried to interrupt. "A police officer has no authority..."

"He has the authority to act on behalf of the city—"

"But not against an officer of my rank, and especially not during wartime."

"Perhaps not, but I can contact people who do. Is that what you want on record, Commander?"

That stone face looked somehow even harder now. "And I have received a communique from your commanding officer authorizing me to use as much force as necessary to remove you."

The officer thumbed his stun baton. It sparked menacingly.

"Will there be a problem, *Lieutenant Commander* Morian?"

She was sorely tempted to smack the condescension right off his face. But his rank stayed her hand.

"No. No problem at all, *Air Marshal* Grig. I'll leave. Peaceably. By myself."

"These people will escort—"

She turned her head. "That won't be necessary."

And she turned and walked away; and surprisingly, no one followed.

She didn't receive any further messages from Richard, but beneath his irritation she could sense a little smugness for putting one over on his sister.

I'll get him back for that.

She was sure he didn't hear that. Despite his complaints, she was *much* better at hiding her thoughts than he was.

———

RICHARD BUSIED himself in the kitchenette, making Danis' favorite—guinea cipollata. He tossed the curled noodles in herbed golden sauce, then topped the noodles with stewed guinea and spooned cipollata over the top.

He could smell every ingredient that had gone into it. He focused on each one, savoring the delicate herbs, the tang of the mustard, the earthy smell of the guinea, and the sweetness of the tomatoes and onions in the sauce.

He didn't care for the dish himself. But he knew that if he focused on each sensation instead of his own tastes, she would receive the message loud and clear.

Unfortunately, you made the other message loud and clear, too. This is barely an apology.

He frowned.

The door opened, almost silently. "Is there a problem, brother?" she asked quietly. But underneath her calm words, he could feel she was simmering.

"We couldn't have had this conversation on your way home?" he said calmly. He needed to remember that, at this moment, he was a brother, not her commanding officer.

"Richard, we both knew that being under your command would make things difficult sometimes, but this sense you have of being my boss even when we're off duty is stifling."

He sighed. "I'm trying to keep my feelings restrained, Danis. So you don't hear everything."

"I've tried to do everything you asked," she said, "but I have feelings, too, and it's unfair for me to have to keep them bottled up all the time."

"I don't want you to." Richard wished he knew how to explain. "I just wish you could rein it in a little. What you did today... You could have killed yourself."

"Rubbish. I knew exactly what I was doing. Richard, I'm not jumping because I enjoy it; I don't. In fact I hate it. I do it because I need to control my fear."

"Danis..."

But before he could say anything more, she broadcast her fears of falling, the ones that first began over the planet Tor.

"This is what I see in my dreams every night, Richard."

She sent him images of her failed ejection from her F-32A. Then the combat jump over Asteroid K-1437.

"What's the matter, brother? Do these images bother you? Because they sure as hell bother me."

He was puzzled. Why didn't he feel these dreams, too? Was she repressing those feelings? "If it bothers you so much, why do you keep doing it?"

"Because I can't afford to be afraid, damn it. You can't, your officers can't, my pilots can't."

"Have you tried talking to someone about it?" he asked.

"I tried talking to you."

Richard was confused. "When?"

"Three different times. I wasn't trying to make it a huge deal, but you kept acting like I was being flippant. So I backed away."

He tried to remember, but with her thoughts drifting

between them, he couldn't remember any of them. "I guess I was distracted."

"And I understand that," she said. "But I'm also dealing with other feelings, and you won't discuss them."

"I understand that you have feelings for Elio," he replied. "I like him. I'm not against you and him, rank aside."

"Of course, rank aside," she said. Her thoughts held a little brittleness. "But you are against him."

"I'm against distraction," he replied. "We're in the middle—"

"Yes, we're in the middle of a war." Her brief flash of anger disappeared. "We've been at war for three years now… Richard. If you found someone, you'd want to—"

"It isn't like that. Whenever you think about him, I can feel it. Your control slips, and I start seeing and feeling everything you do. Is that what you want during your intimate moments?" he asked.

She didn't answer.

"Look, I understand; I really do," he said.

"Richard, it's been years since you had any interest in a woman."

"You're right. I haven't dated since Veya Nance. But this goes far beyond that. You're my sister, and I know you've had physical relationships before. But damn it, there's a difference between knowing and watching."

In response, Danis opened up and released something inside her. It poured over Richard like the contentment of watching a tropical sunset. Every part of him felt fulfilled somehow.

"That's how I feel about Elio."

Richard was surprised that she'd been able to hide the depths of her feelings. "And does he feel the same way?"

"Well, I haven't asked him, but his mood shifts when I'm around. A sort of delighted surprise."

He turned the discussion back to the matter at hand.

"Look, I promise that as soon as we find a way to limit our exposure to each other, we'll revisit this. Until then, please understand that I'm not doing this to hurt you. I'm only afraid of what this might do to our minds in battle."

"That bothers me too, brother," Danis said.

Richard felt a sense of relief, knowing she wouldn't fight him on it.

"But there is one other thing we have to address, Richard."

"Really?" he said." What else is there?"

She grabbed a cushion from the couch and slammed it into his face.

"You got me banned from Resdon," she said with a warrior-like grin. "And that's something I simply will not stand for."

"No, Danis. You did that. Look, I know you're upset and that you're bored, but we need to focus on what's important. I have at least a hundred-and-one things to do most days. You... have little to nothing to do, and that's a problem."

She looked at him but didn't answer.

"But we can't do much about that until the *Avenger* is ready," he continued, "and we have a full complement of fighters and pilots."

"So that's the solution. We move."

"What, you don't like the apartment?" he asked. But even as he spoke, he could sense she wanted something more.

"It's not that, Richard. We need to be back on the *Avenger*. You can be where you can get your hands dirty, figuratively speaking," she added when she saw the look on his face. "And I'll have work of my own to do. Better yet, you'll know right where I am. We'll both be busy, and I won't be causing 'problems.'"

He stared at her, considering what she'd said. It wasn't a bad idea. While he'd enjoyed his time planet-side, he knew his work would go smoother, and a little faster, aboard ship.

"I know what you're thinking," she said. "You know I'm right."

"Fine. I agree," he said, finally. "You have twenty-eight hours to pack and be ready. I'll issue the orders for the recall. They'll go out immediately."

"Good," she said. "I'll pilot the shuttle."

"What? No," he said hastily. "There's no need for you to—"

"No problem, Richard. Why take someone off vacation when I can do it? I'm rated one of the best pilots in the USF, as you well know. So I will pilot the shuttle."

"Yes, but—"

"I know why you're 'yes, butting,' but I need the hours. I have to fly twenty shuttle hours every three months. If not, I'll have to re-certify. And that's not acceptable, is it?" she asked with a sly smile.

He knew why she was demanding it, and it wasn't for the hours. He could see it in her mind. But he needed to keep her under his thumb, at least until they were back aboard, and this was the price she demanded; one last, reckless fling, as it were, before she settled into her routine.

Would I be so compromising if I were in her place? he thought, blocking her from hearing it. *Probably not.*

"Fine," he grumbled. "For the hours."

"For the hours," she said cheerfully. "Now I need to go for a drink."

"What? I thought we just—"

"We did, but we can't get a decent drink aboard ship. Last chance, right?"

"Don't wait up," she said and grabbed her battered flight jacket on her way to the door.

What have I gotten myself into? he thought as the door slammed behind her.

What's the matter, Richard? he clearly heard. *I agreed to everything you wanted. And I got most of what I wanted. So nice compromise, right?*

He sighed. It was going to be an interesting twenty-eight hours.

CHAPTER
TWO

FARDA LAUNCH FACILITY
  Awega City
  Planet Caerus

"CONTROL, THIS IS SHUTTLE 1705 GAMMA," Danis said as her fingers danced over the hologram, "requesting flight plan authorization."

"Flight plan authorized, 1705 Gamma."

Danis smiled. "Requesting clearance to liftoff from pad fifteen."

"Clearance granted. Have a good flight, Shuttle 1705 Gamma."

"Thank you, Control. 1705 out." Danis cut the transmission.

"You know, Richard, this trip would have been so much more pleasant if you hadn't gotten me banned from Som Orsi field."

"I didn't get you banned, Danis. You did that on your own."

"Spare me the scolding. We did that already."

Do you understand what really happened there?

Oh, we're using Psy now?

I like talking, not shouting over the engines.

*So what **really** happened, brother?*

The Air Marshal was furious. Word had gotten around about you pulling these crazy stunts. He was all set to make an example of you.

How? By grounding a squadron commander during wartime?

He could do that, Richard replied.

He can't—

Danis, he was a squadron commander more than thirty years ago. He was reinstated when war broke out. He still has his rank. He could have demoted you back to lieutenant.

That's... highly unlikely.

But beneath her words, Richard could feel her unspoken doubt. It was depressing.

Fifteen minutes later *Avenger* came into view, her dutrinium armored hull glinting copper in the weak sunlight.

She's beautiful, Danis thought.

That she is, Richard replied. *Home sweet home.*

"Avenger Docking Control, this is shuttle 1705 Gamma, requesting permission to dock."

"Permission granted, 1705. You're cleared into bay fifteen."

CHAPTER
THREE

BEYOND THE TAPE

Feducere, Kusam Hills Apartments
  Planet Caerus
  Orso Planetary System

Twelve-year-old Faxil Avestan was sitting on the roof with his father, and he marveled at the expanse of the city laid out before him.

Situated on a hill, the apartments offered a commanding view of the city skyscrapers. Once upon a time, his mother had told him, these were places for the rich to look out upon the gleaming city and the beautiful forests that separated them. But soon one acre, then another, and another were cut down to feed the growing city, until the small manufacturers had grown into colossal factories, spewing soot into the air. Their paradise spoiled, the residents of the upscale buildings trickled away, leaving them for the lower-class population of the city to occupy.

"This part of Feducere used to be for rich people," his mother always said. "Only now that it's falling apart will they let rats like us crawl within the walls."

Faxil wished his mother could be happier. But their apartment, too, was falling apart. And even with both parents working double shifts, they still barely made enough to buy food.

He looked at his father. He rarely had anything positive to say about the city.

"Once upon a time this was where Caerus made its money," he'd told Faxil. "Our engineers and mechanics built the parts for all sorts of things. Gravcars, interceptor engines—even the dutrinium alloys were made here. Everyone knew that we made the best alloys. Well, maybe the alloys from Notor were as good. But then came all those new ships. They use new materials, different alloys—and they don't do half as good a job as a proper Feducere dutrinium alloy. But they saved a few credits and, in so doing, wiped out our entire industry."

Faxil knew that his father was exaggerating—at least a little. There were still lots of factories, and they were still producing.

But even he had to admit there weren't as many lights down below anymore, but it made the view of the city, and the stars, all the more impressive.

He loved the night. They would come up to the roof and look at the stars and talk about things. These were special times, and Faxil didn't want them to end.

His father fell silent.

"Hey, Dad, is something wrong?" Faxil asked. He asked again before he noticed his father's expression, staring at the sky in horror.

Faxil looked up, too.

Usually, it was hard to pick out the defense force ships against the stars, but with a little practice, you could. But now, some of the stars were moving. Sometimes, the little stars came together and made a bigger star.

"Dad, what's that?" he asked, but his father didn't answer.

They watched in silence as blinks of light—explosions more terrible than Faxil could even imagine—peppered the night sky. He knew the defense ships must be fighting the Swarm—strange aliens that looked like melted glass. Everyone had heard the warnings, but it was like they didn't really believe in the Swarm. He'd seen their pictures on the news before his dad had started shutting it off. He didn't know why the Swarm wanted to kill them all, but that's what everyone was saying. He thought maybe if they could talk to the Swarm somehow, they could be friends.

He saw another bright explosion, this one much bigger.

"Faxil..." his father said.

The explosion got bigger and bigger.

"Faxil, we need to get to the basement now!" his father yelled. He grabbed Faxil by the arm, and together they ran back inside.

"Dad, what is it? What's going on?" he cried. But his father wouldn't answer and just ran down the stairs. As they ran down flight after flight, he could see the explosion through the windows; it had turned into a fireball, leaving a streak of light in the sky as it fell toward the planet.

Down one flight after another, they ran, past window after window, and through each one, the fireball grew bigger and bigger until it was all he could see through the window, and still it got bigger. And then there were no more windows, only stairs.

And then there was an earsplitting explosion; the entire building shook violently. And suddenly they were in the air, twisting, spinning as the stairs fell away. They were falling. He was falling... toward the wall, and his dad was right behind him. And then the entire building was on fire. He was out in the open air, still falling. There was fire everywhere; wave after wave of flame blew over him, burning him up, and he screamed and screamed and screamed—

Feducere, Neujaz Apartments

Faxil jerked awake.

It was the same dream all over again. He didn't bother to draw the images from his dreams anymore; he had a whole folder of them, and they all looked the same.

He got out of bed and limped to the bathroom. His leg hurt again, probably from trying to run away in his sleep.

The building hadn't burned away, like in his dream. They'd landed in the basement, and Dad had broken ribs. And Faxil helped him back up the stairs, and when they looked out at the city, their view was marred by a scar at least three kilometers long and one kilometer wide—an entire section of the city was nothing but demolished factories, warehouses, and scorched starship hulls. Later, he'd seen a news show where they had a vid of the crash. Those were the flames he saw in his dreams. The flames that must have consumed his mother.

He saw the ship that killed her every day. Dad had said it was one of the new ships, an Angel-class destroyer, that crashed. Every day Faxil looked out at the hull. He could see the name on the side.

USF-7415 PEACEMAKER

Or at least, that's what it once was. After the fires had fizzled out, several of the letters had been burned away. So someone had climbed up the sides and painted new letters on in their place.

PL*ACET*AK*ER*

Not very original, but it might have been funny if Faxil's mom wasn't buried underneath it somewhere. He didn't draw the hull anymore, either.

What was worse, his dad had started talking to some lady

who'd lost her brother in the crash. Inoiae brought them food a couple times since Dad couldn't work yet and Faxil couldn't cook. After a few weeks, she was coming to visit all the time, and soon she stopped leaving.

He put on some clothes and walked out to the kitchen where Inoiae was puttering around, like she always was.

"Allo, Faxall," she said in her odd North Galactic accent. "Gute Morten. Would you like some brukfrust?"

"Sure, Annoy-ay," he quipped, knowing that she never caught the mistake. But his father... well, he never called her that in front of his father.

She bustled around and quickly served him up some concoction they did in the North Galactic—thin, puffy bread things stacked on the plate. She called them "pancakes."

He told himself that if he didn't eat, it would mean another "talk" with his father.

As he ate, he thought about his Galactic North lessons in school. They'd gone off to live their own way and hadn't communicated with the USF for almost two centuries. Though none of the teachers wanted to talk about it, several students whispered that they were called Pilgrims, or Colonists, even Cowards by some who said they ran away from... something. No one knew exactly what, but they must have been running.

With only one known slipstream, trade was throttled, and the settlers kept to themselves and drove others away.

But they sure did invent some interesting food, he thought as he munched the fluffy pancake. *Too bad that's the only thing I like about them.* He didn't finish, but shoved the rest in his pocket and grabbed his backpack with his sketchbook inside before she could say anything else.

"Faxall, I wan..." But the door had already closed behind him.

He grinned as he coasted down the rails of the stairwell. None of the elevators had worked since the crash, but it was still a lot nicer than old Kusam. After the battle, a lot of people had moved away.

But the smashed hull still lay there, like a gravestone proclaiming the loss of untold thousands of human lives. Including the one that only Faxil cared about, his mother.

When he got outside, he found a beast waiting for him, at least twice his mass, with four powerful legs, a meter-long tail and a pointed snout with razor-sharp teeth. The beast growled and yipped, then ran in circles around him.

"Who's a good khain? Who's a good girl?" he said as he pulled the mashed pancake from his pocket. Kuon—he'd named it—was instantly on the alert, its long, thin whip-tail lashing back and forth as the lithe scaly body danced around him.

"No, no. Sit," he commanded. Kuon proceeded to roll on her back. "Come on, sit up." Kuon instead jumped up and tried to stand, leaning against Faxil until he fell down. He dropped the pancake, and Kuon eagerly gobbled it up.

"What a dumb khain," he muttered as Kuon looked at him for more. "No, I don't have any more. I can only sneak out a little at a time."

Kuon tried to look pleading, but on the angled hunter's face it looked comically angry instead. Faxil laughed and ruffled behind her feathery antennae. "Oh, who's a dummy? Who's my dummy little khain? Is it you, Kuon? Is it you?"

Kuon made a little growly yip and danced some more.

How long has it been now since I found her crawling around in the ruins? he wondered. *Two weeks? Three? It seems longer. She's doing much better now. It's amazing what a little food can do.*

She was more playful than usual. He took a minute to pull out his sketchbook and tried to capture some of her playfulness. *Who would have thought I would have a pet? And a khain? Wish I could take her inside at night.*

Try as he might, his sketch just didn't have the... life he

wanted. It was the difference between a posed photograph and a video still. No movement.

"Come on, let's get going," he said as he shoved his sketchbook into his backpack. "There's nothing for us around here."

———

Faxil liked watching Kuon dance around, looking for more food. He was pretty sure that she'd made a dent in the local rat population. He grinned at the thought as he made his way down through the rubble of the city streets, once filled with gravcars and shops of every kind and people—all the people he could imagine. Even now, it seemed a number too large to count, even if he knew this was only one city of one colony on one planet around one star. It had been... not a bad life.

Then the Blues had arrived and changed everything.

They had strange bodies covered with glass-like armor with a blue glow that shot out of their arms and wiped away whatever it hit. They seemed unstoppable.

He wondered if "they want to kill all humans" was something the news people made up to make them scarier. He'd learned about the word "propaganda" in school before the invasion last year, and the news stories about Blues seemed to fit.

"Hey, blue-licker."

He looked around. *Great, it's Tuptein.*

Tuptein was a bully. Sixteen years old, tall, skinny and dressed like a boy, she and her gang emerged from the alley behind where the grocer used to be. "What are you doing here, glassface?"

"I live here." *You sack of stupid. And who came up with your insults?*

"We don't like having a Blue-kissing human hater in our part of this fair city," Tuptein snapped.

"I'm not a human hater," Faxil said, realizing he was in for it. When Tuptein started calling him a human hater, it meant her goons were going to beat him up. He tried to stall. "And… what? Wait. Fair city?" he said. "Have you looked at this place?"

"The Blues trashed our city," she snapped. "And since we got no Blues here, we're gonna settle for trashing your blueglass ass."

Faxil was becoming desperate. "I'm not a human hater." He looked around. "Kuon?"

"What? Are you practicing your birdcalls?" one of Tuptein's goons sniggered. "Ku-on, ku-on. Or is that something you got from your new mommy?"

Faxil's rage flared, and he bent down, grabbed a rock and threw it at the goon. The boy dodged, and it hit a girl in the gang instead.

"You little prick," she yelled. "I'm gonna cut you a new one," she spat as she pulled a blade made from a shard of glass from inside her clothing and whirled it around in circles as she stepped toward him.

A deep-throated snarl halted her in her tracks. Everyone looked around.

Kuon stood there, long legs tensed, ready to jump. Her tail lashing so hard the air cracked.

"Kuon, here, girl," Faxil managed to croak out more confidently than he felt. She came immediately to his side and rubbed against his leg.

"That's a khain," Tuptein said.

"She's my pet." He managed to sound like he was bragging.

"You can't make a pet out of a khain," Tuptein scoffed. "That's crazy,"

"Maybe it is," he said. "So, how about you stop harassing me? Or should I tell her to bite off your leg? Or an arm?"

Knife-girl quickly tucked her blade back in her clothes.

"Tell you what, glass-kisser." Tuptein laughed. "How about you go down to the crash site and pick out something shiny for me?"

The thought of desecrating the mass grave of *Peacemaker*

filled him with disgust. "I'm supposed to rob a human wreck site just to prove I'm not a human hater?"

"No. I want you to get me something from the Blue ship."

The demand was so audacious that, for a moment, he couldn't even answer. He stared at Tuptein in horror, then said, "Wait—you want me to go beyond the Tape? Are you crazy?"

"The only crazy one here is you," she replied. "Crazy if you want to risk us catching you without your... friend, next time."

He thought about that for a moment. A life constantly on guard, or relative freedom?

The choice was easy.

"Fine, I'll go inside the Tape, and I'll find the glowiest piece of debris I can and bring it to you."

"Good. Because if you don't, I'll have you beat every day until you do." She turned away, snapped her fingers, and her goons followed her into another alleyway.

"Come on, girl," Faxil said with a nervous laugh. "We're gonna go do some grave robbing."

———

FAXIL STOOD BEFORE THE TAPE.

Once, it had been a line of yellow tape with the words "Caution: Authorized Personnel Only." When the tape and the few guards allotted to enforce it had proved ineffective, they put up a fence and assigned dozens of guards. When the addition of shockwire still failed to deter the curious and looters, they erected concrete barriers topped with shockwire, cameras and auto-tracking gun turrets. And across the barrier was a meter-tall yellow stripe reading "WARNING: UNAUTHORIZED PERSONNEL WILL BE SHOT."

Faxil sighed. Everyone knew that the cameras had limited coverage, the turrets only fired warning shots, and the barrier was full of holes. He found a small entrance, too small for the much larger Tuptein and her crew, and ducked through, Kuon following close behind.

The pale hull of the Swarm ship seemed immense. It had sunk too deep for the salvage ships to try and lift it out; the ship's engines would have wreaked havoc on the remains of the city. And who knew how many buildings might collapse under the engine wash?

The fuselage was huge, about the size of two gravtrucks, lying in a crater the length of a sports field and half as deep, and it was studded across its wing-things with what he assumed were weapon nodes. On a human-built directed energy weapon —DEWs as they called them—the weapon was housed in a turret. But here, it looked like a gray egg, and it was disconcerting to see no evidence of the technology that killed so many people. He thought about trying to draw it but couldn't find the right angle to depict the space accurately.

He could see the detritus left by the USF investigators. At first, there had been every kind of news coverage: "Crashed Swarm Ship. Investigations Ensue" or "What new tools can we take from this lucky break?" or "What Swarm secrets will scientists glean from the shipwreck?"

But after a few weeks, the furor died down, and the wreck became just another piece of debris to be cleaned up, at least that's what they told the public.

He made his way to the hole in the side of the ship. Human ship hulls broke when they were damaged, leaving jagged edges. And from what he'd heard, Swarm ships simply cracked apart, but this hole had strange rounded ridges all around, as though something had heated it up and then pushed the hull material aside, making it buckle. He had no idea how that could happen, but he bet the USF scientists had all sorts of theories.

He slipped through the hole and then stood there amazed. Nothing inside looked like a human could fly the ship.

The room, or whatever it was, was huge and round, like the inside of an egg, with USF LifeLights attached to various...

extremities? He tapped the green icon on the one nearest to him, and they all lit up.

The seats, if that's what they were, were attached to every part of the wall, ceiling, floor, walls, whatever you wanted to call them. It was as if they didn't care about gravity. He took out his sketchbook and scribbled a rough drawing.

The next room had some kind of egg-shaped nodes on posts, again jutting from every part of the curved walls. *Holo generators?* he wondered as he walked to the next room. The large screens, if that's what they were, were simply black panels shaped to and inset into the walls. He sketched that room, too.

As he walked on through the ship, it seemed amazing to him how spacious everything felt. And then he found a room that made no sense at all, not that any of the others did either.

It was longer, taller, and the left side was covered in strange-looking depressions that appeared to be shaped like the Blues armor he'd seen in vids. The LifeLights didn't quite reach into the corners.

Do they... attach themselves to the walls when they travel? he wondered. *How could that be comfortable? Are they docking pods?* He tried to sketch the room but couldn't get the shading for the "docking pods" right. There were fifteen of them. He stared at them, wondering how they got in and out of them, and then realized that he didn't even know if the ship was sitting upright. *If they don't care about gravity, who can say I'm not standing on a wall right now? Maybe those are beds.*

But nowhere in the Blue cruiser did he see anything that wasn't firmly attached.

Of course there isn't. He wanted to kick himself. *The scientists took everything they could already. They probably didn't take the screen things because they couldn't cut them loose or something. Or maybe they want the whole ship intact to power up and study.*

Not only had his foray into the alien ship been a total waste of time, but he'd also agreed that Tuptein would beat him up every day if he failed.

Why do I have to be such a loser? he wondered.

He started back toward the hole in the hull. He could probably look for days and not find something for Tuptein. *Is there a chance I could fake it?* he thought as he passed through the openings. *Find something that looks Blue?*

Then he realized he was in a room he didn't recognize, and it had a person-sized hole in the floor. The melted-ridges thing was the same as he'd seen before, but it was in the floor, not on the wall. *If it is the floor*, he thought.

He looked down through the hole. The light was dim. The space below was vast and... *what is that?* There were railings and steel steps. *It must be one of the factories, I think. Hmm, maybe I should check it out.*

Faxil lowered himself through the hole and carefully landed onto the catwalk of the old factory as Kuon boldly leapt from one spot to another. The khain was surprisingly agile. *How can this still be here? Shouldn't the crash have destroyed it all?*

So many factories had been destroyed in the crashes. Millions of lives lost in just a few moments. Yet here was a factory, seemingly perfectly preserved. At least, in part; this part.

Could my mom still be alive? Was her factory not destroyed, too? He tried to shake thoughts of his mother trapped underground, slowly starving—*No, they would have had food,* he reassured himself, however shakily.

From the corner of his eye, in the distance, he spotted a strange blue glow. He shrank back, and Kuon followed, giving him little licks on his hands like she had the day he'd cried over his mother's empty grave.

Blues? How can there be Blues here? Survivors? He realized that he might be the only person who knew about this, and the thought terrified him. *How did the scientists miss this?*

He shook himself. He couldn't just run away... could he?

But I'm here now. And I have Kuon. The khain nudged him reassuringly.

Bolstered by the presence of his loyal companion, he crept forward and looked out and down again.

Trying to keep from shaking, he continued slowly downward. Kuon stayed close, nudging him when he slowed as if she was encouraging him, though he couldn't figure out why. Wasn't she scared of Blues, too?

She's a khain. And khains aren't scared of anything.

Determined not to show cowardice, he made his way down to the factory floor where he stood for a moment, looking around, Kuon by his side. Far away to his right, he could now see the glow was coming from a tunnel bored through the wall. Slowly he approached it, and soon he could see it angled downward into the ground. He reached the tunnel entrance and peered in, and he couldn't figure out why they would—

There was a strange flicker of light. He took a step back. The blue glow was growing brighter, and then he saw it: a Blue trooper pushing some kind of cart to the top of the tunnel, its wheels squeaking.

Faxil froze. The Blue had seen him. It stopped.

What do I do?

He didn't have to do anything. Kuon charged, snarling.

The Blue raised its arm and aimed its weapon at Faxil.

"NO!" Faxil screamed.

The Blue fired as Kuon slammed into the cart perched at the top of the slope. The cart rolled backward, crashing into the Blue, knocking it down. The stream of plasma arched upward and, barely missing Faxil, carved a swath of destruction across the factory wall, slicing through pipes and ductwork and the catwalk.

The cart rolled over the Blue, crushing it beneath its wheels. The Blue exploded, the blast ripping into the walls of the tunnel entrance. Kuon was thrown back. She bounced once, twice, three times, rolled and somehow landed on her feet. She stood for a second, shook herself and looked around.

"Kuon!" he screamed. Kuon looked at him and started toward him. "Come on, girl. Let's go."

He scrambled back up the wreckage of the catwalk. The plasma had sliced through the lower section. Other than that, the rest of the structure seemed to be intact.

He looked back; Kuon was standing at the bottom of the steps looking up at him. "Come on," he yelled. "We need to get out of here."

Kuon limped up the steps. She was moving slowly, limping, but he was sure she—

Another rumble shook the catwalk, and he could see it wasn't nearly as sturdy as he'd thought.

"Hurry, come on. Good girl," he called encouragingly. "When we get home, I'll bring you a whole dinner." She seemed to pick up her pace, and he scrambled across the swaying catwalk toward the damaged section of the wrecked Blue hull.

"Come on," he called again as Kuon made it up to the catwalk. "Let's go—"

He was interrupted by a massive explosion somewhere deep inside the tunnel. The building shook. The tunnel began to collapse. The world flashed white, and suddenly Faxil couldn't see anything but purple. He felt the catwalk shudder and shake beneath his feet. Something brushed against his leg; Kuon had made it.

"Come on, girl," he shouted as, half-blinded, he groped his way along the trembling catwalk, following a pinpoint of yellow in the purple haze, the LifeLights inside the ship.

He scrambled up through the hole in the ship's hull, then turned to help Kuon. "We're out!" he shouted. "Come on, Kuon, we made it." He expected to hear her paws clicking, or her yipping, or even just panting. But he heard nothing.

As his eyes adjusted to the light, he found himself alone.

"Kuon?" he whispered.

He stared down into the hole. Kuon was gone.

He made his way through the ship and out into the open, tears running down his cheeks. *Kuon...*

"I heard something," someone shouted. "Over there."

"There's someone inside the Tape," another voice shouted.

Faxil panicked. He turned and ran and... blundered into the arms of a USF uniform.

"Ho now. What do we have here?" the uniform muttered.

Faxil didn't answer. Instead, he struggled, trying to get free, but to no avail.

"I think you need to answer a few questions, young man."

CHAPTER
FOUR

PREY AND PREDATOR

Freighter *Brigallegro*
Near Planet Thoth
Horus Planetary System

"How far until we reach the Slip point?" Captain Mickle Laitho demanded as his ship burned for the outer system.

"Seventeen thousand two hundred ten kilometers, Captain," the Navigation officer replied.

"Have we lost that signal yet?" Laitho said to the Sensors operator.

"No, Captain. *Brigallegro* is moving as fast as she can," the Sensors operator announced, "but it's gaining on us."

"That Sovereign ship is a little too spry for my tastes," Laitho muttered to himself. "What about those fighter launches we detected from the planet earlier?"

"No pings since, Captain," the Sensors operator replied.

"First Mate, thoughts?" Laitho asked.

"Cap'n, I hate to be a naysayer, but..."

"Say your nays, John."

"We can't outrun them, and if we're caught…" the first mate didn't bother to elaborate. "If we were smart," he continued, "we'd dump the cargo and let them slow for it."

"And you think they would do that?" Laitho asked skeptically.

"If they look to recover it…"

"There's no reason to stop," Laitho said. "Cargo doesn't have many places to go in space. And they might suspect it was a bomb or other sabotage. No, I don't think—"

The ship rocked from weapons fire, and alarms blared.

"Sensors, report," Laitho snapped.

"We… I don't…"

"I said report," Laitho spat.

"I don't know why, but I can't track them, sir," she stuttered. "There doesn't seem to be anything on the sensors."

But a moment later, the sight of an F-32A crossed the forward viewport.

"Can you track them now?" he shouted.

"They're not on sensors," she shouted back as another series of blasts targeted their engines.

Another F-32A fighter cruised by and fired a shot that hit the forward weapons turret. It was followed by a second F-32 that took out the main antennae array, an expert shot, apparently, as the communications console blinked off and reset to default. A third F-32 drew up alongside less than a half-klick off the port bow, matching his speed exactly with its weapons trained on the *Brigallegro's* forward viewport.

Laitho sighed. "I think we're about to be boarded," he said. "Well, if they want us, they apparently can have us. No need to make them work for it."

He got on the comm. "Stand by all hands. We're about to be boarded. Lock down the cargo in the shielded compartment, and make sure you activate the safeties. We don't want to explode, now do we? And if there's a chance we can bluff our way out of this, I want to grab it." He dropped the comm, turned to the Sensors operator and said, "And scramble the sensor rig. Make it look like we couldn't see them coming."

"Aye, sir."

He watched as she input the instructions that would cripple their sensory array to half-range and remove any trace of interference. Then, as the other crew members dashed away to secure the cargo, Laitho rose from his captain's chair—a very expensive and comfortable one, too—stepped up behind his sensors operator, drew his failsafe and stabbed her in the neck.

"Captain. What are... you..." Her words grew faint as she slumped sideways in her seat.

"I can't have you blabbing to everybody about what we were doing," he whispered as her eyes widened in alarm. "You're too excitable, too frantic. You might let something slip. You've become a hazard, my dear."

Her body went slack. He looked down at her, sighed, then grabbed both her arms and dragged her out of her seat.

Where to put her? he wondered as he dragged her limp body along the companionway. *The infirmary would be the most logical place, I think.*

The ship rocked again. "How many warning shots do they need?" Laitho yelled before realizing the truth. The reverberations weren't weapons fire.

"They've activated a lamprey. Prepare for hull breach."

The other ship was about to perform a hot-dock with cutters. *I hope these people don't kill us all; accident or otherwise.*

———

THE *JUSTIFICATION* WAS a sword of law sliding through the black—a metaphor Second-Corporal Lagu Feria wanted to savor before they caught up to the *Briga*-whatever. He was strapped into his drop harness, but his foot wouldn't stop tapping. He really, *really* wanted to get this guy.

Don't think about that right now, he told himself. *Just think about what's coming up. Concentrate on the team. Concentrate on the objectives.*

"Quit stomping your boot, Feria," Master Sergeant Strigett ordered. "You're wearing a hole in the hull."

Beside him, First-Corporal Dusina whispered, "What's got you all worked up, partner? This is a milk-run."

That's not what the captain said, Feria thought. He'd heard the message from Prince Tarak before his yacht had docked. If what he'd heard was true...

Don't think, don't think, don't think. If he thought too hard about what he'd heard, then everyone would know.

And besides, this was a hot-dock. A hot-dock was always a tricky proposition, but proper docking could take minutes, and when getting the jump on smugglers, time was a resource you couldn't waste.

"Is something wrong?" Dusina whispered. Feria could only shake his head.

The red light flared, and the intercom squawked. "Prepare to gravclamp." The humming in the air became a roar as the generators fed power to the clamps. Once they got close, there was no way that the smuggler could escape. The sensation of falling upward headfirst was nothing new to Feria, but he heard someone else moan.

THUNK. The impact against the smaller ship could be felt all across the drop bay. Their helmets sealed automatically, switching to canned air, and Feria heard the whine of plasma torches as the hotcutter went to work.

You grunts know your assignments, MSgt. Strigett barked inside their minds. While it made communicating much easier, Feria still wasn't used to battlefield Psy communications.

Twenty pinpoint plasma cutting heads traced a circle in the hull even as the breach seals fitted into place.

Take your positions and clear your sections. Even for a Psy, the sergeant had quite the bellow.

In seconds the torches had completed their work. The section of hull fell up into the grav clamp and maglocked in place. The gravclamp cut off, and everyone was suddenly falling feetfirst again.

Squad one, debark.

As the harnesses of Squad One released and they were ejected down through the still glowing hole, one of them slammed into the edge but was uninjured by the collision, receiving only a scorch mark to his battle armor.

Squad Two, debark. The next group ejected, the hole cooling rapidly from yellow to orange.

Squad Three, debark.

Before he got the last word out, Feria felt his harness snap away, spit him loose and out through the hole and into the freighter, along with 1st Cpl. Dusina, Strike Sergeant Metlock, 2nd Cpl. Perru, Lance Sergeant Condi, and 2nd Cpl. Humba.

Squad Three. In pairs, Metlock ordered. *Search the starboard side for combatants.*

Feria and Dusina broke away and followed the floor plan they'd memorized in their briefing. He'd been amazed that they had such detailed knowledge of their target, but he didn't complain. Lack of details got people killed. *Well, the wrong people, anyway,* he thought to himself, but he thought Dusina might have caught the gist.

Many doors were open, which made for caution—closed doors usually meant people hiding. Open doors meant people waiting.

Room clear, Dusina sent, and Feria came in and peered into the room beyond. Seeing nothing, he entered, weapon sweeping as he searched for a target.

Please let there be a target.

Please let there be no targets.

He was used to that by now.

Room clear. No exit, he replied and pulled back to investigate the next area.

The desire to avoid conflict, the desire to punish... Feria had seen a lot since he joined the military. But this wasn't the old world anymore, and hesitation meant death, and the boy he'd been didn't understand the man he'd become. And maybe never would. But the man would survive. At least, he intended to survive if he could. But inside, the boy wept.

Feria and Dusina cleared their section of the ship but found only one crew member huddled under a bed, holding a rebreather to his face.

"Get out from there," Feria ordered.

"Do we still have atmo?" the man replied, his voice muffled by the rebreather.

"Did your eyeballs get sucked out of your head?" Dusina yelled. "No? So get your carcass out of there. NOW."

The man crawled out from under the bed and allowed himself to be constrained.

With no other places to search, they took him back to the entrance point, where there were more than a dozen prisoners waiting, their hands clamped behind their backs with wristlinks.

"Where's your captain?" Strigett demanded. "Until we talk to the captain, this ship is officially impounded under the Suspicion of Abetting Enemies Act. Unless this was a mutiny, in which case it becomes Suspicion of Mutiny. Either way, that makes all of you incarcerated until trial."

"That's not how we do things in the Independent Militia of Free People," one of the crew retorted.

"Well then, maybe you should have stayed there." Strigett said and laughed. "Because here, when we're in a war, we don't take namby-pamby rights for granted. We strive for—"

"That's enough," a voice said from above.

Feria looked up and saw the captain hop down into the freighter. *Master Sergeant, I believe we haven't talked in a while,* he sent, very deliberately, to the entire boarding party. *I'll expect you in my ready room when we've finished here, so we can talk about the definition of **inherent rights**.*

Yes, sir, Strigett sent weakly.

It was difficult for the boarding party to see him dressed down like that. Captain Objur had a real sense of command, and he wielded it like a rapier. But to the freighter's crewmembers, it looked like nothing more than a simple stare.

Objur took a portable comm override from his belt, tapped an icon, and said, "This is Arden Objur, and I am captain of the *Justification*. I would like to speak to the captain of this vessel, *Brigallegro*. We will have a short conversation. If the conversation goes well, we will apologize for the trouble, offer you a quick patch to your hull and issue a stipend to have it repaired, and send you on your way. Please come forward, Captain."

He lowered the comm unit.

"And what if it doesn't go well?" one of the crew members asked.

"Then I have to turn it over to my boss to handle," the captain said quietly. "And that will not be pleasant."

Somewhere down the companionway, they heard the sound of a hatch banging and then, "Let go of me. This is my ship, and I have rights, you festering stupid—"

"Your ship? Then I assume you are the captain?" Objur said as Laitho was shoved roughly in front of him.

"Yes, you pus-sucking—"

"I am Captain Arden Objur, and—"

"I caught your little radio show. What are you doing on my ship?"

"I came here to ask you some questions."

"And you had to hot breach my ship for that?" Laitho spat.

Objur smiled—an expression that made Feria shiver. He'd never seen teeth look so... He didn't have a word for it.

"You spent so much effort trying to avoid us that we assumed you were hostile. So here we are. Where's your cargo, Mr. Laitho?"

The freighter captain's face blanched as he stammered, "That's... not my name. I'm Captain—"

"You are Mickle Laitho, with two lapsed warrants for questioning in connection with various questionable activities. Your license under the name Ceni Dezen is technically illegal, but since you're from the Independent Militia of Free People, we don't need to clean up their backlog of petty crime. So, with the knowledge that we really do want to let you go about your business, where is your cargo?"

"We don't have any cargo," he blustered. Even without Psy, Feria and the other members of the platoon would have pegged it as a lie. But this smuggler didn't realize that, not yet.

"You certainly were in a hurry to get away," Objur said.

Laitho smiled. "As it happens, we didn't know you were there. Our sensors are on the fritz."

"Ah, yes. And your sensors officer has, quite suddenly, passed away. How inconveniently unfortunate for me... for her."

"How did you—"

"I have a full dossier on your crew and twenty-four of Border Control's finest combing your ship. Did you think I wouldn't find a dead body behind a false panel?"

"But... I didn't kill her. I only—" He shut his mouth.

"I said if the conversation went well, I would let everyone go. But it isn't going well, is it, my friend? One last time; where is your cargo?"

Laitho said nothing.

"Then I have to send this up the ladder." He thumbed his lapel comm. "Your Excellency? I'm afraid we need you."

In moments a pair of very nice boots appeared in the opening. They were followed by expensive black slacks, a rich demicape, a starched white shirt complete with medals, and... the face of royalty itself: Prince Tarak.

If there's a guy who looks more like a prince than him, I wouldn't believe it, Feria thought as the boots touched down on the deck.

———

LAITHO WATCHED as the prince descended on a dropline, his cape fluttering in the air exchange. *Thinks he's a damn hero out of the fairy stories, does he?*

"Mickle Laitho, my captain has been very patient with you," the prince said. "You have made several obvious and serious mistakes, and to proclaim your innocence now is an affront to my ears and patience. I will not detain these fine men and women any longer than necessary to find what I seek. I will ask you, with the full authority invested in me as both a member of the royal house and a diplomatic envoy with full prosecutorial agency, where—is—your—cargo?"

"I don't have any—"

And that was when his mind came apart.

He felt something push into his thoughts, like a hot knife into butter. It turned his entire self to jelly. He groped for meaning or connection as his thoughts were turned inside out and then discarded until the one he prized most was simply... removed. Then the wedge pulled out, but something remained, tugging at his thoughts, lining them up again, putting them back together like a broken vase, but not quite. Almost but not exactly.

And then it was gone.

He tried to speak, tried to scream at this misbegotten piece of trash who'd violated him. He wanted to tell the prince everything he really thought about their pointless royalty, their useless monarchies, the true freedom of the IMFP. But he couldn't speak. His mouth wouldn't obey. He could feel drool collecting at the corners of his mouth, but he couldn't close his mouth to swallow it.

Don't worry, came the same smug, authoritative voice in his mind. *I'm getting much better at it. I'm sure you'll regain most of your functions in... a year? It's hard to say. I saw what you think of me, but I let you live anyway.*

Mickle Laitho watched the prince speak to his troops.

"I have the location of the secret compartment. You can expect resistance. Take them down hard. Stun batons only."

The prince was so loud inside his head, Laitho's brain hurt. Then he realized the prince was using the override comm. *He wants everyone to know what he's doing. Smarty, smarty...* His brain hurt so much.

The prince turned to look at him and smiled.

Laitho tried to think of why he would do that. It was obvious, really—he just told the crew that if they fired on his soldiers, they would beat them down, but if they surrendered, they wouldn't. But, if the crew shot everyone, then they would look like the sparkly bears that his sister used to like on all her things when she was little. *Wait, that doesn't make sense.* His brain hurt, and he was having such a hard time keeping his thoughts together.

And why was he suddenly "the Prince"? He didn't deserve such... respect, not from him. He was from the Inter... Intim... Independent Free Porcupines. *Wait, the Free Persimmons. The Free Percolations?* His brain was babbling. *What did you do to me?*

Again the prince smiled at him. *Nothing you won't recover from, eventually.*

"There's a section of false wall in the mess," the prince said. "Your target is behind it. And someone get Medical down here."

Ha. He don't know eveyfink.

The drool dripped from Laitho's mouth and his brain hurt.

———

FERIA AND DUSINA followed Strike Sergeant Metlock and the other members of the platoon to the mess hall. Something about the situation seemed off. *Why would the prince send us without weapons?* He directed the thought to Dusina.

Maybe the cargo is explosives, Dusina responded. *We're rated for vacuum, but the prince and his entourage are sans armor.*

You're forgetting everyone on our ship, Metlock barked. *The hole we cut in the hull of this hulk is going to be a problem if we suck the atmo out of both vessels.*

Obviously, depressurization warnings and safety bulkheads would minimize the dangers, but Feria wasn't about to even think that everyone in the troop would hear and he would be ostracized.

"Yeah, that's right," Dusina whispered. "Whatever you were thinking, yep, you would."

It was strange that the way to keep thoughts private in a Psy group was to talk to each other.

The mess hall was, well, a mess. Whoever had been there before either hadn't had time to hide properly or had planned poorly. Either way, the opposite wall was cleared of tables and chairs.

I'm detecting lifesigns with the scanner, Humba sent.

But we have no mental signs, replied Condi.

And that is the nutshell, Metlock responded. *They're scared enough to use brand-new technology to guard against Psy users, but they forgot to activate their own regular defenses. Not that we could have missed the trail they left us. Anyone see the release mechani—*

But the need to open the section of wall was removed when it opened of its own accord, and DEW laser fire poured out.

Combat armor could take a hit or two. But the way the six smugglers were panicking, it was more like ten per person, every second. The team broke into groups, drawing fire into three directions.

Can anyone get a clear mind to poke?

I can barely concentrate on anything.

Who's going to—

But Feria had had enough. *Dusina, cover me,* he sent,

charging forward before realizing he'd impulsively left himself open with no cover fire, but by then, he was committed.

He barreled forward and tackled two of the shooters. In the moments he was exposed, he'd felt at least three shots strike his chest. Not willing to look yet, he forced himself to stand and swing at another shooter and then found himself supported by Dusina while Perru, Condi and Humba subdued the remaining four.

Feria. Are you trying to get yourself killed? Metlock bellowed silently.

No, sir, he replied.

Good. Because now I have to put you in for something heroic, Metlock spat, *and I'd hate to have to pin it to a corpse. Get yourself to Med and get checked out. And your can probably needs to be recycled. Take it to the Armory for inspection. I don't want to see it again.*

Yes, sir, Feria replied. Metlock was a cautious leader, but he'd learned the hard way, if half the stories about him were to be believed. *Did we get it, sir?*

We got something, Metlock replied, *but it's locked up tighter than Uncle Ned's brandy. Not our concern now. Humbo, Condi, keep an eye on this until the prince has it removed.*

Yes, sir, they sent in unison.

Dusina escorted him back to Medbay. "You blithering idiot, what was the point of rushing them like that?"

He sighed. "I've just been on edge lately. I made a mistake."

"It's more than that," she said. "You seemed to forget we didn't have weapons."

"I was just... distracted," he replied.

Are you really trying to hide things? she asked using Psy. *You know I can feel everything, right?*

Feria didn't reply.

Now you're just sulking.

———

"Thank you. You're dismissed," Prince Tarak said to the two soldiers guarding his prize, or his curse. They saluted and briskly departed while his personal prize crew examined the secret hold.

Tarak could *feel* the thing on the other side of the wall. This close, it was unmistakable. The other Psy-Ops might not have noticed its intrusion, but *he* could.

"They fought hard, my Prince," Objur said.

Tarak was glad of the distraction. "Not only that, but they had these." He held up one of the modified halo jacks the smugglers had been wearing. "Not that it did them any good."

"What is it?" Objur asked.

Tarak simply slipped it over his head, and the pulsing from the prize diminished. *It's a poorly modified halo,* he sent. *This shielding is weak compared to ours, but the filter is quite effective.*

Objur gave a slight start. "You've almost vanished from my mind. I never get more than a mental sense of your presence, my Prince, but if I wasn't standing here beside you, looking at you, I'd assume you were dead."

"We have something similar," Tarak said, unwilling to disclose more details. But the secret was clearly out.

"And this one is cleverly hidden in a real halo," he continued. "We could easily have missed it. There's obviously something seriously dangerous going on here."

"What do you think we'll find here, my prince?" Objur asked.

Tarak removed the smuggler's halo, and the sickening aura returned. "I already know what we'll find," he said. "I've had agents watching every questionable ship in every port within my jurisdiction."

"Sir, but you're out of your jurisdiction," Objur said as the prize crew removed the entire wall panel.

"What we have here, Objur, made it necessary for me to apply for prosecutorial status in order to apprehend this criminal. But if they knew then what I know now, they would have rejected my application and possibly would have bungled it. So yes, I'm out of my jurisdiction, but we have what we came for, and that's all that matters."

He felt Objur's attitude toward him change immediately. "My Prince, are you admitting to concealing criminal activity from my superiors?"

"Your loyalty is a fine thing, Objur, but I ask that you look at the big picture. The Horus Planetary Authority may be part of the USF, but they have always played poorly with others. Frankly, they *might* have kept this... prize for themselves, and that *might* have been disastrous."

"You keep saying 'might,'" Objur said.

Tarak could feel Objur's animosity. But the section of wall had almost been removed, and he hesitated to reply.

Objur apparently took his moment of hesitation as a retreat. "What kind of duplicitous royal scheme have you concocted to pilfer items from our jurisdiction, may I ask?"

"I have concocted no such scheme, Captain. But somebody did. I'm just here to stop it."

"And profit from it, no doubt."

"I'm not sure I like your tone, Captain," Tarak said easily. "You are remarkably forward considering you're addressing a royal."

"And you, sir, are very reserved even in Psy, so I prefer to speak, knowing you will betray more in tone and expression than you might suspect."

"I'm well aware of my capabilities, Captain Objur. But let me ask you something..." Tarak said as the prize crew lifted away the panel to reveal the glowing, pulsing, writhing tentacled heart of a Swarm ship, surrounded by machines that clearly disturbed the thing and held it captive.

With the cover now fully removed, Tarak could feel its malignant presence even more. It felt like a mental cancer. Some part of that otherworldly living thing reverberated in his Psy, and it disturbed him greatly. Only now did Tarak realize the effectiveness of the modified shield. *And yet I wonder... could its influence have leaked out? Were the crew members affected by it? They certainly fought hard enough for it.*

"*What is* that?" Objur whispered. Tarak sensed he was on the verge of retching at the invasion of the alien not-mind into his.

"That, my friend, is the brain of a Swarm ship," he replied. "When you hurt its body, it heals itself; it regenerates. When you damage it, it detonates. Can you imagine your government toying with a secret of this magnitude? How long do you think it would be before something goes terribly wrong?"

Objur didn't answer immediately. He thought for a moment, then said, "Given the way they handled the Refractory incident, I wouldn't wish to speculate."

Tarak looked at him and nodded. "Very well, Captain. How would you and your Border Control Psy-Ops like to be assigned to my command for... the foreseeable future? Because, you see, it is imperative that I keep this..." He glanced at the pulsing orb then continued "...this thing top-secret. Can I count on you, Captain Objur?"

He could feel Objur mulling over the possibilities, including the thought of dying unexpectedly, and another of revulsion at the idea of being turned into a vegetable, like Laitho.

"Yes, my Prince," he replied. "I would agree to that as long as we are not required to do anything that might be in conflict with Horus's interests."

"Very good, Captain," Tarak said. "I understand completely. And I'm more than pleased you understand the severity of the situation. I'll reach out to your government, and I'd be grateful if you would brief your crew. We depart the system in thirty-six hours."

After Objur left, Tarak turned to his technicians, who by then looked as sick as he felt, and said, "Thank you for your hard work. Now please replace the panel." Then he turned to the squad leader, Metlock. "Find and distribute these modified halos to those who are required to guard that thing. We're going to be traveling with it for a little while longer." He paused, then added, "And set up the fail-safe device. That thing must not be allowed to..." He paused, shook his head, then said, "Just do it, Metlock."

CHAPTER
FIVE

DISOBEDIENCE

Feducere, Neujaz Apartments
Planet Caerus

Faxil had spent the last week in a detention center being treated like a criminal.

His criminality wasn't doubted. The USF investigators had stressed that. He'd entered a top-secret area, damaged property and equipment, and nearly gotten himself killed.

His father was furious, demanding explanations and screaming at him in ways Faxil had never experienced before. Part of him knew that his father was afraid for him. He even grasped, to the extent that a twelve-year-old could grasp anything, that his father's healed injury made him all the more fearful of any injuries, to himself or his family. But the one thing that Faxil could hardly bear—

"I don't feel I can trust you anymore," his father had said.

He wanted to scream.

How can you not trust me? How am I supposed to trust you?

You just abandoned my mother and found someone else. She can't even speak Standard properly. She's a joke.

He'd told them everything. He'd told them about the hole, and the factory down below, and seeing the Blue, and Kuon saving him—his father had been angry that he'd adopted some strange animal as a pet.

But they hadn't believed him.

Not about the Blue, anyway. His father had already been convinced he was sneaking food out for some reason, and a secret pet, so it seemed, was a good reason why.

If they called me a liar for having a pet and believed me about the alien, I'd be a hero. Instead, they believe I had a pet everyone is afraid of and call me a liar for reporting a secret alien base.

Because of course they'd found no evidence, just rubble. They'd even shown him pictures. The collapse was worse than he'd seen—enough to bury anything... everything. Which they said was convenient for his story—no Blue, no proof.

He'd spent the week in the apartment with Inoiae, kept like a prisoner in his home. Inoiae fussed over him constantly, never leaving him alone for long. She was the galaxy's most annoying prison guard.

For three days he played out the events in his head. But he didn't know what happened to Kuon. He couldn't look for her; for all he knew, she was dead.

Father always said I couldn't take care of anything. Fat lot of help he is, locking me up so I can't look for her. Sometimes his anger at his father, for that alone, eclipsed his frustration about Kuon.

So it was that he was slumped on the couch, flicking the control and trying to find a vid worth watching in the middle of the day, thinking about how he used to go to school.

"What do you want for lunch?" Inoiae called from the kitchen.

"Whatever, Annoy-ay," he said.

After a few minutes of bustling, she came in. She set down a bowl of soup and a sandwich on a plate.

He stared at it. His father never let him eat in the living room. He always said something would get spilled.

"Is this the thing you like?" she asked.

"But... why?"

"Because I thinking it is unfair. You are good son," she said in her stilted accent.

"Um... I... wait, what?"

She dropped her voice to a whisper. "I believe you. You do not making up stories."

He could only stare at her. "You believe me?"

"Yes. I try to tell him, but he is too angry. He doesn't want listen to me. I am very—"

"You believe me. That only makes things worse." He shoved past her, colliding with the small table and knocking over the soup. It fell with a crash as the bowl shattered.

He looked at the bowl and then at Inoiae.

"Why can't you just go back to... wherever," he yelled.

And for the first time, he saw her vapid smile evaporate. Her eyes filled with tears, and she covered her face with her hands.

He felt anger, he felt shame, he felt defeat.

He ran out the front door.

———

"Get him," Faxil heard just before he was tackled by... was it three people?

Tuptein's goons had him pinned down in short order, one gripping his wrists, the other two holding each of his legs.

Tuptein leaned over him, her eyes sparkling with glee.

"So, you take my challenge and disappear for a week. Just like a Blue-bellied coward."

"I'm not a Blue-belly. I was arrested."

"Arrested?" Tuptein sneered. "For what?"

"For going beyond the Tape," he insisted.

Her goons snickered. "Yeah, right."

"What a liar."

"They don't arrest ten-year-olds."

"I'm twelve," he yelled.

Tuptein glanced over at her goons. "My first stint in Detent was at ten. They really don't care how old you are." She looked back down at Faxil. "Where's your little friend? The one that keeps you from getting thrashed?"

Faxil had to keep from spitting at her. "Kuon followed me in. She got trapped somewhere, and I couldn't get back because the USF grabbed me."

"Interesting story." She stood in a thinking pose, tapping her booted feet. "Oh, let him up. You're not gonna try and escape, are ya?"

They released his wrists and ankles, and he stood up, brushing dirt and gravel from his clothes. "I guess not, as long as your bullies don't try to beat me up again."

"What?" one of them complained. "We only did that once."

"It's not like it's personal, man," another said.

"Well, I have decided," Tuptein announced. "You're going to prove to me that you went in there."

"I—what? Are you crazy?"

"Yep."

"But—I got arrested. By military police."

"Who are you afraid of more, me or them?"

He didn't want to admit it, but she had a point. Grown-ups never thrashed kids. Tuptein might easily break his knees with a hammer or something.

"So—why am I taking you to a top-secret area that I got arrested for?"

"I have decided to let you prove that you aren't a Blue-belly coward. That you aren't human-hating scum. That you don't throw rocks at human ships and scream 'I hate you I hate you' and stuff."

He remembered that day. The *Peacemaker*. He'd missed his mom so much that day...

"You mean that's what all this is about? All the crap about being a human-hating coward is because of—that? My mother is dead under that hull, you cross-eyed *moron*. Only an *idiot* would beat a kid up for losing his mom in the worst disaster in history."

The entire gang pulled away. Faxil regretted his words—No, he didn't regret them one bit. He didn't. But he would regret the beating a little.

Instead, she stared at him, her eyes harder than any time he'd seen her before. "My dad was aboard the *Peacemaker*. My mom was ground artillery. They both died. So, you listen to me. Take me inside your little playpen, and we're even. We never touch you again. Deal?"

"Fine." He shrugged as if it weren't any big deal. But inside, he was terrified of getting caught by the USF again. And he really didn't want to think about the Blue.

"Any of you cretins want to go with? See the inside of a Swarm ship?" she challenged her gang.

No one volunteered.

"Gee, it's real easy to call someone a coward when you make them do things you won't," Faxil goaded.

"If you aren't coming, then *fornhal* all of you," she snapped. "Why do I keep a bunch of losers around, anyway?"

She stomped off, with Faxil following. He had to keep his end of the bargain, after all—and if it was just a peek, then maybe he could avoid getting grabbed again.

From behind them, he could see the rest of her crew shuffling along, trying not to look shame-faced at being more cowardly than Faxil.

That put a little spring in his step.

In no time, they reached the Tape. A few moments scouting the perimeter showed another opening they could use. "In here," he motioned to Tuptein.

"Get going, you miscreants," she ordered, and her gang dutifully made their way to the hole in the concrete.

"Now," she demanded, "show me the real thing, Fax. I want to see the heart of this monster."

————

"Jump," Tuptein yelled, and her gang all leapt off the catwalk onto the collapsed rubble. They looked back at her and Faxil.

"What happened to staying quiet?" Faxil insisted. "I thought we—"

"What are you waiting for? Move outta my way," Tuptein snapped. Her minions all scrambled out of the way so their leader could make the jump. Faxil shook his head, then sighed and followed.

They all looked around, the other members of the gang poking in corners and generally gaping at the wreckage.

"So, you weren't making it all up," Tuptein said from his side. "But I don't see no Blues."

Faxil looked around until he spotted the place where the tunnel had been. "They were working over there," he said, pointing. He and Tuptein walked over. "It's weird, though. When it collapsed, it didn't look this bad. But when they showed my father pictures, it looked worse than this."

"Huh." Her grunt didn't inspire confidence, but she said, "Maybe they lied to him. Showed him a picture of somewhere else? Sure made you look like a vong, didn't they?"

He ignored her crass word and looked closer at the collapsed rocks. "Some of these have scrapes on them."

"Well, duh. They did fall down."

"No, I mean—look at these scrapes here. They're all in straight lines. And here on the floor, the same kind."

"So? It just means the USF came in with shovels," Tuptein said dismissively.

"But—" he tried to argue. As he considered it, though, it

was obvious that they would have a difficult time bringing anything heavier in, especially once the catwalk was half-destroyed.

And Kuon wouldn't have been able to escape, either. He'd lived with the guilt for the last week, more guilt than he'd ever felt about anything. But standing here, now, in the place he'd last seen her, it felt like a stab in his chest.

I abandoned her.

"Whatcha thinking about, Fax?"

He didn't want to answer, but she pinched the hairs on the back of his neck and pulled. "Ow, ow, *delfan*. I'm thinking about Kuon."

"What, the khain? Nothing messes with a khain. Your dumb darling is fine."

He whirled around. "Kuon got trapped down here and I ran away. Then I got arrested, and she's maybe been down here ever since. How could she get any food down here?"

Tuptein made a grimace. "Well, I guess she is in a peapod, then. What can ya do?"

"AAAAHH," screamed one of the gang.

In a split second, Tuptein ran faster than Faxil had ever seen. The boy who screamed was being menaced by—

"Kuon," he called. He ran after Tuptein, but as he got closer, his heart sank.

This wasn't the Kuon he remembered. This Kuon had lash scars all over her body, and her eyes glowed silver in the dim light. "Kuon. Stop, Kuon."

But Tuptein didn't stop. She collided with Kuon, knocking the khain away from her lackey. "You wanna piece of my boy? Try a bite of Tuptein Strugere instead."

Kuon dashed forward, and Tuptein took the blow but grabbed Kuon's fronds. Kuon made a pained howl that Faxil had never heard and clawed at the thing hurting her. Tuptein screamed as Kuon gouged her arms.

Kuon growled at her but turned as rocks began pelting her

hide.

"Hey, you stupid beast."

"No one messes with the boss."

Kuon turned to the others, who were immediately frightened and scattered. Kuon started to chase them but turned when the sounds of a sobbing Tuptein reached her ears. With wounded prey and no other distractions, the khain walked slowly toward the weeping girl.

Then Faxil knew what he had to do.

———

Faxil wasn't certain how he knew, but it was the most right and necessary thing he'd ever known. He ran and stood in front of Tuptein. He bared his teeth and growled, snarled, clawed the air, anything he could think of that seemed raw and beastly.

Kuon stopped and snarled back.

Then Faxil did something he'd never thought he could.

He turned his back, knelt down beside Tuptein, and hugged her.

Her shock was obvious. "What are you doing, you spaz?" she said in between sobs.

He whispered, "Play along and cry some more." She needed little encouragement to do that; he bobbed his head next to hers as though comforting her. Then he turned back to Kuon and snarled again.

And Kuon walked over to him, gave a sad, tired whimper, and collapsed on his lap.

This close, he could see the terrible abuse heaped on his poor Kuon.

Blinking through her tears, Tuptein whispered in horror, "What happened to your khain?"

"I don't know," he said. "But how did this happen if she was trapped down here alone?"

Tuptein didn't try to answer.

It took three shirts and a dull knife, but they cut up enough fabric for makeshift bandages for Tuptein and the other one of her crew who got attacked. His injuries were minimal. It took them the better part of two hours to figure out how to get Kuon out of the factory pit. But a little of Faxil's guilt began to subside. He had come back; he had saved her.

"Are you going to be okay?" he asked as the crew helped Tuptein limp back home, wherever that was.

"Yeah." She sighed. "I guess I'll have to crash at my aunt's again. Hope she gets her lazy…" she was saying, but he missed the last part, "…or her *stupid* jerkface guy to… maybe he bought food…"

But then she was around the corner. And he didn't know how he felt about that. *Should I chase after her? Should I try to find out more?* But even injured, she still had her friends to do her bidding. And maybe she didn't want to be disturbed.

That night, Faxil snuck out of the apartment building after his father and Annoy-ay went to bed. He brought a chunk of Gawbos steak he'd found in the back of the freezer. Annoy-ay said it was probably too old and dry to eat, but he'd hidden it away and let it thaw.

Kuon had found him three meters from the door. He didn't know if she'd heard him coming or smelled the raw meat, but she had no problem with old, dry Gawbos.

He sat there, stroking her head—one of the only places she didn't have scars. She looked up at him, and he wondered how he never realized her eyes glimmered silver before. Today was the first time he'd noticed.

While she was trying to eat people. He just hoped that she would remember that Tuptein and her gang had helped rescue her. They weren't her enemies anymore.

Heck, I'm hoping they remember I'm not their enemy anymore, either.

Kuon gave a purr that Faxil could feel all the way to his brain.

CHAPTER
SIX

FRIGATE *JUSTIFICATION*

L-5 Orbit over Geb-nute
Horus Planetary System

ONCE THEY HAD RETURNED to Geb-nute, Tarak had fabricated official documents to show charges of smuggling stolen goods out of the Odin system, dealt with by local government authorities as to the impounding of the *Brigallegro* and all its contents, the incarceration of the crew, and transferring all items of value from the *Brigallegro* to the *Justification.*

Tarak had followed every order he had been given except one, but he'd put his report off as long as he could. He knew what would be said, the arguments that would be made, and what would ultimately be decided.

He didn't need any special powers to know this; he simply knew who he worked for.

He placed the halo on his head, jacking into the Queen's personal meeting chamber, a simple room of smooth stone pillars, a polished floor and a raised dais for her imposing stone throne.

And then he waited.

He also knew what was going to happen. Queen Zara was not a woman to be pushed or rushed into anything.

Finally, Her Majesty appeared before him, seated on her throne. "You have delayed your report to me," she observed dryly.

"There were many details I felt needed to be confirmed before I made my report, Your Majesty," he replied equally dryly.

"You have an astounding facility to say things that are precisely true and yet serve your own interests without my detecting any falsehoods." But the Queen's mouth quirked slightly upward.

"My only interests were to quell the political rumblings before they became ramifications that needed to be dealt with."

"I'm sure," she replied, even more dryly. "How is information containment?"

"My agent was on board and is nearly recovered from her ordeal," Tarak replied. "She was incapacitated by the captain, possibly because he sought to protect her from us."

"Interesting loyalty you breed. What more?"

"We have the entire smuggler crew in the brig," he replied. "They will be delivered to Odin-controlled prisons as time permits. I've also taken the liberty of securing their Border Control Psy-Ops team to prevent any further information leaks."

"I'd have preferred to use our own team for that," the queen said.

"I wasn't in a position to claim them in the time allotted. I used what resources I had and now command a team almost as experienced as ours. Surely you approve of not wasting Odin personnel when others will do the work?"

"Hmm... Devious and loyal. I approve of that in my

servants. You found the despicable thing?"

"Yes, my Queen. Laitho did acquire a second-generation Swarm ship brain. He had it in a protected enclosure far and above anything he should have normally required for his illegal activities. He also had members of his crew outfitted with devices that restricted our Psy-Ops team from tracking their mental traces. Having used one of them briefly, it also may block determined probes from a distance, though their efficacy would require thorough testing."

"Interesting." The Queen sat in thought. She leaned to one side in a manner that he thought looked most uncomfortable and assumed that in her real chamber, the chair she had chosen was significantly more padded than the one before him. He didn't begrudge her the comfort, though—the mere fact that she allowed herself to sit in such a way showed the trust she had in him. He believed it to be far more than she had in her other servants.

Only Prince Tarak knew how much she should trust him. It was, perhaps, less than she thought.

The Queen pondered for several minutes while Tarak waited patiently. As he should.

"Is there any indication that their design resembles the ones we have developed here?" she finally asked.

"I don't claim expertise on the subject," he replied, "but if it was, the design was reconstructed from the base level. The only commonalities were parts readily available from most suppliers."

"And what spectral readings were you able to determine from the controlled explosion?"

He took a deep breath. "My Queen, I regret to inform you that I have not yet detonated the Swarm brain."

"Interesting." Her tone seemed reasonable, but even in a mental conference, her eyes promised punishment for his disobedience. "Can you explain your reasoning?"

"Your Grace, I believe we have an opportunity here to learn

more about our enemy. We have, for the first time, an intact, living specimen of their technology. With caution, I believe we—"

"Caution is a byword I prefer to live by, Tarak." Now her tone brooked no disagreement. But he needed to convince her.

"We are at a dangerous crossroads, my Queen. Our enemy is changing their technology. We can study a live specimen better than mere vids of their attacks."

"And how do you plan to avoid gathering our best minds to study something that could very well decide to detonate and destroy them all?"

"It is a risk, and risks can be minimized. The halos allow for tele-presence experimenting and real-time observation without endangering a single life in the process. The ship *Brigallegro* could itself serve as the laboratory since it already has the restraining equipment in place."

"And what if by taking the safety controls off to study it, this alien brain takes over the vessel and turns it into a Swarm ship?" she snapped.

"We have no indication that they can do—"

"And what if they intend for us not to know this?" she snapped at him.

Tarak tried to keep his patience. He'd expected resistance, but her reaction was even harsher than expected.

"My Queen, surely you realize the strategic advantage that we could gain if we were able to divine the inner workings of this... thing. What if we were able to duplicate some of their technology?"

"Perhaps this is a convoluted plan to acquire one of our ships and copy our own technology and divine its inner workings," she countered.

"Safeguards can be taken to guard against—"

"Silence. Our own history shows a cunning barbarism when dealing with an implacable foe," she said. "From sneaking themselves inside the gates to slaughter and pillage, to flinging diseased bodies into fortified positions, humans have left a trail of misery and destruction during their wars with each other. These aliens have made it clear they intend to exterminate us, to —the—last—child."

"But, Queen Zara, they've already shown a willingness to change tactics—"

"They have no sympathy or remorse for the deaths they wreak across our systems," the Queen continued. "And we will show them none in return."

"But what will we do about the hostages—"

"Enough." Her tone brooked no disagreement. "Now, bring up the screens I know you have already prepared."

Tarak sighed but didn't let his avatar show it. With a simple command, the chamber was filled with multiple camera images of the *Brigallegro* hanging in space, far enough from Geb-nute to limit observation or damage. There were cameras inside showing the mess hall, with its false wall open and the shielded chamber in view.

"Here," Tarak said and motioned to one side at a video moving along at a 2:1 speed, "are the security vids taken during the raid. You can see here..." He paused a moment. "...where the Border Control Psy-Ops team took down the smugglers defending it."

The image had stalled on one of the Control agents tackling two smugglers.

"Experienced, you said," she commented. "Not very coordinated, are they?"

"They have their strengths," Tarak said. "And they were ordered to proceed without sidearms, to avoid unnecessary loss of life."

"The better if you had let it detonate," she said thoughtfully.

Tarak ran the video ahead until the moment he entered the chamber, discussing the situation with Captain Objur, then the resealing and placement of the failsafe. Then he ran it forward to the current moment to show that no one had entered the chamber since.

"As you can see," he said, "everything is in place. Instruments have been recording for the last thirty-eight hours and show no signs of change."

"Well, your technicians are about to have a nice long break," the Queen ordered. "Use the failsafe."

He didn't hesitate. "All teams, failsafe is go," he ordered the ship's crew. "Stand by in three, two, one—"

———

TARAK ACTIVATED the failsafe with a thought.

The failsafe, a modified capital ship DEW laser, fired full power at point-blank range. Intended to penetrate ship armor at astronomical distances, it was no effort to pierce the containment shielding around the alien brain. The interior screen turned white, then black.

Exterior cameras and sensors showed a muted explosion compared to the ship deaths in battle. Large pieces of the *Brigallegro* were still wholly visible, some possibly even salvageable.

"Why do you think the explosion was so impotent?" the Queen asked.

"I wish I could answer that." Tarak sighed, this time showing in the sim. "Perhaps if I had a chance to study one, I could answer that."

"I asked for your thoughts, not your pouting," the queen snapped.

"Perhaps it was weakened by its time in the chamber. Perhaps the DEW burned away so much mass that it had too little to convert toward its death." His frustration slid just a little to the surface. "Maybe it sensed we were watching and chose to deny us the satisfaction."

"That would make them cheeky little bastards then,

wouldn't it?" the Queen said, her jibe not matching the tiny curve of her frown. "I am loath to give you this information myself, but I prefer you to understand the implications. I have been made aware of another of these brains on the planet Citrom. This one appears to be in the hands of a criminal syndicate, the Dawn Fan. Go recover it quickly. And—" Her eyes flashed. "I expect you to report its destruction, not appeal to my curiosity. Understood?"

She was obviously through with humoring him. He knew that if he disobeyed her, she would remove him from his post and possibly shame him too. He was, after all, only her third son. Her merest suggestion would make it clear to anyone that he was persona non grata.

"I understand, my Queen."

She disappeared at his utterance. He removed the halo and found himself in his personal chamber aboard the *Justification*. Waiting for him was his personal aide.

"Sir? We have the first spectral analysis reports for you to look at."

"I'll look at them shortly," he replied. "Clear out the personal training room. I need to think."

There's something more here, something deeper, he pondered as his aide saw to clearing the small training room. Even on a frigate, there were a few luxuries.

Someone is trafficking in these cores, he mused as he hit the padding. *Spreading them about like party favors. But why? What do they hope to accomplish?*

This was the third one he'd tracked down in the last few months. Yet he still didn't know where they were coming from.

But I need to unravel the where, he thought angrily as he placed several kicks against the pads. *And I need to know the why.*

And deeper than even these mysteries, he thought, *I need to find another way of stopping it before it goes too far for any of these short-sighted governments to fix.*

CHAPTER
SEVEN

DESCENT INTO UNCERTAINTY

Regis Magnum Shipyards
Gas Planet Magnum, L2 Orbit
Orso System

DAGON JAX SAT in the command chair of the *Impositor*, overlooking his crew as they scrambled in the face of a Swarm attack.

The Blues were massed in two groups slightly forward, each pressing either low port or high starboard. The inexperienced crew was managing the guns and shields well enough, but he knew there was another threat coming. There always was.

"Maintain your defense," he called as fighters swooped by, two of them slamming against the *Impositor's* shields. "Don't just fire at their positions. Anticipate where they're going to turn. Shields officer; you do the same. Keep an eye on where the attack fronts are moving to and adjust accordingly."

"But sir," one of the crew hollered back. "Isn't it your job to tell us what to do?"

He thought back to the many years serving under Captain Morian, then replied, "The captain's job is to pick the best people and put them where they can do the greatest good. I may not see everything. Are you willing to gamble everyone's lives on the captain's ability to see everything? I think not. Now, adjust the shields to compensate for the group to port? We can't let them—"

Before he could finish, the bridge shook as the bombardment connected, searing through the unprotected armor.

"And now we're going to die because we were too busy questioning the captain during a multi-pronged attack," Jax snapped. "When are we—"

"Sir," the sensor officer yelled. "We have bogeys appearing aft. At least fifty—seventy—more than a hundred. Orders, sir."

"Shields, if we divert all available power to the aft shields, can we hold?" Dagon asked.

"No sir," called the shields officer.

"How much power can you give me?"

"Power cells are fluctuating, sir. We won't be able to redirect in time."

"Then what do you think we should do?" The ship rocked under another forward barrage. "Anyone? I'm open to ideas."

No one offered an idea. He could see their faces. All of them frozen, unable to offer a solution.

"Stars," he muttered to himself, then, "Here's an idea," "Why don't we *turn* the ship? One hundred fifty-five degrees to port and roll sixty degrees."

"Sir?" his tactical officer said, frowning.

"Helm, one-five-five to port and roll." He felt the gravitics shift to compensate for the movement. "That will put the ventral port shields in place to absorb the attack, while the starboard—"

But they had started moving too late. The group to aft had already fired. And even with the attempt to shift position, the blasts ripped through the armor. Engines were breached, and the ship detonated in spectacular fashion.

The red combat lighting shut off and normal lighting was restored. The screens all flickered off, save for the ones showing the replay of the *Impositor* exploding like a barrel full of fireworks. Someone had added a little extra flair to the display. Pieces of the ship were cartwheeling off into space, trailing sparks that snuffed in the vacuum.

All the students stared at the explosion. The vid started over, and they watched the plasma connect with the engines. The hull bucked from the engine detonation before the fires carried forward, bursting out of viewports and seams in the hull, before the final, shattering explosion. Again, there were pieces cartwheeling into space.

Dagon sighed. *Who comes up with this stuff? That looks more like a dramavid than an actual ship.*

"So," he began. "Can anyone tell me what went wrong?"

"Um, sir?" called one cadet. "I think we died."

"If I turn off the safeties in my gravcar and drive off a cliff, hitting the bottom of the canyon isn't what went wrong. It's the inevitable conclusion to a bad decision." He was rather proud of that one. "What was the first thing we did wrong today?"

"Picked a fight we couldn't win?"

"Interesting idea, but no. If the Blues want to kill everybody everywhere, running away just leaves other people to die. Next."

"We didn't just let the AI do the work?" another cadet asked confidently.

And there he is. Vrang Eschiv had on his superior expression again.

"And what, pray tell, would that accomplish?" Dagon asked. He thought back to a time when he'd wondered how he would ever fly the ship as well as the AI. *Oh, to have those days of naivete again.*

"The AI is smarter than anyone," Eschiv said. "So why not have Posey make the calls?"

"You're calling the ship's AI Posey?" Dagon asked, shaking his head.

"Why not, and why not let the ship fight them off? Surely she could have done a better job than we did."

"I'm sure you're right," Dagon said sarcastically. "I can't believe no one ever thought of that. Imagine what fools we've been all this time, letting everyone die while we refuse to trust the AI. Control, replay Scenario FR-1705-T25 on screens one, three, four and six, ecliptic angles, please. AI in control."

The screens switched to a wider angle of the battle without crew performance. They watched as the two groups pressed the bow as before, the splinters that broke off to pelt at the sides more effectively.

Then the aft attackers materialized out of nowhere.

"That isn't fair," the cadet at Sensors called out. "Where did they come from?"

"Swarm ships exit the Slipstream wherever they want," Dagon replied as the AI pulled the maneuver he had called out during the sim. "No, we don't know how they do it yet, but they do."

Vrang pointed to the screen as *Impositor* defended against the attacks for several more minutes before retreating successfully. "See? The AI saved the ship."

"I guess you're right, Eschiv," Dagon agreed. "That sure made me look dumb, didn't it? Control, play T50 this time."

Now the screens showed a much faster enemy. The attacks hammered the shields. And when the enemy winked into existence to aft, the killshot came much faster. The AI rolled the ship and managed to disable several attackers before succumbing to shield failure. "Oh dear," Dagon snapped. "All hands lost. Control, play T99."

The battle lasted only minutes. The Swarm were everywhere, moving in the blink of an eye. Their attacks were furious, forcing the *Impositor* on the defensive—and then the aft force arrived. Before the ship could begin to compensate, enemy fire punctured the aft armor, detonating the engines much like the cadet's run.

"That is the simulation created for the graduating class," Dagon announced to the shocked and dismayed students. "That is the speed and firepower the Swarm exhibits in battle. That is the result of letting the AI make decisions against an enemy it has to see to avoid."

"So what?" Vrang demanded. "You showed us a vid that made your point."

"Not a vid. Realtime AI presentation," Dagon said. "The only thing the AI doesn't get to know in advance is the coming aft attack."

"Then what's the point? Why make a sim that you can't win?"

Dagon sighed. "Control, run FR-1705-actual." He looked right at Vrang. "You want a vid? Here's a vid."

Now the *Impositor* was replaced with a battle-scarred *Avenger*. Instead of the groups of Swarm fighters, there were thousands. And in the background were a hundred Independent Militia vessels, fighting valiantly to save their planet.

The attacks were blinding. The speed was frightening. Dagon could feel himself tensing as he relived the moments over again.

And *Avenger* bore to starboard, rolling and concentrating the bow fire on the dorsal port shields just as the attackers appeared, their massed deathblow caught safely on the ventral starboard shields.

"A *human* saw the flaw in letting the attack continue this way," he said, only a trifle untruthfully. *Leave Commander Haal and her Sight out of this for now.* "A *human* called for the ship to bear starboard. The sim is based on an attack *that I lived through* because a human made a good decision at the right time. We can't always rely on AIs to do the hard work, and we shouldn't. Not just because we should be in charge, but because we understand things even if we don't understand why. Now, I want you to review Sections 133 and 137 of your Operations Manuals—yes, the one with my name on the inside cover. Because I know a thing or two about flying a Defender-class ship."

Haltar Sen's name was on the front cover, not his. *It was mostly Haltar's work. I just helped,* he would say to the class never.

"Remember, it takes over a hundred-thousand man-hours to build a starship," he decided to add. "All those people gave parts of their lives to create something that protects your lives in battle, and theirs, from the enemy. Serve your stations with pride and dedication."

The class filed out, with Vrang quietly mocking his words. "Read the Operations Manuals with pride and dedication. Remember, I know how to write my name in a book."

He considered taking Vrang aside, but several others gave him dirty looks and turned the other way. Vrang was left looking alone and foolish. He finally said, "Whatever," and stomped off the other way.

I don't remember class being this bad when I went through it. Was it this bad?

Dagon grabbed his things from behind the mock captain's chair—clearly against regs on a real starship—and made his way out of the gimbal-bridge. He'd had enough of being the captain for one day. Lieutenant was good enough for now.

———

Regis Magnum Station Hub
    South Plate, Third Zone
    Simulations Corridor

. . .

DAGON ENTERED the express tube and swiped his station ID. The console acknowledged and the car began to lift rapidly, the inertial dampeners protecting him from the extreme acceleration.

He looked out the viewport at the magnificent expanse of space. And below, relative to him anyway, he could see the body of the shipyard. From his vantage point, he looked down into a canyon a half-kilometer round, with dozens of lights winking in areas that manufactured or repaired smaller vehicles such as shuttles or F-32s. And he knew that there was another plate opposite this one, connected to each other by the Control Spindle. But it was on the twelve massive construction arms of the station, like the legs of a spidery moon, that capital ships were born. He could see several partially constructed as he passed, but at the end of the Third Arm was the ship that had saved the human race, almost literally—the *Avenger*.

Dagon tried to put the sim out of his mind as he rode back to *Avenger's* docking port. It wasn't long ago that he wouldn't even have been running the bridge simulations. It felt like a huge burden, taking on so much responsibility.

I mean, I was serving as a second navigation officer. Now I'm responsible for all these kids? He pointedly ignored that several of these "kids" were almost the same age as he was. He'd applied right out of school, and they were coming in years after the crisis started. *Sometimes experience just trumps age,* he thought.

But every time he began to feel as if he had a right to complain, he remembered his roommate, Haltar Sen. And that stopped him dead.

The express car slowed, stopped, and hissed as the pressures equalized. The doors opened, and Dagon stepped into a place that felt more than a little like home.

The air smelled a little different and was a touch more humid. But this was *Avenger*. This was where he belonged.

After the terrible damage endured at the Battle for the Slipgates, *Avenger* had been taken—towed—to Freyja for repairs to the armor, engines, launch bays, and other structural details. But once she was space-worthy, someone up the chain had ordered her brought back to the Orso System for the installation of new shipboard systems. *In a fight for our lives, someone still thinks we need to keep secrets from our allies.*

Even with priority-one authorization, it had already taken almost a year to repair the ship and then replace the systems, instead of doing them simultaneously.

His datapad chirped several times. He'd arrived, and his very presence alerted those who needed a moment of his time. As acting first navigation officer, he did need to have these conversations. But once again, any time he started to feel annoyed at the imposition, he was reminded why he was needed. He took a moment and cleared disruptions to his schedule, then made his way to the elevators. And, moments later, he was in his quarters.

"Hi, buddy. I'm home," he called out, quoting an old comedy vid.

He heard a thud from the sleep area. Immediately he dashed to Haltar's room. Haltar was on the floor, his limbs seizing, his breath hitching with every tremor of his body. Dagon wrapped his arms around the older man and lifted him back to the bed, once again feeling the frailness that had consumed his friend in only six months.

"Come on, man," Dagon said. "Take a deep breath and ride it out. Let the pain go and breathe. You need to breathe."

Eventually, the trembling subsided, and he helped Haltar sit up. He was half-dressed in civvies, semi-formal, his buttons only half done up. *At least he was dressing when I came in,* Dagon thought, remembering the time Haltar fell in the shower. The tremors weren't so bad then, and Haltar had insisted Dagon leave. *Soon, he might not have room for pride and modesty.*

But he never let that leave his lips. "Haltar, you didn't tell me you had a date today. I would have come back early, helped you pick out a tie."

Still shaking from the effects of his illness, Haltar still

managed to give him a stern look. "I'm the oldest person on the ship. If I had a date, you'd try and steal her."

"Oh, come on, that's harsh," Dagon continued to jest. "I wouldn't try to take your girl. But I couldn't help it if she found me irresistible, now could I?"

Haltar gave him a weak punch in the shoulder.

"I don't know why you put up with me," Haltar stammered. "I'm just... a useless—"

"No." Dagon refused to let him finish. "You might be the oldest, but you are without doubt the smartest person too. You have experience that this ship needs. Even if you just take painkillers all day and teach from a chair, you're more valuable to *Avenger* than half the rest of the officers put together."

Haltar sighed. "Better not let them hear you say that," Haltar said. "Such talk can ruin a man's career... I can't just take two and go to sleep, Dagon. To stop the pain, I'd be nearly numb. And it wouldn't stop the tremors."

"Oh, yeah? Who says that you can't—"

"You think Jyra just ignores me? As soon as we docked, she insisted on taking me to see the medical specialist here at the shipyard. He said I have something called Drath Khor degeneration."

"Drath Khor? Sounds like some cheesy villain."

"Take this seriously for a minute, will you, Jax?" Haltar barked.

"I always take it seriously," Jax snapped, then took a breath and curbed his frustration. "I'm sorry, Haltar. I was trying to lighten the mood."

"Look, son, I really appreciate the effort. But I'm dying. And there's not a lot anyone has suggested to fix it. You have to accept that."

Dagon sat for a moment, simply trying to come to grips. *Haltar isn't trying anymore. He's just accepted that he's going to die in pain.*

"So, um, where were you going to go today?" he finally asked, trying to blink back tears.

"That Independent Militia girl, Sasha Crowe, said she wanted to talk to me. I was going to meet her in the Station Mess Three-Alpha at 1800 hours. It's the closest one to here."

"Well... hey. What about using the halo? At least you could talk there."

Haltar managed to give him a look. "Son, you don't get to be my age and turn down the chance to sit with a pretty girl." He sighed. "Besides, I tried to jack into a meeting with Jyra and it went... badly. I seized, and it scrambled the whole thing. She said it was like being in a horror movie."

"You... didn't tell me that."

"And why would I want to?"

Dagon understood his friend's pride, but it still hurt that he hadn't spoken up before. So he decided to push a little. "Hey, I've got free time. I could go to your meeting for you."

"Look, kid, you don't need to—"

"I want to. Besides, why would I pass up the chance to meet a pretty girl?"

Haltar smiled. "Well, I suppose. But get yourself cleaned up. You don't want her to catch a whiff of those feet."

"You going to be okay by yourself a little longer?"

Haltar scoffed. It sounded like a hard breath. "I'll just take my meds and read a book while I wait. I'll be fine."

Dagon went to his room, took off his duty uniform and stepped into the hydro. A few minutes later, he jumped out, grabbed his trusty first-date outfit from the locker and, in moments, had his hair slicked sideways just so. He rinsed his mouth and spit, and on the way out he peeked in at Haltar.

He was already asleep.

But when Dagon looked closer, he saw no pill bottle and no water.

Burying his worry under determination, he left for a meeting with a pretty girl.

Besides, he thought, *I'm betting she didn't request a meeting to put moves on him. I wonder what her real aims are?*

———

Third Arm, Level A, Company Dining Hall
Regis Magnum Shipyards

"It's already 1803. I hate being even three minutes late," Sasha complained to herself as she made her way inside the Three-Alpha Mess. She had dickered over what to wear (dress, modest, moderate-high neck) and then which of her bottles of synth to bring (Bellu Mon, '168). She had hoped to help the senior navigator feel a little bit of posh after eating shipboard rations for so long. Instead, she'd left him waiting.

She entered the mess and realized her second mistake. The Independent Militia of Free People liked to stay flexible, unlike the hidebound Sovereign Systems. She'd made the simple error of assuming that traditional dinners were served between 1500 and 1700. Since she'd been keeping odd hours lately, she normally ate on board her own ship. Allowing for a few late stragglers, she'd thought they would have the mess largely to themselves and not have to shout at each other.

Instead, she'd arrived at the most boisterous time, apparently. Families were in attendance, something that rarely happened shipboard. Many children were shrieking, though whether in delight or agony, she couldn't tell—as an only child whose single mother had fled the Orso System a decade ago, she'd missed the hurly-burly family life.

It was nice to connect with Elio, though, she thought. *He hasn't let his father stamp out his curiosity or kindness.*

She never really thought about the fact that they had the same biological father. He hadn't been there, so it wasn't worth thinking about.

Now she looked in every direction, hoping for a glimpse of the kindly face crowned with wispy hair that she remembered. But instead, she found a lanky young man wearing pressed slacks and a collared shirt, with three fasteners left loose. He waved at her, trying to get her attention. "Hi, um, Captain Crowe?"

Great. I've managed to find myself the only lonely single guy in the room.

But she walked over to him anyway. He looked a little familiar. "Hi. I recognize you from somewhere, I think."

"Uh, yes. I'm Lieutenant Dagon Jax from the *Avenger*. We met after the battle for Freyja."

"Right. Maybe you can help me. I'm looking for the First Navigator. Haltar Sen?"

"Actually, I'm First Navigator now. Haltar's out on medical. And that's why I'm here."

Sasha was instantly worried. "Have you seen him? How's he doing?"

"I see him every day. I got myself assigned to his quarters when he started getting worse. He couldn't even get out of bed for this meeting." To his credit, Jax looked very concerned.

Sasha was beginning to think these navigators were close friends. "All right, listen. I don't want to shout everything over this crowd. Is there somewhere else we can go?"

Jax smiled. "Well, there is a place you can go, but I normally can't."

"And where is that?"

"The Platinum Star. It's kind of a brass-only place a quick tram ride away. I'm just a bridge officer, though—if only there was a captain to pull rank..."

"Oh stuff it," she said. But she couldn't help smiling. "Come along then. You can be my native guide and carry my luggage."

"Yes, ma'am," he said with a mock salute.

———

Platinum Star Dining Room
South Plate
Regis Magnum

"Well, I certainly prefer the atmosphere in here," she said with a sigh. The waitstaff—*Really, a waiter? I haven't seen one of those in ages*—gave Jax a brief glance but didn't press the issue. However, she certainly didn't intend to pour out a bottle of Bellu Mon here, and certainly not with Jax. He might take it the wrong way.

"So what brings you to the station, Captain?" Jax asked her.

"First," she said, "you will not call me captain again. I am Sasha."

He smiled. "If you insist."

"Second, I know five different ways to break your arm. Smile too much, try anything stupid, and I'll demonstrate the first."

His smile grew a little forced. "If you say so, S-sasha."

"Oh, please. If you can't say my name without flirting, just call me ma'am."

"All right, ma'am. Um, well, what's a Militia captain doing here? I mean, this is the Orso System."

"Well, I have... family here," she said, not wanting to go into too much detail. "And the powers that be thought that since I was here anyway, I could be of help to... Marshal Secerna Hyde."

"Marshal Hyde? As in, used to be Commander Flay-Your-Hide?" Dagon asked.

"The same. With my connections, and because I'm not legally a citizen, she was allowed to skirt several loopholes in staffing a project she's working on. While it isn't ready yet, if she can pull it off, it should give us an edge against the Blues sometime soon."

"Can you talk about it?" Dagon asked.

She smiled sweetly at him. "No, Lieutenant. It's classified. Need to know. Hush-hush. Disclosure, tribunal, penitentiary. Not the arc I have planned for my life."

"I understand," he said, looking chastened.

"And what are you doing while Avenger is undergoing her refit, if I can ask?"

"Ahh, I'm not doing anything important. I'm running bridge simulations for a class of cadets. I yell at them a lot. Tell them to keep their heads in the fight or we all die. That sort of thing. It's pretty... I dunno. It seems like they never really get it."

"Oh, it does sound terrible," she said, maybe just a little mocking. "How d'you handle it?"

"Specifically? Well, when things go wrong—and they always do—I ask them what they think the solution is. I ask them for suggestions, too. But they always freeze up. It's like they can't think for themselves. They think the captain should tell them what to do. I had one of them whine and ask why we didn't let the AI fight the ship."

Sasha sighed. "Look, Jax," she said. "Teaching is the hardest job there is. But you're making them think for themselves instead of making them dependent on you. That's good. Because when they find themselves under the command of a captain who's all 'my way, do as I say,' yes, they'll follow orders. But... But, Jax, someday, when it hits the fan, and the captain— or worse, an acting-acting-captain because of a bad run in battle —doesn't know what to do, they'll have an idea. You might have saved their life—and the ship. And second, I hope you had a good answer for the AI twerp."

"Oh, yeah. I ran an AI vid at actual speed, and when everyone died, I showed them the real thing. They'd made a whole simulation out of Commander Haal's twist maneuver at

Freyja. I ran it for them at full speed. They were... more than a little impressed, except for Vrang—that's the AI cadet. He wasn't impressed, or if he was, he refused to show it."

"Well done, Lieutenant," she said. "But enough of that. I'm here to help Haltar."

"Excuse me?" Jax said, "What are you...? I mean, why? I'm sorry. I didn't mean to offend."

"None taken," she replied. "I'm... passingly familiar with your Captain Morian's reputation. I was at the Battle of the Slipgates in my ship, the *Golden Condor*. In the early moments of the Slipgate ambush, your hull took a hit meant for the *Golden Condor*. We weren't going to last through too many of those hits—my *Condor* doesn't have refurbished armor like *Avenger*. I doubt you even noticed it. Well, anyway, I heard about Haltar Sen, and I'm sure he would appreciate me returning the favor. A life for a life as it were."

"He's beyond help," Jax replied. "Our ship's doctor has given up. So has the Shipyard specialist. He's dying."

It seemed so easy when I was going to talk to Haltar. Will Jax act like this is a good idea? she thought.

"I know it sounds... a little like hocus-pocus, but back on Freyja there's a woman they call Mirabilis. There are stories about her; almost folk lore. I've done some digging, and I think I know who she is and where she might be. I think she might be able to help."

"She's a doctor?" Jax asked skeptically.

"No," Sasha said reluctantly. "I think she's got some form of new power that we haven't seen yet."

"Hey, I know a bunch of people with Psy and TK. If you think this Mirabilis can help my friend, I'm all in."

"So..." she said.

"So...?" he repeated.

"Someone needs to go find her," Sasha said.

He made a face. "Who do you have in mind?"

"And that's the problem," she admitted. "I have duties I

signed on to do here, and I can't leave. I have people I trust well enough to stay quiet, but to see the job done quickly? To search thoroughly in each location? I can't say. Do you know anyone you can spare?"

"Nobody comes to mind," Jax told her. He looked disappointed. "All my friends are on the ship right now." He brightened a little. "Maybe if we walk it up the ladder, the Captain will see it as a good idea. He's said a couple of times that he wants Haltar to come back. He and Haltar have been on this ship together for years."

"Well then, I suppose I'll have to make an appointment. When do you think he'll return to *Avenger?*"

"Oh, he got back yesterday. I don't know why. When he left, he told Commander Haal that he wanted to sleep for a year, but he's back in three weeks? Some people just have that work bug, I guess."

"I suppose so," she said with a smile.

Finally, I can repay my debt. I just need to wait another day or so to make my case.

CHAPTER
EIGHT

FRUITFUL MEETINGS

ORSO ROYAL PALACE
  Planet Caerus
  Orso Star System

PRINCE ELIO LORNE rushed down the hallway to the military briefing room as quickly as protocol would allow. There were so many things that needed his attention, and he was constantly juggling them from one priority to the next. *Someday,* he thought, *I'm going to drop one. I just hoped it's one I can afford to drop, and when.*

He'd kept the morning meeting in mind; he really had. He'd even set an alarm. But there were always things to distract him. Nowadays, the distractions were explosive military secrets in the genocidal war being raged against humanity.

Knowing that his reputation for distraction was well-earned, he'd planned to show up at 0940 hours instead of 1005 hours, as he might have several years ago. *Even last year, maybe.*

But he would only be five minutes early. *At least I can hope my father will see the difference.*

He was trying hard to be the new, dependable Elio, perhaps even the Elio who gave small disapproving looks at people who showed up late to briefings.

If nothing else, it might remind them that we're all human. Reminders of our minor flaws are important when we're faced with a war of extinction.

But he knew no one thought that way. Humanity was a condition to be field-stripped and cleaned until it worked like a dependable machine.

When will they see that the Swarm thinks like that and change the way we do things?

Probably never. After all, even Commodore Morian—a hero to be recognized if ever there was one—insisted on his *subordinate* sister keeping things *professional* in her personal life. While he understood the mechanics of it, it rankled that Danis had to put herself on hold so she wasn't a burden to her brother.

He arrived at the meeting and pushed the doors open, only to realize a moment after that he might have allowed himself to be greeted and introduced like the others would obviously have done.

But the room was empty, except for a maid.

Wait. What am I missing? He checked the datapad connected to his arm and found several unread messages, one of which was stamped at 0853 and declared that the meeting would be held via halo to better align with the schedules of everyone involved.

So I stopped working, went through the scrub, and had my valet dress me, so I could jack into the meeting?

Well, it's too late now.

He sat in one of the chairs and slipped the halo on. "Greetings," he muttered to the assembled military commanders, advisors, manufacturing administrators, merchant council leaders and, of course, his father, King Orson Lorne himself. "Did I miss anything?"

His father only gave him a look. Admiral Huis Grig replied, "Of course not, my prince. We were waiting for you."

Great. Early and they still act like I caused a problem, he thought.

"Well, let me not delay you any further," he said. "Let's begin."

The king cast a withering glance at his son, then said, "I would like a report of the new ships we ordered. Administrator Seklom, I believe you have something for me?"

"Your Grace," Seklom replied with a nod of his head. "We at Regis Magnum are happy to report that production of the new Avenger-class ships is ahead of schedule, with four nearing completion. We expect them to be ready for shakedown in... three weeks," he added after consulting his wristpad.

"Why don't you tell us something about them, Mr. Administrator?" the king said. "I'm sure everybody has heard whispers and leaks, so let's all be on the same page, shall we?"

"Well," Seklom said, frowning, "there are significant differences between them and the original *Avenger,* but all in service of protection, of course. We began with the internal structure—while utilizing the lighter construction techniques of modern ships, we increased the actual metal content of the structure by almost ten percent. This allowed us to equip more cubic meters of armor without straining the frame. This also allowed us to reconfigure the drives from the original C-class to the B-class battleship engines. This will give more speed and maneuverability. We have also used the extra strength to give each ship three main guns instead of one. The new Havoc guns are equipped to fire new G-99 rounds. Utilizing the M-99 design, we simply scaled up. But we also improved the traversal—instead of five degrees of radial coverage, each now has eight. And they are placed to fire in multiple forward directions at once, to reduce the enemy angles of attack."

"Good, very good," King Lorne said. "Please continue."

"We upgraded the railguns from the fifty-caliber to twin thirty-caliber," Seklom said proudly. "Using the same firing mechanism design, it increases the force of each round, but as one barrel resets, the second is already firing. It's almost imperceptible to the human eye or ear, but each emplacement will be able to fire nearly twice as many rounds a second, and for almost no more ammunition storage space."

"But how will that help? We need the mass of the fifty-calibers to shatter the enemy," King Lorne replied.

But Father would already know this, Elio thought. *He's asking the questions so others don't blindly agree to curry his favor. It seems I'm still learning.*

Seklom couldn't hide his smile. "Concussive ammunition, sir. The ammo feeds are almost identical to those used for fifty mil, so they require no additional training to use. We've already started installing banks of deuce-thirties on the new ships."

"So, just how effective is this new ammunition?" asked Admiral Grig.

I'm having a hard time believing this, Elio wanted to shout at Seklom. *What were you thinking, installing beta-version weapons on warships going into active warzones?*

"We haven't had many opportunities yet," Seklom admitted, "but using hullscraps from Swarm ships, we were able to test both in atmosphere and vacuum. Every test we attempted shattered the hull into fine sand."

"And what were the results compared to fifty-cal?" the admiral pressed.

"Well, they were destroyed also, obviously." Seklom looked flustered by the question. "But the aim was to create something that would hamper their new healing ability. If they can collect the pieces and seal the breach, make sure they don't have any more pieces."

"But did you bother to test this in an active situation?" Elio asked.

"Umm, er, well no," Seklom replied. "Of course not. We haven't had time to test it in—"

"Then how do you know if—"

"Enough," the king said quietly, cutting Elio off. Everyone became silent. "While I appreciate the ingenuity, I refuse to risk new ships with untested technology." He nodded to Admiral Grig, then Seklom. "We still need to test these weapons. How many banks have you installed on how many of the new Avenger-class ships?"

Seklom looked uneasy. "All of the Avenger-class ships have multiple banks installed. We thought that—"

"I understand," King Lorne said. "And now you will uninstall some of them. Every new ship is to have *alternating* banks of thirty and fifty caliber weapons. Admiral, please appoint someone to determine how they alternate, and make them consistent across all ships."

Seklom looked dejected but nodded his agreement.

Everyone looks on edge, Elio thought.

"Good," King Lorne said. "Let's move on. We must now discuss the enemy. Marshal McAlan?"

McAlan stood, looked around the table and said, "Swarm activity in contested sectors has increased in the last six months by more than fifteen percent. While they haven't yet attacked in force, these skirmishes with our ships require constant maintenance, drain matériel, and keep our crews on a knife's edge. Even with the year's influx of ships from Freyja complementing Sovereign output, we can barely keep the growing number of Slipgates from being rendered unusable. And yet, in uncontested systems, they don't destroy the gate."

"And their purpose in leaving them intact?" King Lorne asked, frowning.

"We don't know, your grace," McAllan replied, glancing at his datapad. "As with so many things, the Blues seem incomprehensible. If there was a way to peer inside their minds, I'd gladly take the risk in order to understand my enemy better."

Elio nodded, thinking about the Swarm ship's core that Kyne Minnah had recovered. Once his father had regained his strength, he had taken the reins of power again and shut that particular research behind a curtain of secrecy that even Elio wasn't permitted to penetrate. *What are you and your team up to, my King? Haven't you had enough of these secret researches? The last one almost killed you.*

"If I find that we developed a way to read the Swarm's collective mind, Marshal," the king said dryly, "then you will be the next to know."

Elio, in that moment, brushed against his father's mind, hoping to glean some slight information. He felt guilty for it and even more when his gentle touch slammed against a brick wall. There was no way to read his father.

Has he gained Psy powers? Or did he train himself to avoid being vulnerable again? What was his recovery regimen? But to all these things, the answers were not just elusive; they were nonexistent.

He checked the chron on his halo. *Already 1017. Is this meeting going to go over? I'm supposed to meet Major Rosst at 1130. Andra's going to be late, and now I am, too.*

———

Gravrail *Expedition*, Passenger Car
    Just outside Som Orsi
    Planet Orso

Andra Graynir watched the world start to take shape as the gravrail began to shed speed. Details that were moments ago blurs of color outside her window began to appear once more. Despite the terrifying speed of the train and its relatively abrupt deceleration, there was little inertia. *I suppose,* she thought, *compared to a starship, or an F32, a gravrail is a simple technology. After all, it only goes in one direction.*

The world outside was suddenly gone, replaced by the inside of a concrete sheath that led into the Som Orsi transit station. She gathered her minimal luggage, and when the doors opened, she stepped out into a bustling crowd of people, all eager to begin their journey or glad to arrive at their destination.

It seemed like chaos to her, and it was: organized chaos, but it was still several minutes before the ebb and flow made any sense to her. After all, this was not how the daughter of a planetary governor was expected to travel.

But now that's all over and done with, she thought with only a trace of bitterness. *Against the Swarm, we're all just people.* She knew her real place now. She was a member of Elio's grand scheme. She was doing something that made a difference.

But the more things are different, the more they stay the same, she thought warmly as she saw her very own fighter jockey waving excitedly, trying to get her attention.

"Gian!" she called and pushed through the crowd toward him.

Gian Vastum grabbed her in his arms and scooped her off the ground in a hug that almost crushed the air from her lungs.

"Gian," she managed to gasp, "you really... must have missed me."

"You have no idea," he whispered. The touch of his breath on her ear sent a tingle down her spine. She never understood how he could manage to do that, but she never tired of it either.

Finally, he set her down, but his hands never left her hips. He leaned down to kiss her.

"Whoa there, flyboy," she said as she pulled back with an impish grin. "What kind of gal do you take me for? This is the gravrail station."

"Well, where do you want me to kiss you?" he asked, his eyebrows just a little too high to be completely innocent.

"Not at all; nowhere. Right now, I'm famished," she replied. "You need to make sure I'm well-fed first."

"Then, as the lady demands," he responded gallantly, "so shall I provide. As it happens, I know a little place about three kilometers from here. I think you'll like it."

———

"NEXT ON THE AGENDA," Marshal McAlan continued, "are the debris fields orbiting the planet. The Battle for the Slipgates cost us dearly, and to add to the injury, we now have millions of navigation hazards to cope with. Our starports are clogged with requests to take off or land. Wait times for clearance are running four hours or more. It's only with the construction of new fields that we've been able to stem some of the congestion."

"What about our military launches?" the king asked.

"My apologies for the omission, your grace. Our military has priority to launch whenever they request. However, this has caused several incidents of angry rhetoric and one act of violence from civilian captains tired of the wait. And I'm afraid things could get worse."

"What about the derelict ships?" Elio asked. "Can they be salvaged; put back into service?"

McAlan motioned to one of the administrators seated behind him and to his right. "Shipmaster Vaskel?"

"We have, of course, towed the largest and least damaged vessels to the shipyards," Vaskel answered, "where they have been thoroughly evaluated. And yes, some of them can be repaired and returned to service. But refitting a ship is no small task, especially with so much damage. The stresses, material crystallization from plasma heating... well, it's all very technical."

"How many can be salvaged, Shipmaster?" Elio asked, frowning.

The shipmaster hesitated, then, in a low voice, "Five, certainly. Perhaps more?"

"You're asking me?" Elio snapped. "Let me understand what you're saying. Of more than three hundred damaged ships of war, only five are salvageable. Some of those ships were brand new. That's unacceptable. To what do you attribute the obviously catastrophic level of destruction of so many capital ships? Is it the construction? The quality or the lack of armor? The efficacy of the shields? What?"

Vaskel looked away and shrugged. "I cannot say, my prince. All I can tell you is that, yes, at least five of the three-hundred-forty-one hulks can certainly be repaired. And perhaps... several more. But frankly..." Again, he shrugged and looked away. "The hulls are worth more as scrap. Even the new ones have been badly damaged by plasma fire. This causes the metals to deform, to crystalize, to weaken. My suggestion is that you have the salvage crews cut the hulls up and send the pieces to the foundries; make new materials from the old. At least that way they become known quantities, instead of stress-riddled deathtraps."

This time, when Elio touched Vaskel's mind, he met no resistance. The shipmaster wasn't lying; not one bit. In a normal combat situation, those ships weren't worth half what an older vessel with railguns was.

Amazing that in only a few short years, we've slid back into projectile weapons and declared our new hull materials and shields almost useless against an enemy that uses plasma weapons and laser-proof armor.

"What about the salvage crews then?" Elio continued. "If we need materials, send them out and clean the mess up."

"That, my prince," Vaskel replied dryly, "would be the obvious answer, but our manpower has been greatly depleted. You yourself saw to that, sire."

That took Elio aback. "I what?"

"When you arranged to send our trained personnel to

Freyja, sire. We had a glut of trained workers, but when you staffed the Freyja shipyards, we lost thousands of available workers. The schools haven't caught up yet."

"Now wait just a minute..." Elio said as he tried to remember the name he wanted. He flicked his mind over those of the members of the meeting and found him present— Mezeke Bohne, Societal Analyst.

Elio reached out to him with his psy. *Mr. Bohne, what was the worker population of Som Orsi and surrounding cities before the Freyja battle?*

"Um..." Elio watched as he consulted something out of his halo's reach. *Twenty million, four hundred seventy-two thousand—*

Wonderful, Elio replied. *And including the recent refugee influx to this planet?*

"Twenty million, five hundred thirteen thousand," Bohne replied out loud.

Every member of the meeting turned to look at him.

Elio smiled. "So we have a hundred thousand more people than before we shipped thirty thousand to Freyja?" He smiled again, then said, "Gentlemen and ladies, I think we have a solution to both problems."

"How so?" asked several people.

"Salvage crews don't require years of training," Elio said. "They need only good and careful leadership; we have that aplenty. Put out a call among the refugees. Offer any with industrial experience a job with the salvage crews. We'll get the materials we need faster, and we won't have to pull personnel from other areas. And we can solve the navigation hazards by towing the largest pieces of debris out to Diminu."

"But how will they be able to work out there?" Duke Rutta demanded. "Diminu isn't a suitable base of operations. It's halfway to Magnum. The planet is a freezing desert of scree. It has no air."

"But we have an orbital station. True, it's badly damaged, but we do. Is that not correct, Duke Rutta?"

"Yes, but—"

Elio smiled. The cantankerous Duke had walked right into the snare.

"But," Elio snapped, interrupting the duke, "it's useless as a defensive weapon, is it not?" He didn't wait for an answer. "As of this moment, it's no more than another piece of space junk. It has a skeleton crew, so I'm told. So let's tow it out to Diminu and reposition the other battle stations to compensate. A skeleton crew, a repair team, and a salvage crew under training wouldn't occupy half of the remaining viable space on the station. And the repair team can expand the available space while the others are working. Yes, I think we can convert the orbital station into a salvage hub in record time."

"Well, I have another matter to bring up," Duke Rutta said, unwilling to let Elio best him again. "We have a veritable fleet of unaligned warships still in our planetary vicinity. While we yet have need of their service, we don't want to come to any agreement we can't afford."

The old Elio would have argued immediately, protesting the words Rutta used to describe the people who had saved them from annihilation, or the implication that they would refuse to reward their rescuers. But now he held his tongue. *Patience,* he thought. *Use your words to strike the important points. Fight for the victories that need to be won.* He'd learned that lesson from spending time with Captain Richard Morian.

Thoughts of *Danis* Morian, on the other hand, threatened to derail his concentration. He tried to put her out of his mind but with little success.

"Have they approached us with their contracts or agreements?" he asked.

"Well—"

Elio tried not to sigh. "The Independent Militia of Free People is... 'independent,' Duke Rutta. They haven't demanded recompense or threatened to leave. We offered them berths for their ships to be repaired, and their crews have, as I understand it, been fully involved in said repairs. Their *entire* crews, Duke Rutta. While we are obligated by the union contracts to relieve our crew for vacations. In time of war?" Elio sounded outraged, though internally, he was smiling. "While I don't suggest we cancel all leave for our military, we could, I think, treat our allies with the deference and respect they deserve. Don't you?"

"Does the prince suggest that he would crawl around in the muck with the laborers?" someone muttered. Elio searched the room for the voice but didn't hear it again. So he ignored it. *Strike the important points.*

"So, that brings me to the third issue," Elio said lightly. "That of the 'unaligned warships,' as Duke Rutta so thoughtlessly calls them." He glared at the duke. Rutta merely shook his head in disgust.

"We need the IMFP to stay close by in case they're needed," Elio continued. "The answer, then, is that we simply offer them contracts to tow the ships out to Diminu and do some initial salvage work. We include a small bounty on personal items from those who died. They can return those, and that will allow loved ones on Caerus to reclaim lost family property. The IMFP would be less likely—"

"But they're pirates," Rutta exclaimed. "We've known this for years. It's why they refuse to live in Sovereign systems."

"The IMFP," Elio repeated, "would be less likely than refugees to steal those items. Only a few people *claiming* to represent the IMFP are actual thieves, while the rest are peaceful traders and craftspeople. While I don't impugn the honesty of anyone," he said and gave Rutta a sharp look, "it seems sensible to trust those who have what they want already. Namely, a home and a paycheck."

"My son has made several excellent points and suggestions," the king said.

Elio, surprised, turned his head to see his father's expression.

There was the slightest hint of a smile on his lips. Elio was elated.

"Sandir Comex, Hal Merca, Pal Jiock." The king pointed to three of the merchant councilors. "You three have interests in metals. And we need that orbital mess above cleared up. While I have Treasury contact the Militia to arrange transport, I want you to organize these refugees into work crews. The sooner we can put them to work, the sooner we can stop handing them free food. My largesse has limits. I suggest you also find experienced technicians to hire as crew bosses, then trawl the established work groups for people with skills to work in space and operate the tools and hire them on as crew leaders."

Elio wasn't certain that it was right for the king to give these orders, but while it could be said he was micro-managing far below his station, it wasn't bad advice.

"Sire, this is a massive undertaking," Sandir Comex protested. "We don't have the liquid funds enough to finance such a massive undertaking. Our holdings are still recovering."

There were always merchants that made their decisions based on the immediate cost, not on the best investment. Comex was one such merchant.

So perhaps father knows best, he thought, smiling to himself. He wasn't certain of that. But one thing he was certain of.

"Fa... King Lorne?" he said.

The king looked at him frowning, his bushy eyebrows knitted together like a couple Rhodian wooly worms.

"Prince Elio?"

"I'd like to be the contact person for this operation. The councilors can make their own arrangements, of course, but I have no doubt Treasury funds will be needed. So it's best someone keeps an eye on the purse."

"Son, aren't you stretching yourself a little thin?" his father asked.

Son. Son. Son. The word reverberated in his mind. Ever since his father had awoken from his coma, he'd been showing uncharacteristically real attention and even affection for his only son.

"No, Father. I'm more than up to the task."

"Very well, then. Have it your way. You have my trust. Do whatever you think best."

He couldn't have asked for his father to say anything more pleasing.

"I will, Your Grace."

The meeting dragged on another hour. Elio waited through several mind-numbing recitations of finance and supply chain issues, but his departure had already stretched past the point of timeliness. But, eventually, his father ended the meeting, and one by one, the halos were lifted. The last two left in the virtual conference chamber were Elio and the king.

"Elio, this is the latest in a long list of responsibilities you've taken. Are you certain you can manage?"

Elio shrugged. "Who else can, Father?"

"It's possible to delegate."

"How much, Father? And to whom? Ugo was my teacher and your friend. But he, he..."

He didn't know what to say.

Especially since Father was the one who orchestrated Ugo's secret cabal in the first place.

There was silence for a minute. Then King Lorne said, "I never intended for you to take so much upon yourself."

"Maybe I need to make up for lost time," Elio said, smiling.

His father smiled back at him and said, "I believe you have another meeting to attend?"

The king removed his halo, leaving Elio alone.

He removed his own halo to find himself alone again. The maid had long since left.

Already late for his next meeting, he hurried from the empty conference room. He was to host the first meeting of the TK Guardians.

Stars, he thought. *Look at the time. I've left them in Major*

Rosst's gnarly hands for forty minutes. I hope the damage isn't permanent.

———

GIAN VASTUM WATCHED as Andra tried to take another bite of Dijia's Dinners justifiably famous Deli-Licious sandwich.

She's beautiful no matter what, he thought.

On a long bun, filled with three kinds of roasted meat, with four specialty cheeses and dripping with the signature herb sauce, it was a wild and earthy taste that Gian had sampled several times while he was dirtside at Resdon.

She opened her eyes long enough to notice him staring. She swallowed part of her last bite and said, "What?" She washed down the rest of her mouthful with a drink and grabbed a napkin. "If I needed to wipe my chin, you could have said something."

"Why? You looked fine to me," he replied.

"Ugh, men," she said before she took another bite. A much smaller one this time, he noticed. After a moment of chewing, she added, "My mother always said men think about only two things: women and dead animals."

Gian thought back to the time she'd snuck him into the governor's residence. There was a whole room devoted to hunting trophies, though he wasn't aware that her father had any interest in hunting.

"Say that again," he said. "I couldn't understand you."

She threw the napkin at him.

Deciding that he could watch just fine with his own food in hand, Gian picked up his sandwich. Nibbling through each bite, despite her head start, he still finished his sandwich before she finished hers.

"How do you enjoy it when you just gulp it down like that?" she asked.

"What do you mean?" he asked. "I tasted every morsel."

"Right," she said skeptically. But her argument bore no heat. She was teasing him, just like she used to.

It's been a hard couple of years for her, he thought. *I'm glad she's finally adjusting to things again. Whatever she's been doing left her frayed for the longest.*

"Well," she said after she finished her own sandwich. "It's been forever since we talked. How have you been doing? How are you doing with the squadron?"

"I mean, wow," he said. "What isn't there to say? I'm trashing the pilot sims—haven't had a problem in one for five months. Um, obviously no recent Swarm attacks. The last one was about six months ago. We were in three different theaters, and I flew wing with Danis. She says I'm doing better, and I even managed to bag the most—What?" he asked. She had a silly smile on her face, and he didn't understand why.

"No, keep going," she said. "Bag the what?"

"Um... in the fight over Asteroid TK-427, I actually got more bogies than Danis, more than anyone did. So they threw me a goofy party and threw glitter all over me. I think I still have some in my gear."

"Oh, absolutely," she said. "I see it in your hair."

"Aw, man." He swiped at his hair several times before he realized she was giggling. "What?"

"Sorry, I couldn't resist."

Beneath the silly smile, he could see the happy smile. The one that had convinced him, years ago, to listen to the crazy girl before he knew she was the governor's daughter.

"I'm glad you're doing so well," Andra said seriously. "So much of what I do is frustrating, even when in pursuit of a higher goal. So it's good to hear that you're doing well, and staying safe."

Not knowing what to say in response, he simply nodded and took a sip of his drink.

It was at that moment a waitress appeared at his elbow. He didn't pay her any mind until he realized who it was.

"I just wanted to thank you again for the other night," she said sweetly. "You really lifted me out of a whole lot of trouble."

"Oh, hey, Bartha." He was suddenly too conscious of Andra's eye on him. "No problem. Glad I could help."

"I'm just glad you let me thank you properly. You were so quick to leave that first night."

There's no way I'm getting out of this with my head attached, he thought desperately.

"No, really, it's fine," he said. "Have a good shift." Catching Andra's eye again, he added, "Um, can I get the check? I think we're ready to leave."

CHAPTER
NINE

Guarded Emotions
Marcatus Avenue
Som Orsi City

"Well, Gian," Andra said as they left the diner. "So tell me about *Bartha* and how you left so quickly the first night."

"It's not like that," Gian tried to explain. "You know it's not."

"Oh, I'm sure it's not, but tell me anyway."

He knew she was teasing—but the tease stung a little. *I spent months waiting to see her, and now this?*

"I took her home in the rain one night. Then I left. The next day she planted a kiss on me. She took me by surprise. I tried to tell her I was taken. But her manager was watching and she ran off."

"Ooh. Tawdry." Andra didn't seem impressed.

"And then I tried eating there before her shift. If I'd known she was scheduled for the early shift today, we would have gone somewhere else."

She said nothing very loudly.

"So, what have you been doing lately?" he asked, hoping to change the subject.

At that, her face brightened. "Well, it's actually been really interesting. I've been..." She faltered. "I can't really say. It's kind of... classified."

"Classified? You can't really say? What's going on?"

She looked around as if to make sure no one was watching, then she took out her ID. And then, removing her Orso resident visa, she revealed another ID card. This one bore the royal seal of Orso on a red background with a black and silver border.

"Wait," he stuttered. "Is that what I think it is?"

"It's a Service of the Orso Royal Family ID. Prince Elio issued it to me," she explained. "Holding one without authorization from a member of the crown family is ten years in prison. But..." She covered it up with her visa again, "...this only says I work for the family, the same as any cook or servant. However, outside the city it works like a badge for the Royal Bureau of Enforcement."

"So... what *can* you tell me?" Gian asked.

She sighed. "A lot of private meetings with... um... doctors and such," she tried to explain. "People who might know things about Heroic powers, scientists who Elio wants to develop resources to track and maybe even improve powers. Since I'm a fairly adept TK, I even do some demonstrations so they can run tests.

"Prince Elio is dedicated to drawing people to his team," she continued. "But it's all very hushed up right now because he wants to avoid having news and press hounding his people with questions, or fakers trying to get assigned to the new *prestigious royal appointment.* And considering a few of the people I've dealt with, Prince Elio isn't wrong."

Gian felt a twinge of... emotion at hearing the prince's name so many times. "So you're working with the prince a lot?"

She shrugged. "I see him two, sometimes three times a week. There's a lot of planning going on right now. He and I have spent a lot of time training together. He's really sharp with his TK now, way better than before. And we trained with a group of marines with TK and Psy." She was flushed with excitement. "When I think about all we've been doing together—"

"A lot of time?" Gian's caution slipped and he interrupted her. "All you've been doing together? You're giving me grief over Bartha, but you're spending all your time with Prince Pretty-boy."

"Gian, what's... I was only teasing you," she said, seeming shocked at his reaction. "I thought you'd be pleased for me."

"But it seems to me like you're falling for him, just like your father wanted."

Andra sighed. She stared at him. Her eyes seemed to sharpen, and Gian felt some kind of force gently take hold of him and pull his face down several inches until his eyes were level with hers.

"Understand something right now, you big dumb fool," she said quietly. "I am not, nor have I ever been, in any way, in love with Elio. When I first met him, I thought he was a pretty boy, a jerk. Then I got to know him a little, and he was kind of interesting. Then he offered me a position and became my boss and, for a boss, he's friendly. He's my friend. Nothing more.

"But I have only ever loved one person enough to commit treasonous crimes. I kidnapped a royal ambassador for you."

The unseen force pulled his head toward her, and she kissed him.

"And if I ever decide to change my mind, I'm certainly not going to hide it. I thought you knew me better than that, Gian."

The velvet-gloved grip on his head relaxed and Gian straightened up. "All right, I'm sorry. I guess... you were giving me a hard time about Bartha, and then you... Well, so I was jealous."

She reached up and put her arms around his neck. "You were always a little like this. I knew that. I saw it when you first introduced me to your friends back home."

Gian flashed back to memories of his old buddies. They'd plotted and planned together to overthrow the governor's influence and live free. They all died in the first Swarm attack. After that, freedom had seemed somehow less important than survival.

"But you were always tender to me," she continued. "You always treated me like... a person. After so many years of being a statue my father trotted out for vids and speeches, I felt noticed. You did so many silly things to get my attention. And when you started trying to get rid of the government, I wanted to see someone like you in charge and let other people feel what I did. But I was so young then and didn't know any better."

She looked up at him. "Elio can't give me what you can. He needs someone who doesn't need to be noticed. And I'm pretty sure I know who that is."

"Who's that?"

"Hush. Forget what you think you know. Just know that I want to share your life because you make me feel like mine is worthwhile."

They stood there in the street, a handful of people passing. One whispered, "Go on. Give her a kiss."

"Well, I am supposed to meet Prince Elio..." She looked at her chron. "In fact, he has a thing today. He's introducing himself to the founding members of his paramilitary group."

"Weren't you invited?" Gian asked.

"Of course I was," Andra replied. "But it would take me at least two, maybe three hours to get to the palace from the transit station."

"Two or three? Andra, I could walk to the palace in less time than that," he said.

"Well, sure," she replied. "But then I wouldn't have gotten to see you, would I?"

"Can I at least walk you to work?" he asked.

"I'd love that," she replied, "but not to the palace. I have one more meeting to attend first. Can you walk me back to the transit station, so I can rent a gravcar?"

———

Sovereign Incarceration Institution *Conquell*
Resdon Military Complex
Som Orsi City

Andra pulled her gravcar up to the heavy gate. The walls were five meters high, topped with coils of shockwire, with a laser enclision fence mounted two meters away. The gate was multiple layers of osmium-steel mesh threaded with spiked barbs. The guards on duty were not regular military; sovereign prisons trained their own guards, and no guard was allowed to serve in a facility that held even one prisoner from their own world. Entertainment vids that wanted a character to be tougher than tough, seemingly unstoppable and occasionally brutal, often turned to using Sovereign guards as heroes—or villains.

One of the guards came to her window. "Identification." The woman's voice was not a request.

Andra handed over her visa and her Royal Service badge. Both were inspected as Andra watched her vehicle being swept by two more security guards.

"You have completed Stage One of entry," the guard said. "Proceed through the gate to Stage Two. Follow any instructions given. If you resist in any way, you will be removed and arrested by local authorities."

"But I have a Royal—"

"Then you will need a royal to officially declare your arrest a mistake and set you free," the guard said. Her eyes were not kind. "They are not known to be lenient to servants who can't follow instructions."

Andra watched the heavy gate open and then drove through. On the other side, she saw a fence built like the gate of osmium mesh and barbs. The concrete wall she passed also had a laser enclision fence on the inside, as did the mesh fence.

Anyone trying to escape here had better learn to fly, she thought. *There's almost no way to avoid bleeding to death or losing limbs.*

She entered a tunnel and found another series of enclision grids; each shut off just before the gravcar touched them, then turned back on after she'd passed. When she reached the guard station, she was ordered to exit the vehicle while an industrial composite scanner identified every material of the car's construction. At the same time, she was put inside a medical scanner, positioned to allow her to stand. The image she saw on the screen seemed to be quite... personal, but she held her tongue.

Once she and the vehicle were cleared, she received further instructions—first, to park in the underground lot beneath the prison. She spiraled several times until she was certain she had reached a hundred meters underground. Then she parked and rode an elevator up for several uncomfortable minutes until she reached Stage Three, where she was confronted by a small desk with a terminal and a gray metal machine with a plastic bin. A stack of clear plastic containers leaned against the wall; each container was filled with a set of white coveralls. And, of course, there was a guard, a huge male whose square jaw looked like it could be used to break rocks. His name badge bore the name Glaud, and a hashbar code. At his waist was a heavy truncheon —no stun capability, she noticed.

"Name?" the guard said gruffly.

"Andra Graynir."

"Home of origin?"

"Planet Tor, Pricus City, Kubernan District, Governor's mansion."

The guard looked unimpressed. "That's different. Home of record?"

Andra realized that this guard saw dozens of Royal-appointed persons. A governor's daughter wouldn't be much.

"Planet Caerus, Som Orsi, Oligere District, Royal Palace."

"Appointment?" The guard glanced at the screen—then looked again. "Wait a—"

She took a breath. "I'm here to see Eugma Zettel."

"No one sees Zettel."

"I think you'll find my credentials state—"

"Zettel doesn't take a piss without the Dominie giving the order. Zettel doesn't get visitors."

"I have a Class One exemption."

Despite what she'd told Gian, her badge wasn't *exactly* the same as a royal servant's. After the guard scanned the embedded code and had a terse conversation with the Dominie that she couldn't hear, she received her clearance.

"Now you need to be searched," the guard said.

"Wasn't I already searched?" she demanded. But his eye twitched, and she remembered the first guard's admonition—*Follow any instructions given.* She tried to put on a meek expression as she raised her arms.

He shook his head. "Remove all items of clothing except for undergarments. Place them in the bin."

Andra almost told him her opinion of the likelihood of that happening—*I'd rather be arrested*—but Glaud held up a hand.

"Look, I get it. You have standards. My job is to make sure none of the prisoners in here can find something as simple as a paperclip. And if the monitors ever caught me abusing my position, I'd spend six months in one of these cells. Remove all items of clothing, please."

Hardly mollified, Andra still needed to do her job. *But I'm going to have a talk with Prince Elio about better briefings in the future.* So she removed her clothes down to her underwear and put them in the bin. And Glaud pushed it inside the machine and then took a security wand from the desktop and went over every excruciating inch of her body.

She couldn't decide if it would have been more embarrassing if he'd leered at her instead of showing no interest whatsoever. Coldly and efficiently, he did his job and finally nodded his satisfaction and went to his terminal.

"Your upper garment has a metal wire." Now his voice almost sounded like he was reading instructions. "I will turn my back. Please remove the offending garment and place it in the bin before putting on a jumpsuit that best fits you. This is for our safety and yours. When you leave, you will be searched again to make sure you haven't removed anything from the prison. You will then be given the opportunity to dress in your own clothes. The jumpsuit will be burned after you leave."

Andra raised her eyebrows but said nothing.

"It is for your safety and well-being," Glaud said quietly. "There are several TK and Psy adept criminals residing until they can be dealt with. Zettel included."

He picked up a breather, handed it to her and said, "Put it on." Then he picked up another and sealed it to his face.

"Follow me," he said and opened the door into the prison at large as she struggled to place the device over her face before the air exchanged.

———

"WHY ARE WE WEARING THESE?" Andra asked, pointing to the breather as they started down the industrial mesh stairs.

"So we can breathe," he replied.

"But why do we need them?" she said.

"If there's an attempted escape, they won't be able to breathe."

That makes no sense.

She walked along a wide catwalk, peering at the rows of cells stacked one atop the other. The visual effect was a child's wall of square blocks arranged in a staggered brick pattern, but each layer lower seemed to pull further back.

"You will be in a small room, separated by a window," Glaud said. "Anything he says to you may be a lie; that's for you to decide."

If she looked over the edge—and it was a long way down—she could see that eventually, another set of cells lay underneath the catwalks upon which they strode. Each cell looked like a cubish escape pod, with a single reader panel on the shell next to the door.

"Anything I say to him will definitely be a lie," Glaud continued. "If you try to correct me, you will be stunned and removed. You will lose your Class 1 clearance and never be allowed to set foot in here again." He glanced back. "Unless, of course, you wish to stay longer."

She ignored his attempt at humor. "Where is Dr. Zettel?" she asked.

"I'm not allowed to say," he replied. "And even then, prisoners aren't allowed to stay in any one place for more than forty-eight standard hours. They are constantly moved. For our safety and yours."

It's like the mantra they chant to keep themselves going, she thought. But she had to admit, if anyone deserved to feel better about their job...

They walked for several minutes, taking metal mesh stairs instead of elevators. When he finally stopped, her legs were burning, and she was dreading the climb back up.

He tapped his wristpad, and a grav platform came out from under the catwalk and locked into place between them and the door to one of the cells.

"But why didn't we take the grav down?" she asked.

Glaud shook his head. "If an alarm sounds, all platforms power off to prevent prisoner escape. So we only use them as a step between walk and cell. For your safety and ours."

He stepped across and held up his wristpad. The panel

purred and beeped, then the door opened. Inside was a clear safety panel, as thick as a starship viewport, with a tiny vox speaker affixed. There was a small table with a blue light and a chair on her side, and a similar desk and chair on the other side. She could see Zettel's living quarters, a spartan affair with only a fixed cot and a small desk.

But it was Eugma Zettel who surprised her the most. He looked like a kindly old man with startling blue eyes and a white mustache, not someone who would assassinate a king. But he was wearing what appeared to be a metal helmet with straps around his neck to secure it in place, and his wrists and ankles each had a strange-looking metal bracelet. He also wore a belt made from the same material.

"Emergency restraints," the guard explained as he took off his breather. "If an alarm sounds, or if you push this button—" He indicated the large blue light. "—his restraints will truss him instantly. You have thirty minutes." Glaud backed away and took a place by the door.

Andra pulled the breather off. "This is a privileged conver—"

"No one visits any prisoner in this facility without a guard present at all times. You can leave now if you wish; your choice." His expression—and his heavy club—brooked no argument.

Andra decided she would simply include it in her report, though how she was expected to conduct her conversation without the benefit of secrecy was beyond her.

"Dr. Eugma Zettel," she said through the vox. "My name is Andra Graynir. I'd like to talk to you for a few minutes."

"Why, of course, my dear," he said with a smile. "I do hope you'll forgive the state of my appearance. I wasn't expecting guests."

"He's lying," Glaud said. "He was informed thirty minutes ago. Before you even arrived."

Glaud, too, was lying, as he'd said he would. Thirty minutes ago she was removing her clothes. But she said nothing.

"Sir Glaud," Zettel replied, "I was merely attending to the social niceties. I meant no disrespect."

Before the guard could continue, Andra jumped in. "Dr. Zettel, I'm here on behalf of the Orso Royal Family," she began without thinking. Then she continued the prepared introduction she'd used for several months. "We're putting together a unit of TK adepts, an autonomous group of civilians outside the military hierarchy. It's thought that too many of our current Heroic forces are members of the military, which could lead to hidebound thinking. We need to step out of the box, so to speak. The group will include people from all walks of life: civilians, police, members of the emergency services, construction workers and so on."

She stopped and frowned; she'd almost forgotten who she was talking to. "You were a member of the research team Marshal Ugo Tan put together," she continued. "You ran experiments on Heroic powers and their holders. You garnered a wealth of information. And then your team tried to assassinate the king because of some inane prophecy."

"Please understand," Zettel said in his kindly voice. "I had no part in that decision. Marshal Tan brought me into his project because he wanted to know about the work I'd been doing on halo technology. I knew nothing about his plot until it was already carried out."

"Halo technology?" She feigned confusion for a moment. She knew full well the many interesting discoveries that had been made in the underground research bunker. Some of the victims had even been able to describe them.

"I was looking at the way we 'jack in' to various meetings and games. Fantastic experiences at our fingertips like never before. But if we can make our brain 'see' and 'feel' and 'hear' things that aren't really there, then why couldn't we do other things? Why not change the way the brain works?"

"You're talking about mind control?" Andra asked calmly.

"You see, this is why my research is so difficult for simple people to understand." Zettel almost waved his arms as if to emphasize his point. But she saw him glance past her shoulder and lowered his hands. "There are many people who suffer from troubles of the mind. Depression, anxiety, compulsions that only make sense to themselves. We have criminals who need monitoring. We have people who suffer brain injuries and cannot speak or walk; we have people who start to decline mentally just after they reach their centennial. I was researching how we might use the halo to help these people to alleviate the obstacles and provide them with a happy and fulfilling life. Imagine a person, if you will, born unable to see because of a simple nerve malfunction? The halo could allow that person to see, while jacked in, of course. It's a problem we've been working on since the inception of the halo. We should be able to create a halo that simply side-steps the problem."

"Everything you're describing is amazing," Andra said. "But you haven't mentioned that you're a Psy, of an advanced level beyond anything encountered so far. Would you like to talk about that?"

———

Conquell Prisoner Area W7-4
Cell #7db41643ed

"Oh, dear," Eugma Zettel said and shrugged. *Well, it wasn't going to stay a secret forever,* he thought. *Even Glaud here knows that much. Likely he would have told her in a few more moments, anyway.*

"I suppose my secret is out now," he said, smiling at her. "I didn't think anyone on the team had figured it out. Tell me, if you please. Who was the deviant that managed to unravel the subterfuge?"

"No one on your team," she replied. "We interviewed your test subjects. The ones who managed to remain lucid, that is."

"I'm afraid I don't know what you—"

"There's no need to deny it," she snapped. "Even if we hadn't gotten it from your victims, we had your notes."

"My notes?" He snarled without thinking. He forced himself back to his kindly persona. "So you found them," he said more genially. "It feels like you simply like catching me off balance. Rather a pity, my dear, since my incarceration leaves me —one-legged?"

"Your notes were very interesting once we managed to decipher them. Don't look so surprised," she added with a tiny smile. "The King's cryptologists assured him that the encryption was a tough one."

"Well, here we are then," Zettel said, his shroud of geniality beginning to loosen. He leaned back on his seat and placed his hands, palms down, on his knees.

"So... my best efforts at confusion and deniability were fruitless," he said amiably. "And what have you come to learn from the *evil* and *devious* Doctor Eugma, eh?" He made a deliberate show of deprecation.

"You, sir, have committed many abominable acts. However," she said and raised her finger as if she was about to make an important statement, "we have no records of your committing heinous crimes against humanity before you were corralled by Marshal Tan and inducted into his think tank.

"It was proposed by some that you were forced into your work. That being so, and in the interests of both justice and the war effort, I am here to offer you a research commission in the prince's task force. It will require you to be under guard and to wear your incapacitory devices at all times. You will never have a moment alone with anyone or yourself. If you are willing to agree—"

"Oh, I agree wholeheartedly," Zettel said enthusiastically.

"Anything is preferable to living out the rest of my life in this box."

"Very well."

Very well indeed, he thought, elated. *The girl looks pleased. As though she's won some kind of victory. How delicious!*

"You will be visited by the king's officials prior to your probationary release," she said. "You will sign documents that state any action deemed dangerous in any way, shape, or form will result in your immediate re-incarceration and a possible re-sentencing."

"Oh, assuredly," he agreed. "I understand that my release is mere sufferance on the part of the royal family. But I will endeavor to please the king—and the prince—with my services, just as I'd hoped to please him the last time."

She cocked her eyebrow at that. "Very well then," she said. "See that you do."

She stood, reaffixed her breather, then turned away and said something to Glaud he couldn't hear. Then the outer door opened, and they left him alone.

Hmm, he thought. *How very agreeable of them.*

———

ALONE HAS A VERY new meaning now, Zettel thought as he lay down on his cot to practice his mental exercises for the morning. As he reached past his helmet's limiter, he tried to touch the mind of the inmate above.

Do they really think they can confine me with my own inventions?

The scientist who reverse-engineered his mental-block halo had done a credible job, but there was one thing Eugma Zettel understood better than all else; never let yourself be cornered. He'd left certain weaknesses within his designs, pathways, if you will. Pathways he could exploit.

Today's neighbor is... Thram Orda. He watched for a few

moments as Thram replayed a few choice moments in his life, mostly reveling in his kills. He had quite a repertoire. But before Thram could exhaust his memories, Eugma had to pull back lest he overreach his strength. *Push and release. Like their horrid physical regimen. Flex and strengthen.*

The unnamed scientist had missed several of Zettel's deliberate flaws, but not all. But the sliver of light he could make out on the other side was enough to make him keep pushing. *Someday, I'll be free of this thing. I will have honed my ability to a razor's edge. And then, my arrogant friends, watch out.*

He reached out below him to find another neighbor… *Apere Ohlra.* He pulled back immediately. The man's taste for women was only made less disgusting by how he chose to fulfill it. The first and only time Eugma had lingered inside such a brain, it had taken days to purge the thriving memory from his own mind.

I would be doing the world a favor if I struck him brain-dead. The worth of humanity itself would be raised a whole percentage point from his demise.

But even with his abilities diminished, not smothered, he couldn't muster the strength to lash out.

So instead, he mulled over the information he'd gleaned from his lovely visitor.

First had been her recent thoughts. She carried them very close to the surface, unlike experienced Psy users. She had great power—her TK was formidable—but not yet truly tested. She'd been awash with emotions about her significant other, an easily manipulated boy who wanted to fly fighters, Gian Vastum. He'd gleaned from her thoughts her intention of being his wife someday. *Two sheep to be led around by the royal wolves.*

Second, she'd extolled the benefits of a Heroic society. He had only caught a glimpse of that project, but she believed people with power wouldn't eventually create a society that favored them and reduced others to chattel. *She even uses her powers on her boyfriend. And he accepts her hypocrisy? But let her have her delusions. She has years yet before her optimism will get her killed. Unless she gets in my way, of course.*

Then his mind had bathed in the emotional tangle that came after he began explaining his technology to her, he realized she had no power in the government, but she did have the ear of one who did. His speech—some of it true—had helped convince her that such things could be accomplished. There was even a twinge of something far away from her, someone her Gian knew who knew someone who might benefit. He would be certain to mention it—if the situation warranted it. If it might possibly enable him to reach past the fence of electronics, guards and royals, to be free once more.

He glanced around his cell. *Soon. Soon I will be freer than this. There is always another step to take toward freedom. And I already know I will be free. Oh yes. One day I will be free again.*

CHAPTER
TEN

GUARDIANS ASSEMBLE

Orso Royal Palace
Conference Room 12-B-3

Meera Seluere wasn't sure what she should have expected a group of TK adepts, or initiates, to look like.

She'd thought perhaps other TK users would look like the soldiers she saw daily in the propaganda vids. Or maybe they would all be slight yet dexterous, with sharp minds and piercing eyes, as the mesmerists of entertainment always appeared.

Instead, it felt like she was waiting in line at a GrabABite quickserve.

She looked around the room. A man dressed in earthy tones with a mop of greasy hair was seated just to her left, and nearby a woman near Meera's age was fidgeting with the hem of her skirt. Behind them was a woman with a wild mass of hair, long and strangely curly. It bloomed from her head like a greeber fern.

She looked to her right. A tall man in a tight shirt and a loose gray-blue vest was seated two seats away. Meera thought the vest might once have been a shirt, but now the sleeves were missing. Two seats further away, a tattooed street tough, and a very lean man with short hair and possibly a temper to match, sat staring stoically at a recruiting poster.

But the one who stood out the most seemed as far removed from the others as she felt close to them. He wore a blue jump-suit, similar to what shipboard contractors might wear, but he wore a sash around his waist and a strip of cloth around his forehead. He caught her studying him and walked over and sat down beside her, a toothy grin on his face.

"Hello there," he said in a melodious foreign accent. "I couldn't help but notice you looking around the room."

She tried not to blush. "Was I that obvious?"

"Amid such strange and new things, how can one not look around and marvel?"

She tried not to blush. "Well, hi then. I'm Meera." She held out her hand for him to shake.

He looked at it for a moment. "May I suggest another?" he asked. He held his hand out in a fist behind her hand. When she made the fist, he touched his wrist to hers, then ran his fingernails up her sleeve. She did the same, a little awkwardly.

"There we are, a proper greeting." He smiled at her.

"It was very different," she replied.

"Yes, I know," he said. "But you see, on my world, touch is a very important sense. We do not like to use our fingers... casually. Touch says many things to different people."

"Oh," Meera said, unsure of what to say next. "Um, they say our handshake came from ancient times when warriors opened their hands to show they had no weapons."

"Ah. And so it is on my world, too. But we wear long,

flowing sleeves. Our greeting checks for knives. So maybe we are more alike than I think."

She found it difficult to ignore his smile; he radiated an infectious joy.

"You haven't told me your name," she said.

"Ahkma doit. My head travels. I am Proose. Vadir Elada Proose Hamanaleckta, but in your way, I am called just Proose."

"So many names."

"Not so, only one. Vadir means—"

But before he could say anything more, a tall, well-built man in a dark blue military uniform entered the room. On his left breast were two rows of medal ribbons. On his head, he wore a side-cap—officially called a garrison cap—a throwback to a time before the Purge. But most conspicuous was his eye patch: black and trimmed with gold.

"Good morning," he barked, surprisingly loud and crisp. "I am Major Avum Rosst. King Orson Lorne has, in his infinite wisdom, seen fit to assign me to your... unit. I will be overseeing your training. I am what some would call a martinet. If you don't know what that means, I will tell you. It means I am one tough bastard, and I will ride you hard. If you graduate—and that's a big if—you will be better and stronger for it. And your ... gift will also be better and stronger for it."

"He doesn't seem like he wants to be here," Meera whispered to Proose.

"If he does not like his king telling him what to do, he should get another king," he whispered back.

"Careful," she said. "You shouldn't talk that way. You'll get into trouble."

"If any of you have previous military experience," Major Rosst continued, "please raise your hands."

Several did.

"Around here, the kings get touchy when you talk about getting rid of them," she whispered.

"I didn't say that," Proose whispered.

"You," Rosst pointed to one of the raised hands. "Stand up and explain yourself."

The man stood to attention and said, "Sir, I'm Jude Cabeus. I, um, was part of the Royal Guard. Eleven years ago." He looked at Rosst but didn't say more.

Rosst gave him a strange look but turned away and pointed at another man.

"I'm Klaus Brekan," rumbled the large man in the ripped vest. He was shaved bald, with a wicked scar down one side of his face. He was the most muscular person in the room. "I was a Marine, stationed shipside. I, uh, made it out. In the battle for Caerus. When she went down."

"Why didn't they assign you to another unit?"

Klaus didn't answer immediately. "I was discharged on medical grounds, sir."

"And yet you're here now, reenlisting, to fight again?"

"I am, sir," the man replied, his barrel chest extended pridefully.

"Good man. And you?"

The woman Meera thought to be close to her own age stood up. "My name is Beko Vissla. I served for two years in the army before I met my husband. He stayed in, and I became a mother. That was twenty-three years ago."

"No marks or commendations?"

"No, sir," she replied. "Just a dirtside grunt. But I do know which end of the gun to hold," she added with a laugh.

"That will be useful." Rosst turned to the others. "The rest of you are new to the military way of life. But while, so I understand, you will not be required to achieve military standards of fitness—" His sour expression told them how he felt about *that*. "—we will be training together to unlock and develop your... abilities and find how and if they will be useful in a combat situation.

"You are not alone," he continued. "There are others who have not arrived yet, in particular your benefactor Prince Elio

Lorne. In the meantime, I have a list of designated pairs for the day. Each day you will have a new pairing. You will stay with your partner each day during training and try to learn about each other's strengths and weaknesses. Do your best to shore each other up, and maybe we can forge something new and exciting together."

It sounded as if he was reading a set speech; one he hadn't practiced.

"Today, we are practicing simple pushes. Each of you will practice rolling small wooden balls away from you. I know that's not terribly exciting, but this is a control exercise. If you manage not to break anything, we'll move on to pulling by this afternoon. Now, Rauf, I'm pairing you with Beko today. Remember the conditions of your parole. Vecht, you're with Klaus. Meera, you're with Jude, and Elaer, you work with Proose."

Meera was a little disappointed that she wouldn't get to continue talking to Proose. She watched him walk over to the frizzy-haired woman and exclaim, "Hello, Elaer. Your hair... is so exciting."

So Meera walked over to the man dressed in earth tones and shook his hand; a surprisingly benign shake, considering her experience with Proose. "Hi, I'm Meera."

"Jude," he said, almost in a whisper. "Want to get started?"

———

Avum Rosst watched his eight new recruits rolling wooden crocket balls along the floor and sighed. He'd been on the orbital defense station *Atollite* when a plasma burst had pierced the hull. He'd made it out of the room before the bulkhead sealed, and all he lost was an eye. But with his remaining eye, he could clearly see that this was foolishness.

Rolling balls around with their minds? Granted, some were better than others. Jude was managing to not only move his away from him, but also made it hop. Klaus had destroyed his first ball in an uncontrolled push, but his second had survived. And the woman, Vissla, she'd managed to roll hers away and then give just a flick to roll it back. *Not in the rules, but I won't press,* he thought.

But the rest were civilians, and it showed. Vecht had already destroyed three balls against the wall, and it looked as if he was about to break a fourth if he didn't rein in his temper. Rauf and Elaer both managed weak pushes occasionally but had no repetition. Rauf kept waving his hands around as though he thought it might help.

It was this or medical retirement, he thought savagely. *I could still take the retirement, I suppose.*

But he knew he wouldn't. The military was his life's blood. And with an enemy so merciless, humanity needed everybody to do their bit.

Some better than others, he thought darkly as he remembered the many recruits who'd managed to stumble through basic training.

He felt a feathery touch on his mind, a simple request to join... someone. He left the room, stepped into the corridor and found Prince Elio Lorne waiting for him.

"Sorry I'm a few minutes late," Elio said.

Rosst had to resist the urge to roll his eyes. The prince's indolence was well known. *It's been over an hour since he was supposed to arrive.* "There's no need to apologize, my prince. I know you have many important—"

"Yes, Major. I was in a meeting," the prince interrupted him. "Enough of platitudes. I can hear your every thought, remember?"

Rosst sighed and nodded. "It seems you have an unfair advantage, Prince Elio."

"In this life there is much that is unfair, Major Rosst. Unfair life, maybe, but we have an enemy to defeat."

He gave Rosst a level look that would have done many a junior officer proud.

"I don't care what thoughts you have about me or the project. I only care what you accomplish. Give them stones, Major, and they will slay giants. They just need the confidence to see it through."

Hmm. Methinks he's gotten a little more backbone these last few years.

You have no idea, Major, Elio responded, pushing into his mind.

Rosst started but kept his thoughts calm. "As you say, my prince. Will you be speaking to the recruits?"

"As a matter of fact, I did have something prepared. Please, lead the way."

Rosst stood next to Elio as he watched each recruit carefully. "Well, we do have some with talent, and some with control," the prince observed.

"You're right, sir," Rosst said. "I noticed that the former military personnel seem to do better than the civilians."

"Yes, I'm sure their previous military training is an asset," Elio agreed. "I understand Vecht and Elaer had a single noticeable burst before they came to us. Meera claims she had several smaller incidents. And Rauf had... well, there's an entire report."

"Is it safe to have a criminal on your team?" Rosst asked. "Should we be training him like this?"

They watched Rauf for an entire minute as his wooden ball made sporadic movements. "You read that report," Elio said, finally. "If he can do that to the enemy..."

Rosst had read the report. Seventeen peace officers injured in subduing a single criminal. But the prince had snatched him out of custody before he could be sent to *Conquell.*

"If he can be an asset, we need him," Elio said. "If the enemy has its way, every human in the galaxy will die. We can only hope to do what we can to keep some of them alive."

The prince shuddered as he said it. Rosst remembered hearing Prince Elio had seen a Blue gasp out the alien threat and expire. He didn't ask, but the prince caught his eye and nodded.

"Well, I think it's time for my speech." Prince Elio stepped forward and raised his hands.

———

FOR SEVERAL MINUTES, while he was talking to Rosst, Elio had been feeling out to the recruits with his Psy. He didn't have to pry deep into their minds; to him, they were an open book. It didn't take him long to understand what they wanted, what they *needed.*

They need a purpose, he thought. *They need a calling. Some of them have the desire. All of them lack guidance. I have to provide that. But first, something to loosen them up.*

"May I have your attention, please?" Elio called out. They all stopped and lined up in loose formation and stared at him.

He was a compelling figure of a young man: tall—two full meters—as were all royals, slim but muscular, and he wore his blond hair a little longer than was fashionable, to his shoulders. His eyes were electric blue, and he bore the Roman nose of his father's line.

"I am Elio Lorne. I assume at least some of you have heard of me?"

His jibe had the desired effect. Several people laughed.

"What? No one? Huh. I think I may need to call my publicist."

Now everyone was laughing, but guardedly.

"I wanted to welcome you to an organization I'm calling the TK Guardians. Some of you might wonder why this isn't a military operation. Some of you may already have heard of TK and Psy units being formed in the military. In which case, I'm sure you're wondering why you're here instead of there?"

No one responded. "So why are you here?" he repeated. *They need to answer the question themselves.*

"Because... we can help?" called out a skinny man with short, spiked hair, who he learned later was called Rauf.

"Because everyone can help," Elio agreed. "We put out calls to increase the peacekeepers and police because they can help protect the citizens. We put out calls for anyone with industrial experience because they can help restart our industries. We put out calls for anyone who wanted to organize the refugees, and they did. And we have people like you, who have a gift that you may be unsure how to use. We will foster that gift, nurture it, develop it and, perhaps, turn it into a weapon we can use against the enemy."

"But our abilities are weak," the woman with large poufy hair known to the group as Elear said. "We've been trying for an hour, and nothing seems to work."

Elio remembered how easy it had been the first time he'd tried to use his TK. He was one of a very few people gifted with both TK and Psy.

He recalled the force Andra had used against her first Blue and inwardly shook his head.

He tried not to think about how easily he and Danis had fallen into Psy communication with each other from the very first time.

"I understand," Elio replied. "I also understand that each of you chose to come here to be tested by our doctors and scientists. I also know each of you has strong TK markers, which is why you eight are the first to be chosen. You eight have the potential to develop and grow your gift into something splendid."

"But how do we do that?" the man called Rauf asked. "What if we're not strong enough?"

"Strong enough to do what?" Elio asked. "Lift a gravcar? Throw a shuttle? The first time I saw TK used against a Blue, it was killed by a rock thrown by a young woman who didn't even know she had the gift. You have the opportunity to—"

"But we're not those kinds of people," the woman called Beko said. "We can't do things like that."

"Not right now," Elio said, "but you can and you will. All you need is training and the will to win."

He waited a moment to let it sink in, then said, "I think you eight are among the most gifted people on Caerus. I also think you have the heart and determination to defend your home. Nobody has ever done this before; not even in the military. You will be the first official civilian group. You won't be sent to the far-flung star systems to fight the war. For you, the war is here, on Caerus. The more groups we have like you to protect the planets, the less the military has to worry about their homes and their families. You can do this. Can I count on you?"

———

MEERA, nervous, stayed at the rear of the group.

She'd heard of Prince Elio, of course, though she didn't admit it when he asked the question. Many women half her age still fantasized about the possibility of attracting the attention of a prince, and rumor had made him out to be kindly and beneficent, unlike his father.

The more cynical rumors portrayed him as a privileged, indolent layabout who never took his duties seriously. But she saw none of that. And, she had to admit, he did cut a dashing figure. His excitement about the project was evident, and she wondered how long it had been since she'd seen that kind of passion in a man.

I'm right here, with a real prince, she thought, filled with awe.

"Can I count on you?" he shouted.

And they cheered, even Meera, waving her arms in the air.

His drive was infectious. It was good to be away from the rut of depression that had shaped her life for so many months.

"Your training begins now," he announced. "You're all relatively new to TK and we have a mix of experience, so our first priority is to pair you with someone you can learn from—"

"Sir," Rosst interrupted him. "I've already divided them into pairs for the day, as you requested."

"Oh? Very good, major. So keep your pairs for today, and keep practicing." He turned to Rosst and said, "I need an escort for today. I'll take... you," he said, pointing at Jude. "You and your partner."

Meera couldn't believe it. *I'm going to spend the rest of the day with the Prince?* she thought, but then she remembered the rumors; Prince Elio was also a Psy, and those kindly eyes held the power to strip your soul bare and reveal your deepest secrets.

It's not just women half my age who can fantasize about a prince, she thought, hoping he wasn't monitoring her thoughts.

———

ELIO OFFERED his hand to Meera. She shook it tentatively, weakly. Even without trying, he could sense the lightheaded giddiness she was feeling, as did most people when meeting a member of the royal family for the first time. He simply ignored it. Then he turned and clasped the hand of a man he once knew well.

"Jude," he said warmly. "Welcome. It's been a long time."

Jude frowned and looked guarded, his memories churning beneath the surface. "I didn't think you'd recognize me. Not after so long."

"I might not have, except for the little scandal it caused when you left," Elio said, smiling. "There's no need for you to explain, not right now. Your reasons were your own, and I am not my father. If you decide to tell me, I will listen. But it has nothing to do with why I made certain you were accepted."

"You... personally chose me?" Jude asked, the astonishment rolling outward from his mind.

"I remember you as a stalwart soldier and a loyal friend," Elio said, thinking back to the many times Sergeant Cabeus had filched goods from the various merchants the king didn't want Elio associating with. Many of Elio's early successes in studying electronics came from Jude's mildly subversive behavior. "I know that without you, the galaxy would be a darker place right now," Elio assured him. "Or worse, a Bluer one."

"I'm sure things would have worked out fine," Jude said bluntly.

Clearly, he doesn't want to talk. Elio thought. *Good enough!*

"Well," Elio said, "I just wanted to say thank you. I didn't have the chance before." He turned and strode away, letting his senses touch the two just enough to know they were following him.

———

"How do you know the prince?" Meera asked, awed.

Jude hesitated before answering. "My father was one of the king's guards."

"But it sounded like you—"

"I'd rather not talk about it," Jude said.

Meera thought he was being something other than modest. *If he knows the prince,* she thought, *why is he being so evasive?*

It was a quiet walk to the royal garage and a quiet ride in the prince's gravcoach, a longer, more luxurious vehicle than Meera had ever seen. It would have felt the height of indulgence had she not noticed the thick wall panels, the powerful hum of the gravfield, and the armed guards in the front and rear of the vehicle. And the armored gravtruck following behind them.

What was it like, growing up like this? she wondered. *If I were reminded every day, every hour, that I might die, it would make me paranoid.* She couldn't yet tell if the prince had risen above such concerns or was merely ignoring them.

"Jude, your job today is a simple prisoner escort," Elio explained en route.

"No weapon, sir?" Jude asked.

"We have armed guards for that," Elio explained. "You're present in case I need something more."

"Understood, sir."

But... why aren't I part of the conversation?

Meera knew that she was still working on her control, but she felt she was a part of the project, too.

After a few minutes more, they arrived at their destination —a squat, imposing building with a sign that read, Detention: Peacekeeping Division Q-15.

The guards exited the vehicle, their movement rocking the coach despite the powerful gravfield. They dispersed around the coach, and when satisfied all was well, one of them opened the door, and Elio stepped out.

"On me," he said, and Jude jumped up immediately. Meera tried to emulate his rigid pose, his stiff walk, but couldn't quite pull it off. Ten meters behind them, the rest of the guards exited the armored gravtruck.

"Follow me," Elio said and walked quickly to the door, which opened immediately on his approach, and, together the three of them stepped inside while Elio's guards formed a semi-circle around the door.

Inside, they were met by a woman dressed in travel-worn clothes and a veritable army of guards, all standing around a single, older man wearing a ridiculous amount of restraints.

"Eugma Zettel," Elio said, loudly, for all to hear. "I am here to release you under Royal Edict 204-15.6, the Wartime Emergency Act, and Edict 117-24.8, the Release of Prisoners for Penitent Labor. By signing this document, you agree to be released from detention to work as assigned and be executed if convicted of sabotage or aiding the enemy in any way. Do you understand?"

"I agree completely," Zettel said. "Just show me where to sign."

The prince handed him a pen. "You've used a biometric pen before?"

"Of course."

And Zettel signed the documents.

Meera had heard of biometric pens—pinpoint lasers that printed the signatures in computer-readable codes, with identifying fingerprints and other bodily information. As long as the documents survived—and they were hardy—they would attest to his complete agreement to comply with the terms of his release.

Once the documents were finalized, copies were made and distributed in osmium-sheaf folders.

"How is your father doing?" Zettel asked.

Elio stiffened, and the palace guards shifted their grips on their weapons. Only Jude seemed to show no reaction.

"You have some nerve—" Elio growled.

"As I explained to your courier here," Zettel said, motioning to the woman, "I merely did as I was instructed by the marshal. I had no part of the plot. I didn't even know of it."

Elio glanced at the woman, and for a moment they seemed to share something.

They're talking to each other through Psy, Meera realized.

Elio nodded, looked at Zettel and said, "My father is well, thank you." Then he motioned to the woman, and together they walked out.

"Prisoner transfer protocols, urchin formation," said one of the gravtruck guards. The detention guards stepped outside and formed columns, and the palace guards escorted the prisoner to the truck. Four guards entered the truck, followed by Zettel, then four more guards.

"We ride in the back," Jude explained.

"Oh," was all she could say before she climbed in, followed by Jude. The doors closed electronically, the locks clunked, the gravengine whined, and the vehicle moved smoothly forward.

During the ride, Meera couldn't help glancing at Zettel. He looked so... pitiful. All those heavy restraints and that oversized helmet?

———

Eugma Zettel sat in the truck, surrounded by armed guards, watched from every angle. And he only wished he dared to smile.

Complete freedom was almost within his grasp.

TECHNICAL DIFFICULTIES

Fellowship Offices, Janati Collegium
Som Vensi City
Planet Caerus

Tenilo Barum sat at his virtual desk, staring at the blank space where his halo call had just ended. He waved a virtual keyboard into existence and called up his own suite of halo programs, including the one that recorded all halo communications.

He needed to review the conversation and everything he'd just been tasked with.

The recording appeared in an instant. He couldn't see himself, of course, but he could see Prince Elio in a remarkable representation of his gravcoach.

"Hello, Professor Tenilo," the prince said. "Congratulations on being offered the status of Visiting Fellow at Janati. I'm sure everyone back home is very proud of you."

"Thank you, my prince," he'd stammered at the unexpected call. "But... I'm sure that's not why you called."

"No, Tenny, I have a project and I need your help," Elio said. "I need solutions, and you're the one person I can trust to find them."

"I'm... it would be an honor, Prince Elio," Tenilo replied. "Of course I'm willing to do whatever I can. I assume it has something to do with the Swarm?"

"No. This is a local problem, and I need it taken care of quickly. If we don't clear away the orbital debris left from the battle, it will cause a major supply chain problem—in and out. And, worse, the military is already hindered in their efforts to defend the planet. While a debris shield might make sense in some instances, it doesn't work for our fighters."

"Understood, I think," Tenilo replied.

He shook his head, staring at the recording. *What was I thinking, agreeing to take it on without knowing the problem or the extent of it?*

"Very well," Elio said. "I have little time, so let's get this done. Are you ready, Tenny? Good, then let us proceed." He cleared his throat and waved a hand. A digital scroll appeared in front of him, and words appeared as he spoke.

"I, Prince Elio Lorne, by order of the king, do invoke Royal Edict 204-15.6, the Wartime Emergency Act, 125-48.4, Royal Claim of Military Salvage In-System, and 75-58.6, the Responsibility of Safe Travel Act, and I do hereby commission Industrial Scientist General-class Tenilo Barum, native to and formerly of the Alastor System, in the work of making our orbital space lanes navigable to common traffic. To this end, there has been decided a number of tasks which must be completed in order to restore respect and confidence in the Crown's ability to provide for the people of Planet Caerus and the Orso System in its entirety.

"One: that the damaged defense platform *Obligation* be

removed from its place in orbit and relocated to a safe and reasonable orbit around the sister planet Diminu."

Tenilo could still barely believe it. *How do you move something like that even when it's **not** damaged?*

"Two: that all debris massing larger than one metric ton be removed, also to Diminu."

How many pieces of debris qualify for that size? There must be a hundred thousand floating around out there.

"Three: due to the shortage of tugs, capital warships and freighters of sufficient size native to the Orso System to be coopted to the task, permission is hereby given to offer contracts to the Independent Militia of Free People whose fleet remains in our system as guests. The contracts would include the transfer of said debris to a reasonable and safe orbit around Diminu, and for the removal of personal effects from the wrecks, including the labeling of said personal effects to indicate any identification data located on ships. It is the Crown's hope that they will render us these services."

Tenilo didn't even want to think of how he, of all people, was supposed to spar with dozens or maybe hundreds of canny ship captains, each looking to fleece him for as much money as possible.

"And four: The name of Professor Tenilo Barum is hereby submitted to the Royal Treasury as an agent of the Crown, paperwork and identity card pending at this time, to be offered any and all *immediate* assistance in the pursuance of these goals."

Even reviewing the video, Tenilo's mind whirled at the enormity of the task and the amount of power he was now entitled to wield. *An agent of the Crown...* he thought. *All immediate assistance... He literally told the Treasury to hand me a blank ledger.*

"Signed, Elio Lorne, Family of Lorne, *regalis pluris centum*, Crown Prince of Caerus, hereditary Seat of Orso and applicable territories. End."

He smiled at Tenilo once again as the virtual document rolled up and winked out of sight. "You'll be receiving the official copy in your folder as soon as it's logged by the Palace officials, but I've already alerted them to your new status."

"But what am I supposed to do in the meantime?" he heard himself ask. "I'm a guest lecturer. I have classes. I have *students*." Students, he suddenly realized, who were currently learning the basic processes for refining starship fuel.

"I'd suggest doing a little homework on the orbital problems," Prince Elio said easily. "And definitely contact Tiger Wok aboard the *Red Dragon*. He's the person who will know best how to approach—Oh my! It looks like I've arrived, and I'm already late for this meeting. Good luck, Tenny. Please keep me updated."

And the gravcoach disappeared, leaving an image of his virtual desk atop his real virtual desk. He shut it off, leaving only one office space in view.

Tenilo immediately began making calls. Not to researchers. Not to Tiger Wok but to the Janati administrators. Someone needed to take his grad students in hand before they blew something up.

———

Tenilo contacted the *Red Dragon* and requested a meeting with its captain.

"The captain is preoccupied at the moment," the comms officer answered after a muffled conference. "I'm certain that he will be available shortly. Do you prefer vid or halo for your communication?"

"I'm sure whatever the captain wishes will be fine," Tenilo said.

The call ended, and he had nothing to do but start requesting reports from the Royal Military. True to his word,

Prince Elio had already cleared the way for him, and his virtual desk was soon overflowing with messages containing ship damage assessments, orbital debris tracking reports, battle analyses with helpful notations pointing to likely Swarm wreckage that could still be recovered even after the past year, and reports of favorable orbits and routes to Diminu. Fortunately, Diminu was on approach, which would present fewer problems;... if he could get things rolling quickly.

Some forty-three minutes later, he received a ping for a vid call. He opened the call and was confronted by a shirtless, bearded Tiger Wok sitting in a very uncomfortable-looking position. His eyes were closed.

"Um, Captain Wok, sir?" Tenilo said. "I was told you were available for a vid conference. Should I call back later?"

He saw an eyebrow twitch. "No need for that," Wok said. "I am merely doing a mild stretch. Keeps me limber throughout the day."

Tenilo hadn't been aware that a pair of knees could touch in that position. "I'm calling on behalf of Prince Elio Lorne, who I know you've dealt with many times before."

"Prince Elio, yes." Tiger Wok smiled as he gently grasped his left ankle and drew it up behind his head. "I know him well. A strong man. A promising leader. Tell me, what brings his representative to me today?"

Tenilo tried to choose his words carefully. "I have been asked to approach the Independent Militia with a request for services."

He saw the eyebrows raise almost enough to expose the man's eyes.

"You are not a stupid man, Mr. Tenilo," Tiger Wok replied. "Yes, I know who and what you are. If you had asked for aid, that would have implied agreements where we have none. And aid is often compulsory in your Sovereign agreements. Your legal scholars would make a fine meal of us then. But services...

that's different. That implies you wish to hire us. Is that not so?"

"Yes." Tenilo breathed in relief. "I have been authorized to offer contracts to any IMFP captain who wishes to take them. We need towing capacity to remove the large pieces of debris in orbit above Caerus and take them to Diminu, the next outer planet from our sun."

Only now did Tiger Wok's eyes open. "Indeed?" he replied as he lifted the right ankle behind his head to join the left. "That's quite a task, my genius friend. Do you have any idea exactly what such a task would entail? Yes, I'm sure you do," Wok answered his own question.

"The immediate concern is navigation," Tenilo explained. "Launching and landing traffic. Right now, the debris is creating vast bottlenecks. Removal will also eliminate the potential for more debris strikes on the surface; the crashes of more than one hundred and forty ships during the battle may have cost as many as thirteen million lives."

"And what about Orso's fleet?" Wok asked. "Is it not available?"

"No," Tenilo replied. "The bulk of the fleet is on patrol."

"I see," Tiger Wok said. "But could there be another reason, something you're not telling me?"

Tenilo was about to disagree, but the captain's eyes were probing, inquisitive, so he decided deception wasn't an option.

"I suspect the prince might have a secondary plan. One of the damaged orbital platforms, the *Obligation*, is to be moved to Diminu as well to serve as a salvage station while it's being repaired. The debris is to be broken up and sent to the factories to be repurposed. But I do wonder if he plans to create an economy on Diminu that draws more people to the planet, thus creating an industrial hub. But I haven't spoken to him about this... not yet."

"You are imaginative and canny, as well." Tiger Wok seemed

to focus inward. Tenilo assumed he was thinking hard on the questions his proposals presented. But it was only when he began to suspect the captain had fallen asleep did he speak again.

"While your Prince Elio is also shrewd and canny, many of our military ships do not have the towing capacity that you may require. But I will ask the other captains if they are willing to help."

Tenilo knew that though Tiger Wok denied that he held any real position among the Independent Militia of Free People, things had a way of going exactly the way he wanted.

"I will be creating an office to..." *What? As yet, I have no idea.* "For now, you may give your captains my contact details. They can contact me. Messages will be forwarded."

Tiger Wok lowered both ankles, then moved to his stomach and lifted his entire body off the floor on just his hands, arching his feet toward his head. "I would like to ask one further question," he said. "Why did you approach me first?"

Tenilo smiled. "Prince Elio assured me that you would know how best to approach the other captains." *At least, I'm sure he would have, had he been given the chance to stay and complete his briefing.*

Tiger Wok smiled in return. "Again, he proves himself shrewd and wise. Perhaps if there were more rulers like him in the Sovereign Systems, we might get along better together. I will have my financial officer draw up a sample contract, and we can discuss details later."

Tiger Wok signed off, and Tenilo looked at the pile of other things he needed to accomplish.

Now I need to add "finance minister" to the list of things I need to learn today.

———

FACULTY LABORATORY SIGMA - Office
Janati Collegium

TENILO HAD BEEN LOOKING at the design specs for the damaged orbital platform and the damage reports supplied by the Royal Military for so long that his eyes felt like they were full of sand. But he was now certain the orbital burn engines weren't damaged beyond repair. A few quick repairs, a steady hand at the controls, a little finessing, and it should be able to move, albeit slowly, under its own power. There was no need to recall a carrier to tow the massive station almost one-hundred-seventy-million kilometers to Diminu. It would take months, but it could be done.

Tenilo rubbed his eyes and checked the chron. *Oh, blazes. It's 0235? How did it get so late, I mean early?*

He checked his messages. From every IMFP captain had come the same message. *We don't have the towing capacity for that large a vessel.* The ones that could have teamed up cited the precision flying needed to accomplish the goal, something they weren't willing to risk. With so many Sovereign ships out on patrol or defending Slipgates, they didn't have the raw power to move the largest wrecks.

Another message caught his eye. Something from the Delat research team about clearing the orbital scraps left by the damaged ships. *Oh, it's only 1838 for them?* he thought, only a touch bitterly. *Might as well see if they stayed late.* So he sent a message saying he was available to jack in. The response was immediate, and he found himself in a lab-like meeting room.

"So, you intimated that you have some ideas?" he asked.

"We can't do anything about the largest pieces—" Alphor began.

"Obviously," Tenilo interrupted, unable to hide his sarcasm entirely.

"Um, we tried to come up with something for the smaller ships—" Betta said.

"I've already taken care of that," Tenilo interrupted again.

"But we still have the detritus left," Alphor said. "There's a half a million kilos of nuts, bolts and paperclips left up there, and it's all going to prove a navigation hazard for decades."

"And a good deal of it is non-magnetic," Betta added. "So even if you used mag-tractors, it would still leave a lot of hazardous debris."

Tenilo resisted the urge to glare. "So, you don't have any ideas?"

"Well, we ran through a list of things that won't work," Alphor said. "That counts as progress, right?"

"Give me the list," Tenilo said, trying not to sigh.

Tenilo mused over the list for a minute. *There has to be a way around this,* he thought. "What about grav-tractors?" he asked, fearing he already knew the answer.

"Prohibitive energy expenditure," Alphor said immediately. "That one was so crazy we didn't even write it. Grav-tractors only beat the energy-cost curve by focusing on a single area. For any ship smaller than, say, a Class-C, about a hundred square meters is sufficient. Only a carrier or maybe an Angel-class battleship would have the reactor capacity to create the wider-area coverage you would need. Even if you could, the power consumption would require at least one ship's reactor just to keep up, perhaps two."

"But doesn't the mass of the object matter in the equation?" Tenilo said. *Why is this the same problem? I was trying to solve something else, but it's the same thing.*

"Well, yes, it could if you were still working in a relatively pinpoint manner," Alphor explained. "What you're asking is to turn a penlight into a searchlight by giving it a bigger battery. The penlight itself can't make more light."

"I disagree," Betta jumped in. "You could technically make the penlight better by giving it a larger bulb. But the rest of the light still isn't going to support that level of power without burning up."

"Are we talking about the grav-tractor now, or the flashlight?" Tenilo asked.

Alphor and Betta looked at each other for a moment, then began shaking or nodding heads so oddly that he began to wonder if they had developed Psy with each other. "Definitely a grav-tractor," Betta said.

"So, is there another technology that will allow us to clear the debris from orbit?" Tenilo asked. *I'm sure there's a way to do this. Why do I feel like the answer is so obvious?*

Suddenly it hit him.

"We're chasing after the wrong problem," he said. "We don't need to gather the debris. We just need it moved."

"But isn't that what we're—"

"Listen," Tenilo said. "How hard would it be to make a low-orbit satellite with, say... a frigate's grav-tractor set to wide extra-orbital dispersal, but that only operates for seconds at a time?"

"But what would that accomplish?" Alphor asked.

At the same time, Betta blurted out, "Of course. Disrupting the debris into a decaying orbit. With optimal orbital coverage, you'd have metallic rain in a week." She paused. "But wouldn't that be dangerous... falling? You're suggesting most of it would burn up on reentry, I assume?"

"I could make a second one with the mag-tractor," Alphor burst in. "As the steel and Osfec debris decays into the lower orbits, the mag will grab it. You'd have to clean it off in a few weeks, but between the two, you could make real headway at clearing longitudinal orbits one at a time."

"And that would give you nonferrous disintegrating debris, a pile of scrap to throw in the furnace, and a lot more launch windows," Betta finished, smiling proudly.

"I like it," Tenilo agreed. "Submit the proposal to the

committee with my name in third. I'll authorize the Treasury. We need these things in the air now."

"But why your name?" Alphor asked. "Are you trying to steal credit?"

Tenilo rolled his eyes. "Are you kidding me, really? Prince Elio ordered them to fast-track anything with my name. I'm just getting you into production a month early." He pulled his halo off. His eyes barely opened.

Really? Trying to steal credit on a floating tractor beam. He could hardly believe the audacity of it. And while he had more important things to worry about.

He tried to stand and stumbled.

Like sleeping. I should definitely do some sleeping.

He made it to his cot, but sadly his shoes never made it off his feet.

———

TENILO DREAMED.

He was trapped in a burning building, flames everywhere. Each time he tried to escape, there was a locked door. *Unable to comply,* the building kept saying. *Doors are sealed due to the emergency.*

"Let me out. I'm going to die."

Normal operations will resume shortly.

"But by then, I'll be dead."

Doors are sealed due to the emergency.

"The emergency is that I need to get through the door."

Normal operations will resume shortly.

He beat on the door. "Let... me... OUT!" he screamed, throwing himself against the door. It opened, and he fell through... And landed on the hard floor beside his cot.

"Well, who wants to untangle that nightmare?" he muttered as he struggled up off the cold concrete. "Ugh. I need a hydro."

He hobbled into the communal staff facility down the hall

—that no one was using at 0545 in the morning—and stepped into the hydro. As the hot water beat down on him, he tried to figure things out.

The gears started spinning. *I have a problem because sensible ideas are being prevented for nonsensical reasons. Or nonsensical ideas are being prevented for sensible reasons? But those ideas make situational sense, and I just need a way to override sense to make things happen—Yes!*

He had it, the solution he needed. He literally jumped out of the hydro, struggled into his clothes, and rushed past a startled young woman, yelling, "Yes! Yes! Yes!"

———

"Let me get this straight," Kyne Minnah's vid image said as he wiped his hand across his face. "You had a dream?"

"About being in a burning building. With locked doors," Tenilo repeated.

Kyne laughed. "A bad dream and then an idea to use brute force. You're suggesting an AI that can override Sovereign safety systems and fly the whole ship?"

"No," Tenilo explained again. "It doesn't need to fly the ship. I need an AI to translate and act on or retransmit remote instructions. But it needs its own secure comm to receive the instructions."

"And you need this in a week?"

"Yes. Well. Yes," Tenilo stammered.

"Don't ships have remote systems for that?" Kyne asked.

"But the ships are damaged, and they're too big to tow. I need an AI that can override all the safeties."

"Can't the ships' AIs do that?"

"Any that still function won't initialize systems without redundancies. If we copy the same AI to each vessel with intact drives, we can link them together through comms and fly on the same headings. Any deviations due to ship damage can be accounted for by the replacement AIs."

"And who all's going to fly this abomination?"

Tenilo frowned. He hadn't considered how he might manage that part.

"Do you really have sixty or so alternate bridges and the personnel to man them in order to fly remotely?" Kyne asked.

"Look," Tenilo replied testily. "It's not a pretty time for either of us tonight, and I've been twisting my brain inside and out for two days. This is all I could come up with. I have full authority and Treasury backing to get this accomplished. They want the orbital mess cleared yesterday."

"I can understand that," Kyne replied.

"So when can you have a simplified AI ready for me?"

"Oh, please. You really expected to wait a week? I have something I call an Essential Intelligence, or EI. It doesn't class as an AI, but it does have the computing power. Think of it as a Guardian-class ship processor in a modern housing. And there's no pesky rules-following because it has no inboard personality, none at all. Not even the fake kind they have on some of the older starships. It's only smart enough to do what it's told; nothing more."

"But what about the—"

"Communication rig?" Kyne smiled. "Broadband multi-spectrum transceiver, ten by twenty-five centimeters. Guaranteed no signal degradation over five hundred kilometers in ideal conditions. The math says it'll get static every time you get hit by a meteorite."

"What about less-than-ideal conditions?" Tenilo asked.

"Well, there's a reason the military hasn't taken it yet," Kyne replied. "As long as you have reasonable line of sight, it should work fine. I'll have the prototype delivered to your office at the Collegium."

They exchanged a few more brief remarks and ended the call.

Even with the head start Kyne had offered him, it might still take his technopathy to integrate them and bypass the ships' security. Tenilo started looking over the list of engineers and technicians Elio had provided.

We need at least fifty of these things produced in a hurry, especially if I'm the only one who can install them. I hope Elio's collected the taxes this month, because I'm going to wreck his balance sheet.

CHAPTER
TWELVE

ANOTHER BAD IDEA

Feducere, Factory District
Planet Caerus

Faxil was out walking with Kuon when he found a beautiful Pasarian daisy that had managed to grow out of the rocky debris.

"Where did you come from, little guy?" he asked, taking out his sketchbook.

He lightly sketched the rubble behind it for placement, then started creating the rubble in the foreground. He had just started on the flower itself when he felt a sudden sense of alarm. Kuon gave a startled yip and crouched, growling and lashing her long tail.

"What is it, girl?" he asked.

"Yo, pencilhead. What you doing today?" Tuptein called as she and her gang appeared from behind a building.

He sighed in relief. "I'm drawing this daisy growing out of the rocks here," he replied.

"Why you care 'bout some lame flower?" she asked. "You're not going all wimpy on me, huh?"

He turned his head a little to look up at her. "Last month you beat me up. I didn't know there was anywhere else to go."

She turned her head away but didn't reply.

"It must be a tough flower," he said, trying to change the conversation. "There's not much here to grow flowers with. But it managed to fight its way up and bloom."

"Huh. A tough flower? Never thought 'bout it that way." Tuptein came closer and knelt down to look at the blossom. "Keep kickin' it, little pansy."

"Daisy."

"Whateva." She shuffled her feet. "Hey, ya wanna go poking around awhile?"

"I wanted to finish first," he replied.

"Okay. Yo," she yelled to the others. "Circle back in five."

Her gang waved back and took off.

"At the risk of offending you," he said, knowing that with Kuon nearby, he stood an even chance of coming out unscathed, "why are you being nice to me now?"

She was quiet for a moment, which was a good sign.

He took the time to try and get the petals right.

"Nobody hugs me," she said in a low voice. "Not for a long time."

He stopped sketching to look at her. "No one?" he asked incredulously. "What about your aunt?"

She glared at him, but it seemed a reflex. She picked up a stone and threw it across the nearby intersection. "Didn't know her before The Battle. She doesn't do nothin'. She doesn't care. Doesn't feed me. Hafta get my food from somewhere else."

Faxil returned to his sketching, but his mind was whirling. He'd fed Kuon, and she'd become his friend. He'd hugged his bully, and she'd become an ally.

But while he pushed his father away and refused to deal

with his stepmother more than necessary, they still showed him affection and caring.

I think I still don't understand people, he thought. But he decided that maybe he needed to do more for Tuptein. *I understand about repeating things to get the same result, at least.*

He finished his sketch of the flower. He looked at it, then at the flower itself. There was nothing wrong with the drawing, but somehow he'd failed to capture the *life* it showed. There was a resistance to futility in the real one that he hadn't gotten right.

He folded his sketchbook shut. "Okay, what was it you wanted to do today?"

Tuptein smiled. "I wanna go check out that factory they put behind the tape yesterday."

"Really?" Faxil couldn't believe his ears. "After the last time, you want to get in more trouble?"

"No trouble." She shrugged. "It's new. They don't know all the holes yet. No cameras."

"So why's it behind the tape, then?"

"I dunno. Let's find out."

He really wanted to protest, but from the stories she and her crew told, they'd been doing this a lot since he'd gone in the first one. Something about proving they weren't as afraid as him.

I know what I saw. There was a Blue down there. And where did the scars on Kuon's back come from? Something was down there the whole time.

But he didn't know how to convince anyone that what he was telling them was true.

Unless someone else finds them, too. He looked over at Tuptein. *I know if she sees one, she isn't going to keep quiet.*

"I'm ready to go. Are you ready?" he asked.

Tuptein smiled and cracked her knuckles. "Yeah. Let's go."

He whistled for Kuon, who came bounding up, a wriggling rat in her jaws.

"That's disgusting," he said.

At the same time, Tuptein murmured, "That's so cool."

———

"So how did you get your aunt to take care of your scratches?" Faxil asked as they made their way to the factory.

"As if she'd bother," Tuptein scoffed. "I know a guy. He's kinda creepy, but he knows bandages and stuff. He was happy to help."

"A creepy guy?" Faxil didn't like the sound of that. "What if he tried something weird?"

"I told him I'd cut him if he did," she replied, whipping out a glass shard crudely taped to a stick handle. "And he knows how many crew I roll with."

Faxil looked back at the motley group following them, and wondered if they'd know what to do without her explicit instructions. But he said nothing.

They reached the hill overlooking the factory, and Faxil tried to comprehend why they'd blocked the place off. "It's just in the middle of nowhere," he said as he scratched behind Kuon's feathery antennae. "It's not even near the other crash sites."

"I heard that they captured a buncha Blue freaks and they're torturing on them in there," one of the crew said.

"Yeah? Well, I heard that they only got one. But they cut him open and left all his guts hanging out, and they're studying how to kill one easy," another said.

"You dummies." Tuptein stopped and turned to face her lackeys. "Everyone knows that the Blues are made of like, super rock armor. When you break it, they explode."

"That's not what I—"

"Stuff what you heard," Tuptein shouted. "If they did catch one, they'd be figuring out how to make some wicked laser guns that would burn right through the bastards instead of juicing them up."

Then she turned to Faxil. "What do you think they're doing?"

He was surprised that she turned to him for ideas, but he wasn't about to let the opportunity slide. "Clearly, the factory isn't destroyed," he said in the most authoritative voice he could manage. "But it's big, and it has a roof that isn't straight or flat in a lot of places. "If some small piece of debris came tumbling down, it could have punched through the roof, and they wouldn't find out for weeks. I mean, with all the other, really obvious places to look."

"See, guys? Told you he was smart." Tuptein slapped him on the back.

Faxil tried not to feel embarrassed, but he was sure his face turned pink. *Me, smart? I'm not...* His thoughts turned in a different direction. *Wait, she thinks I'm smart? She tells people how smart I am?*

"Well, who's ready to go break the tape, then?" he said with much more confidence than he really felt.

That was answered by a ragged chorus of cheers, and Faxil began marching down the rubble-strewn street toward the factory, Tuptein just behind him. *I have no idea how I ended up the leader for today, but I hope I don't do anything to screw this up.*

———

As THEY CREPT through the abandoned factory, Faxil couldn't help but feel like they were crawling through an empty tomb, like the ruins of Imhoteptra in the movie he'd seen, though his father didn't know it.

The crew spread out, each one acting like it was some kind of wacky adventure.

Faxil knew better. There were deadly aliens under the surface of the planet; he'd seen one. Kuon's wounds were evidence enough for him that something still prowled in the darkness. She stalked along beside him, her meal long vanished but her eyes darting in every direction as though she was looking for more food. He admitted to himself the real reason he was here—if this area was taped off, it meant that something was here. And that the government knew it.

If only he could find one piece of evidence... maybe people would believe him.

He crept as silently as he could, the others creating enough noise for thirty, especially the one who kept calling, "Yoohoo, Blue bastards. Where are you? Hide and Seeky, find you quee-kie."

Faxil peered into the dark corners, the shadowy places—and then smacked himself. *The Blues can't hide in corners. They glow all the time. It would be stupid to—*

He suddenly realized that maybe they didn't glow all the time. Maybe they went dark when sleeping, or maybe their glow was some kind of communication system; how they talked to each other.

The one I saw before was glowing. Does that mean there were a lot more down there?

He shook himself out of his hysteria. He was making up things about aliens, then using them to justify other unknowns. He needed to keep a clear head.

But I'll be checking those dark spaces anyway, he thought.

He saw a large shadowed place behind a large machine. But there was a strange color glowing in the darkness, almost like a blue glow. His heart pounding, his breath rasping, he crept forward. The closer he got, the more obviously it—

"What is it?" Tuptein asked in his ear.

Faxil jumped and screamed. He whirled around to see Tuptein, who yelped at his scream and stumbled backwards. Faxil tripped over Kuon as she tried to scramble out of the way, and he fell half on top of Tuptein.

Numerous thoughts and emotions ricocheted through his head: from anger to frustration, from fear to embarrassment. "What were you doing?" he finally managed to gasp out, but her expression changed, and he instantly regretted it.

"Get off me," she screamed and shoved him off as easily as a grown-up might. By the time Faxil had gotten up, Tuptein was standing, her fist balled and her crew gathered close.

"What the matter, boss?" one of them said before she smacked him.

"The little creeper do something stupid?" asked one of the girls. "We gonna whip him good?"

Tuptein's face looked flushed and red even in the dim light. She stood there, breathing heavily. Finally, she relaxed her fist.

"I thought I saw a blue glow back there," Faxil said and walked around the side of the machine, but there was nothing there. *Of course there isn't. After all that commotion, it had plenty of chances to get away.* Kuon went further, sniffing the ground and making low growly noises.

He turned to find Tuptein and the entire crew standing behind him.

"Think we should leave him here for the USF to find someday?" one of the crew giggled. Faxil's blood froze in his veins. Kuon immediately turned and snarled at the giggler.

"No," Tuptein said. "He leaves, we leave. Right now. And if I ever find one of you touched him instead of me, I'll break your arm off. Understand?"

Faxil reached down to stroke Kuon's head, trying to get her to calm down, but she'd already relaxed, scratching at an itchy scale and licking his hand when he lowered it.

"We're gone," Tuptein ordered, and the crew followed her out.

Faxil was suddenly left alone, in the abandoned factory, where he thought he might have seen an alien.

Regardless of the danger from Tuptein or her crew, he had no desire to stay another minute. He turned and fled in the same direction, not stopping until the bright sunlight shone down on him.

———

DINNER THAT EVENING WAS STRAINED. Annoy-ay didn't say anything about him being gone, and his father didn't seem interested in talking. They just picked at their food in silence.

Faxil didn't know what to say or do. He wasn't sure what the problem was.

Dad's datapad beeped on the table by the door. He walked over and put it on. Faxil could see the years of grime caked into the edges; the pad had been used when he bought it but still cost them a week's grocery bill.

"Yes?" he said, a little irritated to be called during dinner, Faxil was sure. Then his expression changed. "Yes sir, Mr. Omakoto. They what? That's insane... No sir, I mean... no disrespect, honored sir, but that would be a great boon for my family. Yes, if they need an experienced fitter, I'll sign up."

A few more polite phrases, and he took the pad off again. "Oh, this is... I can't believe—" His smile was bigger than Faxil had seen since before his mother died. "Oh, Inoiae, they put out a call for all experienced shipyard workers. The government is putting together a repair force for the damaged orbital platform, and they're paying. They say it will be four months, maybe five, and I'll make more than I would in a year. Training begins in three days for weightless transitions. This is... I can't believe it." He grabbed Annoy-ay in a bear hug and lifted her clear off the ground.

"Stop that," Annoy-ay scolded. "Put me down now. I will not be reason you hurt again, can't work." But she was smiling too. And in their eyes shone something Faxil didn't understand.

"I'm right here," he said, wishing his father had paid him any attention.

"Faxil." And his father scooped him up too, clenching him

tight and swinging him left and right, just like he'd done when Faxil was little.

Then he set Faxil down and gave him a level stare. "Look, I know things have been difficult lately. You and I haven't seen eye to eye. And maybe I should have taken more time letting you get to know Inoiae. But I need you to understand something.

"My responsibility is to take care of my family. Today, that means taking a job where I must leave for a few months and come home with a huge paycheck and my old job guaranteed, or they might hire me to do other work for the government. Either way, son, this is big. This is *huge.* So I need you to buck up around here. You aren't going to be just Faxil Avestan. You'll be the man of the house. You need to care and protect. Inoiae is going to need you, and like it or not, you'll need her. Make the best of this time you'll have together, please?"

Faxil couldn't deny the strength and determination in his father's eyes. "Sure, Dad. I'll do my very best."

He'd waited years for his father to look this way again.

And then he heard it all fall down.

"Well, we've got a busy day tomorrow. You run off to bed, and Inoiae and I will plan a little party. And I'll need some work clothes that aren't beat to rags, and—"

"Goodnight," Faxil said, but nobody heard him. He went to his room and shut the door.

"Man of the house... care and protect..." He threw his jacket against the wall; it hit with an unsatisfying thump. "Go to bed like a child. Be a grownup and leave so the adults can kissy-face and all that weird crap."

He turned out the light and flopped down on the bed, still in his clothes. He'd rather fall asleep than listen to the "adults" act "grown-up."

But as much as he tried, he just couldn't stop hearing things. First, it was the synth glasses clinking. Then it was the whispered conversations in the hall, as if he couldn't hear. But when he heard their bedroom door try to shut three times, he knew they were definitely "adulting." Once their door closed, he grabbed his bag and his lifelight and snuck out the front door with no one the wiser.

———

FAXIL PICKED his way across the familiar landscape with Kuon at his side, only now, in the darkness, it was transformed into a confusing maze of strange spires and contorted shapes that only his light and closeness could properly reveal. As he picked his way back to the factory, one thought kept humming in his mind.

Protect. Protect. Protect. I tell people there are aliens under the streets, and no one believes me. How can I protect anyone?

He would go back, and he would find evidence. He would take that evidence to someone and make them believe. One person, that's all he needed. Just one.

As he drew closer to the factory, he began to feel like the noises around him had changed. Odd rustling sounds, the skittering of stones. But then he heard a muttered swear, and he knew what the noise was. He cut to the left and found Tuptein scrabbling around some debris.

"What are you doing here?" he demanded.

For the first time in his memory, the bully looked flustered. "I, um, I was... I'm heading back to that factory," she finally stated. "I decided to go back and explore in the dark because I'm not afraid of anything."

Faxil thought that was a strange thing to say. "Well, I'm going back because I need to know if that glow we saw was a Blue."

"What are you talking about?" she said defensively. "I didn't see a Blue."

"C'mon, you were standing right next to me," he pressed. "You saw the glow too, didn't you?"

"I... don't know what you're talking about. I told you I didn't see nothing."

But Faxil was certain she was lying.

"Well, since there's no reason to be afraid," he said, "I don't suppose you'd like to go along with me? Maybe hold my hand if I get scared? It's pretty dark, after all."

"Yeah, sure. Whatever," Tuptein said.

So they crept down to the Tape and slipped past the shoddy barrier once again. They both had lights, and once inside they turned them on. But their paltry beams could barely illuminate the cavernous work spaces.

"It was so much easier to see during the day," Tuptein said.

"I guess it looks dark compared to the light outside," Faxil agreed. "But yeah, whatever leaked through the cracks during the day sure isn't there now."

It took a little doing, but he managed to retrace his steps back to the machine he'd seen earlier. It still stood there, large and imposing. He wasn't certain Tuptein recognized it until he tried to walk behind it and she clutched his wrist.

"What are you doing?" she demanded.

"I'm just looking," he replied.

"Well, let's look somewhere else."

Faxil tried to yank his arm away and walk forward, but she held on tight, pulled along with him as he went around the corner. "Wait, you stupid brat. You're acting like—"

But when he shined his light in the secluded corner, there was nothing there.

"See? I told you," Tuptein said weakly. "Let's just go. Nothing here."

But he shined the light lower. In the accumulated grime of months or maybe years, there were clear footprints—except there weren't any human feet shaped like that. Three large toes in the front and an odd heel shaped like an eight. And there were a whole lot of footprints.

"Look," he whispered.

"I don't want to look, okay?" she said.

"But there really are—"

"I saw it before, all right? I saw the glow. Can we go now?"

He looked at her. *Really* looked at her. For the first time, he saw fear on her face. And he couldn't believe how vulnerable she looked. She wasn't a bully at all; she was a scared girl.

"Look," he said to her. "I understand if you're scared. I'm scared, too."

"You are? I mean, of course you are," she said, a shadow of her tough voice returning. "Anybody should be scared of a Blue."

"Even you?" he asked.

"Yeah, maybe even me."

"Well, I have a duty now," he said, recalling his father's words. "I need to care and protect. I need you, and you need me, okay?"

Her expression was one of pure shock. "You... need me?"

"Yes. I need to follow this trail and find some kind of evidence. If we know the Blues are here, somebody else needs to know. We need proof."

She seemed like she wanted to say something else, but instead she nodded, her mouth set in the stubborn expression he knew so well now. "So what are we going to do?" she asked.

Her fear and her bravery were warring with each other, and he didn't want to risk her fear getting the better of her.

"In the other factory," he said, "they had some kind of hole drilled in the wall. I think we can follow these footprints and find out what they're doing. But you can wait at the entrance; you can wait to hear from me."

She didn't look scared now. She looked genuinely frightened. "W-what do you mean?" she asked.

He tried to make it sound the least dangerous he could. "If we went in together, we might both be spotted. But if I go down alone and get spotted, you have a chance to escape and warn other people."

Nope. That sounded really dangerous.

"Why are you being so stupid?" she asked.

"I gotta be brave," he replied. "I guess it's just a boy thing."

She punched him.

"Ow. What did you do that for?" he asked.

"To show you that girls can do boy things too, you jerk."

He rolled his eyes. At least she wasn't halfway to cowering anymore. "Follow me," he said, shining his light on the floor. He could hear her behind him, huffing in… anger?

Better angry than scared, he thought. But then he could hear Kuon's muffled purring of comfort. *She's petting Kuon? Those two have come a long way.*

He found the hole in the floor after about five minutes of careful searching. Down below glowed a strange orange color, with occasional white flashes like he'd seen before. "This must be it," he said as he shucked off the backpack and dropped it to the floor, opened it, took out his sketchbook, then said. "Watch this for me, okay?"

Her only answer was a snort.

Yep, We're definitely back to regular Tuptein. He lowered himself carefully through the broken concrete floor. Kuon followed closely.

———

It took a few minutes for him to climb down through the tunnel to a point where it leveled off, then it continued on for what he knew was a lot of meters before going down again, and he wondered if he was now in a different building.

This factory was in much better condition than the one he'd just left.

He dropped out of the tunnel onto a steel catwalk and looked around. And there it was: the blue glow.

He crept forward, Kuon on his heels. The glow grew brighter and, suddenly, he saw them. Five Blues, the ones he'd heard they called Troopers. They were walking near each other, but they slowly got closer and closer until they locked into a pattern, an X made of five Blues. *How weird is that?* he thought, his hand on Kuon's muscly neck.

"I... think we need to follow them, girl," he whispered. Kuon uttered a low growl, her antennae flicking like they did when she was nervous but ready to go.

He crept along the catwalk, trying not to make a sound. The Blues moved onward, still in formation. The catwalk ended and he had to climb down the stairs. He hurried to catch up, Kuon following silently.

He caught up in the next room, where the Blues were fiddling with some kind of device near another hole in the ground. Suddenly there was a flash brighter than he could ever have imagined.

It was brighter than staring into the sun, yet it had flashed only for a micro-second. Faxil blinked and blinked, trying to make the purple image go away. When it finally did, he saw the Blues lowering huge metal containers into the hole. As he watched, as one went down, another one came up, filled to the brim with... what?

Feeling enormously brave, he crept along, taking short breaks to quickly sketch scenes of the Blues doing... whatever they were doing. He followed the container to a place where at least a hundred other Blues were gathered... *well, a lot, anyway.* And he and Kuon hid behind a large machine. What they were doing, he had no idea. But he sketched madly, trying to grasp the essence of what they were doing.

They were using some sort of big electromagnet thing to sift through the contents of the container, pulling up a mound of iron nuggets or something and putting them aside. Then they used another device to start sifting out other materials.

They're... they're mining. But for what?

There was only one obvious answer. They had landed here

on purpose and were secretly stripping supplies from Caerus to... do something. Whatever they were doing, it would be bad.

"We need to tell someone," he whispered to Kuon.

He turned to leave and felt something yank hard on his shirt.

A piercing *breeeep* sounded, and all the Blues looked his way.

And at that moment, he realized he might not be telling anyone after all.

The lever he had accidentally hooked when he had turned swung back into position. Trying to free himself, he smashed his hand on a panel of buttons. The machine clanked to life and released him, and he ran for the catwalk stairs. Several of the Troopers ran ahead of him—so fast—and tried to block his way.

Attack, he heard, or felt, clearly in his mind.

He had no idea where the thought had come from, but Kuon leapt into the air, letting out a banshee shriek that pierced Faxil's ears. But strangely, it seemed to affect the Blues as well.

They halted just as Kuon crashed into one, teeth clamped securely against the Trooper's wrist area. With a terrifying ease, Kuon tore the wrist and part of the arm loose. Another Blue tried to grab her, but her tail cracked like a whip against the Blue's chest, cracking it like a window.

Faxil could only stare in amazement as parts of the armor broke loose and fell to the ground. Faxil grabbed the largest piece, hoping to use it as a knife or something—just as strange feelers came out of the exposed chest and tried to snatch it back.

The feelers yanked, and he pushed. The shard sank into the center of the feelers, a pulsing white... thing. The Blue tried to push him away, but the chest erupted in a flash of light, and Faxil was thrown backward from the explosion. When he looked, the Blue was just... gone.

Amazed at what had just happened, he looked back to Kuon, who was battling another Blue. This time she attacked the leg, forcing it to fall to a knee. When it did, Kuon's long lashing tail wrapped around the neck and ripped its head clean off.

Leave.

Not wanting to ignore good advice, no matter where from, Faxil ran for the stairs as blue plasma blasts arced past him. He could feel their heat. Kuon began shrieking again, and the blasts stopped for a few moments. By the time the blasts started again, he and Kuon were up the stairs and heading up the tunnel back to Tuptein.

He tried to scramble up, but in his haste he couldn't find any purchase. "I need help!" he yelled as Kuon clawed her way out.

Tuptein leaned over the edge, his backpack dangling from her hands. "Grab on!" she shouted.

Faxil grabbed on, and Tuptein heaved with a strength Faxil might envy at any other time. But as she pulled, Faxil's sketchbook tumbled away, along with his pencils.

"NO!" he screamed as Tuptein hauled him out of the hole. "My sketchbook."

He turned to go back, but she grabbed his arm, swung him around and smacked him. "Run, you idiot."

The plasma that blasted out of the hole shocked him out of his stupor. He began to run, but Tuptein was faster, and her greater mass pulled him along as her powerful legs pumped with a vigor he couldn't match.

They got to the factory door. Tuptein yanked it open and shoved him through... and screamed.

Only after the scream did Faxil register the sound of plasma and the sizzle of cooked meat. Tuptein, still screaming, fell on him, and even in the moonlight he could see the raw burns on her bare skin, half her shirt having burned away. He grabbed the other arm and struggled to drag her away. Fortunately, he heard no more plasma shots.

Kuon was underneath her burned side, trying to support

the weight. Faxil, in a spare moment of thought, wondered how she knew to help Tuptein. They quickly dragged her back along the tunnel to the abandoned factory, then struggled out of the hole in the Tape, where he once again found himself surrounded by guards.

Help. Run. Faxil didn't know what those thoughts meant. It was so confusing.

"Somebody get on the radio," one of them shouted as he knelt beside Tuptein. Another took off a backpack and started pulling things out. He sprayed some chemical on her arm, and she screamed even louder than before.

"Stop it, you're hurting her!" Faxil yelled, but one of the guards picked him up and pulled him away, no matter how much he struggled. She continued screaming as the spray began to foam on her arm, then the one kneeling beside her unwrapped a bandage and wrapped it around the foam.

"One-Zero-One, Ten Niner, we have a severe burn victim," the person with the radio said. "Two juveniles, one female approximately twelve years old. One male, also about twelve. Found outside at a breach in the perimeter of the Obstructed Zone One-Three-Four. Request immediate air evac for the girl... Yes, air evac. First aid has been applied, but we may have second, even third degree burns here. She needs the facilities at Regional, not the med tent we have out here."

It wasn't until they shoved him into the emergency skiff that Faxil realized just how badly Tuptein might be hurt.

CHAPTER
THIRTEEN

ABOARD THE AVENGER

Regis Magnum Shipyards
South Plate, Third Arm Drydock
Avenger, **Officer Quarters Deck**

Commodore Richard Morian checked himself in the mirror one last time. His eyes had crinkles in the corners, and his uniform felt slightly loose down the sides, as if he'd lost weight.

It felt good to be in his uniform again, though—three days aboard ship without it had begun to grate on him. He didn't want to discount the time he'd had to rest and remove himself from his daily duties after his tour of duty aboard the *Intrepid.* Even though he'd need the time off to recharge his batteries, so to speak, he never really stopped being the captain. It had been a refreshing breath of air after his time on the *Intrepid.* He'd seen a play, he'd watched some news like a normal person, and he'd spent entire days barefoot.

Now, as he looked in the mirror, he saw the statesman he was becoming.

He had no doubt that he would now be remembered for all of Sovereign history as the man who had won the first battle against the Swarm, and the second, and the third. There was no way to avoid that. And should there come a time when his duty called him to be something other than a captain, he would feel compelled to take it up.

Councilor Morian? *Ambassador* Morian, striving in his waning years to keep the bonds of humanity forged strong?

Politics? No thank you. And yet...

What about Admiral? he wondered idly but dismissed it. There was no real way to achieve that. He'd spent too many years bucking the wishes of those in power to assume that they would put aside their prejudices even for a Hero of Humanity, or whatever inane title they slapped on him. Even if he was promoted, it would likely be a ceremonial title, something they gave him with a hefty stipend as he retired from service and disappeared from view, considered too toothless and lame to be any more good—

All this over a few crow's feet? he chided himself. *Hell, I'm only forty-two. I have a good hundred years left in me yet.*

He looked again, leaned forward and stroked his black hair. He didn't have any gray hairs yet—and likely wouldn't for another forty years, if Haltar Sen was any indication.

The thought of his senior navigator touched his heart. He checked his chron; he had thirty minutes before he was required to be elsewhere. So he decided to make a visit.

He made his way down to the officer's quarters deck and went to the room Haltar shared with Dagon Jax. He tapped the annunciator screen and waited for the door to open.

Lt. Jax opened the door, looking a little rumpled. But when he saw Richard, he straightened up. "Captain Morian, sir. I... uh..."

"Relax, Mister Jax," he replied. "I'm here to see Haltar. Is he awake? Feeling like visitors?"

"I'm sorry, sir," Jax replied. "Haltar's not here. He had an appointment this morning; for tests down on South Plate. He said he'd be gone most of the day."

Richard sighed. "Perhaps I should have just contacted him. I thought spontaneous would feel a little more…"

"I understand, sir," Jax nodded. "Like it was heartfelt? Instead of just checking off a list?"

"Yes," Richard replied. "I think that's exactly how I would describe it."

Mister Jax is growing wiser as he ages, he thought. *Better than some I've known.*

"If you want, sir, I'll let him know you stopped by."

"Thank you, Mister Jax, that will do fine. Will I be seeing you on duty today?"

"Sorry, sir." Jax gave a sleepy smile. "Just came off duty. Nasyn should be at the helm right now. He'll be replaced by Teth at midday."

"Very well. Enjoy the rack time, Mister Jax."

"Aye, sir." Jax gave a salute, looking ridiculous in his sleep-wear, but he returned it anyway and then stepped away.

Morian checked his chron. He would be expected on the bridge in a few minutes.

He rode the lift, hoping that there would be something positive to accomplish that day, some obstacle he could leap to make a difference in his sour mood.

Not likely. We're in drydock. What possible obstacle could there be?

Avenger **Hangar Deck**
Muster Room B

. . .

Danis Morian looked behind her. Jackknife and Gian were at her right and left. *As it should be, I suppose,* she thought.

She still ached over the loss of so many friends, but she had to persevere. *It does no good to fight and quit. You must fight on until the end.*

She entered the room to find two neatly arrayed platoons of twenty; one wearing the standard blue pilot's uniform, the other wearing the new, dusty orange TK copilot uniform with the star-and-fist patch Danis thought tacky, but that decision had been far above her pay grade. And in the rear was the person who'd brought them all together. Danis hadn't had a chance to meet her yet.

"Congratulations," Danis barked to the room full of Academy graduates. "Half of you have been deemed worthy to ascend to the exalted rank of fighter pilot. Some of you already hold the title. Specifically, the three people standing in front of you. We have survived too many battles to count. It's my hope you all will do half as well.

"To the rest of you... your TK abilities have been deemed strong enough to be a positive reinforcement to a fighter pilot. This is not something new, though it still is relatively rare among the Sovereign fleets. I was the first to implement the idea." She flushed a little, remembering the times when Elio was in her fighter, dodging and fighting the Blues. But before Richard could rain on her memory, she pressed on. "You will be tested; I can assure you of that. If you pass, you'll be assigned to a pilot, permanently. If not... Well, we won't dwell on that.

"I understand several of you pilots also have TK abilities. *You* should understand that your gift only makes it more dangerous for you; distracted pilots don't survive."

She waited for any comments, but there were none.

"Now, for introductions. To my left is Senior Lieutenant Jona Canif, callsign Jackknife. Frankly, he doesn't answer to anything else. To my right is Senior Lieutenant Gian Vastum, callsign Joker. And I am Commander Danis Morian, squadron commander; callsign Domino. Notice that my name is not sir. It is not ma'am—" She resisted the urge to glance sideways. "—and it is not 'Hey, Danis.' Isn't that right, Flight Leaders?"

She heard Gian grunt in annoyance. It was hard not to grin. "In front of any officer higher ranking than myself, you will call me Commander or Commander Morian. Don't screw it up, or you will be on KP duty for a week. Any other time, my name is Domino. Don't screw that up, or you'll be on *latrine* duty."

The shock on some faces was too much, and she finally cracked a smile. "Callsigns will be given as they are earned. Earning one requires the approval of a flight leader or at least five flightmates. Try to avoid earning names like 'Fireball' or 'Smokebomb.' Such callsigns will not be approved. Since this is a reorganization, we will be working in simulated combat scenarios in real fighters. The reason for this is that TK doesn't work in sim. Maybe someday.

"Some of you will be washed out if you can't perform up to the level I require. This isn't a condemnation. It's just reality. My goal is to keep you alive. More training or experience might bring you along, but I will not be providing it. This is wartime, and I don't have the luxury of coddling my pilots. Do you understand?"

A chorus of "Yes, ma'am" sounded, with more than a few "Yes, Commander" and a handful of "Yes, Domino."

"Excellent." She clapped her hands. "We already have a duty roster for tonight. Anyone who called me Commander, you're assigned to KP for the afternoon. If anything is wrong with my dinner, you'll hear about it. Anyone who called me ma'am, I expect the heads in Section Three and around the hangar bay to sparkle."

There was a chorus of groans that quickly cut off at her stern look.

"Now, we are fortunate—oh so fortunate—that in recognition of *Avenger's* fine service these four years of the war, we have received not a squadron of F-32As. We haven't received two short squadrons of F-32As. No, in the wisdom of the military brass, we have been presented with two short squadrons of... B-29 fighter bombers."

Though she heard no outcry, she could see the stricken look on the face of every pilot on her left.

Barge-drivers, fruit-bobbers, hull-bumpers, and less savory nicknames ran through Danis' head. She did sympathize, though. "These will be on loan to us from the Regis Magnum shipyard while we are in training mode. They have heavy armor and will resist taking damage a little better while we bump into each other, so I was so eloquently told. Though that wouldn't *happen* if we had something that went faster than a walk."

This earned a chuckle.

"When we are ready to officially recommission, we will receive our full complement of fourteen *F-32Cs* fresh from the factory. I am assured the 32C is, in every way, a superior craft to the F-32A." A small *whoop* sounded, though she wasn't certain how she felt. To Danis, piloting the F-32A was like wearing a second skin.

"Duty rosters are forthcoming. Each of you will be paired up with a copilot for a week. You will eat together, train together, bathe and sleep next to each other, *if appropriate*—and then switch until you find someone that fits. Again, this is wartime, and we need effective teams. This isn't a meet-cute, and anyone found having *any* kind of relationship during this time will be summarily ejected from the program. Any questions?"

Nearly every hand raised.

"Let me qualify that," she said. "Are there any questions that don't pertain to me or my previous battle exploits?"

Every hand went down.

"I don't mind telling stories," Danis said with a wink, "but the proper place is on a barstool, and you'll need to bring plenty of cash. Flight Leaders, anything you wish to add?"

She'd already instructed them to be stoically silent.

"Then you are to report to any assigned duty stations in fifteen minutes. Dismissed."

As the new pilots and copilots trailed out, the woman in back walked forward. She wore several battle ribbons and a medal, a seven-point star on a blue square. The closer she got, the more Danis realized just how short the woman was. They exchanged salutes. "Greetings, Commander," she said. "I am Lieutenant Commander Axi Quento. As you are aware, I am here to assist in training exercises."

"Welcome. I'm happy to have a third flight leader," Danis replied as Axi shook hands with Jackknife and Gian. "But I understand you're an Academy instructor. Why are you out here?"

"It so happens that my son is enrolled in the Academy right now. I took a brief leave from duty to avoid a show of favoritism." Her mouth quirked in what might have been a frown of disapproval. "Not that he gets it from me, but you understand."

"I do indeed." There had been a few pilot murmurs a long time ago about her serving under her twin brother. She'd been able to solve it with a simple training challenge. She'd smoked every one of their fighters in sim while piloting a shuttle. "I wish we'd had the opportunity to meet before this. I'd have liked to introduce you."

"Oh, there was no need. Almost everyone is a former student. And this is not about me," Axi replied. "You establish authority, establish command chain. They know I am here if they need me. No worries."

"Well, then," Danis said, "I think you deserve a bite and a sip. And I want to hear how you earned the Azimuth medal. Let's head down to the mess, and you can fill us in on your roster. Let us know if there's anyone we need to keep an eye on."

"First, watch Brigan Uan," she said with a smile. "He is a fine pilot, but he causes trouble."

"Sounds like my kind of cadet," Jackknife quipped. "Think he needs a new pair of boots?"

Danis glared at him. "If I see those boots again, I will space them."

———

REGIS MAGNUM SHIPYARDS
North Plate, Specialty Medical Hospital
Skiagraphic Holo-Imaging Center

COMMANDER MANDA HAAL sat next to Haltar Sen as the doctors detached the almost empty bag of murky substance that had been fed into his arm through an IV.

"It will take approximately ten more minutes for the solution to permeate the cells," the skiagraphicist said. "Once we reach saturation, we'll activate it with a mild electrical stimulation. The reaction between this electrical charge and your nervous system will give us the ability to take extraordinary readings of your entire body."

"You hear that, Hal?" Manda teased. "They'll be able to find all the puppy dog tails you were made of."

"Nonsense," he wheezed. "The universe stopped using puppy dog tails back in the aught-thirties. They became too expensive. Now they just use lizard tails instead."

Manda laughed, but it was a little forced. Only weeks ago, he'd sounded far more robust than this, *and back then,* she thought, *he sounded plenty bad. Now he sounds like he's dying. But he keeps fighting. It's almost heroic how he's able to keep going.*

They chatted quietly for a few more minutes until a nurse came in and pressed a small instrument with a circular metal pad to Haltar's skin. "I'll speak with the doctor, but I think his readings are about right," the nurse said. "They'll take him in shortly."

"What do you know—" Haltar cut off with a raspy cough. "A doctor said ten minutes and he meant five instead of fifteen. What's the universe coming to?"

Manda could only laugh with him. It helped to hide the tears she wished she could shed.

I won't; not in front of him. Not while there's a shred of hope left.

She followed the hover-gurney as they went to the Nimbuskiagraphics chamber, where they floated the gurney into place, locked it into the clamps on the machine, raised it slightly and then stepped away. Manda watched as hundreds of tiny trilodes whirled a complicated spiral around the gurney, and her friend.

The flashing lights at first seemed hypnotic, pulling her into a trance, and the faster they spun, the deeper the trance became. And then she realized it wasn't a trance; she was having one of her visions. Except... nothing was happening.

She was surrounded by pinpoints of light; each one was moving, leaving a trail behind it. It was like watching blinkbugs in timelapse. Except, they flew in straight lines and made precise turns, and the lights didn't fade.

What is the meaning of this vision? she wondered. *And why is it so... abstract?*

But the more she watched, the larger the traceries of light became and then they began to form a complete picture. Her head started to hurt, but she tried to ignore it to keep the vision. She realized she must be seeing something at play, a complex working whose purpose would only be understood when—

A hand landed on her shoulder, jerking her out of the vision. She looked around. One of the technicians had simply stepped to her side to speak to her.

"What we're doing now is scanning his body for micro-electrical disturbances," he explained. "The entire room is a ferromagnetic cage, and the machine itself is shielded like a military bunker against outside wavelengths. The only free electricity in the room is inside our bodies, and even then, our effects are minimal compared to the chemicals we injected."

"So exactly how do those work?" she asked, trying to casually ignore the pounding headache her visions always brought.

"The fluid contains microparticles of several electro-sensitive metals. We can change the composition to detect different anomalies, but this solution is geared toward mapping his nervous system... I think we're about done."

Manda turned her head to look at the skiagraph floating in front of her; it wasn't good.

Several places were marked by subtly changing colors, indicating damaged nerves close to the surface of the skin. The various aches and pains that Haltar had complained about for the last several years were likely located in those areas, and that made sense. But other, larger nerves were marked with angry red symbols, and when she moved closer, she could see the damage.

It was like the nerves were... frayed, or nibbled. In reality, those nerves were simply missing... *sections?*

She couldn't imagine the agony it must be causing.

And when the doctors stepped away to confer, none of them had happy looks on their faces.

As much as I hurt right now, his pain is so much worse, she thought as she stepped forward to hear what they had to say.

———

Marshall Secerna Hyde's schedule pinged at her while she was working through a folder of virtual documents. She swiped several aside before she located the schedule she was looking for. On it was an official meeting with Commodore Richard Morian, marked *Tentative Date/Time.*

What's this about? Rear Admiral Neboda had ordered her to brief the commodore once he returned to duty. She remembered setting the meeting more than a month ago, but there shouldn't be any reason for it to—

A flashing light on her armpad caught her eye. She tapped it. It opened to reveal she had three priority messages waiting. *There's always somebody's priority message waiting.* But one of them announced the unscheduled return of Commodore Morian.

He's returned? I wasn't expecting him for weeks yet. But her notification had been set to coincide with his officially resuming command of the *Avenger.*

Festering pustules. Project Glass is only now beginning to bear results. And Project Champion still needs further testing.

Technically, she didn't need to get his approval for anything. She was, after all, a Marshal, and he was only a Commodore. Yet despite the difference in rank, he was the one who had the ear of the throne.

She'd been placed in charge of important projects that would have fallen apart without her clutching them together. He was an *accomplished war hero,* the victor of several campaigns against the Swarm, while she had spent the entire war planetside. Having the approval of such a *prominent military figure* could only help maintain the funding for her projects. *So says Admiral Neboda.*

Needing the approval of such a strutting cockerel, especially one who ranked so far below her, irritated her to no end.

Well, we'll just have to see how it turns out. Maybe he's only half the pretentious twit I've heard about.

She punched in his comm code and waited for him to respond.

———

RICHARD MORIAN'S wristpad announced a priority incoming comm. He checked the display and found it to be from Marshal Secerna Hyde. *I recognize that name. But where have I heard it before?*

Without immediately being able to place the marshal, he

retired to his ready room and flicked the incoming vid to his table. A woman's face appeared in the holo above his desk. Her hair was cropped shorter than men's standard. Her body fit and blocky. *Ah, yes,* he thought. *Project Director Hyde, from the T-99 initial trials and the flechette missile trials for the F-32C when I was aboard the Intrepid.*

"Good morning, Marshal Hyde," he said. "To what do I owe the pleasure?"

"Good afternoon, Commodore Morian," she replied caustically. "I am currently working on several projects here at Regis Magnum, one of which will certainly concern you personally."

"Me, personally?" Richard was confused. "I wasn't aware that—"

"I refer to the new Avenger-class ships, of course."

"Ah, of course." Richard had heard encouraging news about the ships that would bear his mark. "So what can I do for you?"

"Admiral Neboda... insists that having your approval of the project will... streamline certain funding issues. He's of the opinion that you can provide a helpful push in the right places to increase our funding, allow us to expand operations and achieve completion sooner."

He remembered Secerna Hyde as being a woman who had no problem speaking her mind, often verbally lashing certain people with her extensive vocabulary. For her to seem so meek and timid... *Either Neboda filed the rough patches to glass, or she really needs my support. But what other ramifications might I be missing?*

In a way, it didn't matter what the ramifications were. The Vindication Fleet was a necessary addition to the USF—a fleet of ships specifically constructed to harass and tear down the Swarm occupations in more than thirty systems.

The Avenger-class ships were being constructed to be able to counter everything they had learned about the Swarm so far and, hopefully, a few new tricks as well.

And yet, the ramifications were still there. Richard refused to step into a trap just because it lay in the middle of the path he needed to take.

"Marshal Hyde, I of course am willing to offer any assistance I can. But professionally, I really have to ask, is there more to this request? I'm not keen to offer my support blindly or needlessly."

"This is just like I thought," Hyde suddenly scowled. "I don't understand why I even need to be pushed through this—"

"Marshal, while I hold the lower rank, I do ask to be spoken to with respect."

"Well, that's what it always is, isn't it?" Hyde's square jaw set into a stone block. "Respect for the war hero. Accolades for the triumphant captain. You even managed to claim a decisive victory in a fifty-year-old—"

"Marshal, I have no idea what you're talking about," Richard insisted.

"Awarded Knight-Captain at twenty-eight, weren't you? Youngest ship captain ever. While everybody else had to work their way up the ladder like normal people. Then you act like a pretentious twit for the next six years until you become the Hero of Tor."

I have no idea—How did this become personal?

"Marshal Hyde, I was granted Knight-Captain by the late King Lorne for valor after three ranking officers were killed in the Battle of Osiris. His son, the current king, apparently posted me to the oldest ship in the fleet as punishment for some slight of which I never learned. If I appeared to you to have an attitude, I assure you it was discipline and belief in the necessity of my role in the fleet that kept me going."

He thought of those moments above Tor, as the *Mariposa's* Captain Paris disobeyed orders and walked into the enemy path because she thought he was a cold-hearted bastard. "And I claim no heroism over Tor," he continued. "My duty required me to leave the battle. It was the actions of others that forced me to intervene to the extent I did. And it was only my posting to *Avenger* that brought me to attention now—"

He drew a deep breath. He needed to keep his anger in check. "Marshal, I was simply in the right place, at the right time, with the right people. Everything we know about our enemies we found out by accident. And luckily, I refused to let my antique weapons fall into disrepair because I wouldn't let someone's *fit of pique* keep me from doing my duty."

Marshal Hyde's expression only softened a hair. He still saw that stubborn jaw set. "Thank you for explaining, Commodore. I request that you meet me at 1700 tomorrow for a briefing on the status of Project Vindication."

"I accept the request," he replied. "Am I to bring any particular officers with me?"

"Bring whoever you like," Hyde said almost offhandedly. "I'd offer a meal afterward, but I have another meeting scheduled. Those of us who work on the station get blessed few opportunities to take a vacation. Hyde out." And her image disappeared.

"Simply amazing," Richard muttered to himself. "I wouldn't have believed she, a marshal, could feel and act that way."

He chuckled. "Or that she could go so long without swearing at me. She really was restraining herself."

He tapped the contact for his executive officer, and Lieutenant Commander Jadern's face popped up over his datapad almost immediately.

"Commander Jadern reporting, sir. And may I say it's good to see you back at the helm."

"Had any troubles during my absence?" he asked.

"No sir. No troubles," Jadern replied, struggling to hide a smile. "Just unrelenting boredom, I swear."

"I'll bet. Well, I have a command appearance to make before Marshal Hyde tomorrow at 1700. Look through the roster for that time and find anyone who might have some interesting things to say during a ship inspection, put them on the schedule to join me, and include yourself."

"Are you expecting problems with the new ships, sir?" the XO asked.

"No problems. Just unrelenting boredom, I hope."

Jadern's mouth quirked up in a smile but then settled into a serious expression. "You hope, sir?"

"Are you private?"

"Yes, sir."

"Marshal Hyde was unexpectedly hostile toward me during our vid."

"But sir," Jadern protested, "isn't Marshal Hyde the one who—"

"Indeed," he replied. "Which is why I'm feeling suspicious. She isn't the type to seek out a lower officer's opinion. And given her stated feelings toward me, there must be something else at hand. So I understand Admiral Neboda set this up. And he set it up because... why?"

"Perhaps because you're unbiased, sir?"

"Or overly biased," he replied. "They claim they're making a fleet of ships like the *Avenger*, but the scuttlebutt while I was on *Intrepid* suggested they keep adding new ideas. And, as you know, Jadern, new ideas have a way of going badly awry."

Jadern looked at him skeptically but said nothing.

"Assemble that roster," Richard said. "I need to ponder this a little longer."

BED AND BANDAGES

Feducere Regional Hospital
Kherton Building, Second Floor
Epidermal Emergency Unit

Ospes Warthon stood at the EEU nurse's station chatting with Taisa Jan when the head nurse walked by. "Spes, how many times do I need to tell you—"

"Yes, ma'am. Sorry."

"Now, what have we got going on in room 223?"

"Unidentified juvenile female, burns along—"

"I understand the injuries just fine," she snapped. "Why do I have one, and who is the boy?"

"I wish I could tell you," Ospes replied. "She's still out, and he tightens up whenever anyone speaks to him."

"Is that supposed to be a figure of speech?"

"No, ma'am. He actually hugs himself. I've seen it a few times. Some kid thinks he's due a thrashing when he gets home;

doesn't want to say who he is. Thinks the punishment will go lighter somehow."

"Hmf." She started to walk away but stopped and turned. "Why don't they think further ahead?"

"Dunno? But funny thing. The longer the kid's gone, the more likely the parents are just to be happy to find him."

Jan stood there a moment longer, then said, "Start digging. If you can get him to say anything, it'll be easier to keep him talking. Whatever you can get will narrow the search." Her eyes flashed. "Whatever these two did for her to receive extensive second-degree burns, he needs a thrashing."

With a sigh, Ospes made his way back to room 223.

"Hey kid, I'm back," he said in greeting, but the boy just tightened up. *Great. Already hugging his legs.*

"Look, kid. You gotta know your parents are worried sick, right? When they know where you are, they'll come down and wrap you up and take you home."

"No!" he shouted. "I won't leave her."

Well, this is interesting. He's barely said three words.

"Well, how about her? Tell me her name, and we can see about telling her family what happened. Maybe you're scared, but do you want her family to worry?"

He was silent for a minute. "Doesn't matter," he muttered. "She don't care."

Wow. She was right. Now we can probably start looking at single mothers. "Why wouldn't her mother care?" he asked.

"Mom's dead. Tup says the one she has now ignores her a lot, has a lot of loser boyfriends."

Surrogate parent. Check for repeat domestic abuse calls, with different perps. He tried to think of a name that might be shortened to Tup.

"Tup," he said, feigning thoughtfulness. "That's an interesting name. Is it short for Tuppance? Tupper? Tupriana?"

"No. Tuptein—"

A name.

"—isn't her real name. It's just what her friends call her."

Ospes sighed. "Do you know her real name?"

"Of course not," the boy scowled. "Why would I? I'm not her friend, am I?"

And then he burst into tears.

Well, this is unexpected and awkward. But he entered the room and sat down beside the boy. "Look, kid," he said. "I don't pretend to understand why you're making the decisions you are. Heck, I'm just glad this girl's got fresh bandages and an IV of happy-juice. But the one thing I will tell you; if kicking two guards in the shins to protect her isn't friendship, then she's a fool to turn you down. Maybe you should ask her about it."

He wiped his eyes.

Ospes was about to say something more when his radio squawked. "Hey, Spes," came Narci's voice. "We got an ID on the boy. Faxil Pellere, mother Kvone Pellere. Last known address was in Khusam Apartments—demolished, of course. Kvone died in The Battle, though. Factory didn't evac in time. No other known relatives."

The boy's eyes went wide. "Hey, kiddo, I'll be right back." He hurried out into the hallway. "Star's sake, Narci. I was sitting next to the kid."

"Well, the kid is now Faxil," Narci said. "And this says he has nobody."

"Look, he's dressed and fed. This isn't some street urchin lost in the cracks. And neither is the girl. By the way, do a run on teen girls with the name or alias Tuptein. It's all I got out of him before you mentioned his dead mom."

"Well, if he's got someone else, who is it?" Narci asked. "Birth certificate doesn't list a father."

"I'll see what more I can get out of him, but I'm not expecting a lot."

He went back to find the boy had disappeared.

How? I wasn't but a few meters away. But somehow, he'd vanished.

———

Faxil had heard everything.

His father wasn't his real father.

He didn't have a father.

He didn't even have a real last name.

He knew how to run silently. You learned how to do that since The Battle. But this was a hospital, and it had an army of nurses and doctors everywhere, and those muscly guys they always had on the vids to hold people.

And security. Don't forget the security, like the guy you were just talking to.

But that wasn't what he wanted to forget. He wanted to forget the words "no known birth father."

Who is he, then? Faxil wondered. *He lived with Mom and me for years. My whole life. Why would she do that?*

He thought of Tuptein's explanation of her aunt, lazy and dependent on loser guys to keep her afloat. *Is that what he was, just a loser guy my mom let live in the house?*

And now his fake dad had found a new fake mom, and his whole family was fake. He didn't even know where Kuon was or where she went to when he wasn't giving her leftovers. *Do I have anything in my life that isn't fake?*

———

Ospes looked impatiently in every nearby room in the hospital, looking for his escaped juvenile. He dreaded calling it in. With the head nurse already on his case, he didn't want any incidents on his report. He might even get reassigned. *No, I really think Taisa is interested, finally. But if I don't catch the kid—*

He heard a sob coming from Room 255. He checked the nameplate. Empty. He pushed the door open slowly and found the boy crying softly.

"Is it okay if I come in?" Ospes asked, hoping not to startle the kid, Faxil, he remembered.

Faxil looked up at him and nodded.

Ospes sat down on the floor next to him. "So… you want to talk about it?" he asked.

The kid didn't say anything.

"Sometimes, it helps to talk about it. Even to a grown-up. I mean, maybe I know someone else who had your problem, and I can tell you what they did. You know, if it helps."

"Who's my dad?" Faxil asked.

"Well…" *That was a loaded question right off the bat.* "I assume you know where babies come from?"

The jest didn't land well. But he did look up, his tear-stained face twisted into a grimace of a sad-smile. "Of course."

"Well, there's a difference between fathering a kid and being a father. Believe me, I know. I didn't have a dad until I was, well, almost your age."

Ospes tried not to let old memories dwell, but… *The kid needs some truth right now.* "Mister Tried-Once found out Mom was pregnant and ran off. She raised me for ten years by herself, until the day a construction worker saw me get chased by a couple drug dealers I'd pissed off. He whipped them good and took me home. Next thing I know, he's coming over for dinner twice a week, then he says he wants to be my daddy."

Ospes couldn't help but smile at the memory. *People just don't much care for shiny weddings anymore.* He remembered himself in the little blue suit, a perfect match for the groom's.

"And that… was the best thing that ever happened to me. He was a great dad. And he's why I decided to be a person who helps other people."

Faxil just sat there, sniffling. But it seemed like he picked up the important parts, at least.

"Why don't you tell me a little about your buddy in 223, huh?" He wasn't just trying to get the kid to talk. He knew the boy needed to say something.

"Well... she's really tough. She has a gang, and they run around and have, I dunno, adventures and stuff. I never had any friends, so I just stayed home and worked in my sketchbook..." He trailed off, and a tear trailed down his cheek. "I can't believe I lost it. It had all my good stuff in there."

"But why did she get a gang?" Ospes tried to keep the conversation steered.

"Well, after the crashes, her mom and dad were dead. They were both military, but different kinds? I forget. And her aunt ignored her, so she was tough and got a crew together. And they went around... doing stuff. And then they started picking on me, and after a couple weeks, I kinda ended up in the crew. But not really, you know? They didn't see me as crew, even if they listened to her. And they were afraid of Kuon. Kuon really protected me."

"Oh? Who's Kuon?" he asked, hoping for another angle of inquiry to pursue.

"Kuon's my pet khain," he said. "She likes pancakes and stuff, and sometimes she'll do tricks for me. And when we found Blue Troopers under that factory, she ripped one of their heads off with her tail. It was kinda cool. And I think maybe she can hear my thoughts?"

So he draws all the time and has a pet monster who eats pancakes, and they kill aliens together. Ospes had a feeling that some of this was either an overactive imagination or psychological damage. *Way* above his pay grade.

"So, how about we go back and sit with your friend, okay?" he said instead. "Because I'm getting old, and I just don't fit on the floor like I used to."

Faxil gave him a look he recognized. The *why is this grown-up so weird* look. But he got up, and so did Ospes.

It's okay, kid. Give it a few more years, and you'll be the goofy grown-up who gets the weird looks.

He almost followed him back into the room, but his radio

hissed. "Narwhal calling Osprey, Narwhal calling Osprey. Mission Earthworm is a go. I repeat—"

Speaking of weird grown-ups. "Narci, I'm out of the room. Did you find anything?"

"Yep. Put out a photo of the kid, the Hills district responded. Says they had him a week ago. Nerfs didn't even update his record, only entered it locally. What a buncha—"

"Is there someone coming to get him?" Ospes interrupted.

"They contacted the kid's dad, like before. He was a contact number on the local files. They didn't even know he was missing. All riled and heading your way."

"Good. Hey, anything about the girl?"

"Nothing on first name Tuptein. No juvie priors on any name starting with Tup. Last names include Tupia, Tupek, Tupelo, Tupi, Tupinambus—"

"And are any of those a teenage girl?"

"If they are, no priors."

Ospes resisted the urge to swear. "Hey, thanks for the quick work."

"No problem. Apparently they were just bored. You know? Alien invasion means everyone stays home."

Ospes knew it was the opposite. Looters had been rampant even during the debris falling from orbit. It was getting harder for security and peacekeepers to stay on top of things.

"Whatever. Talk later. Ospes out."

Now his only hope to help this girl rested in her waking up and talking to him. *If she's half the firecracker Faxil says she is, I'm going to have a rough time of it.*

———

Faxil sat with Tuptein again.

"You know," he said quietly, "I've been confused for a while. I mean, I kinda understand why you started picking on me. The *Peacemaker* killed my mom. Not on purpose. But I threw rocks at it because... what else could I do? And your dad, and your mom... I understand. Tough girl being tough.”

He thought he heard her breathing change, but she didn't move. So he continued.

“But then you started being nice. Just a little, you know? But it was nice, being nice. I mean being treated nice. And then you got hurt, and I had to save you. And when... I hugged you, and it felt special to me, too. I guess what I'm trying to say is... tonight I learned I don't know what a family means. So I'm gonna make it up. I wanna say that if you want to be my family, instead of living with a mean aunt, maybe we could try that. Whatever that means.”

He wished she were awake, so she could say something. When she didn't, he covered his face in his hands. “Oh, who am I kidding? I could practice that forever, and as soon as I say it, you'll just beat me up. Tuptein doesn't need some skinny snot for family. You have your whole crew.”

“Ss... ss... stupid,” she mumbled.

He instantly jumped from the chair and ran to the bedside.

“Ss... stupid jerk. Not gun... beat ya up,” she managed. “Ya... kinda cute... fer *snot*. Keep ya.”

His eyes began to tear up, but he forced them back. “Tuptein. You're okay. I mean, you're not okay, but you're awake. How are you feeling?”

She glanced at her arm, swathed in bandages. “Ow. Ow.”

Faxil winced at the memory of her bubbled, scorched flesh. “Yeah, it was pretty bad for a while. And they have you on something called ‘happyjuice.’ At least that's what Ospes called it.”

“Lutanyua,” she murmured. “Pain relief. Big dose... you can remember old things real good.”

“How do you know that?” Faxil asked.

“Pashel sold it for a while. Fifty cred a dose. Think I got like five cred worth right now. Cheapskates.”

"What do you mean, you got five creds? And who's Pashel?"

She groaned. "They only gave me five creds worth."

Faxil decided to ignore the comments. "Tuptein, I'm so sorry. You got hurt because I was too weak and slow. You shouldn't have to protect me like—"

"Pinari," she interrupted him.

"—okay, like a... pinari. And I—"

"My name's Pinari. Pinari Tudein," she said.

From outside in the hall, Faxil heard a "Yes!" and a radio click, but this was more important.

"Your real name is Pinari?" he asked incredulously. *Pinari, like the little bush in the old forest? With the pink flowers?*

"You got a problem with—"

"It's beautiful," Faxil said.

She reached out with her uninjured arm and pulled him close. "Better not have a problem," she mumbled as her strong grip on his shirt slacked almost immediately.

He sat with her and watched as she slowly drifted to sleep again. Shadows passed in front of the doorway behind him, but he refused to look. Everything he needed right now was in this bed. And he would watch over her.

"Faxil?"

The voice whispered from the doorway was familiar, and yet not. For hours he had imagined his father's voice, but this wasn't what he sounded like at all.

He turned and saw his father, alone, tears streaming down his face.

Everything I need is right... right... right...

There was no reason that he couldn't need two things.

He ran to his father's arms, and they sobbed together for what seemed like forever.

———

Eventually, the crying ended, and Faxil allowed himself to be walked out into the small waiting area. He sat with his father and Annoy-ay.

"Son," his father said, "earlier tonight I said to you that I needed you to be a man and protect Inoiae. And you ran away and ended up in a hospital."

"But, I was—" Faxil tried to explain.

His father held up a hand to stop him. "I can't call you a man who protects and tell you I don't trust you. So I decided that I need to listen to my heart. Your recent actions are strange, and you do things I don't understand. So please help me understand."

So Faxil told him everything.

The rage he felt when his mother died.

The bullies who chased him and hit him.

Meeting Kuon and taming her.

Trying to solve his own problems by buying the bullies off.

The pain of losing Kuon underground.

Saving Tuptein and saving Kuon.

Continuing to do dangerous things because, for the first time, someone respected him.

His absolute feeling of betrayal when his father found another wife.

And then, he paused. *I've said so much. But I can't let this go. I let everything else hide inside me for so long. I want... I need to say this.*

"I heard the security person," he said. "He said my name isn't Avestan; it's Pellere. He said that you're not my real dad."

His father's mouth dropped open. Faxil had never actually seen a real person's mouth open like that. Then his father began to cry again. He continued to cry long after Faxil would have thought a man could have tears.

Finally, he said, "When I met your mother, we were stupid people having reckless fun. Then we had a fight, and we broke up, and I didn't see her for two years. The next time I saw her, she had a one-year-old baby... you."

Faxil couldn't believe any of this was happening. *This is how I learn the story? Why? Why is it like this now?*

"I asked her if the child was mine," his father continued. "She refused to answer me at first and then denied it fiercely. I wasn't the one. I should just go on and live my life, just like I'd told her when we fought. But I'd grown a bit since that fight, even if she didn't seem to have. She was broke and angry, and she could barely take care of herself. But she gave everything she had to you."

Faxil thought of his mother, how her eyes always looked haunted, scared of things around corners.

"So I started showing up, helping to carry groceries, bringing her clothes I'd found at thrift stores or charities so she wouldn't freeze. And finally, I got her to admit that she hadn't been seeing anyone before or after me. And that I was your father. Well, by that time I was practically living with you both. I tried to marry her, make it properly official, but she said a few shirts didn't..." He looked at Annoy-ay. "...buy me any favors. So I lived in your house, and I took care of you. We shared expenses at a time when things were economically terrible, and she survived and you prospered. And the more I watched you grow up, the more I wanted to be there."

Faxil was beginning to understand. "But she didn't?"

"Not for a long time. Sometimes, it would feel like maybe she'd forgiven me, or at least forgotten for a while. She would let me get a little closer, and I would think that maybe things were getting better. But the one thing I realized after she died... was that I never said I was sorry."

He sighed. "She never let me get close again, Faxil. As much as I cared about her and you, I think the only reason she let me stay was because of you. I... killed some part of her, Faxil. I made a terrible mistake, and it shaped the rest of her life. Not just you —oh, she loved you. She once told me that she'd planned to give you away, that she couldn't bear to have any part of me near her. But the moment she looked at you, she knew she could never do it."

Faxil got up and hugged his father, his actual and real father. And he let Annoy-ay hug him too because he knew she cared, and maybe he didn't have to dislike her.

"No, you don't," she whispered.

He didn't know how she knew that—had he whispered it? No! But maybe he could stop making fun of her name. Inoiae was kind of a cool name, even if it was hard to say sometimes.

"I'd like that," she murmured, right next to his ear.

He realized that she really was like a mom. She could tell what he was thinking.

———

DAGON JAX HAD MADE up his mind. After sitting with Haltar in Medical again this morning, he knew he could delay no longer. He showed up for duty twenty minutes early, his uniform the sharpest it had looked since his last Academy inspection. He found Captain Morian on the bridge, watching over the refitters as they re-installed control panels and checked power levels, without ever seeming to stare. Dagon always wondered how he did that.

Before he could say his carefully rehearsed lines, Captain Morian spotted him. "Lieutenant Jax? You're a bit early for your duty shift. Come to relieve Lieutenant DeLong?"

"Oh, um, I mean—" He steeled himself. *This is no time to appear weak.* "Captain, may I request a moment of your time?"

"Certainly, Mister Jax," he replied. "Come to the ready room."

Dagon took a deep breath. "With your permission, sir, I'd like to apply for leave."

The captain look surprised. "I don't understand. You could just ask Commander Haal if you needed a few—"

"No, sir," Dagon insisted. "I need to leave the ship."

"Explain, Mister Jax."

"Haltar Sen is my teacher, and he's my friend, and he's dying. Captain Crowe thinks she knows someone—"

"Sasha Crowe from the IMFP?" the captain asked.

"Yes, sir. She said there's someone who they call Mirabilis there on Freyja. She's a healer; she makes miracles... Well, the name makes sense when I say it—"

"And you'd like to take a detachment and go look for this woman in IMFP space without diplomatic authorization?"

"I guess that's what I'm asking, sir."

The captain lapsed into silence.

Well, he didn't reject it outright, Dagon thought. *That's a good sign, isn't it?*

He waited far longer than he'd expected. *What the hell was I expecting? "Sure, Jax. Take a shuttle and a squad of marines. Fly off into another system without a senior officer to tell you what to do, and grope around until you find some lady who goes by a codename." How did I sit on this for so long and not think one thing about how I would actually do it?*

Eventually, the captain spoke. "I understand your desire and your concern for Haltar, Mister Jax. Were I in your place, I would argue for our friend as well. But regulations say that irregular leave off-ship like you suggest constitutes *positum absentia,* or dereliction. I cannot and will not grant it."

Dagon's spirits fell. But he respected his captain too much to rail against what he could see as a barrier over which he couldn't pass. He prepared to salute and leave and tell Sasha Crowe they had to find another—

"However, I am perfectly within my rights as Commodore to authorize an away mission, with all necessary personnel and equipment, for whatever reason I choose as long as it doesn't cause a diplomatic incident. So I'll choose a commander to lead the mission and a shuttle to carry four, maybe five others. Agreed?"

Dagon was relieved. The captain was going to do it. Even if Dagon wasn't going along. Then he had an idea.

"Um, sir?" he ventured. "I notice that you haven't assigned a pilot for the shuttle. Permission to volunteer?"

"Why, now that I think of it," Morian said with a wink, "you would be the perfect person, wouldn't you? As long as you make certain your position as instructor is covered before you leave."

Dagon could barely contain his enthusiasm. "Yes, sir. Absolutely, sir."

"Good man. File a plan of action by... 1200 tomorrow. Dismissed."

Dagon snapped to attention and threw him a salute. Morian returned it, smiling, and Dagon turned and left the ready room, already pondering who might take his instructor position for a week or more.

I could ask Gian if he could—oh, Danis. She still totally owes me for the ride from Typhon. I mean, kinda. She'd totally do it, right?

CHAPTER
FIFTEEN

THE COGS OF WAR

Combat Training Square - "The Incursion"
Resdon Military Complex
Som Orsi City

MEERA STUMBLED behind an outcropping of rock, trying to heave her weapon into line with the attackers. Blues were striding indefatigably over any obstacle, firing their plasma rifles over and over. Meera fired staccato bursts at one, then a second. The bullets slammed into the second, causing it to explode, but the first one, undeterred, fired again, this time catching her in its beam. Meera screamed in frustration as the sim kicked her out. She found herself in the Waiting Room, as the sim-selection menu had been dubbed, watching the ongoing battle as if it were a giant vid.

She could see everyone going through the exercise. Klaus, the big, scarred veteran, easily wielded the large weapon, using the simple TK sim-commands to knock his opponents backward before striking. His shots clustered neatly in the chests of the Blues, causing each of them to explode. He was supposed to be her partner for today, but he'd said little and seemed nervous. She couldn't imagine why he would be afraid of a mother twice his age and half his size. *Maybe he just isn't interested in carrying an untrained civilian through the sim.*

Jude, her partner from the first day, was ignoring the TK commands entirely. He simply took slow, methodical shots that destroyed each target. She remembered hearing that he was a hunter; his method seemed appropriate until she remembered the conversation he'd had with Prince Elio that first day. *Palace Guard... when and where would he have learned to shoot like that?*

Jude's partner for today was Proose, who was surviving the battle handily. But the longer she watched him, the more she noticed that he spent more time dodging than firing. Each of his "near misses" would have been close enough to cook his skin in real life.

He's taking advantage of the weaknesses in the sim, she thought. *That's... cheating.*

Jude made his way across the field, firing at targets of opportunity, with Proose somehow dancing right between several of the Blues. They fired at him, but his reflexes got him through time after time as the deadly beams disintegrated the Blues in their own crossfire.

Now that's definitely cheating, she thought angrily. *The briefing said they can absorb most kinds of energy, including plasma. The sim is simply not accurate, and his score is... oh, it's zero. So his antics aren't doing anything to help him. Hah!*

She turned her attention to Rauf. The pardoned criminal was using a pair of pistols, firing both at the same time like a hero out of a Frontier Planet vid. But she couldn't see any evidence that he was using his TK commands.

His partner Vecht, the mechanic, was having trouble with both his heavy rifle and his TK. She zoomed in on him, watching his anger increase until he rushed at his enemies, throwing his rifle at one of the Blues. He was quickly cut down, though ironically, his rifle smashed a Blue's head in. It didn't explode, but it did fall over "dead." He appeared in the Waiting Room. "Stupid freaking pile of crap!" he screamed, trying to flail or kick at some imaginary foe before grabbing at the representation of his halo. He instantly disappeared.

Looks like they'll be requesting a replacement halo. Again. She'd tried to talk to the volatile man, maybe find out why he was so driven, but he'd quickly grown frustrated and excused himself from the conversation. She wondered how he'd gotten on the team.

Beko, the other veteran, seemed to be doing well at the sim. Like Klaus, she made simple TK commands to slow their approach and fired her rifle. While not as accurate as the former space marine, her shots were good enough to put her score near the top.

Elaer was at the top. Ignoring the entire training premise and scoring equation, the frizzy-haired woman was flinging rocks with deadly accuracy. She shattered the carapaces of each foe, and with each death, her score climbed, even with the point reduction for "accidental kills."

Suddenly Rauf was standing beside her. "Stupid sim. Cheating bastard."

"I noticed that it doesn't mimic real life very well," she agreed. "But you were doing very well with your pistols."

He muttered something in a language she didn't understand.

It was at that point she took notice of the conversation going on behind her.

"Not TK. This is not TK." It was a vid image of Dr. Zettel in his helmet arguing with Major Rosst.

"This is the most advanced sim-training we have against the Blues," Rosst explained. "And it has controls that mimic the use—"

"Mimic." Zettel managed to inject the single word with a

cubic meter of condescension. "You cannot mimic it. This is no more practice of TK than lifting a sandwich is exercise."

"Dr. Zettel, the goal of the sim is to practice techniques in conjunction with battlefield weapons—"

"You have it all wrong, Major," Zettel interrupted him. "TK is the weapon, Major. You teach tricks and nonsense. TK is instinct."

"So how do you suggest we do live-fire exercises, Doctor? Have the Guardians practice on each other?"

"Pshaw," Zettel's avatar said. "These people will not learn by warring against each other. They are too afraid."

Meera wouldn't listen anymore. She stomped over to the pair. "Excuse me, Doctor," she said to the floating vid. "But I came here to kill Blues. I am not afraid. You give me anything real, a straw dummy over this mess, and I will practice until I can set things on fire with my mind."

"Ah-hah. This one has spirit." The image of Zettel clapped his hands. "I think fire is probably beyond you, my dear, but I think the major has some dummies we can try. Don't you, Major?"

Major Rosst's avatar looked thoughtful. "Well... We do have those prototypes from the marshal's program. But they weren't very useful before."

"Trust me," Zettel said, more calmly now, "when they have a real enemy, they can let go of their controls and act on instinct."

Major Rosst considered that. "I suppose we can give it a try," he replied slowly.

Before he could go back to his usual rancor, Meera added, "And I'd like to train with pistols. The rifles are too heavy for me to handle."

A look of resignation crossed the major's features. "I suppose one more won't hurt anything," he said, though far less caustically than he'd been when considering her earlier complaints. "Meera, we'll meet again at the Excursion Field at 1330."

"Yes, sir," she replied, throwing him a salute to thank him.

He even smiled a little. "Good job," he said, then left.

Meera was elated. Finally, things were going better. She'd felt like such a failure the entire week of training.

———

Major Rosst removed his halo and stared at the good doctor sitting at a desk nearby.

"I'd better not find out this is some kind of trick," he said.

"Why would I trick you?" Zettel asked. "There isn't anything I want more than to study these... Heroic powers. And besides," he said and motioned behind him at the two Conquell guards, "I would have to be very sneaky to accomplish my getaway plans without being, you know, shot."

"Has he done anything suspicious while I was otherwise engaged?" Rosst asked the guards.

"We are under specific orders, Major," one of them replied. "If we suspect he is doing anything other than discharging the duty assigned, he is to be killed without prejudice."

"You should see how hard it is to convince them my lavatory visits are a military necessity," Zettel said, smiling. "But never mind. Do as I suggest, and I promise you will see results."

"I'd better," Rosst growled. "Because I don't like being manipulated."

Unconvinced but left with few options if he was going to report any successes for the week, Rosst left the Incursion and made his way to Deep Storage. Despite the name, it was only one floor below the surface, but he was required to show his ID twice and pass through three biometric scans to reach the Prototype Champions locker. There, he found what he was looking for, and the remote key to control them. He inserted the key into his datascreen, and a holo appeared of the various basic maneuvers they could accomplish, as well as limited in-battle responses and attack patterns. He double-checked each one; all nonlethal weaponry and safety padding to protect the recruits. He activated all thirty.

"Well, time to see if you were worth the ridiculous expense," he said as he walked out of Deep Storage, not having a clue that Dr. Zettel had seen everything with his Psy.

―――――

Combat Training Field - "The Excursion"
Resdon Military Complex

It was almost 1330 and Meera could barely contain her glee. She was finally going to practice real TK again.

The other pairs had arrived slowly, one after the other. Jude and Proose had been the last pair to leave the sim. Beko and Elaer were talking animatedly together, and Meera wished she could find some way to fit herself into their circle of two, but the roommates seemed fast and inseparable friends. Rauf and Vecht stood together, arguing with each other.

Meera stood next to her partner Klaus on the field. It seemed as if he was trying to avoid looking at her.

She summoned up the courage to speak to him. "Have I... offended you somehow, Klaus?" she asked, a little more timidly than she'd wanted.

Klaus looked down toward her. She thought it might be the first time he'd actually made eye contact with her.

"Um, no, ma'am," he replied.

"Well, you haven't spoken to me all day." She tried to give her best stern-mom expression, but even Sorge had been small compared to this mammoth-sized man.

"I, um, uh..." the man stuttered.

She fought to maintain her frown, though it was almost comical how she had defeated him with a few words.

He closed his eyes and hung his head a little. "All right, I'll be honest," he said. "I didn't know what to say to you."

"To a partner?" she countered. "To a civilian? To a woman?"

"To, um, a hottie mom."

She blinked. And then blinked again. "I have never heard a discriminatory compliment. Congratulations."

He seemed about to say something more, but suddenly Major Rosst's voice cracked across the field.

"Re-CRUITS. Fall in." There was a brief shuffle as everyone but Rauf lined up. He simply strolled to his spot on the end.

"It has been suggested," the major began, "that our training sims aren't working for some of you. As much as I dislike proven military tactics being ignored, I've decided to grant an exception. This afternoon, we have at our disposal a series of prototypes from the Military Research Facility at Regis Magnum. We gave them a shakedown in combat training—they were less than effective. However, each of these prototypes are worth a half-million creds, or so I'm told. So please try not to break them."

Dr. Zettel stepped up beside him. *Look at him sweating,* she thought. *That metal helmet must be miserable in this sun.*

"Recruits," Dr. Zettel shouted, "we are outside and fighting real enemies because TK is not something you can pretend to do. Playing with balls is more effective training than the sims. Take the control you have learned and use it. Push your enemies down, lift them into the air. They are programmed to hit you physically but not hard."

"Use caution and stand by your partners," Rosst added. "Remember, nothing beats another pair of eyes and hands. Work together, learn what each of you can do, and what you can do together."

And with that, the mechanical warriors crested the hill

behind Rosst. Each had a heavily padded glove on one hand and a splatterball gun in the other.

The splatterguns opened fire.

———

SUDDENLY MEERA WAS YANKED sideways and pulled behind a rocky outcrop. A moment later, the splattershots impacted, sending a yellow spray of paint to every side.

"Well, now is really real," Klaus said with an irritating smile. "What do you think of live-fire?"

"I don't know what to think," she wailed.

"Well, the point is to not die," he said. "You get hit with the paint and you die!"

"I figured that part out."

"I know my TK pretty well," he said. "How about you?"

"I'm... I'm not very good, Klaus," she said as she tried to look around the edge of the rock. "I only seem to be able to use it when I'm upset."

She felt a hard pinch on her bottom.

"What was—" She looked back to find Klaus grinning at her. "Did you just—"

"Didn't touch you, I swear," he claimed, holding his hands up. But the pinch happened again.

He touched me like that? He touched me.

She felt it again. He was grinning at her, his hands still in the air.

"Why you..." And she felt the power surge through her. It connected her with the entire world, and the entire world was hers to command.

And she commanded his large, muscular body to slide out into the line of splatter fire.

In moments his entire right side was pocked with yellow paint.

"Hahaha," he yelped in glee. "That was amazing," he yelled.

"So what can you do to them?" He pointed at the robots, who layered him with a fresh coat of yellow paint.

Meera turned her attention to the three advancing robots. Even through the rock, she could sense their movements, could feel the impacts of the splatterballs as they hit the rock. Oddly, she couldn't seem to feel them before that. So she hadn't tried.

As they walked, she found that they each had a specific pattern of movement, but on the leader's seventh step, they all landed at the same time. *Five, six... now.* She seized the landing feet and held them fast. The one with the fastest walk tripped; its momentum swung it sideways into the second, who collapsed into the third. In seconds they were all collapsed and inert, their programming apparently designed to signal "defeat" in non-optimal conditions.

"Meera, that was amazing," Klaus exclaimed. He seemed about to hug her but glanced at the layers of paint on his arm and reconsidered.

"You... you..." she fumed. "How dare you do that to me? I hardly even know you." But her anger died away and she smiled at him.

"Can you still feel the power?" he asked.

She reached out like before, but the power was gone. She no longer felt anything at all. She was devastated.

She simply stared at him and shook her head.

"Look, partner," he said, his face serious. "I know I did a medium-bad thing. But I was all caught up, and you needed to be mad. I'm sorry if I offended you."

"Well, I don't accept," she said and turned and walked away.

Elsewhere on the field, it seemed things were going well. Jude was throwing rocks. They were large and slow, but they connected solidly enough to knock the robots down. Elaer was using a piece of osmium cable she'd found to strike or trip the robots, and Beko seemed to be trying what Meera had done— holding the legs down while she picked them off one at a time, hitting them with a rock.

Then she saw Rauf. The lanky boy was *physically assaulting* one of the robots. The splattergun fired at point-blank range, but the shots veered away from Rauf's body like water parting around a stone. He gave the robot what appeared to be a powerful uppercut and it lifted off the ground and flew backward to land on its back and lie still. She stared at him in awe. She would have sworn he didn't actually touch the machine.

"Yeah!" Rauf yelled, his tattoos flashing in the sun as he jumped in victory. "Knocked the bastard into the middle of next week."

Then the remaining robot shot him. His tattoos disappeared under a coat of yellow.

"Exercise halt," Rosst's voice rang out. The robots stood up on their own and remained at attention, all but the one Rauf had knocked across the field.

"Well, that was... interesting," Rosst declared. "Everyone visit the wash station, then we'll reconvene."

———

"Well, that wasn't a total catastrophe," Rosst said when they'd reassembled. "Though I do wish you hadn't broken that last one, Rauf. As I said, these are expensive."

Eugma Zettel gave all the appropriate nods, but inside he wanted to mock the fool. *Not a total catastrophe?* he thought. *He literally just watched his recruits unlock powers they'd never known in the space of twenty minutes. And he thinks it's a mediocre performance? Idiot!*

"Well, Major," Zettel said lightly. "I think the results are... impressive, and I believe the injured robot can be repaired with a minimum of fuss."

"Oh, you do, do you?" Rosst said, his disbelief clear. "And where do you think we will find such a repairman?"

"Wait for the debrief," Eugma insisted. "I think you will agree that today was a good day." He brushed against Rosst's mind, just a hair. "In fact, with your permission, I'd like to set up one or two tests in the debriefing room? Just to show you."

He felt Rosst's resistance, and he teased his mind again.

"Fine," Rosst said, finally. "If I have something concrete to show in return for the damage to that robot, maybe I'll have something to report to the prince."

"Ah, yes, concrete," Eugma laughed. "An excellent idea. I will have some brought in."

He could feel the contempt Rosst had for him, but he didn't care. He had the perfect plan to escape, and Rosst was playing perfectly into it, with barely any help from Zettel at all.

The major is less suited to judging the worth of these soldiers than I am to judge a pie-eating contest, he thought moodily.

Zettel turned to his guards. They were wearing security halos to prevent him meddling with their minds, should he somehow escape his helmet. *And yet they never thought to protect anyone else against me? I could simply command anyone around me to attack the guards. Fools. All of them!*

"I have instructions from Major Rosst, yes?" he questioned the guards. "I am to request materials for a debrief test."

"Go ahead," Guard One snapped.

"Nothing electronic, nothing mechanical," Guard Two added.

"But I need to bring the broken robot into the debriefing. Surely that doesn't violate the spirit of your orders?"

The two guards turned away and conferred silently.

"You may request workers to bring in the robot," Guard One finally said. "You may not touch it or approach it to within five meters. If you do, you will be terminated without warning."

"On my word," Zettel said with a smile.

An hour later, the team had gathered again in the debriefing room. On one side of the room was a pile of concrete blocks, against the other wall the damaged robot.

Zettel was forced to stand against the back wall with the guards lest he be too close to the tests.

"Well, Doctor," Rosst said, "I hope you're going to impress me."

"Of course," Eugma replied.

He raised his voice. "Attention, recruits. I want to congratulate you on a fine performance. I think the results are... impressive. Rauf, I'd like to begin with you, if I may."

"Let me guess, you're mad I busted the bot?" Rauf replied.

"No, not at all," Zettel said lightly. "But we'll talk about that in a moment. I'd like to ask..." He looked at each of the group in turn, then said, "Elaer. Could you throw one of the concrete blocks at Rauf?" Then he turned to Rauf and said, "About halfway, you, Rauf, will simply catch it with TK."

Elaer easily picked up the reconstituted stone and threw it. Zettel closed his eyes and the block fell to the floor.

Elaer looked dumbfounded.

"Did you use TK, Elaer?" Zettel asked.

Elaer nodded.

"Then you must do better," Zettel said. "Rauf, you scored an impressive blow earlier this afternoon. Elaer, throw the block at Rauf so he can punch it."

Elaer slung the next block faster than Eugma could correct—

Rauf, taken by surprise, caught the block directly in front of his face. It disintegrated, leaving a fine coat of gray powder hanging in the air before sliding down an invisible barrier.

Elaer looked terribly shocked. "I'm so sorry. I didn't think—"

But Rauf sprang forward, lashing out at Elaer, but before he could reach her, Beko used her TK to catch Rauf's feet and hold onto them.

"Let me go. I'm gonna punch—"

"Rauf. Control yourself before your parole is revoked," Major Rosst shouted, but Rauf wasn't listening. So Zettel poked the rage in Rauf's mind. Rauf recoiled and turned, looking for whatever had distracted him, but the moment passed, and he calmed quickly.

"I am very sorry, Rauf," Zettel said carefully. "Elaer does not know her strength yet. That was my mistake. But you see? Rauf has a TK bubble. It protects him and allows him to strike very hard. But he doesn't have distance yet. With practice, he will improve. But now we have a team member that deflects projectiles and can use great strength. Rauf, could you punch the stack of blocks for me?"

"Pleasure." Rauf punched the stack of blocks, but it was clear to all that they began to disintegrate under the force of his blow *before* he reached them.

"Excellent," Zettel said, clapping his hands. Obviously, he was thrilled. "Rauf," he continued enthusiastically, "you see this as a battle strength now, but when you learn to control it, you may be able to lift vehicles. Imagine picking up a gravdumper as easily as a puppy.

"Now, for Klaus. Big, strong Klaus. I would like you to push the block out of..." He looked around the group. "Beko, would you please hold the block aloft in your hand?"

Beko lifted the block, and Klaus easily pushed it away. It crashed against the wall.

"I hope your demonstration involves fixing the damage to this room," Rosst said caustically.

"Add it to budget requests," Zettel said and ignored him. "Beko, stand much closer and do the same."

The result was predictable; the block flew across the room even faster than before.

"Now, Klaus, hold the block yourself and push. Push hard."

Klaus stared at the block in his hand... and it broke in half and the two pieces flew across the room. "How did I do that?" he asked, still staring at his hand.

"Your strength is proportional to distance," Zettel declared with a smile. "Look at the wall."

They all turned to look at what Zettel had seen from his

further vantage point. A jagged piece of the block was embedded in the wall.

"The closer you are to your target, the stronger your TK will be," Eugma explained. "Throwing a rock, or any kind of ballistic missile, will be deadly; simply pushing back at the enemy will merely distract them. You are not weak, Klaus, but you do have strength you didn't know. And now for Elaer—"

He continued, explaining Elaer's skill to her, but as Zettel suspected, she feared her TK and used props as a crutch to control her strength. But he didn't mention it.

He also explained Vecht's sense of machinery. Simply by touching the broken robot, several of the broken pieces were reshaped and reinserted into their original places. Pieces knocked askew were reconnected. By the time he was done, the robot could have passed for new, and Zettel insisted he made note of the parts that needed to be replaced. And, for the first time, Vecht was smiling.

He explained Jude's issues as one of size. His skills lay in smaller projectiles. With a simple thought, Jude had gathered a hundred of the broken concrete shards and began twirling them around himself, much to the amusement of the rest of the group.

He watched Meera's expression each time he ignored her. And when everyone else had had their moment, he handed the meeting back to Rosst, who grudgingly offered praise to the people he'd presumed useless only hours ago.

As his guards escorted him out, he felt Meera's resentful gaze upon him.

Exactly as I planned.

———

WHY NOT ME? Meera thought. *Why didn't Dr. Zettel have anything to say to me? Didn't I do well, too?*

Maybe she hadn't done well. After all, she only did the same thing Beko had done, but Beko had also pelted her enemies with rocks. She, Meera, hadn't rushed the robots or disabled them with real TK. She'd just tripped them.

Meera thought back to her emotions at the time. Just before the robots had arrived, Klaus had told her she was "a hottie mom." That had set off a firestorm of confusion in her mind. It had been years since she'd thought about men that way. Graben had damaged her self-image, the bastard. And then she'd had children to raise. She hadn't cared to seek out anyone to fill the few empty minutes she could spare for herself each day.

Maybe... I'm always going to be second-rate. I was Graben's second choice, wasn't I? I just wasn't good enough for...

Then again, Klaus had looked at her. Not leered, as she might have expected a young man to do. And he'd given her a compliment, if not the one she was raised to expect. But—

But there was no way to misinterpret Klaus' casual use of TK on her. It was an inappropriate liberty, plain and simple. She wasn't going to accept that from him, or anyone.

And she was going to tell him so—

"That was a great job," he'd said. "That was amazing, Meera."

Maybe I... Maybe I... No. I'm going to visit the doctor.

———

BACK IN HIS CELL, Doctor Zettel smiled. *I look forward to it, my dear.*

CHAPTER
SIXTEEN

POWER DEPRIVED

REGIS MAGNUM SHIPYARDS
North Plate, Second Arm
Office Delta—Security Specialists

"YOU'VE all had a week to find out," Marshal Hyde snapped at her specialists. "I want to know everything about this technician de Cevoir. Where did she come from? What are her loyalties? Her school records. Her logins on this base. I want answers, and I want them *now!*"

"It says here that she was a citizen of Tor when the Swarm first attacked," the one called Heng said. "Her family fled, first to Odin, then here. The records are spotty but seem legit."

"Kasa de Cevoir is considered a prodigy," another called Marst said. "She graduated from standard education three years early, then began advanced schooling. She earned two degrees in three years, Chemistry and Engineering. She took an advanced degree in only two years, Materials Science. And... earned a first-level degree in Classical Instruments."

"And yet none of this explains how she was able to forge a clearance almost equal to mine in the fifteen minutes that she left her station," Hyde observed. "Dig deeper. I want to know who the hell she is."

"Something strange here, Marshal," the woman called Lutcho said. "de Cevoir has a clean record, no apparent complaints. And yet, in a high-clearance system search, there's evidence that she was in line for disciplinary action several times, but the complaints have been wiped from the system, or she was suddenly transferred to another department."

"What kind of evidence?" Hyde demanded.

"Records of partial drafts, ma'am. While no actual papers or communiques exist, there appear to be several draft backups lodged in various points of the system, citing an insubordinate attitude and disrespectful behavior."

"Conclusions?" Hyde snapped.

"If it was only once, I would think that perhaps they managed to work something out without official paperwork," the specialist replied. "But the repeated offenses, and then the current situation, I can't imagine how it means anything other than she was somehow able to delete negative content from her record."

"So, people, it appears we have a spy in our midst," Hyde said. "Any thoughts on how she was able to forge that clearance?"

"Um, no, ma'am," Marst replied; the rest of the specialists merely shook their heads. "The data log shows guest access," Marst continued, "then suddenly it changes to admin access. Then the creation of a new account, then she was able to access the security feeds."

"Search the system. Find out if there's any evidence that suggests previous intrusions that match the data. Now, what about her activity before the incident?" Hyde asked. "Is there any indication that she was directly involved in the catastrophe?"

"No, ma'am," Heng replied. "Cameras show her at her station. Data logs show that she was entering data and other such activities alongside the others as was required of her. Nothing appears to be amiss."

"Is it possible she was able to fake those activities?" Hyde asked thoughtfully.

There was silence.

"Um, last week I'd have said no, ma'am," Marst replied. "But this week has been... unusual."

"Indeed it has," Hyde answered.

"Ma'am, I would like to point out what might not be immediately obvious," Lutcho said.

"Go ahead."

"Post-analysis of the incident shows that the electrical contacts generating the energy incinerated several seconds before loss of containment."

"So?"

"Technical Observation Five had significant damage from the aborted explosion. If she had meant to sabotage the experiment that way, she'd have died. Even without the possibility of a hull breach, that station would have been flash-burned."

"And she hasn't exhibited any of the traits of a failed martyr," Hyde mused. "So, for the time being, she's been tentatively cleared of any wrongdoing in regards to the containment failure. So what else was she planning to accomplish?"

No one spoke.

"Well?"

"Um, Marshal," Heng said. "At this point, we just don't know."

"Then you'd better come up with something, and soon," Hyde snapped and then turned and stormed out.

And now I have the meeting with Commodore Morian in twenty minutes, she thought savagely. *Suction-feed my schedule to a slobbering sycophantic sacerdot.*

Regis Magnum Shipyards
North Plate, Second Arm
Meeting Room Two-Gamma

Richard Morian was the last to arrive at the meeting. Nearly everyone in the room stood and saluted. "At ease," he said as he returned the salute and took his seat at the table, as did everyone else, with the exception of Sasha Crowe, who merely grinned and waved.

He smiled back at her. *Living the life of a free woman, she might say.* He was curious to find out why an IFMP captain was attending the meeting.

Manda Haal was there, as he might have expected—she knew more about a ship's bridge than most. Dagon Jax and Haltar Sen were also in attendance, but that was understandable. Haltar was, in his opinion, the best navigator in the Sovereign Systems. Haltar looked... fine, but from the reports he'd received from Dr. Jyra Dowd, the only reason he was still on his feet was the medication.

Looking around, he saw his XO, Michael Jadern, talking to his chief engineer, Maxim Volkov, along with three of his subordinates, and Science Officer Dr. Herrick Tobbs standing with Lieutenant Commander Corin Fargo, who would evaluate the new weaponry. But...

Danis isn't here. At first it seemed strange. He'd been catching glimpses of her mind constantly, and though her feelings for Elio were buried in the constant work of training the new pilots, he'd felt her determination to do everything she could to shut him out. So it was with some surprise that a barely familiar face walked over and saluted him.

"Captain Morian, sir," she said crisply.

"Lieutenant Commander Axi Quento, I presume?" he

replied as he stood up, her dossier sliding into his mind—*Was that Danis?* he wondered, and he felt his sister's quiet chuckle. *She's getting better at hiding herself.*

"Yes, sir. I was asked by your XO to attend. Commander Morian asked that I extend her apologies for skipping, but she has a training exercise scheduled."

"I see. And when was this exercise added to the schedule?" he asked.

"Five minutes after she received your communique, sir." Quento wasn't able to hide her grin.

Well, he would miss Danis' opinions, but she was obviously in one of her impish moods. *Let her have it.*

"So, what experience do you bring to this discussion?" he asked, flitting over his memory of her dossier.

"I was squadron commander for three years before marriage," she recited. "When I got pregnant, I moved over to Material Management Operations for five years planetside, then took a posting on the carrier *Prince Royal*. I was second-supervisor to the frigate-bay repair crews. When I decided my boy was old enough, I returned to flying as an instructor."

"An impressive and relevant list of talents," he said. "But, why the changes?"

"A bit personal, sir, but politely, I wanted my son to get to know me. I always knew I'd be flying again someday—and when I became an instructor, he fell in love with flying just as I had. So, he understands me, and I him."

"Well, we're glad to have someone with as much experience —" But he cut off as crisp boot-steps announced the arrival of two Lieutenant Commanders.

"Marshal on deck," they announced.

———

"MARSHAL ON DECK," Commanders Kinna and Fen announced, then rotated to face each other and snapped to attention, as did everyone else in the room. Except Sasha Crowe, sitting in the back.

Please tell me this isn't what I think, Sasha thought.

In strode an impeccably uniformed Marshal Secerna Hyde. Not content to dress in shipboard or jumpsuit, she was in her full regalia, medals gleaming, jacket shoulders pressed and lifted, her flared khakis tucked into her boots.

Oh, it's worse. Sasha wanted to groan. *She's going to power-trip the meeting.*

She marched to the head of the table, saluted, then said, "Greetings, Commodore Morian, captain and crew of the *Avenger*," she began, without releasing the ease. She looked around the table, then said, "I am pleased to announce, firstly, that repairs to the *Avenger* are almost complete. You have had a very important role to play in the war so far, and I can assure you that despite all the damages and... sporadic repairs, your ship will soon be at the very peak of its fighting capabilities. We require only fifteen more days before inspections are completed, and you will be ready to depart for your next adventure."

Sporadic repairs, huh? Sasha thought. In less than a sentence, the marshal had insulted the entire colony of Freyja and their excellent shipyards, which had operated for decades without any Sovereign interference whatsoever.

I don't miss sitting next to the woman every day. But it seems like Secerna misses punching me down. I can't stand her.

"And I am happy to report that the first four ships in the new Vindication fleet, the *Absolution, Benediction, Censorious,* and *Darsana,* are all ninety percent complete. The Second, Third, and Fourth Fleets are at forty-five percent. Their structural work and hulls have been completed, armaments are being installed, and interior work is underway."

Nobody moved except Sasha. She shifted in her chair, happy to be unnoticed a little while longer.

She knew the marshal hadn't invited her to this meeting. In fact, if Jax hadn't mentioned it while bouncing at Morian's approval of the Mirabilis hunt, she might have missed it entirely. And she knew exactly why she was being excluded.

Because I have a big mouth. And I like Richard enough to butt in.

Secerna continued her little speech. "Some of the new features we've pioneered for the Vindication Fleet are impressive. We have new armaments—twin-barrel thirty-caliber railguns with concussive rounds. These will be in addition to the standard fifty-calibers you're used to, but we believe the fleets will eventually shift completely over to the new weapons. The concussive rounds add the same impact to the target, with almost twice the rate of fire and decreased weight per round. They will be much more effective against the new breeds of Blue that are able to repair themselves... by scattering or shattering their armor. They'll be open to killshots."

Secerna paused to collect herself; Sasha could see she'd gotten worked up. *I never could fault her enthusiasm or dedication,* she thought. *But everything else...*

"Analysis of fighter attacks on capital ships has revealed several key points of failure. We've reinforced the armor and added flechette missile launchers to guard those key points. Enemy fighters planning to attack those sections will be unpleasantly surprised."

She smiled at this, and Sasha felt... *Okay, that grin is just a little creepy.*

"Finally, we've taken advantage of the stronger internal structure to add three main guns instead of just one. The Havoc cannon uses G-99 shells, an upscaled version of the M-99. Set to proximity, and at release, you have a cloud of self-guided ballistic missiles. Each gun has a wider angle of coverage. The two fore guns combined can cover almost twenty degrees to port and starboard, and eight degrees vertical. The rear gun is partially camouflaged between the engine housings to maintain the element of surprise."

Sasha technically agreed with all these innovations, but she was reminded of what she'd heard an old general once say. "No matter how many wars we fight, we only ever plan for the previous one." *These new ships could be proof against the tactics of yesterday,* she thought, *but the Swarm always seems to be a step ahead. And these new ships are definitely two steps behind.*

Sasha stood up, stretching languorously. "I think they've stood at attention long enough, don't you, Marshal? And I'd like a word, if you don't mind."

She could just make out Secerna's face between the others. Her jaw clenched a little tighter, but she maintained her composure.

I always forget that she can actually keep her temper in check. When she needs to.

But Sasha had called attention to their stance, and Secerna could either refuse to put them at ease, or give in to Sasha's suggestion and effectively yield the floor.

"At ease," Secerna bit out.

Sasha fought the urge to sashay to the front of the room. *Better to not cause the wrong distractions.*

"Greetings, everyone. For those of you who haven't met me, I'm Captain Sasha Crowe. I've been Director of Project Vindication for six weeks now, a demotion of sorts, mostly because Marshal Hyde and I haven't been working well together."

"Aren't you speaking a little out of turn?" Secerna asked, the veneer of politeness thin enough to cut her.

Sasha ignored the comment. "I only found out about this meeting at the last minute, despite it being largely about my project. I assume an oversight was made—" *A deliberate one.* "—but I'm happy to give you the report myself. And frankly, the project isn't going well."

"What do you mean, not going well?" Richard asked. "Marshal, why the disagreement?"

"She doesn't disagree," Sasha said quickly before Hyde could. "The problem is the timetable."

She set her proj on the table in front of her, and with a

touch on her wristpad, activated the presentation she'd cobbled together. "Marshal Hyde was ordered to pioneer a new capital starship in eighteen months. No starship has ever been put into production within eighteen months—in fact, the usual time is five to seven years."

"Given that we are simply modifying a C-class Defender," Hyde butted in, "it was believed to be a minor problem at best."

The *Avenger's* Chief Engineer, Maxim Volkov, spoke up. "Permission to speak, ma'am?"

"Permission de—"

"If there are shipwide modifications underway, that always causes a problem," he blurted out.

Hyde glared at the engineer for interrupting her. Sasha watched him turn red, then pale as he realized he'd made an enemy of the Marshal. *Richard can protect him. I think.*

"But he's right," Sasha concurred as she flicked to a readout of the structural materials. She understood a little of it herself, if not as much as the people who created them. "Instead of shaping and drawing out girders and supports, these new materials are foamed composite poly-alloys that reduce weight and material consumption. They are pocked throughout like honeycomb, giving them incredible strength—I've seen the tests. Then, each layer is a different alloy with a different stress factor, meaning that they're less likely to bend and warp under strain."

"Then why the negativity?" Richard asked her.

Hyde stood in front of the holo display. "Because she doesn't like the fact that I—"

Sasha slammed her hand on the table. "The V-One fleet is a literal test bed. The structural materials are supposedly improved, but we haven't even done proper shakedowns on the new ships, let alone tested them in combat. While they have done stress and plasma tests under controlled conditions, we haven't done a tenth of the abusive testing that a properly planned ship of the line would undergo. And as she has said, there are already two dozen more of these ships in various stages of construction."

"We are in the middle of a war," Hyde shouted. "If we don't forge new weapons, we will—"

"I have questions about the new weaponry," Lt. Commander Fargo said.

"Which ones?" Sasha asked, glad to interrupt another tirade.

"Those thirty-calibers, ma'am."

Hyde responded, "They are a marvel of engineering, you ungrateful—"

Sasha was through being polite. "What the marshal means," she shouted over Hyde's indignant response, "is that they haven't been battle-tested, and one out of thirty tested broke down in field trials. And the ammunition—"

"What happens if the ammunition falls in the gunnery section?" Fargo asked.

"They can't, you peon," Hyde yelled. "They're packed in noxygel to retard combustion. When you feed the cases into the batteries, it breaks the seal and the noxy breaks down. There are no safety problems."

"Not yet," Sasha contradicted. "But if there ever was, it would go in the books."

Then Richard spoke up. "Pardon, Marshal Hyde? I myself am concerned about the main guns. Three weapons larger than our own Big Charlie? How is the structure modified to handle that?"

"Captain," Manda suddenly shouted. "Something is very wrong. I can feel—"

"I've had enough of this," Hyde hissed. "This is my meeting. I am the only one who's supposed to be talking. And I've had enough of all your insubordination. I will have you all put on report, and *you*." She jabbed a finger at Sasha. "I don't care what I have to do to cancel your contract. I'll shut the entire station down if I have to—"

The lights flickered once, then the room was pitched into darkness.

———

Danis Morian watched from a distance as the newly trained pilots of her command dodged and weaved through the blackness, fighting each other.

She'd grouped them into flights of four and set them into the new sim named Facade 101. It was a simple trick and one that she expected would work well. Each flight saw itself as human. The others were Blues.

It's almost ingenious, she mused as her pilots frantically wheeled around each other, taking shots as fast as they could. *Swarm battles always feel like you're fighting on multiple fronts,* she thought, *as if each of their leaders is committed to an overall plan we can't see, or even comprehend. Since we can't predict their plan, we plan not to predict.* Since each flight saw four other groups as Swarm, and "Swarm" enemies were never shown firing on each other, the pilots had to learn to react as if the killing blow could come from any direction at any time.

Which is exactly what would *happen, but in human battles, we can estimate where the safe zones are. Blues pop up where you least expect them.*

Confident that learning proceeded apace, she glanced at her other screens, where Gian and Jackknife were busy running the TK adepts through Pilot Training 101. Using F-32 trainer modules, they were being given basic training on takeoffs, landings, and flying techniques. *I wish the Academy had done this work for me,* she wanted to grumble.

But she knew that there was always the chance to save someone. She'd been blown out of her cockpit in the first battle with the Blues, over planet Tor. She'd had to rescue Elio from a wrecked battleship over Caerus. If teaching the TK copilots how to actually fly might save a life or two... Well, that was a good enough reason.

The weight of the lost Ranger pilots pressed on her whenever her thoughts traveled down this road. *So many friends gone. And why? Why did they have to die, fighting against an enemy on some sort of religious purge?*

She felt Richard's emotions spike. *I thought I was keeping myself contained better than that,* she thought just before the sim crashed.

She waited for the screen to light up, detailing the error. But nothing came, and the hatch didn't open automatically.

She pushed it up with her own strength and began to climb out, only to find that the entire simulator room was dark, and the other pilots were all beginning to shout.

"Everybody calm down," she heard Gian call out. "Whatever is going on, it's temporary. Lift up your hatches and exit calmly. Stay next to your simulators. The lights will resume shortly."

The clamor dulled to a persistent murmur. She could hear the canopies' inert hydraulics hissing in protest as the students climbed out, the stamping of shipboard boots as they scuffed on the floor.

The lights still hadn't come back on. The only illumination was the faint orange glow of the hallway tracking lights.

"Orders, Domino?" Jackknife asked, and she realized that indeed, everyone was waiting on her.

"Everyone close your eyes," she replied. "Let them adjust to the darkness for a moment. When you open, you'll be better able to see."

She could hear the difference in their voices after she gave them clear instructions. Panic was giving way to calm.

I was never this... frantic, was I? She remembered her training, her first days in the cockpit, and remembered she'd been twenty-five. She'd trained long and hard to reach the position where she could apply for pilot. The ranks were difficult to break through, back then.

The median age of her group of forty was twenty. *That means some of these people are barely out of school. They haven't been at the academy as long as I've been fighting this war. And I'm supposed to make them into... me?*

She pushed the thought aside. *No distractions right now.* "Open your eyes," she said quietly, and the room became full of soft gasps of relief. Now the room was barely lit by the orange trackers, but the room had shape and a path. She led them out into the hallway.

"What happened?" she heard someone behind her say. "What's going on? Have you ever seen a station go dark? Is it the reactor? No, this station has a whole bunch of reactors. One wouldn't—"

She closed out the chatter and concentrated on Richard. *We have a blackout down here. What happened?*

We don't know, he replied. *Most of the communications are out, too. Datapads work, but only short-range. The station structure blocks digital signals, and the repeaters need electricity.*

Danis had no idea how to solve this. And maybe she couldn't. *So,* she attempted a moment of levity. *How did your meeting go?*

Oh, the one you skipped?

Oops. But he didn't sound mad. That was a plus.

Um, I had super-important training to watch, I promise.

Would you believe that this is the best part of the meeting so far?

She laughed. Everyone looked at her in the dim orange light.

Gotta go. She broke connection and turned to her pilots. "I have bad news. Power is out all over the station. We don't yet know the full extent of the problem because comms are all also down except for short-range. So we are going to do this old-school. Follow me to the hangar bay. As we go, we'll stop at every emergency locker and pull depresh suits."

"Um, Domino?" one of the pilots asked. "Why not just kit up everyone right away?"

"That would be a nominal course of action, except I don't know if the station is going to depressurize," she explained. "What I do know is that other people will find that locker and panic when it's empty. But we are going to sit by our fighters. If there's an attack, someone needs to be ready to vac-walk through an airless hangar and launch. And that someone is going to be us."

———

Manda Haal watched the drama play out before her. It sickened her to no end that whining careerists like Hyde still clung to any shred of power they could. Even putting her loyalty to Richard aside, Hyde was the most petty, shrill, annoying ranking officer she'd had the misfortune to—

Her vision swam before her, and she plunged deep into Seeing. It came without warning, as always, but this time was different.

Something was about to happen—a great darkness would descend upon them, but it would be temporary. They would be blind, but eventually they would see again.

They would find a woman. Manda had no idea who she was, only that she had caused the darkness. From the woman emanated a blurred nexus of confusion and chaos.

She saw death and destruction everywhere.

She saw starships exploding in the vastness of space.

She saw starships exploding around Magnum itself.

She saw Swarm ships decimated under a thousand barrages from human fleets; she saw the Swarm destroying everything in their path, then she saw Swarm ships retreat en masse as the humans cheered their victory.

She saw hundreds, thousands, maybe millions of lives, loves, and children perish or prosper. She saw entire planets razed to ashes, entire planets raised in celebration.

She saw Captain Morian lead valiant charges against the enemy and defeat them.

She saw Captain Morian wild-eyed and cursing as his ship was torn to pieces under him.

She saw Captain Morian cold-eyed and merciless, ordering the deaths of those who had betrayed him.

And she saw herself a thousand times—dead, alive, alone, with friends, entwined in the arms of a man she couldn't see—

How? What? She wanted to scream as the image of herself was torn away in the tumult. *Wait. I've waited so long. Who is it? What do I have to do?* She *pulled* at her visions and somehow gained a level of control she'd never had before. She saw herself again and again—

—the bridge was aflame as she burned in agony—

—the viewports shattered, and she was drawn to oblivion—

—a shuttle explosion engulfed her—

—shot in the darkness—

—stabbed—

—beaten to death—

—and again embracing, kissing, loving someone whose face she couldn't see—

But finally, the vision dissipated and she once again found herself looking at the woman. Alive, dead, shot, strangled, stabbed, alive, helping, betraying—

She had no idea how one person could be a lynchpin for so much, and she had no idea how to sort the torrent of images that battered her mind. Every timeline tumbled one atop the other, and she couldn't make sense of any—

It stopped.

She found herself clutching her head, her eyes clamped tight.

"Captain," she shouted. "Something is very wrong. I can feel—"

"I've had enough of this," Hyde hissed. "This is my meeting."

She tried to tell him, tried to shout over the angry marshal. But her voice was too weak, the pain and exhaustion slamming into her harder than ever before.

And then it happened. She knew as the darkness descended, even as others gasped in fright. She forced her eyes open, but of course... there was nothing there.

CHAPTER
SEVENTEEN

SHADOW OF CORRUPTION

Justification **Crew Quarters**
Inbound to Planet Citrom
Naranj Star System

"Attention, all hands. Attention all hands," the intercom crackled to life. "All ship's crews to duty stations. Shift change will be in three hours. All combat marines are to report to muster rooms immediately."

"Time to get up, Feria," First-Corporal Dusina said. "Prince Tarak has another mission for us. And this time, don't try to be a hero."

Lagu Feria opened his eyes to find his view blocked by a mass of tight braids before Dusina rolled off the outer edge of the bunk. She always took the outer edge.

"Up, second-corporal," she barked as she pulled her braids back into the ponytail she preferred. "You need pants."

"Four days in this damned destroyer," Lagu groaned, "with nothing to do and no information, and suddenly his High-Waisted Pantsness decides we need to gear up and get ready to deploy."

"Quit your whining, Lagu. If you recall, you're supposed to take orders from me," Dusina scolded as she pulled on her shirt. "And am I 'nothing'?" she snapped, insulted. "You've been doing 'nothing' for four days?"

"But I liked the orders you gave an hour ago better—ow," Lagu said as his pants collided with his face. "That was the buckle."

"Well, maybe you should belt your mouth shut," she retorted. "Just because I'm a flirt doesn't mean I don't have feelings. Jerk."

But she smiled as she said it.

He rubbed his cheek. The buckle had stung. "Well, at least we won't be bored today. Time to go kick some ass, I think."

In only thirteen minutes, Captain Objur and the twenty-five members of Border Control Platoon 27, who were now under the command of Prince Tarak after the success of their last mission for him, were assembled in the muster room, along with two other platoons Prince Tarak had taken aboard en route. Lagu had met some of them during the three days since they'd boarded. They were good soldiers, but all of them were Psy.

The prince seems to have a vested interest in certain types of people, Lagu pondered as they waited.

At fifteen minutes and thirty seconds, Prince Tarak swept into the room, flanked by two operatives in paramilitary attire. Their faces were covered, and they moved stiffly. Lagu wondered what was wrong with them. *They don't seem to have mental auras,* he realized. *Some of those smugglers had halos that blocked Psy. Maybe these guys are special infiltrators?*

"Thank you, Captain Objur, for meeting with us," Prince

Tarak began. "Thank you, Sergeants Strigett, Toccare, Volen. We have arrived at Citrom, and we will be debarking in two hours and twenty... seven minutes. Under the Sovereign Edict 235-47.39, regarding Interplanetary Commerce and Trade, criminal elements of Citrom have been proved to be involved in conspiratorial acts against the hegemony of the Sovereign Stars. Since I, in my capacity of prosecutorial authority on Geb-nute, have discovered these criminal acts, I am authorized to act in accordance with... a great deal of very pompous language that I'm not going to recite to you now. The point is we are now en route to a holding pattern in orbit, where we will disembark in drop shuttles. The transponders have been equipped with programming that will allow us to see traffic patterns without having to go through the onerous burden of requesting clearances."

"Pardon, sir, but why?" Captain Objur asked. "And, for that matter, how?"

Tarak stared at him, then said, "I have received intel that another of the... things we recovered and destroyed at Geb-nute has been obtained by a criminal organization called the Dawn Fan. We are to remove it from their possession with all haste and prejudice, as well as anything and everything that could possibly be connected to it."

"Prince Tarak, sire," Master Sergeant Strigett said. "With all due respect, are you telling me we flew to the outer expanse of Sovereign territory to bust a few *narcotikas*?"

"With respect, Sergeant, it's because I ordered it so." The prince had a thin smile that didn't reach his eyes. "Nevertheless, these aren't narcopeddlers or protection racketeers. Somehow this group has become the premiere source for Swarm salvage. They are providing matériel salvaged from various battlefields to interested parties. Matériel that is already considered Sovereign property under the Royal Claim to Military Salvage. More importantly, they are using this matériel not just for profit, but for development. And the last thing any Sovereign government needs is Swarm technology being used on-planet by criminal or disloyal actors. Datapads up!"

Everyone in the room pressed the "accept link" button, and the pads all trilled for a few seconds as information streamed in.

"You, each and every one of you, now have the basic tactical information of our strike on the Dawn Fan site. Study it thoroughly. Be at your assigned drop shuttle in two hours, at... 21:30 precisely. And," he said and smiled, a real smile this time, "go to work knowing you're about to make Citrom a much better place."

———

Planet Citrom
Ligarch's headquarters?]

Praeser carefully balanced the tray of fine crystal as he entered the office of his master, Hirana Ligarch. His master was a harsh and exacting leader, with a network of spies throughout the Sovereign Systems Upon the carefully etched tray were the master's afternoon staples: three small sandwiches of Ortavian raikh with vagary cheese, a glass of Epos synth—a vintage older than Praeser's father was when he died—and a pelum fruit, cut into thin wedges.

Master Ligarch had no need to explain why he preferred fruit worth a single credit when so much else was within his reach, but sometimes Praeser wondered.

Praeser also carried a report from one of Master Ligarch's many employees, serving in other places such as the peacekeepers, the pharmaceutical industries, or the ranks of parliamentary aides.

He placed the tray upon Master Ligarch's desk and stepped back, awaiting his master's response.

As usual, Master Ligarch began by swirling the chalice

lightly to inspect the scent. He inhaled deeply but did not drink. Then he methodically ate the pelum a bite at a time, interspersed with bites of the sandwiches. He sniffed the glass several times but didn't drink any until the end of his meal. Finally, he lifted the envelope with the report, glanced at it, looked at it, then looked at it again, this time in anger.

Praeser remembered a time when his master hadn't been so quick to enrage, but those days were three years in the past.

"Why wasn't this brought to my attention sooner?" Ligarch demanded.

"My apologies, Master," Praeser replied, trying not to cringe. "I was not given to know what it contained. If it is a matter of urgency, I can only tell you that it came from Mister Belos, who often delivers messages from the Spaceport authorities."

Master Ligarch's eyes narrowed. "I will have Fiestro speak to Mister Belos later. Now, I have business. Come with me to the dressing room."

Praeser followed obediently. He began undressing Master Ligarch, pulling the shirt away to reveal the marks that had appeared after the Swarm attacks began. He began to fit a white shirt upon his master.

"No, you fool," Master Ligarch snarled. "I have business to attend. The black shirt."

Praeser didn't know what the ⚡⚡ marks meant—they looked like lightning bolts—or why they were there. He only understood that they appeared before and when his master became angry.

But that didn't matter. If Dewos Above meant for his loyalty to be tested, then he would prove himself the more honorable for serving.

———

Planet Citrom

Lagu Feria's stomach struggled to reach equilibrium. The drop shuttles had done just that; *drop*. After a screaming ride down through the atmospheric night, the shuttles rocketed across the cityscape only a hundred meters above the rooftops.

In the enhanced vision of his goggles, buildings flitted by in shades of infrared and ultraviolet, entire neighborhoods of grav traffic leaving trails of reflective energy as they scattered. Then the shuttles had abruptly halted before a monstrous building, clearly what once had been an intersystem-funded manufacturing concern before it had fallen into disrepair.

The drop lines had fallen, and Border Control Platoon 27 was out in moments, firing at anyone below and securing a foothold position just inside the building's perimeter fences. The prince's shuttle hovered above, his strange specialists sniping at any visible observers or guards visible.

Platoon Twenty-Seven, you have your objectives. Strigett's Psy voice sounded harsh. *Secure and defend, then push forward.*

Lagu and Dusina dashed forward toward the northeast corner of the building, firing at anything that moved, while Strike Sergeant Metlock and Second-Corporal Perru each led their pairs to positions near the known exits.

Dusina pulled her doormaker from her belt and slapped it in the position where schematics indicated there would be no structural beams. "Two minutes to make a boom." She grinned at Lagu. "Fun, fun, fun. Maybe if you get a promotion, you can have fun, too."

"I had plenty of fun without one earlier," he snapped as he edged backward to a safe distance. "And if it's so much fun, why doesn't Metlock do it?"

"Have you ever seen Metlock have fun?" she asked. "Hey, you feel off. What's up?"

Lagu replied, "I guess I'm pondering the morality of the 'guns blazing' approach the prince ordered."

"This is a major crime hub," she replied. "Most everyone

here is involved with a dangerous crime of one sort or another. Simple."

He thought about that until she said, "Party time" and hit the detonator.

The reports of simultaneous explosions all around the building shook the night air as Lagu jumped through the smoking hole, sweeping the room, with Dusina close behind. His Psy sense didn't perceive any life, but with the new halos that wasn't a given.

He fired a quick spray across the exposed furniture, the high-impact shells exploding anything they hit into flinders and shrapnel.

"Room clear," he shouted as Dusina took point to the next room. A quick spray of bullets and a "Clear" later, Lagu ran through and checked the next room.

They proceeded in like manner, occasionally firing frag grenades down hallways they didn't have time to explore, until they reached BC-27's meeting location. They were mere moments behind Metlock and Perru.

You're late, First-Corporal Lady, Perru mocked.

Yeah? I got to use a real bomb. Dusina made a rude gesture. *You just had doorbells.*

Yeah? How many frags did you set off?

Enough, Metlock ordered. *Dusina, you take point down a level. Perru, you follow and assist. Condi and I are meatshields up here. Go.*

Dusina and Perru took off for the stairs, with Humba trailing Lagu by a step. *Why's Met staying behind?* Humba snapped. *Is it that bad downstairs?*

The sound of DEW fire erupted behind them.

"They have DEWs in here?" Perru shouted, verbally. "Why aren't we packing lasers?"

"Because we're here to break Blue toys," Dusina snapped at him. "If they have Blue armor, lasers lose instantly."

They clambered down the stairs and through the next stairwell, halting abruptly because there was no floor there.

"What the stars?" Humba muttered.

They were standing over a three-story underground complex created by the destruction of the two previously existing floors. The broken concrete of their floor ended about a meter from the opening. And below, they could see every kind of...

Pieces of Swarm starfighters lay everywhere, some of them suspended from cables. Technicians looked like they were trying methods to reassemble the pieces into a complete ship. There were bodies of Blue soldiers, somehow not entirely destroyed. There were scorch marks on the walls—clearly someone was experimenting with reactivating plasma weapons.

What's the call, Corporal? Lagu asked.

Dusina glared at him. *Duh. Back in the stairwell, and keep running.*

They cleared the next two flights without problems, but when they reached the door, it was fused shut. "You got any more doormakers?" Lagu asked.

"No, he only gave me the one," she grunted. She pulled against the door, but it refused to budge. Lagu reached out to Metlock and Condi—

Nothing? From either? Some strange pressure was affecting his mind, and he didn't like it.

"What about frag grenades?" Humba suggested.

"*Fornhal,* no," Dusina said. "In this enclosed space? The shrapnel-bearings would ricochet right up the stairwell."

Lagu reached out to the other BC-27 teams and couldn't find them either. The pressure increased.

"Well, do you have any better ideas, *First-Corporal?*" Perru demanded.

Lagu shoved Perru for his tone. "Has anyone been in contact with the other teams?"

Dusina's mind focused for a moment. "That's funny. I don't feel anyone else."

Humba and Perru immediately tried as well, but Lagu knew what they would find.

"It's like they aren't even there. And when I try, I start getting a headache."

"There's something badly wrong in this area," Lagu surmised. "Maybe it's Blue, or maybe it's human, but whatever it is, it's blocking Psy. My guess is it's interference from something inside that room, because we could connect earlier, and now we can't. And if our teammates had died, we would have felt it."

"So now what?" Perru demanded.

"I guess we need to go up a floor and find our way down," Lagu said.

"But how—"

"It doesn't matter," Lagu insisted. "We have a job to do. In fact, we have two now. If this door is sealed, the others are too. We need to spread out and blow the doors open."

"For the other teams?" Humba asked.

"Maybe. But also because we might not have a good route back up."

"You heard the fool," Dusina barked. "Up and jump."

They ran back to the previous floor and opened the door, where they were confronted by several options; none of them good. "Don't you sometimes wish we'd gotten TK instead of Psy?" he asked Dusina.

"Why? I'd just push you around the harder," she said with a smile. "This was your crazy idea, so go first."

———

PRINCE TARAK's shuttle landed just beyond the three-story building. The ramp dropped down with a tremendous bang and he marched out onto the concrete pad, halo on his brow and a heavy TC5 railgun in his hands. He paused for a moment, his right hand held high to halt the assault troops jostling for position behind. He could feel every marine already in the building. He could hear their thoughts. He could see through their eyes. They were performing exactly as he would have expected. But since studying the strange new halos, he was beginning to understand the flaws.

He could sense the muffled presence, though not specific thoughts, of the criminals inside. He touched the minds of his squad leaders to let them feel his presence.

And, sure enough, ambushes that might have proven costly moments ago were now foiled as the squads retaliated with prejudice. He received several thoughts that indicated the criminals were using DEW weapons. *They're experienced professionals,* he thought. *And they have combat armor.* But he knew as well as the soldiers how little protection that provided against directed energy weapons.

He felt one fall, then another, and another. And even as he felt the enemy presence dwindle, so too did the numbers of his troops. *But it has to continue,* he thought savagely, gripping the TC5 so hard his gloved fingers ached.

With a thought, his twenty-strong royal guard surged forward, weapons sweeping wide as they sought the prize— someone with information.

His Psy-Ops troops having drawn off the low-level enforcers, he walked calmly across the concrete and entered the building, his guards surrounding him, silent and efficient. They met no resistance.

Once he reached the reinforced bunker at the center of the building, though, it was a different story.

He felt the Psy attacks begin. Though none of them was a match for his strength, the sheer number could be dangerous. He parried their mental attacks and struck back with his own, but with so many targets, he could barely inconvenience one before another took its place. He was wasting time and energy, he realized. *I have to put an end to this,* he thought, *and quickly. Guards! Breach!*

All twenty opened fire together with their heavy DEW lasers and carved the reinforced bunker wall to pieces. The bunker, at some time in the distant past, had been reinforced with dutrinium sheet, but under the terrible, concentrated barrage of the energy weapons, it began to slough away. Once the gap was large enough, his troops leaped through, one at a time. The fighting was intense, but slowly his guards began to make headway.

While some of his enemies were wearing halos that shielded their minds, somewhat, and made them difficult to attack, his guards were totally immune to Psy attack. And, by the time the criminals discovered that, it was too late; they'd been completely overwhelmed.

Prince Tarak, the way now clear, stepped through the hole and continued on to find several of his guards under attack by criminals using TK. Several of them tried to rip the weapons from his guards' hands, but it soon became apparent they lacked the raw strength to do so. And once the guards cleared their weapons from the TK attackers, they quickly cut the enemy down.

Merely minutes later, the immediate area around him had been cleared without a single loss. All was quiet.

Prince Tarak, satisfied with his own progress, reached out to the rest of his teams to see how they were doing, but without success.

Captain Objur; report position and progress. Nothing.

He frowned, concentrated and repeated the thought. Still nothing.

Strigett, Toccare, Volen, report!

But there was no reply. He reached out to their minds, but there was nothing. The thought waves were silent. It was as if they all had died.

He cleared his mind, then closed his eyes and scoured the

building. There was... something... He stepped forward, passed through one room, then another, his guards following closely.

He stopped, closed his eyes again, turned his head slowly from left to right... *There!*

He opened his eyes to find himself staring at a blank wall. He smiled. Behind the wall—he knew—was a computer system junction. He handed his railgun to one of his guards, then stepped forward, laid the flat of his hand on the wall, closed his eyes again and reached inside the system. For a second, he was almost overwhelmed by the sheer number of gigabytes that were skittering through the ether, but he quickly stabilized, then concentrated. He was inside the security system, the entire building laid out beneath him, all three floors and a vast basement. And while he couldn't access the visual images of the monitoring systems, he could sense the frenzied movement below. People moving around, everywhere—people his Psy could no longer locate.

He broke the connection and stepped back, away from the wall.

Psy-jamming? Now we know. This will bear investigation. But for now, I think we have what we came for.

He could feel his target just ahead. He stepped forward and walked several meters to the end of a wide corridor, where he was confronted by a simple wooden door. He nodded to the captain of his guard. The man stepped forward, grasped the door handle and pulled. It opened easily, and Prince Tarak couldn't help but smile at the man's restraint. He'd expected him to blast through the door with his DEW rifle.

The captain stepped aside, and Prince Tarak entered the central chamber; a simple office with a single desk and a chair. Behind the desk, a balding man aged about fifty was leaning back in his chair, his crisp attire marred by a worn sweater jacket.

"So you've come," the man said. "I told him you would. I

told him this might not be enough." He waved his hand around. "But he did not believe me, so he sent them away."

"Sent them where?" Prince Tarak asked casually as he searched the man's eyes and gently touched his mind. And he wasn't surprised to find the man weary of knowing, of watching the events he predicted come to pass. This man was no longer surprised by anything, including life.

He's a Seer.

And his attempt to pierce the man's thoughts further was halted.

"I don't wish to tell you, of course," he replied. "But I will. They went after the girl. I warned him the girl was a danger. But he believed he'd covered all eventualities." The man sighed. "How stupid of him. He has no idea how many eventualities there can be. And thus, my loyalty is repaid... though poorly."

Prince Tarak tried again. The man wasn't wearing a halo, and yet his thoughts, every thrust, were thwarted.

"You will take me to your ship, of course," the man said, resigned. "I'm not a danger. Your medical team will discover that. But I must tell you that I do not plan to speak about these things."

"And I must tell you, I plan to speak of them at length," Prince Tarak replied. "After I make certain no one can profit from this... wanton betrayal of humanity."

"You speak as if you or I are still human." The man giggled. He held up his arms. "Your tin soldiers may take me now."

Two of them restrained the man at Prince Tarak's silent order—just as the entire building began to shake violently.

"Ooh, how exciting," the man said dryly. "I wonder what will happen next?"

―――――

THIS CLOSE TO THE DOOR, Lagu could make out thoughts on the other side. He knew that someone was alive, and that meant that everyone else might be, too. Though it was difficult, he conveyed the danger to the rest of the team and they moved away.

Lagu checked the chron on his wristpad. *Five, four, three— launch now.*

He launched his remaining frag grenades at everything that resembled a door. Across the room, he could hear the rapid *choom, choom, choom* as his team fired their grenades, but by then, he'd ducked under a heavy table.

The explosions shook the entire sublevel. Debris rained down in every direction, and Lagu leaped out into a vast cloud of dust. It was several seconds before it settled enough for him to see the results.

The doors were twisted and mangled but still in place.

A laser beam burned through the filing cabinet next to him. "Stars!" he shouted as he ducked back down and returned fire. His enemies didn't seem to mind the needle-like rail-gun rounds streaking by at more than three times the speed of sound, their lasers pinning him down. He could see them angling to the sides—if he let them, they would corner him.

Guess it's time to be stupid.

No! He felt he could hear Dusina's warning as he dashed to the left, firing wildly.

Ha. That'll show—

He saw the laser flash a moment before the area in front of him exploded. The force sent him flying backward through the air, smashing through everything in his path.

Must have been a power cell... he thought as he picked himself up and, without thinking, threw himself to the left just as another laser flash cut past him and blasted through the wall behind him. He looked around, trying to find a way out of the killbox and instead found salvation in the form of a weapon unlike anything he'd seen before.

It appeared to be part Blue Trooper's plasma weapon and

part... he had no idea what, but it did have what seemed to be a ridiculously large power cell grafted on.

He tapped the power icon. The weapon began to hum and a green light appeared in the power cell window.

Guess we'll find out just how good their R&D is, he thought as he stood, shouldered the weapon and touched the trigger.

In less than a micro-second, a beam brighter than the sun blinked on. When he was able to look again, there was a path of destruction carved all the way across the room and through the adjoining wall, and the one beyond that, following a scorch mark as wide as his hand. His foes were nowhere to be found.

He blinked, stared down at the weapon and found the power setting. *Hey, hey,* he thought. *This thing is set to "vaporize." Let's see what else we have here. Ah, here we go. I'll set it back to "Cut." That way, I won't kill our friends.*

Stand away from the door, he warned, then aimed the weapon at the adjoining wall and touched the trigger. And a fine hairline beam of destruction carved an opening. He kicked it and the chunk of masonry fell in, and the rest of his team scrambled through.

"You ever see anything like this?" he yelled, holding the weapon up for them to see. "I found it over there." He pointed. "There are two more. Grab 'em and let's do this."

———

"So, you're the man who guards criminals' precious commodities?" Prince Tarak said as he marched the balding man out of the building, surrounded by his guards. "You gave up rather quickly."

"And why wouldn't I? I see all eventualities." The man shrugged. "I foresaw your coming. But I follow the path of my life. He calls me his Bishop."

"What do you mean, Bishop?" Prince Tarak asked.

"Oh, it's a very old game," Bishop replied. "Chess. A checkered game board, with pieces representing the members of ancient Earth governments. King, Queen, Bishops, Rooks, Knights and, of course, Pawns. Each one moved a certain way. The Bishop could see the board but only move on one color, diagonally across the board. I must say, the name suits me well."

"Let me guess—Pawns were the ones that were sacrificed for strategy?"

Prince Tarak's forces cleared the bunker walls and made their way to the entrance.

"I see you understand the principles, at least," the man said and giggled. "But I'm afraid you are about to meet a Rook or two."

Prince Tarak immediately threw up a mental shield as a dozen attacks came at once, far more powerful than any so far. Together, they tested his ability to repel them.

It was while he was fending them off that Bishop was able to twist out of his grip. He had a hidden weapon and pointed it at Prince Tarak's head. "Stay your hands, or your prince dies." He barked the order, then giggled. "Drop your weapons. Now!"

At a nod from Prince Tarak, they all complied.

"I'm afraid mine was the better strategy," Bishop gloated. "Your pawns will be removed, and this entire incident will be no more than a footnote in the Sovereign histories. Histories that will not survive much longer," he added as his soldiers poured into the room.

"I know a thing or two about Seers, Bishop," Prince Tarak muttered though he was still concentrating on fighting off his Psy attackers. "Your abilities are limited."

"The limits of my ability do not concern me so long as I gain the desired results," Bishop sneered.

"Very well, I will play your game," Prince Tarak said. "I will make two moves. The first, I will order my guards to kill all of your soldiers. What's the second one, d'you think?"

"You will... eat a sandwich?" Bishop said, obviously

confused. Then he recovered and screamed, "Kill all his soldiers now."

The sound of DEW lasers quickly abated as Prince Tarak's twenty guards used their enormous strength to physically crush Bishop's soldiers, and with a twist of his mind, he disposed of the last of the Psy attackers.

One of Bishop's soldiers tried to get up, but the heavy metal foot of one of Prince Tarak's guards stamped on his chest and crushed the life out of him.

Bishop's hand wavered, and the pistol drooped.

Prince Tarak reached out, took it away from him and pointed it at him.

———

Using the prototype plasma weapon, Lagu Feria made short work of the enemy blocking his way.

He learned to blink as he touched the trigger and thus avoided the purple floaties in his eyes.

He looked around. He was on his own,

He shrugged. What he couldn't understand was why the enemy persisted. *Against weapons like these, Sovereign forces would flee the field and regroup.* And while he knew they'd faced similar weapons wielded by the Swarm troopers from the beginning, he also knew it took an inordinate amount of guts to charge the Swarm bastards. *But these criminals throw themselves at us, seasoned Sovereign marines, with no strategy at all. It doesn't make sense.*

But soon, the room was quiet except for the humming of machinery.

"Attention," he felt Dusina call out faintly. "...room not cleared. Commence grid search in pairs or..."

He reached out to her but couldn't find her. *So, this is simple,* he thought. *Grid search in pairs. Clear the room.* He reached out to the other members of the team but found only an unfamiliar mind, a member of another team. At his touch, she began to make her way toward him.

As she came into view, he saw her face was covered by a tactical mask and she was carrying a skinny-barrel DEW rifle, a different kind of weapon to those issued to his team.

She was much smaller than most marines; slight, girlish. Most of the female marines he'd known were physically imposing and worked out constantly, but not this one.

Hey, she reached out to him. *I'm Hallie, well, my real name is Hallaba.*

Hey, Hallie. I'm Lagu. My partner just called for a grid search in pairs. You want to join me?

She nodded. *I didn't sense anything.*

Audible call, he replied. *They're using a Psy blocker. Psy works at close range, but that's it.*

The prince will destroy it, Hallie replied. *Don't know why. For someone so interested in new technology, he destroys a lot of research.*

They made their way across the vast room, checking under stainless metal research tables and inside storage rooms, but they found nothing.

You're so tense, Hallie said. He could feel a giggle in her thought.

Hey, I almost got wasted, he replied. *I got shot at by these floppers. With no backup. They're crazy.*

Seems that way, she replied.

Hallie had a strange tingle to her mind. Something he'd not encountered before. He wanted to poke it, test it, but Psy etiquette was drilled into all Psy-Ops troops from day one: never intrude into your teammates' minds. It destroys camaraderie to know that the people you're supposed to trust have violated you.

If you're thinking about me, stop it! Mission first. Mission only.

He smiled to himself and refocused on the search.

They cleared the room, and Lagu flung open the door and yelled, "Clear," then stepped into an even larger room where he found the rest of his team.

I seem to be the ranking member, Dusina reached out. *So I'm calling it. The room is clear. Corporal Rutger, radio the prince and tell him we have the labs secured. And then we wait until he gets down here.*

CHAPTER
EIGHTEEN

———

Prince Tarak, accompanied by half his android guard, made his way down through the building to the lowest floor. He could feel the oppression of the Psy jamming increase. He knew that his Psy-Op soldiers weren't sensitive enough to have detected it in the heat of the battle. And he could only hope that the losses were limited to those on the floors above.

He found the stairwell door opened into a freefall down two more stories to the basement floor, but his Psy-Ops were moving around below. He'd received a transmission that the room was secured—but without Psy, he couldn't be certain. The struggle down below was too fierce.

So he called down.

"All team members, report."

Each of them called out a positive report: no movement. The monitors showed no signs of life. Weapons were hot and ready.

He made his way down to the end of the stairwell, where he found the door had been either melted or burned away. *Plasma weapons,* he thought. *I bet there will be an interesting story in the debrief.*

But for now, he followed the unusual, Psy-blocking force to the center of the cavernous room. After a few minutes of searching, he found what he was looking for: a large, rectangular metal plate and twin metal disks seemingly set into the concrete floor. He could feel the rhythm of computer language emanating from the disks, and he knew. He knew that somewhere below was something new. Something wonderful... or terrible. *But will it help win the war? Or will it destroy all it touches?*

He turned, looked at his guards and said, "Step back and wait here until I return."

He reached through the concrete with his technopathy, activated the elevator controls, and slowly, the metal platform sank into the semi-darkness.

At first he could see little, but then, as his eyes became used to the dim blue lighting, he recognized them: human computers. But these weren't the slim, beautifully designed versions you could buy in the stores. Nor were they anything like those that adorned the homes of the well-to-do. These were parts ripped from every conceivable product, wired and spliced together, the result of some madman's artistic dream. But that wasn't what frightened him. It was what it was all connected to that did that.

He'd seen or been a part of numerous salvage operations since the war began. Queen Zara had sent him to investigate dozens of locations trafficking in Swarm technology. But here he found the writhing, pulsing hearts of a dozen or more Swarm ships, all interconnected with human technology.

And it gave off a constant psychic pulse, like an oceanic tide of mental sewage, constantly flowing and retreating.

He looked around the room and could see a section, an area that had been reinforced with the same technology that had contained the single Swarm brain he'd destroyed on the *Brigallegro.*

Except, the containment field they're using is only enough so they *can't feel it anymore,* he thought. *But if I could feel it up there on the top floor of the building, what was that kind of exposure doing to the people who worked down here?*

Queen Zara would order him to destroy it immediately. And, unlike in times past, he fully agreed with her. This abomination reeked of psychic trauma.

The mental miasma was powerful and would likely contaminate whoever worked on it for more than a very short period of time.

Which means, sadly, that I must learn something from it before I end its misery.

He slipped one of the negation halos he'd taken from the *Brigallegro* onto his head. It didn't stop the tidal wave of sewage, but it did help mitigate it.

And so, knowing he was likely risking his life, he reached out and touched it.

His technopathic senses permeated the human-designed technology and beyond, touching the Swarm tech beating softly beneath.

You! the whisper echoed through the profundities of his mind.

Prince Tarak's presence in the world disappeared.

CHAPTER
NINETEEN

TOO MANY CROOKS

Regis Magnum Shipyard

Dagon Jax couldn't remember a time when he'd been so thoroughly engulfed in darkness.

"All right, everyone, stay calm," Morian shouted. "Calm down. Obviously, the station still has power. Feel the breeze? That's our air supply. It's still working. So it might only be the lights."

"Morian, why are you taking charge?" Marshal Hyde said. "I am the superior officer here."

"And these are members of my crew for whose safety I am responsible," Morian retorted. "Now, reach out, group together and make your way to the door."

Dagon reached, groping, and found Haltar.

"Hey! Watch it, kid. You're messing up my hair," Haltar's voice seemed uncharacteristically strong, and then he chuckled.

"Consider it payback for all the times you ruffled my head and called me kid," Dagon replied as his other arm found a pilot's jumpsuit. "Who do I have here?" he asked.

"Commander Axi Quento," she said quietly. "And I was standing next to Commander Haal, I believe?"

"Yes," Haal replied. "But I'm down here. My head..."

"C-c-commander?" Dagon stammered as he knelt down. "Hold out your arm. I can't find you."

He reached with both hands, groping, and eventually found a shaking hand.

"Commander, are you all right?"

"My head. It hurts, Mister Jax," she replied.

"Here, let me help you up," he said. He grasped her arm and helped her up, and she sank into his arms.

"Just hold... I need a minute," she whispered.

Dagon's thoughts were racing. Manda Haal was in his arms, trembling with pain, and he didn't know what to do to comfort her.

He closed his eyes, remembering times long past. The Battles of Tor and Luna had been the first shots fired in the war against the Swarm. And while *Avenger* was being refitted, there had been a celebration given by the Governor of Tor. The crews of the surviving ships had all been invited to celebrate the victory and mourn the losses.

On the third day, when the celebrations had begun winding down, Dagon had caught sight of a beautiful woman in a long blue dress the color of the morning sky. She was tall, almost a full two meters, and her long blonde hair was arranged in the manner of the Torian women.

And so, not recognizing her in civilian dress and a little the worse for the celebratory punch, he decided to walk over to the beautiful young woman and introduce himself.

And then Captain Morian had joined her and called her "Manda."

And then he recognized her; Commander Haal, the career-driven and humorless officer. But ever since that moment when he saw her in the morning sun, a halo of gold around her head, he hadn't been able to get her out of his head.

And now, the object of his most secret, fervent desires was asking him to hold her.

His thoughts continued to whirl. He'd latched onto every bit of relevant information he could find. She liked chordochime music. She preferred vid shows with planetside instead of shipboard stories. She owned a small trove of *real* books—

"Hey, kid," Haltar called out. "Where'd ya go?"

"Um—" He didn't want to abandon Haltar, of course not. *But, um, clearly I've been ordered by a superior officer to give aid and comfort to, the um... the superior officer.*

"Pardon me, Commander Quento," he said. "Our Senior Navigator could use a hand?"

"Of course," Quento replied, and Dagon breathed a sigh of relief as Manda Haal—Commander Haal— gripped his uniform with almost crushing force. A thought wormed its way past his infatuation—*She's in a lot of pain. A LOT of pain.*

"Reaching for you, Haltar," he said, waving his hand around, but found the pilot jumpsuit again. "I mean, Commander Quento."

"Follow my voice," Captain Morian called as they edged their way toward the increasingly visible doorway and the light beyond.

They reached the hallway to find that even emergency lighting had refused to power up, and the way was lit only by the tiny orange tracking lights that ran along the ceiling.

Haltar looked bad in the orange lighting, but when Dagon pressed him on it, he said irritably, "Look, Jax, I'm not great, but I can manage. Let's leave it at that."

Dagon thought of Manda Haal still hanging onto him. "She's in terrible pain, Haltar. D'you have any of your pain pills with you?"

"Are you crazy?" Haltar replied.

At the same time Commander Haal said, "Absolutely not."

"Look, I'm sorry," Dagon said. "But we have a real situation here—"

"That's enough, Mister Jax," Haal said as she pushed away from him. "Another word and I'll put you on report for harassment."

"He's got a point, Manda," Haltar whispered. "Not the strenjucha, but I have some strong antinausea so I can keep food down. You could take one of those. It will stop the dizziness, at least."

Commander Haal glared at Dagon for a moment but then said, "Fine."

She reached out to Haltar, took the pill—it looked huge to Dagon—and dry-swallowed it.

Dagon's attention was momentarily distracted by two voices behind him. He turned to see Sasha Crowe and Axi Quento.

"I know the business, trust me," Quento was saying.

"I'm not questioning your acumen, Axi," Sasha replied. "Quite frankly, I don't care. I'll lose my contract, but it will be worth it if it puts Hyde behind a reception desk. Stand by for transfer."

They raised their datapads, and Dagon heard the trilling noise that meant that Sasha was sending files to Quento.

And the trilling continued and continued.

What the heck is she sending her?

Then he looked back the other way. Commander Haal was walking, only a little unsteadily, to Captain Morian.

"Permission to speak, Captain?" she said.

"Of course."

"There's an unknown target it's extremely urgent that we find her. I know where she is. Who can you spare?"

"Spare? Manda, people all over the station are panicking. I just had a message from Danis, and she's preparing for war with a host of cadets."

"Sir?" she emphasized. "This is *vitally important.*"

Dagon saw Captain Morian's eyes change, even in the dim light. "Who do you need?"

"I'll go," Dagon said and stepped forward. He turned and looked at Haltar.

Haltar gave him a stern look and pointed back toward Commander Haal. He'd be all right without Dagon.

Haal looked at him, heaved a deep breath, then said, "Fine. That's one. Who else?"

The captain looked uncertain for a moment. "Manda, we don't have any combat marines here. This is a group of bridge officers."

"I'll go," Quento said. "I have combat experience, sir."

"More than a hair, Commander, but yes, and thank you. Chief Volkov, can you spare two of your people?"

Volkov pointed to two, a burly man and a slender woman.

"Well, then," Haal said, "let's go find this... whoever she is."

REGIS MAGNUM SHIPYARDS

MANDA HURRIED ALONG THE DARKENED, empty corridors, her impromptu group following closely behind. Even in the dark, she felt as if her steps were perfectly planned.

Even now, after more than three years, she didn't fully understand her gift. It wasn't something she could call on whenever she wanted; it came and went, and it always left her with a knowledge no person should rightly know.

Do I see the future as it's been written? she had often wondered. *Or do I see the future at the point where it becomes written?*

She thought of the battles where she'd known ahead of time that enemy forces were arrayed against them. They'd survived those moments with nothing but minutes of warning from her. And they'd been nearly destroyed when her visions had suddenly changed.

Could they influence the visions? she wondered. *If their decisions ripple to me at the time they make them, then could they change their plans at the last minute? Or would planning to change the plan negate my warning entirely? And who are* they?

Whatever else she might wonder, the vision she'd just received might have given her a clue. She had seen an event that hadn't yet happened and wasn't yet written yet—at least, that's what she thought—an event that was perhaps a focal point for events that would take place days or even months away, and she had to find out.

The woman could live or die, and never know who would pull the trigger or plunge the knife. And Manda could only hope that she could get there in time and make the right decision.

And if being there is the wrong decision, she thought as they hurried onward, *I've already lost.*

More than any other time, she wished she hadn't been gifted with the power of Sight. The uncertainty of it caused her to be hesitant, fearful of making decisions without it, even as she feared making decisions based on it without foreknowledge of the outcome.

She came to an intersection, a confluence of four hallways. She stopped and stared back and forth, not knowing which one to take.

She closed her eyes. *The one to the right? Yes!* It felt right. *Here I am again, trusting a power I barely understand.*

"Wait here," she said. "All of you."

"Ma'am—" Jax began to object.

"I said, stay here, Lieutenant," she snapped and immediately regretted her harshness.

Inwardly, she shook her head as she turned and began to walk away, only to hear footsteps echoing behind her.

She stopped and turned. Dagon Jax was following her. "I gave you a direct order, Mr. Jax."

"I'm sorry ma'am," Jax replied. "But... we're bridge crew.

You know I can't let you do this on your own. I would be charged with dereliction if anything happened to you. So, order or not, I cannot allow you to do this alone."

She stared at him for just a moment, then sighed and said, "Very well. Follow me." Knowing full well he would have followed her anyway, regardless of her rank and orders.

The thought was somehow comforting as she picked her way along the darkened hall.

No one wants to be alone, she thought.

———

REGIS MAGNUM SHIPYARDS
Detention Block A-23

ALONE IN HER CELL—BEING held on suspicion of spying after getting caught using a datascreen to access secure, unauthorized data—Kasa Su-Mei waited. The featureless room would have bored any other human, but Kasa wasn't any other human. She had hundreds of petabytes of information stored in her implant. She could peruse vids, all of her recent conversations, documents, files...

Unfortunately, that also meant there was nothing new to watch. *Still,* she thought, *it beats staring at the wall.*

But she waited, and she waited, until only twenty-seven seconds earlier than she'd anticipated, the power went off and she was in darkness until... the dim orange of emergency lighting snapped on and bathed her tiny world in tangerine-colored stillness.

Kasa had always had a good sense of time, even in a cell surrounded by... nothing, and she'd been able to predict the power outage for the station lighting *almost* to the minute.

Wirelessly, her implant hacked the electronic locks. The door opened—her nanomod eye activated, showing her things no human could see. The entire makeup of the shipyards was rendered as a three-dimensional model downloaded into the memory core implanted in her temple. Shielding the core, a thin Terrium metal foil acted both as a scanner block and a decoy—her medical records stated the head wound she'd received during the Battle for Tor had necessitated the insertion of a med plate that covered the very real hole.

I offered my life in exchange for my parents' freedom, she thought as she followed the diagram out of the cell block to the public hallways, hacking one closed door after another as she went.

Hirana Ligarch had no problem taking my implants two steps further, she thought as she passed through into the detention center reception area, still unopposed in the total darkness.

She had almost reached the main intersection, when her eye picked up a signal from two people—not station personnel, but Ligarch soldiers.

I guess they're here to rescue me? she thought as she approached the final pair of doors that led out into the station.

The doors opened, and the two Ligarch soldiers stepped through.

The signal she received from their implants displayed their names and identified them as members of the Tupeti, which she knew meant they were special forces trained to infiltrate, steal, kill, and destroy.

They must be here to rescue me, she thought. *That's not what I expected; not at all.*

She planned to make her way, on her own, to the escape point as the original plan called for.

"Tachier, Stakon," she greeted them. "I am glad to see you... Ughhh." She stopped talking when Stakon punched her in the stomach.

Stakon was huge; an enforcer and, standing two-point-two meters tall and weighing in at one-hundred-forty kilograms—

not a single gram of it fat—he was one of the biggest men on the Ligarch payroll.

With one huge hand, he grabbed her by the neck, lifted her off the ground and threw her across the hallway. She slammed into the wall and slid to the ground.

"What's—" She managed just a single word before Tachier backhanded her.

He leaned in close. She could smell his breath. "You were caught," he whispered.

"Yes, but it's not like—" But he struck her again. Her head slammed back against the wall.

"It doesn't matter," he said, then stood upright and kicked her in the stomach. "You were caught." He kicked her again, "And that means you've been rendered useless."

"Let me," Stakon said as he stepped forward, leaned over and grabbed her by the neck. Then he gently, almost reverently, lifted her off the ground.

"Sssssstak—on, wha..." she choked out.

"You have failed in your responsibilities," Tachier said, standing on tiptoe so he could reach her ear.

"I can... still..." she tried to say, "be... usssseful?"

"Our employer," Tachier said, "has decided his investment hasn't delivered and so must be... liquidated."

"Not iffff... I'm dead."

"I'm sure the moderate return this raid will furnish will balance *your* account." Tachier sighed. "And, of course, your parents will continue to work."

Her eyes bulged, though from rage or lack of air, it was difficult to say.

"An' you already been replaced," Stakon laughed. "Ya not one of us no more."

She clawed at Stakon's unyielding arm, tried to kick him, anything to get a breath of air. But to no avail.

"You there," a voice behind them shouted. "Drop whoever that is and put your hands behind your heads."

If Stakon hadn't turned slightly to see who was yelling, she wouldn't have managed to see either of them, but she did, two figures in shipboard uniforms; not station jumpsuits like the one she wore. Both were armed. Neither looked confident.

She heard the woman yell, "That's her. She's the one. Ohhh. I can feel it changing. It hurts."

Stakon smiled and squeezed a little more. The emergency lighting suddenly seemed so much brighter. Her head was spinning. She kicked, flailed her arms, trying to hit him, but he just seemed so... far... away...

The crack of a pistol. The thud of a body. *Huh?* she thought, vaguely curious as Stakon suddenly dropped her. She fell to the floor, coughed, then choked as she gulped lungfuls of fresh, precious oxygen.

Her lungs heaved as she rolled to one side, watching as Stakon rushed at the two intruders, swinging his arms, his pistol seemingly forgotten.

He batted one of them into a wall, then punched the other and grabbed her arm. She watched as he wrenched her around and threw her like a limp towel to the floor with a resounding thud. He turned back to the young man, who now had his pistol aimed shakily at him. She winced as he fired. The shot hit Stakon squarely on the chest. The giant merely laughed and punched him again.

Ligarch wouldn't send them without armor, Kasa thought fuzzily. *Where's Tachier?*

She craned her neck around and found him lying on the ground, his hands clutching his neck, a puddle of crimson pooling around his head.

Lucky shot; clipped him just above the collar. Ah! There's his pistol.

"You have failed in your responsibilities." Those words had completely changed the equation.

She crawled over and grabbed the weapon. Surprised by

how light it was, she realized it wasn't a kinetic pistol; it was a DEW.

Of course. The military switched to older tech sidearms when they realized the Blues were impervious to directed energy weapons. But Ligarch, he has no such needs, does he? And kinetic body armor is useless against DEWs.

Carefully, using both hands, she aimed the weapon at Stakon's huge back just as he pulled back his fist to deliver a killing blow to the woman.

One for the team, she thought as she touched the trigger. Die, you son of a snake!

———

Regis Magnum Shipyards

MANDA WATCHED the beast of a man effortlessly throw Dagon aside before turning again to her.

"Little bitch," he whispered. "I kill you now." He grabbed the front of her uniform, heaved her high in the air and drew back his fist, smiling at her as she waited for the blow that would kill her.

But all she could think was, *I hope Dagon's all right.*

Then she heard a crack, saw a flash of light, and the hand and arm holding her went limp, severed at the elbow, and she dropped to the floor, Stakon howling.

She heard the sound again and saw a thin beam of energy punch through Stakon's head from back to front, and he dropped to the floor in a heap; dead before he hit the ground.

A DEW pistol? she thought. But where? How?

She looked over at the woman she'd been trying to rescue. She looked as battered as Manda felt... and she was holding a DEW pistol in both hands.

Suddenly, her Sight began to flicker; not as intense or overwhelming as before, but debilitating, nonetheless. Several possible deaths she'd seen before flickered through her mind before fading away, to be replaced by a new series of possibilities that flashed through her mind too quickly for her to grasp onto them before they were gone.

One of us was going to die here, she thought as she tried to remember what she'd seen. But it was all too hazy. What she did clearly remember, though, was that had not Jax insisted on accompanying her, she would have died alone. By refusing to obey her order, he'd saved her life. *And the others, too...*

It all seemed so fragile. Her Sight allowed her to know things but not understand them. *If only—*

"Commander," Jax shouted, and she realized that she'd momentarily lost touch and he was trying to pick her up, get her into a sitting position. "Commander, please say something."

"I'm all right, Mister Jax. Thank you," she said, trying not to groan in pain. "Check on the girl."

Jax hesitated.

"Do it now, Jax," she snapped as she struggled to her knees.

He nodded and did as ordered, while she remained on all fours, head down, breathing hard, trying to pull herself together.

Dagon reluctantly went to the girl who was lying propped up against the wall. If anything, she looked worse off than Manda. But then the bloody corpse on the floor moaned. "Help me," he mumbled. "I'm dying."

"Commander. This man is still alive," he shouted and dropped to one knee at the man's side.

The man, whose name Jax learned later was Tachier, was lying on his back, clutching his neck, his head surrounded by a pool of blood.

Not carotid artery, Jax thought. *Apply pressure. First aid locker?* Jax looked around: nothing. *But didn't I see... Has to be. Station protocol: One every hundred meters.*

He jumped to his feet and ran along the still darkened

corridor and, sure enough, as he came to an intersection, there it was, on the wall, a large white box with a red cross.

He wrenched open the doors and rummaged in the dark until he found a package of field dressings and some bandages. He grabbed them and turned and ran back to where Manda was now on her knees beside the girl.

He ripped open the sterile packaging, crouched down beside Tachier and began to apply the dressing.

"He's evil," the girl muttered. "He just tried to shoot you and murder me. Why are you trying to save him?"

Jax glanced sideways at her and couldn't help but wonder the same thing himself. This guy and the dead monster had tried to kill them all.

"I can't just let him die," he said. "Besides, he may have valuable information."

He turned again to Tachier and applied the bandage.

"There. That should do it."

———

Kasa's mind was whirling. *Oh yeah, Tachier is going to have a lot of information, all right: about me.*

She'd gotten caught by the USF Security Corps. Ligarch had sent his goons to find her and kill her. She'd killed Stakon with Tachier's pistol. There was no way this was going to end well for her. She needed to kill him before he could reveal what he knew. The only thing she had going for her was that he wasn't likely to incriminate himself... not immediately, anyway. She had some time to form a plan.

She heard footsteps. Three more people in shipboard uniforms came running along the still-darkened corridor.

"We heard a gunshot," one of them shouted. "What happened?"

The one she'd heard the commander call Jax stood up and said, "We have one dead and two injured. Commander Haal needs to be taken to the Med Bay. This one," he said and looked down at Tachier, "must be kept under close guard. He tried to kill us. I'll stay with this one until you get back."

It wasn't until he knelt beside her again that she noticed he only had two pips on his shoulders. *A Senior Lieutenant giving orders for a Commander?* she thought. *Either the other three are enlisted flunkies, or he's earned some real respect.*

"Sorry I haven't checked on you yet," he said. "How are you feeling?"

"I'm fine," she said, struggling to sit more upright. "What ship are you with?"

"I'm sorry?" he said, seemingly startled by the question.

"You're wearing shipboards, not a jumpsuit," she said.

"Ah. Yes. *Avenger,* USF2918C, Lieutenant Jax, ma'am."

"Kasa de Cevoir," she said. "And I barely rate a *miss.* So don't *ma'am* me."

"Very well, miss," he replied with a polite smile.

All this cutsie banter is great, she thought, *but if he's only a lieutenant, he isn't going to get me anything I need.* "Um, can you help me up?" she asked.

He helped her to her feet. She thanked him, then blinked on her nanomod eye and scanned the area for a terminal; any terminal. *If I can just get access, maybe I can see about reversing some of this. And, not incidentally, making sure Tachier doesn't spill his guts.*

But there were no terminals.

She shut the eye down. In this darkness, she couldn't risk the flicker of images across her cornea to remain unnoticed. *Ligarch only spent twelve thousand on this thing,* she thought. *Tight-fisted... Why couldn't he have sprung for the direct optic nerve upgrade?*

"Can we go somewhere else?" she asked.

"I would like to," he replied, "but this section of the station is new to me." He picked up Tachier's pistol. "I was following the Commander. She... she seemed to know her way around."

Okay, she thought. *Now that somehow sounded suspicious.*

"But I'm sure someone will be back to get us shortly."

She stared at him. In the dim orange light, he looked decidedly nervous.

How could he be so commanding one minute and now so inexperienced? Something must have been driving him; loyalty to his commander? Whatever it was, he's lost his confidence. Maybe I can... I need to get to a terminal.

"Listen," she said, "I know my way around the station. If you tell me where you started, I should be able to find it, even if I need to check a terminal."

"Meeting Room Two-Gamma. But most of the power is out," Lieutenant Jax said. "Terminals should be out too."

"Nope. They're fine," she said without thinking.

"How do you know that?" he asked, frowning.

"Um—" *Idiot. You messed up again.* "I heard one of those guys mention it."

Jax continued to frown. "I think... yes, that makes sense... I think. So, which way do we go?"

"Um, this way... I think," she managed to say without incriminating herself further.

She glanced at him and saw that he'd also retrieved Stakon's pistol.

Sloppy of me, she thought. *Now he has three weapons, and I have none. I'm defenseless.* She blinked on her eye as he followed along behind her. *Well, there's nothing more I can do now. I must try to earn his trust. I need to find a terminal.*

CHAPTER
TWENTY

THE PLOTS QUICKEN

Meeting Room Two-Gamma?

Sasha Crowe flipped through the different settings on her wristpad. *No signal. No signal. Feed unavailable. No—wait.* She was receiving analog signals; old technology, but it was occasionally useful during salvage operations and other EVA activities.

"Sasha?" Secerna Hyde snarled. She was fuming. "It seems there are intruders on the station. How can that be? To my certain knowledge, there's been no inbound traffic during the last forty-eight hours. Sasha? Are you listening to me?"

Sasha looked up from her datascreen. "I'm sorry, Marshal. Your guess is as good as mine."

"Are you certain you know nothing?"

Sasha heaved a deep breath, her anger beginning to boil deep in her gut. "Yes, Marshal. I assure you that neither I nor mine have any idea what's going on. But I'm going to find out, and I'm going to do something about it."

Hyde tried to stare her down, but Sasha was more than a match for the insecure marshal.

Hyde turned away, defeated.

Uh-oh, she's decided to pick on Richard. That should be fun.

Sasha suppressed a smile and continued to work on the analog signal she was picking up. It didn't seem to be random or environmental. It was coming in short bursts, and even with the gain turned up, she could only make out hissing garbles. But then...

"Secerna," she said, "I think I might have something. I think someone is trying to communicate."

"Is that so?" Hyde snapped. "What are they saying?"

"I don't know," she replied. "It's... garbled. I think it's being run through a scrambler. Either that or it's encrypted. It's old tech; not my field of expertise, I'm afraid. Nor that of any of my crew, that I know of." She paused for a moment, then continued, "If we could contact Tiger Wok, he might have someone."

"But we can't, can we? Communications are down." Hyde seemed to find the small victory over Sasha empowering. "Well, I have a solution," she continued. "We already have a security program in place for just such a situation." She turned to Richard and snapped, "Morian, I'm commandeering some of your crew to act as guards. I'm going to the North Plate Central Hub. Once I get there, I can activate it."

"What kind of security program?" Richard asked skeptically.

Oh no! Sasha had a sinking feeling in the pit of her stomach. "Secerna, you can't be talking about—"

"I certainly am," Hyde said, cutting her off. "Project Champion will be proven today."

"But—" Sasha tried to argue.

"Say another word, Crowe, and when this is over, I will have you arrested. Do what you apparently do best—look at your screen and complain about how something needs to be fixed. Commodore, I require your men. Now!"

"Marshal Hyde, with all due respect," Richard replied—and Sasha could tell exactly how much respect he felt. "That's not going to happen."

"Commodore Morian," she snarled. "I am a Marshal of the—"

"You are a scientist," he stated firmly. "You are not and have never been a field commander. I will not, and under article 127.5 dash three dash—"

"When this is done," Hyde shouted at Richard, "I will have you stripped of your commission and your uniform processed into cleaning rags, you mutinous scum. And you, Crowe... Your contract is officially in default. You will find yourself in prison and your people exiled without a credit of the money you signed on for."

"Marshal Hyde. I must remind you that I am a military officer of the United Sovereign Navy in a time of war," Richard replied calmly. "And we are under some sort of concerted attack. Captain Crowe is the daughter of King Lorne. Somehow, I don't see your authority overriding either one of us. Now, I suggest you calm down and let the professionals try to figure out what's going on."

"I will not suffer another moment of your overblown pretensions, either of you," she snapped, then turned on her heel and walked away. "I will go myself," she yelled over her shoulder, "and I will find a thousand loyal soldiers. And I will take back this station from whoever has invaded it, and then I will come for you; both of you."

Sasha groaned in relief, and Richard sighed. "I wish I knew how I offended her all those years ago."

"Believe me," Sasha said. "I've worked with her for months, and I can tell you, it doesn't take much. She's got a chip on her shoulder the size of an asteroid."

Morian just shook his head.

"But returning to the question at hand," Sasha said. "I'm receiving some kind of encoded analog transmission, and I think it's coming from somewhere right here on the station."

"Analog? You mean like radio?" he asked. "But how can you find that?"

She smiled. "We copied the basic designs for your datapads years ago," she said. "But radio works really well in debris fields and with only minimal power, whereas Sovereign x-ray signals take a transmission boost to get past the chaff."

Richard looked thoughtful. "An ancient philosopher once said, 'Humans have no idea how much of their technology can be used as a hammer.'"

"Are you quoting that horrid little book at me again?" Sasha glared at him.

"All I'm saying is, you don't have the knack for reading their communications. But we can disable theirs."

"You mean... blanket jamming? Yes!" Sasha switched to broadcast. "Crowe to *Condor*. Do you read?"

"Yes, Captain," came the tinny reply.

"Asteroid, Bakshish, Crater."

There was a slight pause, then, "Acknowledged! On my mark: three, two, one!" and the transmission cut off, replaced by a hissing sound.

"There," she said. "We're now in blackout, but so are they."

"So what is this 'Project Champion' the marshal seems set on using?" Richard asked. "You didn't seem too... enthusiastic. Is it some kind of weapon?"

"Oh no. It's nothing like that," Sasha said sadly. "But it isn't going to go well. The stupid things can barely march in a straight line without an AI controlling them."

———

Jax followed the young woman—Kasa—down a corridor he thought he'd taken before. As she went, she looked at each of the doors, lit only by the tiny orange emergency lights, until finally she stopped, nodded, stepped forward, looked at Jax and said, "There should be a terminal in here."

She activated her datascreen and tried the door handle—it

was unlocked—opened the door and stepped inside, followed by a deeply confused Jax.

Using the glow from her datascreen, she quickly found what she was looking for and sat down. A few quick taps on the keyboard and she had the terminal operating.

"I'd never have thought to use my datascreen like that," Jax said.

"How often are you in total darkness, Jaxie?" Kasa said, smiling up at him in the soft light from the terminal.

He nodded, thoughtfully. He couldn't think of a time in his life when he'd ever been in total darkness.

Her fingers flew over the keys so fast he could barely see them.

"You're really fast," he said, impressed.

"I should be. I earned three specialist degrees in five years," she muttered as she continued to type.

"You don't do that without knowing how to type," she continued. "You have to create a lot of papers for the professors to ignore. I once had a prof tell me that my immaculately researched, incredibly detailed, and concise thesis on the metallurgical properties of Osfec-12 in starship construction needed to be ten thousand words longer."

"Um... how long did it take you to do that?" he asked.

"About two hours. The scrolling was the longest part."

As he watched her work, he could see the data flickering by at speeds his eyes could barely follow. *I hope this isn't going to take two hours,* he thought as he leaned back against a nearby wall and folded his arms.

———

Regis Magnum Shipyards
   South Plate, Third Arm Drydock
   Avenger, **Med Bay**
   Avenger?'

Manda Haal heard Jax say, "Commander, are you all right?"

"Mister Jax," she mumbled, "thank you for your assistance. I don't know if—"

"Manda, open your eyes."

That's not Jax.

She opened her eyes. The light hurt her eyes. She closed them again.

"Open your eyes, please, Manda. I need to check them."

She did as she was asked. *Too bright!* She tried to turn her head away, but she couldn't. Someone had a hand on her forehead and was shining a bright light in her eye.

The light clicked off. She blinked several times. Dr. Jyra Dowd was standing over her. "You mistook me for Lieutenant Jax," she said.

"I thought I heard his voice," Manda said.

"Oh, really? Then perhaps I should check your ears, too."

Manda tried to smile. She was more than familiar with Dr. Dowd's bedside manner.

"Is he all right? Mister Jax?" she asked.

"As far as I—" Dowd was interrupted by a knock at the door. It opened, and Richard Morian stepped inside.

"Captain," Manda said and tried to get up.

"Stay put. That's an order," Morian said with a smile. "I'm glad to see you're feeling better."

"Better?" Manda was confused.

"Don't you remember?" Richard said. "You took quite a beating. Commander Axi Quento brought you in. These two also had to be carried in. Oh, and Haltar's in Medbay Two."

Manda looked to her right and saw the two men who'd tried to kill her and Jax.

The wounded man was restrained on the bed next to her. His bulky companion was on a gurney covered in a white sheet.

"Doctor," Morian said. "I need to talk with your prisoner. Remove his restraints, if you please?"

Manda saw the clamps open, and she entered the Sight.

"Richard," Manda whispered. She wanted to warn him, but she knew it was going to happen, no matter what she said or did.

"I am Commodore Morian. What's your name?"

The captive remained silent.

"Why are you here?" Richard asked gently.

Again, the prisoner said nothing.

"Why did you attack two members of my crew and at least one other person? Your punishment will not be pleasant. Help me, to help you. Talk to me."

"Hah," Tachier said. "I await the pleasures of your merciful justice system. It will be as a paradise compared to what awaits you."

Richard frowned, pulled up a chair and sat down. "That's better," he said. "So, what awaits us?"

"You have already been betrayed by those closest to you," Tachier whispered. "Even though they don't see it yet, they serve his Will, and they will usher in your downfall. And it will begin—AAAAHHHH."

His shriek was unlike anything Manda had ever heard—except in her vision. She didn't know where it came from or how, but she knew Richard couldn't prevent it.

Dowd ran to Tachier's bedside. "His readings are off the charts," she shouted. "What's happening?"

"AAAAAHHHHHHH," he continued screaming.

"Open his shirt and get out of my way," Dowd snapped.

Richard wrenched the shirt open, and Dowd placed the pads on his chest.

"Clear," she shouted, but Manda knew it was over. She turned her head to look at Tachier and saw the scar on his upper left forearm. It was the one she'd seen in her vision: ϟ a single lightning bolt.

The medbay autodispenser buzzed and injected something into the prisoner's IV.

"What's that?" Richard said.

"I don't know. I didn't prescribe anything," Dowd said, frowning, and glanced at the terminal. "Twenty micrograms of —but that's a lethal dose."

It took only a moment of thought for Manda to make the connection. "That means... someone wanted him dead," she said. "It also means someone is hacking the station systems, and there may be more than one traitor among us."

Morian stared at her for a moment, then said, "That would present an intolerable situation. How do we find one traitor among this... this debacle, much less two?"

CHAPTER
TWENTY-ONE

THE ENEMY OF MY ENEMY

Planet Citrom
Naranj Star System

Prince Tarak opened his eyes to find himself wrapped in a warm, velvety blackness.

Get up, a voice said, deep inside the darkest corners of his mind.

I need to get up, Prince Tarak thought. *But I want to stay down. It's so warm and peaceful. So... peaceful... Isn't this what I want? Peace, stability? I can have that here.*

There is no peace, the voice said. *I have always sought conflict.*

But if you simply stopped, Prince Tarak thought, *there would be peace; no... conflict.*

I thrive on conflict, the voice boomed inside his head. *I search out iniquities and eliminate them.*

As do I, Prince Tarak thought. *If not, I would have no purpose.*

Humans have no purpose, the voice echoed through his mind, reverberating, grating. *They are minuscule, inferior, unneeded. As the ants are to you, so you are to me. They are iniquities that must be destroyed.*

Finally, Prince Tarak understood.

"You are the thing we fight," he said aloud, his voice flat and lifeless in the featureless void. "You are the Swarm."

I am the Will. You are nothing.

"If we are nothing," Prince Tarak shouted, "why have you not already eliminated us? For four years, we have denied you. How can we be nothing? Ants build thriving civilizations beneath our feet while we ignore them. If we are ants to you, then why d'you not ignore us and let us continue on with our minuscule existence? The truth is, we are too many and too resilient to allow you to simply eliminate us. We will fight you forever until we stop you."

I am the Will. I have forever. A single thought spans entire generations of your families. You will be eliminated.

"You are wrong," Prince Tarak shouted. "If we have to, we will fight for generations. You will not win."

I Will you to despair and die.

"You can Will all you want," Prince Tarak shouted. "It won't work. We will defy you. Your soldiers and your ships are not undefeatable. And we're forever learning. Go back where you came from and leave us in peace."

There can be no victory over my Will. We will wear you down. You will suffer the slow but inevitable loss of your existence.

"Then the last human will spit his defiance in your face as you crush him," Prince Tarak snarled.

So be it, the voice said calmly. *I Will you all to be crushed. And I Will it to begin... with you.*

And suddenly, the warmth was gone, taking the comfort with it, leaving Prince Tarak floating in a sea of cold, of emptiness that chipped away at his resolve, his very being. He wanted to shout his defiance at the Will, but the thought of uselessly shouting into the empty void made him feel weak and impotent.

He mustered his mental reserves, cloaked himself in the power of his Psy, and willed himself to be whole.

"I can be whole," he whispered to himself. "I will not succumb to this emptiness. I will center myself, and *I will* return to my world."

And then... he sensed another presence.

Who are you? the presence asked.

He heard it. He felt it. It was much like the one before, but as an infant might be compared to a full-grown marine.

"I am Tarak," he whispered. "I am a human. The Will has declared it will destroy me and my people and that it would begin with me. Have you come to kill me? If so, I defy you."

I... am Dek-On-Pen-Nwn-Dwo.

There was a moment of silence, and Prince Tarak again, for that brief moment, felt the oppressive emptiness, and in that brief moment, he prepared himself to die.

But then, the voice said, *I want my people to be **free.***

PRINCE TARAK AWOKE, opened his eyes, breathed deeply, then looked around. At first, he saw nothing, but it was warm, and he knew he was lying on his back.

There were people. He could feel them everywhere. He could feel them all the way out to the edges of the city and beyond. He knew where each and every person, animal, and insect walked, slept, and burrowed.

What happened to me? he thought. *My power has been enhanced. Whatever gods there might be in the universe—*He stopped short.

He'd met a god. Or at least something more god-like than

anything he'd believed in before. And it had sworn to destroy the human race.

And if I feel all this after mere moments in their world, what must their power be like?

He pushed himself upright, pulling the electrode patches off his chest, to the consternation of the medic.

"My prince," the medic pleaded, "Please lie back and rest a while longer. We're trying to evaluate the state of your health in the wake of the incident."

"Incident? What incident?" he gasped as he staggered to the door, then out onto the shuttle's ramp and stopped, his hand on the bulkhead, head down, breathing hard. He looked up, and he knew. A pillar of smoke some thirty meters wide and a kilometer high was billowing out of what once had been the three-story building.

"Prince Tarak, Prince Tarak," the medic babbled. "No one knew where you were. We couldn't find you. The techs and soldiers were removing everything we'd found, but you... you were nowhere to be found. It was only after one of the Psy-Ops mentioned having seen you in the sublevels—"

"Were any of my people killed by the explosion?" Prince Tarak interrupted him.

"Well, no, sir," the medic replied. "That's the strange thing. They should have been, but by some happenstance, everyone was outside. They all recall being ordered to leave the building, but no one gave any orders to evacuate."

Prince Tarak didn't believe in happenstance.

Luck is for those without understanding.

And suddenly, the place the Will intended to attack became clear to him. But the plots involved... they weaved and intersected to form a tapestry more complicated than Prince Tarak could ever have imagined.

After its defeats, the Will had set in motion a series of events —some of which Prince Tarak himself had participated in—

diversions that would create the perfect storm of confusion to cover the real attack.

"They found you curled up next to the machine, sire. You seem to be in excellent health, but we really—"

"I have business," Prince Tarak said sharply as he turned and walked unsteadily back into the shuttle.

He stood for a moment, his eyes closed, then opened them and pulled on his shirt. After a few moments of deep breathing, he turned again, stepped out onto the ramp and then walked purposefully to the shuttlecraft where they were holding his prize prisoner.

Bishop looked at him and giggled.

"What was that thing below the basement?" Prince Tarak snapped.

"Didn't you figure that out?" Bishop said. "It's a device we created for talking to God."

"I don't believe in God; any God," Prince Tarak spat. "And if it was, why would it bother to tell me its plans to exterminate the human race?"

He probed Bishop's mind, only to find it blank.

"Not so easy, is it?" Bishop said with an annoying grin.

Tarak launched an all-out assault on his mind, but each of his quick, deft attacks was met only with blankness. It was as if Bishop was wearing some kind of protective halo, but he wasn't. In the end, Prince Tarak had to give up.

"Tell me about your God," Prince Tarak said finally.

"He's not really *my* god," Bishop replied. "I just work for his disciple."

"And he protects your mind?"

"No," Bishop said. "He just taught me how to frustrate you."

"Tell me how the Will intends to attack the Orso System," Prince Tarak demanded.

"Oh, no, my Prince," Bishop said. "I couldn't tell you that. That isn't how it—"

Prince Tarak, his anger rising, closed his eyes and dipped into the well of new-found strength. His head swam, every nerve in his body tingled and, with a single thought, he reached out, gripped the shields that kept him at bay from Bishop's mind, and wrenched them aside.

"Wait!" Bishop gurgled. "What... are... you..."

"You are right, maggot. I am frustrated," Prince Tarak snarled. "See how it feels now!" And he stabbed deep inside the man's mind and began to read his thoughts.

He was aware that the man was gasping and that the medic was urging him to stop.

No! I will not stop, he thought savagely. *Somewhere in here, there must be a way to stop this from happening again. There must be a weakness I can exploit or some flaw in their tactics. I have to find an answer. Give it to me.*

When he finally let go, the man, the Bishop, was no more, and Prince Tarak let his mindless body slump in his restraints.

"My prince, what have you done?" the medic cried out. "Even you can't execute a man like that."

"I merely interrogated him," Prince Tarak stated. "It was the only way. He was able to block my... my more... conventional method." *Even though I invented this method only months ago. How did he learn how to block me? No one else has... ever!*

The medic was calling for help, even as he ripped the man's shirt open to reveal a strange-looking symbol branded into the man's chest: ⚡⚡. More medics rushed in and crowded around Bishop, discussing whether or not there was a chance of reviving him.

But Prince Tarak knew better. He'd destroyed the man's mind. Bishop had committed abuses more terrible than even Prince Tarak wanted to think about. And Bishop had committed them all in the name of his mysterious leader.

But Prince Tarak couldn't stop thinking about the abuses. The man's thoughts reverberated through his mind. Everything he'd overseen was there for Prince Tarak to see, understand and duplicate.

And the terrors of every human Bishop and his cohorts had abused or killed were also there for him to see as well. Their faces crowded his vision. They wouldn't leave.

He went back to his shuttle, to his medbed, and lay down. He closed his eyes. The faces were still there, staring at him reproachfully, and he promised them he would find the one who'd orchestrated their pain and eliminate him.

Eventually, he fell asleep, their cries of pain still echoing in his mind.

CHAPTER
TWENTY-TWO

ON THE PRECIPICE

PLANET **Caerus**

Som Orsi Training Center

Meera Seluere waited until after training hours, until everyone else was headed to the mess hall, and then she headed down the secluded hallway to see Dr. Zettel.

I know he's considered a criminal, she thought. *But... he's almost always nice and helpful. Why are they so paranoid about him? Because of his Psy, I suppose. I wonder what he's done.*

She arrived at his door to find two guards wearing light combat armor and armed with stun batons.

"I'd like to see Doctor Zettel," she said.

They looked at each other, then one of them knocked on the door. It opened a crack, the guard leaned forward and there appeared to be a brief conversation. Then he turned back to her. "You may enter. But you must not touch the doctor. Do you understand?"

"I do," she replied.

Followed by the guard, she stepped forward through the door to find... not a single room but a nice, comfortable apartment. Soft harmonance music played in the background—something she'd never heard before. Several comfortable chairs were scattered throughout the narrow parlor, and she could hear clinking sounds coming from... *a kitchen?*

"Come in, my dear," Dr. Zettel said lightly.

He was stirring a pot of noodles and tasting a green-flecked sauce; his battered metal helmet glinting under the overhead lighting.

"Hello, Meera," he said, then he looked at the pot and said, "aspanakh. Would you like some? I'm afraid I didn't make much, but—"

Meera glanced at the guard. He was shaking his head.

"No, thank you, sir," she said politely.

He shrugged. "Ah well. It needs a little more time, anyway. What can I do for you?"

The scene was surreal. *He's bustling around a kitchen making dinner while wearing restraints? While guards stand by with batons?*

"Earlier today, you talked to everyone about their powers," she said. "But you didn't talk to me. Why not? Is it because mine is... is useless?"

The doctor's face fell. "Oh, Meera," he said consolingly. "No. Of course not. I didn't mention you because I thought you understood your power. I didn't mean to slight you."

"Understand my power?" Meera repeated. "No! I don't. It's as alien to me now as it was when I first realized I had it. I can only use it when I'm angry or upset. And then it goes away."

"Ah," Zettel said, nodding. "Now that's far more common than you may think. Take Rauf, for instance. Do you think his TK is different than the rest of you? It isn't. He only uses his TK the way he does because that's how it first manifested. He was in danger, he protected himself, and he survived. So that's how he *thinks* to use his power. You likely manifested during an emotional moment, did you not?"

Meera thought back to the first of her "accidents" after

Sorge's death. She'd reached for a glass jar on the spice shelf. It fell off the shelf and shattered, spilling the cepa all over the floor, and she'd... exploded.

"So the first step," Dr. Zettel explained, "is to find your trigger, then identify what it *causes*. May we try an experiment?" He held out a spoon. "I know you can't touch me, but think about the thing that upsets you most while thinking about moving the spoon."

She hesitated, then... *I want... I **need** to understand my power. For Sorge.*

Even now, it surprised her to think of Sorge, to feel the decades of happy memories flooding back, all of them tarnished by her anguish. But inside her misery, she found something more, a shining light that touched the spoon, felt its contours, the gentle curves.

And then it began to lift gently out of the doctor's hand.

———

ZETEL WATCHED the spoon clatter to the ground. He saw Meera's face turn to disappointment.

He fought the urge to crow in delight. *It's there. I knew it. She's no simple TK. She had great power, possibly more than any I've met except for the prince. And all the fools in her life treated her like a piece of garbage.*

"Now, that sensation you felt as you lifted the spoon," he said quietly. "Wasn't it... just incredible?"

She nodded, slowly.

"You could feel it, couldn't you? Every little curve and nuance. I think you might even be able to tell me the metals it's made from?"

"Oh, I don't think—" she stammered.

"You don't need to think, my dear," Zettel said as he picked up the spoon. "You already know, don't you?"

She hesitated. "I didn't always do well in school," she said, "but I remember iron is magnetic, and I can feel the tiny magnetic waves... or whatever. It's different than the other metal. Um, it feels like a coin. Nickel? Is it nickel? And there's something else mixed with it... If it's a steel spoon, then I guess it must be... carbon?"

Zettel smiled, a real, genuine smile. He felt like a proud grandfather. *But enough of that,* he thought. *I have places to be, and they aren't in prison.*

"Now, reach out beyond the spoon," he said. "Feel the world around you."

He waited as she closed her eyes. Her breathing slowed, and his did as well. He watched as her body shifted, her face flickering from emotion to emotion.

"I feel... the room," she whispered. "I can feel the halls, and the rooms. I feel the people in them."

He could feel them too—brushing up against her mind—and he learned everything she learned, and slowly, in the depths of his mind, he was able to build a map of the entire base.

"I can see... everything," she said, her voice full of wonder. "It's so beautiful."

But Eugma wasn't listening. He was feeling something happening elsewhere on the base. Through the girl's power, he sensed the sudden busyness in the comms section. He wanted to focus more, find out what was happening, but her attention slowly widened and drowned out the specifics.

"This is wonderful," she whispered but was interrupted by the buzzing of her datascreen.

The contact broken, Zettel's very normal view of the world snapped back into being, and he forced himself not to stagger at the sudden change. *If I show the slightest weakness, they will suspect.*

Then he realized that it wasn't just the girl's datascreen that was buzzing. The guards' comms were beeping too, and so was the vid screen they'd grudgingly allowed him. It was the base PA system.

"Attention! This is an emergency message. I say again, this is an emergency message."

The datascreens blinked, and the scene on the vid changed to one of the front of the Royal Palace, and a man in uniform stepped up to the podium.

Marshal McAlan, Zettel thought.

"Good evening," McAlan began. "As of four o'clock standard time this afternoon, we have lost all contact with the Regis Magnum Shipyards and are thus in a state of emergency. All military personnel will report to duty stations immediately. All leaves are canceled. To our civilian population; stay calm. We have no reason to think this a concerted attack on the shipyard. You have nothing to fear at this time."

———

MEERA COULD SCARCELY BELIEVE what had happened to her. The sensations she'd felt were... *fantastic, that's the only word for it.* A whole new understanding of... what, she didn't know. What she did know was that some kind of... door had opened for her. And it was a joy to unlock her powers?

She could feel everything in the room. She touched a small table, and it rocked. She touched a chair, and it scooted a centimeter. She felt the woodgrain of the table, the upholstery of the chair, the stuffing that had been replaced... She felt the dirt in the carpets—*Oh. If I was the cleaner here,* she thought, her mother instincts coming to the fore, *I'd give these carpets a good vacuuming.*

"Shouldn't you be reporting for duty?" Zettel asked.

"No. I'm not on duty... Doctor. This is wonderful. But—" Even in her euphoria, her old doubts surfaced. "But is everyone else able to do this so naturally?"

"Naturally?" Zettel looked shocked. "My dear, I've never met a TK with this ability."

"But, when the others—"

"Miss Seluere," Zettel interrupted her, "no one else I know of can feel the entire world the way you do. They use their TK as a blunt instrument. Think of it this way; the others trying to… solve a puzzle while wearing heavy gloves. You can solve the puzzle while blindfolded, just by feeling the curves of each piece." He narrowed his eyes. "How many things did you move that were unfamiliar to you? How often did you manipulate things that were strange and new?"

She thought back. The incident in the kitchen, knocking her jewelry box over, smashing her bedroom furniture—of course—the wooden ball after an hour or so… Klaus, her partner, who had upset her after he touched her. And the robots she tripped, but she'd already been angry at Klaus, so…

"Doctor, I… I don't know what to say," she said. "If there's anything I can do. You know, I mean, because of your—"

"Think nothing of it," Zettel said. "Helping you has been its own reward."

Her datascreen beeped again. This time it was Prince Elio Lorne.

"Attention, everyone," he said. "Because of the situation at Magnum Regis, we are on standby. You will ready yourselves for imminent deployment. I know your training is incomplete, but if the shipyards are under attack, they must be defended. We meet in Conference Room 12-B-3 in fifteen minutes, battle dress required. Elio out!"

She looked at the doctor. "I need to go," she said. "But thank you. What you've done, how you helped me, it means the world to me."

And she ran out of the apartment, her heart alternatively pounding.

———

DEEP DOWN, Zettel wished, just a little, that he felt guiltier about using the naive woman the way he had. But then: *Even among the new ruling class, there will be those who lead and those who follow. And I intend to lead.*

He briefly thought about Bissette, one of Ugo Tan's Seers in the underground chamber of the Royal Palace. She had been the most gifted of Tan's kidnapped group, and she'd remained lucid longer than most, almost until the end. He'd felt for her as he now did toward Meera.

Bissette was dead now, killed along with the rest of Tan's Seers during Elio's purge, but she'd whispered to him one night.

The secret won't survive!

What secret? he'd asked.

Your secret, our secret, she'd replied. *All this will be undone, and at the worst of times.*

The worst of times? Why? he'd asked.

All the Seers will be set free.

Bissette's eyes had shone. *But they haven't seen what I've seen. They don't know what's coming. But you...* she'd said as she touched Eugma's face. *You will be imprisoned for your crimes. Then you will be set free by your captors, and you will escape this world. Then you will ascend to greater power than you can dream of now. But I can't foresee what you will do with it.*

Why not? he'd said.

Because I can see Tan's decisions, and the royals, and yours, she'd whispered as tears streamed down her face. *You will make terrifying decisions. But when you are asked the most important question... I can't see the answer. I only know that you are the danger. Can you make the better decision, Eugma? Can you?*

She'd died that night. It wasn't uncommon for one Seer or another to die from the constant cocktail of drugs Ugo Tan had ordered. It took only a little extra that night to make certain she didn't speak of the future she'd foreseen for him. He'd even made it look like she did it herself.

He wasn't going to let anyone stand between him and the greater power. He was destined to—

"Doctor Zettel?" Guard Two said crisply. "We have received orders to move you to a secure location."

"Why? What for?" he asked.

"We have our orders," the guard said. "Pick three items and prepare to be moved."

It was moments too soon for Zettel to enact his plan. So he picked up a book and a small carafe of synth—not potent or particularly good—and said, "Will there be a glass where we're going?" he asked. "Or should I take one with me?"

CHAPTER
TWENTY-THREE

SUPER CARRIER COLOSSUS

Planet Diminu

Orso Star System

Tenilo Barum sat in the control center of the *Colossus,* his technopathy skittering across the ship's remaining systems, constantly monitoring every flicker and fluctuation. He wasn't certain which ones did what, but after twenty-seven hours of connection, he knew the difference between "normal" and "abnormal" and was trying his best to keep everything balanced, notwithstanding he was tied into the other ships in his little convoy, dozens of damaged capital ships, each being gently persuaded to fly in formation.

At nearly two kilometers in length and over a half-kilometer at its widest point, the Angel-class supercarrier *Colossus* had served as the home of eight frigates, dozens of support craft, and two entire wings of fighters. It had been the largest and most ambitious ship ever built, almost bankrupting the government of Dianesis.

Before the Swarm attacked, four years earlier, the ship had boasted enough DEW weaponry to burn a continent to a cinder, and enough missiles to fight any single fleet to a standstill. By its presence alone, it had cowed three rebellious colonies into surrender.

But none of that mattered to an enemy that counted its soldiers as cannon fodder and possessed weapons that could burn through its energy shields.

Following the appearance of the Swarm, all Angel-class ships had been frantically refitted with railguns, their shields and armor replaced as quickly as possible.

Unfortunately, the *Colossus* hadn't been fully retrofitted before the attack on Caerus, and its shielding had been torn to pieces by Swarm weapons. But, by some fortune, it hadn't suffered irreparable damage to the comms or the engines, but with over a hundred major hull breaches and so many systems down or destroyed, the AI's safety systems had refused to accept commands. With the AI bypassed and the remote systems connected to Kyne Minah's EI processor, it served as Tenilo's flagship for his enterprise.

An enterprise, he thought, *that, thankfully, will be ending soon.*

He could see Diminu in the viewport now, a tiny dot of irregularly reflected light from the formerly volcanic planet. The surface had been explored three or four times. It was a ball of ancient silicate lava flows that gifted the planet with a palette of unlikely colors; streaks of black obsidian amid the ivory silica.

"Bridge crew," he called, "report status, or whatever it is I'm supposed to say."

A chuckle came over the comm systems as the remote crews back at Caerus Officers Academy began sending reports to his datascreen. He watched the numbers scroll by; he didn't understand most of them, and he didn't have time to learn them. But with the application of his technopathy, he was able to fake it.

Comparing the numbers allowed him to order the *Vigilant* to reduce power from its number three reactor—because of minor fluctuations—and recommend that the *Altostratum* run diagnostics on the hull integrity in the aft section.

Some of the ships were held together with hurriedly welded spare girders and he didn't want to lose any now that the goal was in sight.

The hull report came back positive, so he figured the problem was likely a sensor glitch. He gave several pieces of advice, took some, and reported some as errant.

I can't wait until this is over.

"Prepare the orbital insertion calculations," he ordered. "I don't want to collide with any of the debris the IMFP has already dumped out here."

He received a chorus of "understoods" and then leaned back in the captain's chair.

Suddenly, his sense of the other ships flickered and died. "I'm losing signal," he shouted, jerking himself upright in the seat. "Report fleet status."

"All ship functions normal."

"Nothing to report. All ship systems normal."

And one after another, they continued to report all was well with the fleet.

"Something's wrong," Tenilo said. "I'm not receiving comms from the other ships. Scan for interference. I need to regain control."

"Sir, planetary broadcast," someone reported. "Broad spectrum, all channels. Readjust all frequencies to 289.5 GHz."

Tenilo's fingers danced over the hologram, delicately tuning his equipment, and was instantly reconnected to the rest of his fleet.

"What's the broadcast?"

"The palace just announced that we've lost contact with Regis Magnum Shipyards," the voice replied.

"Any reasons given?" Tenilo asked.

"No, but it doesn't sound good."

"Do we have imaging?" Tenilo asked as the problem

tumbled through his head. "We need to know what's happening."

"Sir, the military is claiming no knowledge of what's happening."

"Well," Tenilo replied thoughtfully, "that makes us the closest to Regis Magnum. I want all scanners fully active, maximum power and range."

"Won't that tip off the enemy to us, sir?"

"Enemy?" Tenilo snapped. "What enemy? The Swarm? No, Lieutenant. The Swarm always knows where we are and that we're going to fight. This is something else. Give me full active scanning. Now!"

Every ship in his makeshift, crippled fleet activated scanning, the fields a part of his consciousness as he monitored the systems using technopathy. Before they could report, he was receiving the information. But what he saw wasn't what they were looking for.

The debris field around Diminu was much larger than it should be. By his count, there were twenty-seven more active signatures than he had accounted for. *But if I add in the number of IMFP ships that we're towing, then there are only three more.*

Had the Blues already found the wreckage over Diminu and slaughtered the IMFP ships?

So maybe I was wrong, he thought. *Maybe it is the Swarm.*

"Sir, radar says there are multiple contacts around Magnum."

Tenilo frowned. "I know that," he said. "But where exactly are they?" he asked.

"On the far side of Magnum beyond the shipyards," the lieutenant responded. "Nothing is moving. I think they might be hiding there in the sensor shadow."

"And we have enemies hiding right here," Tenilo shouted. "Look at the readings around Diminu. Activate all weapons systems."

"Sir, we don't have weapons officers at the remote helms."

"Then get some!" Tenilo shouted. "And do it now. The situation here is critical."

He sat in the captain's chair of the formerly most feared vessel in Sovereign space, hoping they could get a handful of weapons officers in place in the next five minutes.

Because his scan now showed that three vessels were already moving toward him.

———

TENILO DREW CLOSER TO DIMINU—AND so did the three enemy ships.

As close as he was, he could now see their glow, but the signatures were much larger than he'd expected. As they moved into view, he saw the familiar Blue fighters stream out.

"They've created carrier ships," he called over the comm. "Inform Command the Swarm has carriers."

And he waited.

And waited.

The fighters streaked closer. He activated whatever shields were available just before the enemy found their range and started firing.

"I need weapons officers!" he yelled as enemy fire splashed across the shields.

"We have one," someone replied.

"Then get him to the *Colossus* remote station," Tenilo ordered.

"Sorry, sir, he wasn't at the *Colossus* remote location. He's logging into the *Fusillade*."

Tenilo reached out across the x-ray comms connections and found *Fusillade* in the middle of the pack. He was instantly aware that her bow shields were malfunctioning.

"This is fleet command," he called over the comm. "All ships, adjust formation. *Safe Harbor* and *Penumbra* take the lead, with *Fusillade* behind. Cover that ship. It's the only offensive capability we have."

Just as the ships settled into position, the enemy carriers began firing. Though smaller than any USF carrier he'd ever seen, it easily ranked larger than a frigate, possibly as large as a Defender-class light carrier. But that wasn't all; the carrier's weapons were far more powerful as well, and they were driving a wedge between several of the salvaged ships.

Then *Fusillade* opened fire.

Aptly named, it rained hot ammo through the void. And the weapons officer was doing well; his targeting was spot-on. In minutes he'd destroyed a half-dozen fighters with his initial volley.

"Great job, Fusillade," Tenilo shouted, jumping up and down in his seat.

But then, the enemy began to shift positions. "Fusillade! Come to—um—ten degrees to the right," Tenilo ordered.

"Adjusting to starboard, zero-one-one point two, firing now."

As the enemy ships shifted to split *Fusillade's* firepower, they opened fire on *Safe Harbor* from an angle that prevented *Fusillade* from having a clear shot.

"Shields are at seventy percent," Tenilo muttered as the readings flashed across his mind. "Sixty percent... fifty-five..."

"Where are those weapons officers?" he shouted.

"We have weapons officer boarding *Vassalus*... now."

"We have weapons aboard *Firestorm*."

"Weapons officer, logging into *Bistardis*."

Tenilo let out a breath of anticipation he hadn't realized he was holding, and the reports came streaming in:

"Acquiring targets."

"Acquiring."

"Firing."

"Fire all."

"Firing now."

Space lit up with streaks of white and blue light as the ships traded blows. As more and more calls from arriving weapons officers filled his ears, the more he wished that someone had arrived for—

"Weapons officer for *Colossus,* signing in, sir." The voice was a deep baritone. "How may I direct your antipersonnel communications today?" his weapons officer said. And Tenilo could feel the grin on his face.

Tenilo smiled. "Let's tell these Blues that they called the wrong number."

"Aye, sir. Weapons... on line. Multiple targets acquired. Firing... Now!"

Tenilo felt the great ship respond. Damaged as she was, she still had one of the most formidable weapons platforms ever built.

Dozens of batteries swiveled to face the enemy. And in a single glorious moment, the officer fired, and the sheet of fiery death streaking toward the Swarm doubled.

The entire ship vibrated slightly under the simultaneous output of every railgun aboard. But as Tenilo marveled at the exuberant display of marksmanship, first one ship, the *Repulse,* then another ceased firing.

"Repulse. What is it? What's happening?" he yelled, standing up and then sitting down again.

"Sir," Repulse replied, "the autofeeders aren't responding."

"Diagnostics. Report damage to railguns," Tenilo yelped.

"No damage, sir," Repulse replied. "Batteries one, three and six are out of ammo and—"

And Tenilo realized his mistake. While weapons officers were able to fire their weapons remotely, they needed gunnery crews to reload them, and there were none aboard any of the ships in his fleet; they were running with... not even skeleton crews, just the minimum to operate essential and life support systems.

A real captain wouldn't have forgotten that detail, he

thought savagely. *But what choice did we have? Most of the ships are little more than derelict. Stars, we were lucky some of them could still fight.*

"All weapons officers," he called. "Conserve ammunition. Once it's gone, there will be no more. Restrain yourselves. Wait for clear shots."

His orders were confirmed by a chorus of *affirmatives,* but it did little to assuage the sinking feeling in the pit of his stomach. *I'm going to die. Here, on this behemoth. Alone.*

We need to be there, at Regis Magnum, not here, he thought. *We can't do anything for the crews and ships that died here, but we could, maybe, save the shipyards and everyone in them.*

"Navigation. We aren't going to fight our way through this. Give me a course to Regis Magnum."

"Sir, you want the fastest course, or the most direct?"

"Explain," Tenilo said.

"The most direct course would be to haul to port. But getting the rest of the fleet to follow would be a chore and you'd probably be shot to pieces. The fastest would be to do a gravity assist around Diminu since we were heading for orbit anyway. You'd pick up enough speed that you might outrun some of them, and you'd get a nice momentum pickup if you run hot. But—"

"No buts. Set the course," Tenilo interrupted and ordered the fleet to follow his lead.

The flight plan began streaming across his console. The mathematician in him wanted to run the calculations himself, but he didn't have time. He set course and speed and sat back and waited.

"I have to warn you, sir," Navigation said, "that if you apply more speed than those calculated, you risk destabilizing the ships. And that would not be good, considering the state they're in. There's no telling how much damage a hot burn could cause."

Tenilo felt the massive ship shudder under the combined

fire of the Swarm carriers. "They're going to take a lot more damage from those dreadnoughts," he replied. "If we can withstand the worst of the atmospheric shockwave, the other ships will stand a better chance of survival."

He felt the subtle effect as *Colossus* entered the planet's gravitational well and began to compensate. Even though Diminu's mass shadow was much weaker than most planets, the ships still picked up speed. And though the enemy fighters had little trouble maintaining their harassing fire, the carriers were losing ground.

His ad hoc fleet continued to pick up speed as they dove toward the planet.

Tenilo's plan was to increase the speed, then decrease the angle of attack, orbit the planet and then slingshot away on an elliptical course that would take the fleet to Regis Magnum. It was a plan he knew required orbital calculations he couldn't spare time for—his consciousness was spread throughout the ships now, monitoring each one for any hint of instability.

Vassalus began to quiver: microtremors that might not even have registered at the remote stations. But Tenilo could sense it.

"Vassalus, break formation and dive now," he ordered.

The remote bridge crew hesitated, then followed the order. But the rear solar assembly began to tear free, the debris crashing into the *Ibehrtus*. *Ibehrtus* decelerated—causing a shift in formation—and collided with two other ships before the rest of the fleet was able to adjust course and avoid more collisions. All of this threw the formation askew, and several vessels lost their exit vector to Magnum.

"Tenilo Barum," came an officious-sounding voice. "You are to cease your actions and return to the field of battle."

"Who is this?" Tenilo demanded.

"Lieutenant Commander Aboter, OIC Remote Control. Those ships are Sovereign property. You cannot remove them from their designated location over Diminu."

"Have you not noticed there are three enemy carriers and

hundreds of fighters over Diminu? Get it together, Commander. I'm trying to save your sovereign fleet and the shipyards at Regis Magnum."

"These damaged ships are the property of the royal military, and as such, they are to be returned to battle immediately."

"Well," Tenilo snapped as his concentration flickered, "how about you get your... How about you help me save this wreck of a fleet and move it to Magnum and neutralize the mess over there? Surely the shipyards are more valuable than this collection of space junk."

"We have no actionable intelligence that anything is happening."

"How do you figure that?" Tenilo shouted. "You have an official royal announcement that the station is cut off, and you have our radar readings that suggest a Swarm attack."

"We have no confirmation of those readings," Abotur replied, "but we do have a verified enemy sighting at Diminu. Now release your hold on the ships so they can be piloted."

"Wait." Tenilo felt the tug on control systems from far away, and yet he was so deeply integrated into the systems that he was unconsciously fighting them off. "You mean you... you can't override me?"

There was no answer.

"Yes!" he yelled. "So, I, Tenilo Barum, royal envoy to Prince Felder of the Alastor Sovereign System, do hereby declare and announce that I, independent of any governmental entity, have decided to take control of these, um, forty-three vessels and will take them to a destination of my choice."

"Then you will have committed an act of piracy, Tenilo Barum," Aboter said. "You still have the opportunity to—"

"Poppysocks," Tenilo said, sitting up straighter in his captain's chair. "Do you have even the least idea who and what I am? Every one of my friends in this system outranks you. Furthermore, I am an Agent of the Crown, to be rendered all available assistance. That's *all* assistance, Commander. But, if you want the excitement of logging me as a pirate, you just go ahead, and I'll see you at your court-martial. Tenilo Barum out."

Tenilo reached the exit vector and, together with the rest of his ragtag fleet, he hurtled out of the planet's gravity well, and the other ships followed, their remote crews locked out of their systems. He increased speed, feeling the strain all across the fleet as he pushed past Mach 35 toward Mach 40.

Though he, himself, was under intense pressure, he still hoped he could reach the station in time.

CHAPTER
TWENTY-FOUR

CENTRAL CONTROL

Kasa de Cevoir flicked through all of her previously targeted systems. It had been almost an hour. The station computer was in shambles. And it was her fault. Her timed virus had done a lot of damage, but she'd managed to halt the worst of it and start everything back on the road to recovery.

I sure won't get the chance to fix it myself, she thought. *If I have any brains or luck, or both, I'll ditch this guy and find an escape pod as soon as the lights are back on. The last thing I need is for Hyde to find me...*

Then she realized that Hyde's wrath was nothing compared to that of Hirana Ligarch.

If I want to survive, she thought as her fingers flew over the holos, *I need to disappear. I need to find some worthless, out-of-the-way, miserable planetoid that has no contact with any of the Sovereign Systems. Somewhere out in the IMFP, maybe. Falsify records, report my untimely death, escape under an alias. I can live on rations and water.*

Such a life seemed bleak and hopeless, but one thing she'd learned: you grab opportunities when they present themselves.

Any kind of living was preferable to dying under Ligarch's cruel gaze.

So she readied a timed report of her death to go out in twenty-four hours. She created a program that would undo some of the damage her virus had caused, while looking like the station's computers were enacting repairs to the code from backups. She set a timed program to destroy her records entirely in seventy-six hours. She set another program in the observation system to seek out her image, delete it, and corrupt any footage that contained any recognizable portion of her face.

But there's someone who doesn't need the computer to find me, she thought. *Tachier can tell them everything. And if he does, they'll never believe any of the reports or records. They'll hunt me down, with all the authority of the royals behind them. And while they might not draw it out as much as Ligarch would, I doubt they'll let me live.*

"Hey, Jaxie, can you... um... check the hall?" she asked. "I thought I heard something."

"Of course," he replied.

As Jax left the room, she did a quick search for information on Tachier. *Ah, he's in the medbay.* She was about to move on when she noticed that a group of three people had recently transferred through the airlock onto a small shuttle bound for *Avenger.*

She, of course, had had to leave those systems operational for her scheme to work.

As Jax left the room, she pushed through the firewalls that protected the ship's computers from people less like her. She found the medbay, and the life-support system monitoring two patients. One of them was moving, the other mentally active but unmoving. *Tachier, tied to a bed, obviously.* She inserted a tiny bit of code into the system. It would be quick, clean, and unnoticed... until it was too late.

She swept her trail all the way back to the terminal, where

she left several innocuous inquiries into the station systems and a confirmation that repairs were underway.

"Well, I have good news," she announced when Jax returned. "The systems are being patched and restored from backups. We should have things back to relative normal soon."

"Glad to hear it," Jax said. "This orange is beginning to—"

He was interrupted by an alert that began scrolling across the holographic display.

"Wait," Kasa snapped, "there's something—"

ATTENTION! ALL STATION FUNCTIONS HAVE BEEN ASSUMED BY CENTRAL CONTROL.

ATTENTION! ALL STATION FUNCTIONS HAVE BEEN ASSUMED BY CENTRAL CONTROL.

ATTENTION! ALL STATION FUNCTIONS HAVE BEEN ASSUMED BY CENTRAL CONTROL.

"Jaxie, get out of here, now!" she screamed.

And, as Jax flung himself out into the hallway, she leapt over the desk and threw herself into the air. She felt the door clip her decksoles as it slammed shut behind her.

The orange lights flickered twice, then were replaced by the more comforting yellows of the emergency lighting system.

"Hey, that's better," Jax said. "Now I can—"

"No," Kasa said, panting. "Someone just hijacked the station's computer systems."

And I'm the reason why.

AVENGER

Medbay

Manda lay on the medbay gurney, fully dressed in her shipboard uniform, clutching her temples as the visions streamed through her mind.

I want it to stop, she wanted to wail, but the images

continued to flash through her consciousness at breakneck speed.

She saw hundreds of futures—death, destruction, agony, and woe. She saw Blues annihilating vast numbers of humans. She saw humans destroying Blues. She saw humans fighting humans. She saw the Sovereign rulers crushing dissent. She saw the IMFP plowing through the Sovereign defenses. She didn't know why or if all these futures could come to pass, but she had to do... something.

And everywhere, she saw the enigmatic symbol, ⁊, a phantom that drove entire governments to war with each other. *I need to act if I can. I need to stop this... this civil war from happening.*

But the images continued to stream past, a river of misery—

And then she saw something.

She seized the images as she had before. Somehow she managed to hold on.

She saw a strange force of Blues, Blues that didn't glow— *What are they? A stealth enemy? Why have they changed?*— marching through Regis Magnum, murdering everyone in their way.

And there was the second vision—where she stood beside the humans on the station, and they triumphed.

Why is it me that changes things? Is it because I warned them of the attack? Or is it something I do? I know... I think... I must...

She had an answer. She got up off the bed, grabbed her pistol from the top of the bedside cabinet, holstered it, and walked out of the medbay.

"Manda, where do you think—" Dowd called after her, but Manda ignored her and headed for the shuttle bay.

She walked quickly—as quickly as her painful condition would allow—and as she walked, she noticed a marine, one of *Avenger's* crew, approaching from the other direction. And recognized him.

"Senior Lieutenant Pazon," she said, her insides twisting.

Pazon saluted. "Yes, ma'am, Commander."

"I need you to come with me," she said.

He hesitated. "But, ma'am, I am on orders from my—"

"I said I need you to come with me."

"No, ma'am. I was ordered to report for brief." He thumbed his comm. "Major Kagen," he said. "Sir, I have been detained—"

Manda had had enough. She pulled her pistol. "Cut the comm. Now."

His mouth dropped open. He turned off his comm and stared at her. "Commander. What is going on?"

"Lieutenant," she said, "I have an urgent task, and I need you to help me. Now please accompany me to the shuttle bay."

It took her almost five minutes to reach the shuttle bay. By then, her arm was aching from holding the pistol.

"Why are you doing this, Commander?" Pazon asked.

"I'm a Seer," she said, "and I had a vision. You were part of it. You have to help me. We must save some people."

"Then why not do it right and get official help, more people?" he asked.

"Because that wasn't in the vision," she replied. "Now get in." She pointed to the ramp and followed him into the shuttle.

She heaved a deep breath, nodded, then gestured with the pistol and said, "Good. Now sit there and belt yourself in."

Manda watched as Pazon did as she asked, then she slipped into the pilot's seat.

"It's been years since I flew a shuttle, but this is an emergency," she said as she looked over the controls, assuring herself that everything was as it should be.

"Ma'am, I really must protest," Pazon said respectfully. "This feels a little like a... kidnapping."

"Nonsense," she replied. "You're not a kid, Pazon. You're twice as big as I am."

The adrenaline coursing through her body was making her feel giddy.

If it wasn't for the imminent takeover of the station, I'd feel like a teenager.

She belted herself in and began tapping the icons that would turn on the shuttle's system. The holograms rose in front of her. Her fingers danced. The screens lit up. The engines hummed.

"This is Commander Haal, First Officer, *Avenger*," she said over the comm. "Open the shuttle bay doors. Emergency protocol One-Alpha-Five-Five-Zero-Two-B." She scanned her badge, and it transmitted her authorization to the station's AI, and the door began to open.

"Commander Haal," Richard's voice came over the comm. "What's the emergency? You can't just commandeer—"

She tapped the comm off and launched, scraping the edge of the bay door.

"Did you... just steal this shuttle?" Pazon asked from the seat behind.

"No. I borrowed it," she said, trying to sound light and humorous, but inside, her stomach was in knots and her heart was pounding.

———

REGIS MAGNUM SHIPYARD

"Get into your suits," Danis ordered.

As several of them began to grumble, she turned again and snapped, "Anyone who wants to fly with me WILL learn to follow orders. Life support could fail on this station at any time. Now do as I ordered. Do it quickly and double-check your seals. We need to get to the bombers, ASAP."

"Why are we even bothering with the bombers?" someone asked. "Isn't there a hanger with F-32As near here?"

"Maybe," Danis snapped, "but I know the bombers were

just serviced for live-fire training, because I ordered it. I can't say the same for a hangar full of docked fighters."

It had been an arduous task collecting forty-three suits from the various lockers here and there around the North Plate, but they'd managed.

As a chorus of "ready" sounded throughout the atrium, she heard running footsteps approaching.

"Everyone against the wall. Sidearms!" Danis shouted.

They moved quickly. Danis to the left, with Gian and Jackknife on either side.

But it was only Axi Quento, panting as she rushed into the atrium and skidded to a stop.

"I knew it." Quento laughed, her sides heaving. "Domino Morian would find a fighter if her leg was broken."

"Why are you here, Commander?" Danis asked. "This is not a training exercise."

"That I know," Axi said with a grin in her clipped version of the Standard language. "And I ask question. I ask that you surrender command of squadron to me."

Danis lifted her arm and took another quick glance at the active scans of Regis Magnum. Translated into a holo, it revealed a bitter reality. There were capital ships and fighters converging on the station from beyond the planetary sphere. And they didn't respond with Sovereign transponders.

Danis shook her head, looked at Quento and said, "Excuse me?"

"With due respect, Domino, I know it is much I ask. You have thousand hours in seat. I almost match that, and I two thousand hours teaching. You, Gian, and Jacknife form heads of three flights, I fourth. Please let me do what I do best; yell at rookies."

Danis opened the locker next to her and yanked out a vac suit. "Get ready, Acting Squadron Commander. What's your call sign?"

Quento laughed. "Crash."

"Wait a minute. Crash?"

Quento laughed. "I have accident in training? Someone rhyme Axi Quent' with 'accident.' Now I am Crash. I will crash hard."

"Not filling me with confidence here, Commander," Danis said dryly.

"But you already promoted me," she said with a grin, then turned and shouted, "Listen up! I am Crash Quento, and you *will* do as I say. Pair up, pilot and TK. No one leave partner, get to fighter. Run Checklist five, and launch. Form up outside. Go!"

The entire squadron roster immediately bundled together. Gian and Jackknife paired with their TKs. Danis, however, had not assigned one to herself.

She looked around and noticed a tall, slim young woman she hadn't seen before. She appeared to be younger than Danis had been the first time she'd climbed into a fighter.

"What's your name, soldier?" she asked.

"Jennat Mefta."

"TK?" Danis asked.

Mefta nodded.

"Welcome to the other half of the Domino team," Danis said. "Let's run."

She palmed the hangar bay door open, and everyone dashed toward the bombers. But just as most of the pilots and TKs had cleared the hangar bay door, alarms began blaring and the door slammed shut, gravity shut down, and the launch doors began to open.

What the hell is happening? This will kill us all.

The doors stopped moving; the gap between was little more than a meter wide. But the atmosphere was escaping, and the pilots and TKs were grabbing their helmets, some falling to their knees, tumbling in the low gravity.

"Get hold of something and push off," Danis yelled into the suit comm. "Get to the bombers."

But while some managed to stay alive a little longer, many had already stopped moving and were being swept toward the bay door and out into the black.

Why! she wanted to scream. *It was a simple order—double-check your suit seals.*

But for those, it was too late. They'd already learned the hardest lesson: grow lax and you die.

Danis and Mefta gripped the ladder and floated into the B-29 bomber nearest the bay door. All the bombers were now hovering above the hangar deck. The suction had abated to a gentle breeze; the hangar almost devoid of air. She powered up, activated the seals and switched over to flight comms.

"Bay twenty-seven? This is Domino Morian, Three Alpha Three Twenty-nine-Eighteen Avenger. Do you read?"

"This is Twenty-seven," a voice replied. "We tried to close the door but could only halt it. Sorry."

Sorry? she thought. *That it?* "Well, what's done is done. We're launching. Open the doors, please."

The doors opened, and what was left of her two squadrons eased out of the bay into the black.

Someone's going to pay for this, she thought darkly.

REGIS MAGNUM SHIPYARD

Manda landed the shuttle without incident in the South Plate shuttle dock. After she felt the docking collar connect to the starboard portal, she rose from her seat. But no sooner was she on her feet than the shuttle dock alarms began to blare, the emergency lights flashed red, and there was a sudden hiss of escaping air.

"Ma'am," Pazon shouted. "The docking seals aren't connected. Seal the hatch, we've got—"

"Atmo loss. Yes. I know." She slapped the controls to seal all hatches, something clicked, and the pressure quickly stabilized, just as she realized the shuttle was still moving.

"We didn't just lose atmo," she said. "Gravity in the shuttle bay is out, too."

"So what do we do?" Pazon demanded.

"We use breathers," she said without thinking. "We need to get to the access doors."

"Ma'am, with all due respect, a breather's no good; even a soft vacuum will kill you. And without gravity, it's even harder to do anything without injuring yourself. Trust me, this is my job."

"Then get me across now," Manda snapped. "Do whatever you feel is necessary."

"Check the emergency storage," he said.

She nodded, opened the cover and found several skinsuits and atmospheric filter masks.

"Okay, that's not terrible," he said. "These aren't vacuum-rated, but if you seal them, they will slow bodily air loss. I can get you across in that."

She slipped the pathogen-resistant suit over her uniform and fixed the mask tightly over her face.

"We've got about thirty seconds," Pazon said. "Keep your eyes shut tight, and don't breathe unless you have to. The less air inside you, the less will be sucked out through your skin."

She knew he was exaggerating, but not by much.

"And you realize that this might kill you?" Pazon added. "I think I can do this, but it's something I've never practiced with a civilian and non-vac gear."

"I have every confidence we will succeed," she stated and activated her air reserve to protect her face. "Wait, I'm not a civ—"

"Get ready to fly," he ordered as he slammed his fist against the Emergency Override, and the air disappeared around her. Her skinsuit began to inflate. He grabbed her with both hands and threw her down the docking shaft.

She flew in a straight line along the tube but clipped then slammed into the edge of the bulkhead and bounced sideways. She struggled not to gasp in fear, and tried to blindly arrest her spinning and bouncing, but only succeeded in striking something else before she contacted something large and solid, moving at speed.

Pazon had launched himself after her with sufficient force to catch her and continue his trajectory. He clutched her to him, taking the bone-shaking thump at the end of the tube with his back. He pounded on the controls, only to fail. The door was sealed.

Manda struggled for her badge. It was in her shipboard uniform, inside the skinsuit. She opened the skinsuit and reached inside, feeling the loss of air as she fumbled for the card. She found it, wrenched it from the suit, slammed it against the panel, took a deep breath and screamed, "Emergency override, One-Alpha-Five, Twenty-nine Eighteen Avenger."

The door opened, and Pazon shoved her inside.

She landed on her back on the gravity-induced floor. Pazon stumbled in after her and slammed his fist on the controls. The door slammed shut, and atmo began circulating back into the passage.

Manda ripped the mask off her face and lay on the floor gasping lungfuls of air. Pazon sat beside her for a moment, staring down at the floor, breathing deeply, then he seemed to gather himself, rose to his feet, bent over, grabbed her skinsuit and hauled her to her feet.

"Get it together, Commander," he said. "We've got work to do, right?"

She nodded, but as she did so, another vision flashed across her mind, and then another. The first showed Pazon alive and celebrated as a hero. The second showed him dead, with Manda mourning him.

No! No, no, no, no!

She took one last deep breath, then said, "Let's go,"

She was determined to do everything in her power to make sure he survived.

It was at that moment she felt someone touch her mind. *Manda, what's wrong?* The voice was familiar. *Is there anything I can do to help?*

———

MAGNUM REGIS STATION

Central Computer Core

Marshal Secerna Hyde marched forward at the head of a hundred soldiers and more than thirty of the station's crew. They'd brought her safely to the central computer core. For obvious security reasons, access was restricted to only those with the highest possible clearance; Hyde was one of only a dozen such people.

She inserted her badge into the reader. The lanyard dangled as the computer processed her credentials. She gave her print scan, her retina scan, and a blood sample—which was also measured for lividity, active cell count, known narcotic and sedation compounds and decayed protein structures.

When she finally gained access, she turned to her followers and said, "I will activate the defenses from here. We will quickly take back *our* station from these invaders, whoever they are."

Her rapidly assembled corps cheered her words, and she felt a moment of pride.

Did Morian manage any of this? No, he didn't. He couldn't. And as I step up to the next level, I will make sure to do it on his prostrate back.

The doors opened, and autoturrets whirred to life for a split second... and then fell silent.

Whoever destroyed our systems will find themselves hung from a docking claw, if I have any say, she fumed as she entered the core chamber where a single holo terminal awaited her.

She sat down, linked her hands together, cracked her fingers, flung her arms in the air, and then began.

First, she entered her information, security clearance and passwords—a lengthy string of data that would be gibberish to anyone outside the command structure—and then she entered her Military Research Protocols. Finally, she brought up the Champions project, entered the activation codes, and then confirmed.

"There! That did it," she muttered and breathed a sigh of relief as the computer showed the robots activating. Their processes initialized and synced with the station's AI. *Once the station has control of a hundred unstoppable robot soldiers, it will only be a matter of hours before the halls are swept clean of trash.*

She began searching the security systems, looking for the intruders. *There must be an army of them if they thought they could take over the entire station.*

The feeds were dark, showing infrared images only. They showed no one in the halls, no one in the bays. No one in the armories. Just small amorphous blobs indicating one piece of machinery or another.

She entered commands to rewind the footage to the last known movements, minus one minute.

Dozens of cameras showed movement. While a few had station personnel marked by badges, several showed strangers in infrared. Hundreds of them. And all were disappearing down the docking tubes to the ships under construction.

"Stars!" she yelled. "Stars, stars, stars." She shut down the terminal, jumped out of her seat and ran out into the corridor, the security doors closing automatically behind her.

"Follow me, people," she shouted. "We need to get to the Vindication Fleet docks and quickly. The bastards are taking the ships."

She led them to the deep storage bay and palmed the door controls. As the door slid ponderously open, she yelled, "Here are the soldiers who will help us regain—"

The terrifying roar of weapons fire shattered her world.

Behind her, soldiers and crew screamed, fell, and tried to run as the USF Armored Champions Division fired a wall of bullets into the crowd. Several tried to return fire and were immediately cut down. Others retreated, found cover, and were pinned by the haze of bullets.

Hyde knew the Champions—in case of a Swarm incursion—had been armed prior to storage. She also knew that each of them carried fifteen hundred rounds of 6mm railgun ammo, and they weren't even firing on full auto.

One of them aimed at her and fired. She dove to the side, hit the ground and froze, hoping the Champions would assume she was dead.

This is absurd, she thought desperately, as she lay among the dead. *My people designed them. Surely they wouldn't—*

But it all made sense. When hit by a kinetic projectile, Blues shattered and died. Movement was the primary indication of the enemy. There had been no need for more complicated targeting, *except for identification imagery, which we neglected to include,* she thought savagely.

And she lay there, listening as the Champions murdered the people they were supposed to save.

———

AVENGER

Command Bridge

Richard Morian was in the ready room on the *Avenger,* searching for Manda. He could feel snatches of her emotions, but something was wrong. She was... determined, in a way he'd never seen before.

Manda, what is wrong? Is there anything I can do to help? he called to her.

Richard, she sent back. He got the impression she was

running. *I had a vision. All our people on the station—they're in danger.*

Everyone on the station is in danger, he replied. *But what—*

You don't understand. They're inside. There are enemies inside the station, and they're everywhere. I think they're going to take out the main computer—I think?

Morian was stunned. *How could the Swarm have gotten into the station? And why would they? We have never practiced for such a situation.*

He was about to reach out again to Manda when alarms began sounding. He broke the connection, jumped up and ran to the bridge. "What's happening, Mr. Jadern?" he snapped.

But before Jadern could answer, "Sir, we've received numerous alerts almost simultaneously from Regis Magnum," Sandra Lowry called from Comms. "We have several alerts of an attack near the computer core, and we have enemy incoming."

"Enemies?" Morian's adrenaline spiked. "Are we certain?"

"We have Swarm energy signatures inbound, multiple contacts." The call came from Lt. Janis Samms, sensors officer. "They're coming around the curve of Magnum now, sir."

"Why didn't we have any warning?" Morian demanded as he scanned the massive tactical hologram floating above its generator on the command well deck.

"I don't know, sir," Samms shouted. "I'm looking at the feeds, but they don't match our sensors. I mark at least thirty Blue contacts. And... sir, some are much larger than usual."

"How large?" Morian asked sharply.

"Almost as large as we are, sir," Samms replied.

How did they hack the nav satellites before they got here? And why would they send soldiers inside a space station? Especially if they appear to be attacking it from space? Stars! Whenever the Swarm does something new, it never makes sense.

Suddenly, new alerts began flashing on all screens.

"Comms. What's happening now?" Morian said, trying to keep his tone even.

"I don't know, sir... No! Wait. We have multiple launches from the drydocks. Identifying—*Benediction, Fearful Symmetry, Dursana, Censorious, Expiation, Absolution, Gerrhonotus.* Sir, these are all Vindication ships. The most completed ones."

Morian stared at the holo. He could see the ship's signatures, the debris floating away from the ships where they'd broken away from the docks.

"Even partially completed," Morian said in relief, "those ships will be a welcome addition to... What in the name of..."

Even as he watched, the ships turned and began to regroup in battle formation.

"They're attacking the station!" Samms shouted as the ships opened fire, destroying structures and bays across the station hull.

"Where are the station shields?" Morian said, an icy calm to his voice.

"Still down, sir," Samms replied.

He closed his eyes for a moment, then said, "Mister Jadern, launch from the dock and get us over there. Do it now!"

"Aye, sir... Sir, the dock is not retracting. It won't disconnect."

"Then break it," Morian ordered. "And get us between the station and whoever that is over there."

"But what about the Swarm ships?"

He felt Danis' promise of vengeance, a far cry from the whoop she made every time she launched her fighter.

"Leave them to my sister," he said. "Thrusters, if you please, Mr. Jadern."

The ship shuddered violently. They heard an ear-splitting creak as *Avenger's* thrusters powered up. Then there was a mighty cracking sound as the massive docking collar was torn away. The ship jolted violently, and Morian grabbed onto the command rail as *Avenger* suddenly surged forward.

"Damage report, Mr. Volkov?" Morian said over the ship's comm.

"Hull damage minimal, Captain," Volkov replied. "No breach."

"Seventeen degrees to port, Mr. DeLong," Morian snapped out the order. "Roll three degrees to port."

He checked the screens.

"Ms. Fargo. Open missile bays one through twenty-five and fire at will, at the Vindication fleet," he ordered. "Let's see if we can distract them a little."

Less than five minutes later—almost in slow-motion, so it seemed—he watched as two-hundred-fifty M-99 five-megaton torpedoes streaked across the blackness to strike the seven familiar profiles of the Defender-class ships and explode. A series of huge explosions chained across their hulls. The damage was extensive but not crippling.

"My compliments to a fine barrage, Ms. Fargo," he called. "Continue to fire at will." But he could see they'd already raised shields to ward off further attacks.

"Targets of opportunity, Ms. Fargo," he said and then directed his attention back to his navigation officer.

"Mr. DeLong," Morian continued. "Insert us between the station and the fleet."

"Captain," Volkov shouted. "Our shields won't be enough to hold them back."

"We'll last longer than the station hull will," Morian replied. "Divert power from reactors two, three and four to the starboard shields."

"Deploying shields to starboard," Volkov said. "Shields at one hundred percent and holding."

Morian could little more than watch as missile after missile exploded against their shields. *Avenger* slipped between the Vindication fleet—believed to be the master stroke that would end the war—and the giant station that built them. *Without some saving grace,* Morian thought, *the fleet will indeed be the end of the war... Just not as a victory for us.*

CHAPTER
TWENTY-FIVE

UNDERMINED

Feducere City Hall
  Planet Caerus
  Orso Planetary System

"...and that's where we stand," replied Ms. Certis, the adoption attorney.

Faxil watched her holo maintain an almost perfect expression of fake concern. *I bet she'd be real concerned if she'd seen Blues hiding under the city.*

"So," Faxil's father said to the woman, his tone snarkier than Faxil had ever heard from his father before, "until we have sufficient financial leverage to adopt Pinari, she'll remain in the care of her aunt, her only family member, who's a known drug addict, demonstrably abusive and neglectful."

Whew, he's really angry, Faxil thought.

"We really don't have the manpower to deal with such problems," Certis explained. "Everything is still in turmoil since the Slipgate Battle."

"Is not fair." Inoiae stomped her foot—a movement mostly lost to the holo. "Law is supposed to apply evenly. Aunt is not caring—why can't we?"

"Ma'am, if you were applying to adopt one of the recently orphaned children who don't have any home at all..." Faxil watched as Certis' expression changed to one slightly more hopeful, but still fake. "I assure you your application would be fast-tracked through the system in two days, probably less."

"So the obvious solution," Faxil's father said, "is to arrest the aunt and her drug-dealing boyfriend, or whoever he is, and then Pinari'd be in the system, right?"

"She would be placed into the city's juvenile-care system," Certis said condescendingly, "awaiting her aunt's release or incarceration, which would be months, perhaps even years. And even if she *was* put into the adoption system, she would still be placed in order of records entrance. You would have to have face-to-face interviews with—and reject—at least a hundred children from your adoption district before you got to her."

And, for the first time, Faxil saw her composure crack and show some real emotion. But she quickly covered it up. "Believe me," she said, "your heart will break long before then."

Maybe she looks fake because it hurts to be too real, Faxil thought. *It must be hard trying to help kids when everyone else is so concerned with their own safety.*

And suddenly, it all made sense to him; it wasn't that people refused to believe him about the Blues. They just didn't want to. They couldn't handle any more pain, so they just believed that the Blues couldn't be here.

Kuon raised her head and growled.

Faxil was still startled every time Kuon did something like that in the apartment. After all, she'd only been allowed in for the last few days. Every time he noticed her, he felt like he would be in trouble.

But instead, his family had quickly acclimated to the extra body lying near doorways or couches or beds. And Kuon seemed very happy to finally be near friends, though Faxil noticed that she especially perked up around mealtimes.

"Hey, Dad?" Faxil said.

"Faxil, please, it will have to wait." His father turned again to the holo. "So again, the only way is to secure a large amount of money as proof that we'll pay the system to have her?"

"This conversation doesn't have to be like that, Mr. Avestan," the attorney replied.

"What about my posting to the salvage crews around Diminu? Doesn't that paycheck count for anything?" he said.

"A job posting is not cash in hand," Certis replied. "And it also highlights the fact that you, one of the primary caregivers, would be absent for long periods of time. And while that isn't the detriment it would have been a year ago, it would still be a major concern."

Kuon's growling grew louder until she barked, once, then repeatedly.

"I don't believe you have a dog mentioned on your application," the attorney said.

"It happened recently," Avestan said before turning to Faxil. "Quiet her down."

"Are you aware that having a large animal makes it less likely that an adoption would be allowed?"

"She's not that big," his dad outright lied. "And she's sweet and well-behaved. She's just sitting too close to the audio feed."

Kuon broke away from Faxil, stalked over to the door and continued to growl.

Suddenly the screen began to flash.

"Attention! Attention. This is an emergency message. This is an emergency message."

A vid appeared, an image of the Royal Palace and a man in military uniform stepped up behind a podium.

"People of Caerus, I stand before you today with a message of the utmost importance."

"Look, thank you for your time, Mr. Avestan," Certis said. "We'll talk again soon, I'm sure." And she shut off her vid.

The emergency message continued, unheard, **"We have lost all contact—"**

"Faxil, I'm not blaming you," Avestan said, "but Kuon might have just shot our chances." Faxil's dad looked over at Kuon, who was continuing to bark and growl. "What is it? What's going on?"

Danger danger...

The feelings radiating from Kuon set Faxil on edge.

"It's Kuon," Faxil replied, his heart rate increasing as he ran to the window to look outside, Kuon following him. "She's telling me we're in danger."

Inoiae looked at him, concerned.

"Kuon is talking to you?" Avestan asked, frowning. "Do you know what's upsetting her?"

"—we do not believe there is any reason to fear at this time—" the uniform droned on.

"Kuon, what's the matter?" Faxil asked, standing by the window with Kuon at his side. He was certain she could understand him and that somehow, she was able to communicate with him.

Hate... hate, hate... bite, bleed, kill!

"She's... upset. She acts like this when there's Blues around," Faxil said, "and she really wants to hurt something." He swallowed, unsure how this would go. "The last time she acted like this was at the factory where Pinari got hurt. And it was after that I began to hear her."

Avestan stared at him, then at Kuon, who tilted her head, then he looked at Inoiae. She nodded.

"You mean the factory where you claim to have seen Swarm soldiers?"

Faxil drew up as much courage and determination as he could muster. "Yes, sir. And I did see them. They hurt Kuon. You can see the scars. Look."

"Look at me, Faxil," his father said. "Are you absolutely sure? If you're making it up—"

"I'm not," Faxil cried. "You have to believe me. I have to protect my family."

"Well then," his father said, "I think we need to go and find out what's going on down there. Can you lead us, Faxil?"

Faxil bit his bottom lip, hesitated, then nodded.

Avestan turned and said, "Inoiae, get some sturdy clothes and supplies—water, flashlights, rope, whatever you think we'll need. Faxil, get dressed; get ready. I'll make us something to eat."

"What—you're making dinner? Now?" Faxil was dumbfounded.

His father grinned. "Never go looking for trouble on an empty stomach, my son. And that goes double for a khain."

Kuon stopped growling, turned her head to look at him and yipped her approval.

———

SOM ORSI TRAINING CENTER

Meera, now dressed in her Royal Army fatigues, raced to the conference room. She got there to find she was the last to arrive, and Prince Elio was already standing before them, as was Major Rosst and a woman she didn't recognize. *Wait—I do know her. She's the one who was there when we picked up Dr. Zettel.*

"Good. Now that you're here, Meera, we can get on," Prince Elio said. "First, let me introduce Andra Graynir, Royal Envoy and Agent of the Crown. She has extremely powerful TK.

"My intention was for her to work with you in your training, but unfortunately, that will have to wait. As it is, she and I will be accompanying you on your mission."

Meera tried not to wobble. *Prince Elio will join us?*

"Now, I have to tell you that we are receiving disturbing reports from all over Som Orsi. Hundreds of people have reported seeing Swarm soldiers. As the first reports came in, they were dismissed as hysteria, but no more. We are also receiving reports of a concentrated Swarm attack on Magnum Regis. I also have to inform you that we are now under a full military emergency." Prince Elio looked at each of them in turn, then said, "Questions?"

It was Klaus that spoke up. "Will we be going to Magnum, sir?"

"No," Prince Elio replied. "We will not be joining the defenders on Magnum. Those ships left at full burn almost thirty minutes ago. All military personnel left planetside are now part of urban pacification." He looked at his chron, then looked up at them and said, "We leave in five. Get to your assigned gravtrucks and be ready to protect your homes."

There was a rush to the door. Meera, at the rear of the group, happened to notice Major Rosst wasn't moving.

"Major, sir," she said, "aren't you coming with us?"

He smiled at her and said, "I have a small part to play here before I can leave."

Meera couldn't remember ever seeing him smile before.

"I'll be leading a platoon that is currently... preoccupied," he said. "They will be arriving soon, and we'll cover the flanks. Plenty of action for an old horse like me."

"I'm sorry I didn't do better in training, sir," she said as she turned to leave.

Rosst stepped forward, touched her shoulder, and said, "Wait!" She turned to look up at him.

"Young lady," he said, "and I can call you that as I am more than twice your age—it is not my place as a trainer to tell you how well you do. It's to tell you where you're lacking. Most trainees view their trainer as an enemy and vie for the only real win—respect. While I haven't been with your team long enough, you have all impressed me, especially you. Now go and impress the prince."

Barely able to contain her smile, she saluted him and fled to her gravtruck.

"If this was flight school, they'd have given you the call sign 'Overdue' by now," Andra yelled at her. "Now get in."

As Meera jumped in the back, Andra slammed the door and the gravtruck surged away.

Meera, her stomach churning, watched through the armored slits as the world flashed by so fast she was unable to see much of anything. At speeds approaching two-hundred-fifty kilometers per hour, the ride was short, and it seemed like only minutes later that the truck came to a stop.

"Pair up, you rookies," Andra shouted as she jumped out into the sunlight.

Meera quickly found herself next to Jude. He gave her a quick nod. She returned it, looked around and saw... She couldn't believe her eyes.

They were at a crossroads just inside the Feducere city limits. It was hot, dusty, with a warm breeze stirring the dust. The streets were deserted except for—*No!*

Marching toward them through the streets, dozens of Blues were firing their plasma weapons seemingly indiscriminately in every direction, raking buildings and killing anything that moved.

Meera stood still, her eyes scanning the streets, recording everything, even the tiniest detail: every crack in the pavement, every stressed girder or joint, every ruined building, every soldier, enemy or friend.

She watched as Jude began flinging pebbles at the enemy soldiers, striking them with pinpoint accuracy at speeds in excess of Mach 1, shattering their armor, penetrating deep inside.

Meera felt the explosive concussion as their bodies shattered and, without thinking, she reached out and seized the broken bodies and hurled them at the still advancing enemy, taking them out one by one.

"Hey, you've been holding out on us!" Jude shouted.

"No," she yelled back jubilantly. "I only figured it out about twenty minutes ago."

Meera tried not to think about the people that must have died in the shattered buildings. Instead, she concentrated on a downed light pole. Effortlessly, she lifted it a meter off the ground and threw it at a group of six Blues. It smashed into them, sweeping them away to crash into the building behind them.

But then, the building above them began to rumble. The ground began to shake. She looked up. The building, all eight stories, was beginning to break up; it was collapsing before her eyes. Dust and debris were raining down on them. The front wall began to crumble under its own weight. Meera could see large chunks of masonry break away and fall toward her. She concentrated, tried to steer them away, but it was too much for her. A large chunk of the building broke away and fell toward her.

She screamed, ducked down, her hands clamped over her head, expecting to be crushed under hundreds of tons of brickwork.

But suddenly, Andra was there, and Meera could feel a change in the mindspace around her. She looked up. The massive chunk of brickwork was hovering more than fifty meters above her head, crumbling, bits and pieces of debris falling all around them.

The entire wall teetered, then started to fall toward them, held only by a single girder. For several moments it hung there, and then the girder snapped and the eight-story wall slowly began to tilt and fall.

Again, Meera screamed and covered her head, but nothing happened. She looked up to see Andra holding back almost half of the slowly collapsing building. Meera was dumbfounded to see such power.

"Hey guys," Andra shouted. "Move out of the way. I'm going to let it fall. Watch out for collateral damage."

Meera stood up, turned and ran, then turned again and watched in amazement as the crumbling debris began to fall and surround Andra like a planetary ring of destruction.

———

BEYOND THE TAPE

Faxil did not feel comfortable sneaking around beyond the tape again with his family. Kuon seemed excited, alternately rushing this way and that, circling the tiny group, darting ahead, scouting the way.

No danger. Faxil felt the khain's thoughts.

But before he could say anything, Inoiae said, "I hear. I hear Kuon say something."

"She said there's no danger," Faxil said.

"It feel like word 'calm' to me," Inoiae replied.

Faxil couldn't be certain when he started picking up Kuon's hints and warnings, but he found he was pleased he could do something special.

He felt his father put a hand on his shoulder. He looked up at him, questioning.

"Son," Avestan said, "I've been meaning to... I have something I need to say. I know this is a difficult time for you... and I've been... selfish. I should have listened to you. I was wrong when I didn't believe you." He paused for a moment. Faxil looked up at him. "I should have spent more time with you, talked to you more, but I didn't because I didn't know how. Then I met Inoiae and the loneliness went away. So I moved on, dragging you along behind. I didn't respect you or your feelings as I should have."

"I understand," Faxil said.

"Well, we're a family, right?" Avestan said.

"Yes, Dad." He turned to look at Inoiae. "Mom?"

Inoiae began to tear up. "Yes. I be your other mom."

Other mom. It was such a simple idea, but one that had never occurred to him before. He could simply have another mother. Not a replacement but adopted. Like he had with Kuon, and Tup—Pinari.

Kuon pushed in between them, and as Faxil absently reached down to stroke her antennae, he realized his father's hand was already there, stroking her neck. Inoiae joined them, and the simple act of touching Kuon turned into a family hug —the first ever, as far as Faxil could remember.

"You are in a restricted area," he suddenly heard. They all turned to find five security guards staring at them in the dim light. Kuon began growling, her tail lashing.

"My name is—" Avestan began.

"It does not matter," another guard said. "You will leave now."

"My son says that there's suspicious activity here," Avestan replied. "I demand to see for myself."

"Your son lied to you," the first guard said.

"There's nothing suspicious," said another. "You need to leave, now!"

"Leave, or we will be forced to detain you," said a third.

"There is something wrong," Inoiae said. "These people; they do not feel right to me."

"Why are you not wearing USF uniforms?" Avestan asked calmly.

"Husband, they are not human," Inoiae whispered, but the guards heard her.

"We are human," one of the guards said—though Faxil couldn't tell which one it was.

"We're not leaving until we find out what's going on here," Avestan said.

The guards looked at one another, nodded, then pulled their weapons.

Kuon immediately jumped forward, snarling. She grabbed onto the arm of one of the guards, but despite her size, the guard effortlessly batted her away and marched forward, indifferent to the blood that streamed from his arm.

"You will now be detained," one of them said.

"Move!" Avestan shouted, shoving Faxil and Inoiae violently aside as they opened fire. The railgun fire was deafening. Concrete chips peppered Faxil's jacket.

"Now you stop!" Inoiae shouted.

They took no notice, pointed their weapons at her and fired.

But their arms flew upwards, the heavy railgun rounds streaking harmlessly over their heads.

"Inni, get moving. We need to get out of here," Avestan shouted.

"No," she yelled back. "My family run from Riadoaik. They run from Haiobuok. We come here for better life. I have better life now, and I WILL NOT RUN AGAIN."

This time the weapons aimed skyward, and the guards emptied their weapons, hundreds of rounds, into the air.

They looked at their weapons, tossed them aside and came forward with purpose.

Kuon charged, her tail slashing at the men who no longer acted human.

Avestan grabbed a metal bar lying on the ground and attacked first one, then another with vicious swings. One of them came at Faxil, arm swinging, and he froze in fear—

But Inoiae stepped in front of the blow, and the guard stopped moving. "You will not hurt *my Faxil*," she snapped.

The arm blow halted inches from her body. The guard reached for her with his other hand, his fingers clawing at her throat. But Inoiae simply caught the wrist and twisted it, and the guard was suddenly facing the other way, grunting in pain despite his now obvious inhumanity.

"You see, Faxil," she said calmly as she smashed her other arm down on the guard's elbow, shattering it. "Why do these humans not be people? I not know. But humans they are." She viciously kicked the man in the ribs, and Faxil heard a sickening crunch as the ribs gave way. "And humans, they break."

"But he is still a person?" Faxil said.

"No," she replied as she kicked the guard in the head and, with a final gasp, the guard lay still.

"I see eyes," she said. "No person there. I feel many new things in my thoughts. I feel you. I feel Kuon. I feel nothing in him. Only distant command to kill us."

She turned to another guard, lashing out with powerful strikes. Faxil couldn't believe this small woman was capable of such fury. Her second victim was soon on the ground, his hands to his throat, gurgling his last breath.

Faxil looked over to where his father had two of the remaining guards at his feet, the pipe thick with blood, and a bloody gash on his face. Kuon was standing over the fifth guard, a hunk of dripping flesh in her mouth, but when she looked at Faxil, she dropped it.

"Come here. Look," Inoiae said, crouching down beside her last victim. She pointed to the dead man's forearm, and the strange symbol burned into his skin—ら.

Avestan nodded and bent over his victims. "Same here," he said, "both of them. Who are they? What..." He obviously didn't know what else to say.

"Let's go," he said. "I want to see what it is they didn't want us to find. Lead the way, son."

Bolstered by his father's brave words, Faxil pointed. "The hole is over there, under—"

But before he could say more, and before they could move, the ground began to shake violently.

"Get down," Avestan cried out, grabbing them, one on

either side. Inoiae fell to the ground, Avestan on top of her, covering her with his body. Faxil fell to the ground beside them, Kuon next to him.

The shaking increased exponentially, accompanied by loud rumbling, an ear-splitting screech and a deep throbbing hum.

The ground continued to shake beneath them as they huddled together.

Faxil couldn't help himself. He had to look. The ground in front of them slowly erupted upward as a massive ship—its shields shimmering electric blue—rose slowly from the depths.

———

SOM ORSI TRAINING CENTER

Eugma Zettel sat quietly in his cell, a tiny space with featureless walls, a blank steel door and two guards outside. *They think they've taken every precaution*, he thought, *but they're wrong.*

He reached out and seized control of their minds and bodies. One stood still, his body rigid. The other withdrew a key, inserted it, turned it, and the door opened.

Zettel released his hold on the two guards. It was very difficult to maintain control of their bodies through his helmet. But he'd practiced for so long...

Released, they looked at each other, nodded and drew their batons. He struck out at their minds. They dropped to their knees, their hands clamped over their ears, screaming in pain.

He wrenched at his helmet, trying to find a way to pry the strap loose. "I've got to get rid of this thing," he muttered as he ran out into the corridor. "A knife... No... scissors. I need to find an office—"

He rounded the corner at a run and ran straight into Major Rosst. Rosst was holding a chair.

Before Zettel could react, the chair slammed into his face.

He staggered backwards, raising his hands, but the chair slammed into his head again.

Dazed, barely able to stand, he tried to strike at Rosst's mind, but it wasn't there.

The chair came down again, striking the helmet, and Zettel had the distinct impression his head was inside a bell.

"I never trusted you," Rosst snarled, "you insufferable little bastard. But you knew that. You poked and prodded my thoughts for weeks. I knew something was wrong. Never before have I acted the way I have since I met you. Then the prince told me he could feel you manipulating people—not until today, mind you. So he gave me this." He pointed to the halo around his brow.

My design, Zettel thought. *They used my own design against me again.*

"And the privilege of being the one to tell you that you will never escape. Understand, little pig?"

The chair rose again, and Zettel raised his arms and gave up. He slumped to the floor in surrender. His head began to buzz painfully.

"What... is... that?" he stammered.

"It's a toy one of our specialists designed," Rosst replied with a smile. "It broadcasts thoughts. Not real ones, of course, more like background static, so I'm told. You won't be able to think or do any damage for a looong time."

Zettel could barely see his guards. They'd recovered from his attack but were *very* angry.

"Take him back to Conquell," Rosst snapped. "He's violated his parole. We will not make the same mistake again."

CHAPTER
TWENTY-SIX

FIGHT IN FLIGHT

ODIN FRIGATE *JUSTIFICATION*

Second-Corporal Lagu Feria jogged along the corridor to the meeting room. When he arrived, he was saddened to see just how many of his comrades were missing.

The squads were lined up, as he expected. But there were so many holes in the ranks, most of them sergeants. Master Sergeant Strigget and Captain Objur stood at the head of the gathering, talking quietly to each other.

Dusina was there, standing in her place, hands clasped behind her back, hair neatly tucked beneath her cap.

"You were up early," he whispered. "How so?"

"I needed a walk," she replied. "Everything's upside down now. I needed to think."

Lagu nodded. Ever since the raid, her mood had been off and, well... she didn't come to him at night.

We lost a lot of people, she reached out to him. *It's... devastating.*

She heaved one of her irritable sighs and shook her head.

He was about to ask her what she was thinking but was

interrupted when Prince Tarak entered the room and they all snapped to attention.

"At ease," he said. "There are some things I need to talk to you about before we get down to business."

Lagu was surprised at how casual the prince was. *Is it just for show?* he wondered.

"First, we just entered the TK-421 Slipgate and are en route to the Orso System. Caerus is under attack, and they need help. Can we get there in time? I don't know." He paused, looked around, then continued, "If not, they'll need aid and recovery. We can help with that."

Lagu hoped they'd be in time.

"Second, I want to thank the Horus Border Control Unit 27 and their captain for joining us in this endeavor," Prince Tarak continued. "While I hadn't expected to take any losses on our previous operation, we certainly did, and the mission turned out to be far more important than I realized. Instead of a simple salvage bust, we uncovered evidence that there's a vast conspiracy against the Sovereign Stars. And without the four teams of BC 27, we wouldn't have been prepared for what we found. In short, I believe we would have failed. The enemy was prepared for us. They knew we were coming. A fact which supports my conclusion that had it not been for BC 27, they might have gotten us all."

He took a deep breath and continued, "After communication with Geb-nute, I am inviting any and all of the remaining BC 27 agents to join my task force. If you cannot or do not want to serve me in this endeavor, please take a step forward and transportation back to Geb-nute will be arranged for you."

He looked around, waiting. Not a single border control agent stepped forward.

"Good," Prince Tarak said, nodding. "I thank you for your support. Now, Captain Objur will give you your new assignments."

Everyone snapped to attention as Captain Objur stepped forward.

"We'll begin with some promotions," he began. "My only regret is that every one of you receiving a promotion will be doing so at the cost of another. First Corporal Vaqui Dusina?"

"Yes, sir," she snapped to attention.

"You are hereby promoted to Lance Sergeant and given command of Team One. Congratulations."

"Thank you, sir," she replied in the tradition. "I will discharge this duty with honor and vigor."

As Objur moved on, she whispered to Lagu, "Obviously you're a corporal. I'll make you my second."

Lagu thought of all those times they'd shared a bunk and now he could feel her new authority driving her passion onward and upward. And he knew her promotion meant that he would rarely, if ever, rack early or sleep quietly.

But for some reason he couldn't fathom, his thoughts turned to Hallaba , someone he'd met. But someone he somehow felt a strange connection to. He was intrigued; he wanted to know more about her. Never before had he felt the tingle between minds that he did with her.

"What's wrong with you?" Dusina whispered.

"What?"

"What just happened to your brain? It's like—"

"Second-Corporal Lagu Feria?"

"Yes, sir?" Lagu replied.

"For distinctive gallantry and tactical thinking, you are hereby promoted to Lance Sergeant and command of Team Three."

His thoughts were thrown sideways. *Wait—I'm what? I just jumped rank?* He'd thought maybe, eventually, he'd get promoted, but—

"Um, thank you, sir," he replied. "I will discharge my duty with honor and vigor."

He could barely stop fidgeting as the captain finished the

roster, assigning members from different units to the open slots. And then, by some weird coincidence, he heard Hallaba Ulsare assigned to his team. After they were dismissed, he tried to talk to Dusina, but she simply turned and marched away.

"Hey, what's the deal?" he said as he jogged to catch up. "Aren't you happy you got promoted?"

"Hey, aren't you happy *you* got promoted?" she mimicked as she turned the corner.

"I'm surprised is what I am," Lagu protested. "I had no idea, but this is a huge deal, right? Who hears of a nobody getting pushed up to lower noncom?"

"*Nobody,* apparently," she snapped. "That's who."

"Wait," he said. "Are you angry that I was promoted? Why would that upset you?"

"I picked you as partner," she said, "because you did what you were told, and you didn't act like you wanted to run off. Well, congratulations."

"But I don't want to run off," he said. "We're the same rank now, right? There's nothing anyone can say about us now. I mean, everyone kind of knew, but we can just date openly and stuff now, right?"

She stopped, turned to look at him, and said, "Do I ever act like I want to *date* a man?"

"I mean, we're in a relationship. Right?"

"Stars," she said and rolled her eyes. "Call a puppy a wolf and give him a pack and he thinks... I don't do 'relationships.' I don't do 'dating.' I just do lots and lots of sex because that's what I want; that's what I need. You think I spent all my time with you? I didn't. I knew you weren't going anywhere. And, like a good puppy, you waited for me. But I already knew you didn't want to wait anymore."

She waved her hand at him. "Get along, little doggie. Go find your pack and tell them how happy you are to be the big bad wolf." Her gaze shifted behind him. "And be sure to invite your new bi—"

"Cor—I mean Sergeant Dusina?" newly-minted First-Corporal Humba called from the end of the hall. "Master Sergeant Strigget needs a word."

"Whatever," Dusina snapped and turned and marched away.

———

REGIS MAGNUM SPACE

Danis hauled hard to port on the yoke, streaking past the lumbering ship just in time to avoid a stray missile from *Censorious*. "Why are our own ships firing at us?" she yelled into the comm.

"Don't know—station securi—at this ti—"

"And we don't have station communications up yet?" Danis shouted as she narrowly avoided another missile. She flipped the B-29 into a tight, twisting turn and, as she swept by *Censorious'* starboard missile battery, the B-29 launched one of its own, and then she watched her screens as the capital ship's launcher exploded in a spectacular ball of flame that died away quickly in the vacuum.

The B-29 was a fighter bomber, an amazing machine, maneuverable, loaded with firepower and a sweetheart to fly. It was not, however, an F32A. Its primary weaponry was its complement of sixteen M59 50-megaton Lance missiles; the B-29 was a ship-killer. Its capacity as a fighter was defensive. Its secondary weaponry was its quad, 55-caliber railguns and, as sweet as the B-29 was, Danis missed her 32A.

"Whoo," she yelled. "Must have caught one in the tube. Jennat, was that you?"

"Yes, ma'am," came the quiet reply from her TK.

"Don't be shy, Jennat," Danis said as she reversed her engines and tipped the fighter-bomber over into a side-on loop, dodging a Swarm fighter. "Be creative with the power you have, but don't forget to let me know what you're doing," she yelled as she fired a stream of fifty-five millimeter railgun rounds into the Swarm fighter, sending it spinning away minus half its port wing and the two weapons platforms mounted thereon.

"But I'm not very talkative," Jennat replied.

"Today is definitely not the day for that," Danis said through her teeth as she fired at a second Blue as it leveled off and tried to match her heading. "Can you do anything about him?"

She watched as the Blue fighter veered away. Danis turned hard to starboard to match its trajectory and fired her railguns, catching the ship just as it sideslipped away from her. It exploded beneath her in a ball of brilliant blue fire.

"Too late," Danis yelled. "Hold on. Here we go." And she rolled the B-29, dropped its nose and slid into a long spiraling dive that brought the B-29 onto the rear of two more Blues. Firing quad streams of railgun rounds as she hurtled by, one of the Blues shattering into millions of tiny shards, and the other turned and hurtled away.

"Domino!" she heard Jackknife shout. "On your six. Incoming."

She slammed the B-29 hard to starboard just as Jackknife's railguns shredded the Blue that had followed her dive.

"Thank you, Jackknife," she shouted.

"All in a day's work," he replied. "Saw them coming for you."

Danis rolled her eyes. It was yet another non-admission that Jackknife had the Sight.

Danis glanced at her screens. The amount of information streaming across them was unimaginable, daunting and, for a lesser pilot, almost unfathomable. She shook her head, sat up in her seat and looked out through the canopy. Space in all directions was a mass of craft of one sort or another: Blue fighters. Huge Blue ships the like of which she'd never seen before. USF fighters and bombers. Eight Vindication ships, one of them with malfunctioning shields, firing on *Avenger*.

"Domino to Crash," Danis said into the comm. "We see malfunctioning shields on one of the cruisers. Looks like... *Benediction*. Advise."

"Kill it," Axi shouted. "Enemy is in control. Take it out."

"Domino Flight, on me and follow me in," she called. "Lance missiles. We're going to try to peel one of those parasites off my brother."

One after another, the ten B-29s in her flight swooped in. "We have a weak shield in the aft docking junction," she shouted. "Concentrate your fire there. Firing two..." Her fingers hovered over the console as she counted down as the distance between her and the *Benediction* closed. *Four... Three... Two...* "Now!" She yelled as two of her Lance missiles streaked toward the great ship's aft docking junction. She made a hard turn to Port, dropped the B-29's nose, and hurtled away—her speed approaching Mach 10—down and around in a great circle that brought her once again face-to-face with the wounded *Benediction.*

It was at that moment someone on the *Benediction* finally noticed them and started firing. Fortunately, the gunners, so it seemed, weren't experienced, and the streams of railgun rounds tracked poorly.

"One more time," she called. "Follow me in. Watch out for those railguns."

Each of her ten fighters, one after the other, unleashed its missiles.

"Penetration," called Domino-six. "We have a confirmed hit inside shields."

"I'm going for another run," called Domino-nine.

"Negative, Nine," Domino called. "Return to forma—"

"But I have a great shot," the pilot yelled, cutting Danis off as he swooped in and fired a pair of Lance's... just as one of the *Benediction's* aft railguns erupted with multiple streams of fire moving too fast for Danis to see. Ten brilliant white lines of gunfire sheered two of Nine's upper port engine struts. The engine, one of four, died, and Nine's bomber went into an uncontrolled spin.

"I've lost steering," he yelled. "Can't pull it—"

"Rotate your upper starboard engine forty-five degrees clockwise. Cut power to your remaining port engine and stabilize."

"Not working—can make—aft junction."

"Nine, pull out of there. Do as you're told."

But Nine wasn't listening. He plunged into the *Benediction's* aft docking junction, firing all ten of his remaining missiles.

Danis watched as the *Benediction's* aft dock blew apart in a blinding flash of white light. Explosions rippled through the great ship from aft to bow until, with one last cataclysmic explosion, she disintegrated.

"You know," Jennat whispered, "it's kind of ironic, don't you think?"

"What do you mean?" Danis asked. "What's ironic?"

"Well, it's just that... well, a benediction is the end. But this one was the first—"

"Two of our people just died, Jennat," Danis snapped, interrupting her. "So shut up and shove something."

ONE THOUSAND KILOMETERS OUT FROM REGIS MAGNUM

Tenilo didn't even bother to keep track anymore. He'd been flying so fast, for so long, with his mind stretched so far, that it didn't even matter. He was a fleet of ships. He knew he could look at the camera systems and find himself slumped in the command chair of the *Colossus,* surrounded by food waste.

He'd not risen from the chair for a hundred million kilometers.

Ahead was the Regis Magnum Shipyards. With his mind tied directly into all the systems, he could see the battle unfolding as easily as he might see a three-dimensional holo in the war room.

It was worse than he'd ever imagined.

Sovereign ships were firing on the station, Swarm fighters were flocking in every direction, and the new dreadnoughts were firing on the incomplete ships in the docks, destroying all the progress that had been made building the Vindication fleet.

And in the center of the conflagration, just as he'd expected, was Captain Morian, his shields failing, his ammunition almost exhausted. It was little surprise to note that *Avenger's* entire compliment of DEWs had been removed during the recent multiple refits. *Avenger's* armament had been reduced to nothing but missiles and railguns.

Colossus, on the other hand, and the rest of his ragtag fleet—

Tenilo redirected all power to the DEW weaponry and activated them. During the USF-wide refit of 3279, they'd never bothered to remove them from the gargantuan vessel. The ship was so vast that they'd simply added one-hundred-seventy railgun turrets to the hull. *Less time and less effort*, Tenilo assumed. *Hah!* And their shortsighted thinking would serve him well.

"Avenger," Tenilo reached out to Morian. "This is Colossus. Are you there, Captain Morian?"

"Who is this?" Morian's reply felt... uncomfortable.

"Ah, Captain Morian," Tenilo replied happily. "It is I, Tenilo Barum. I and my fleet are here to help. Please get out of my way. You have exactly two minutes and thirty-three seconds."

"What?" To Tenilo, Morian now felt outraged. "Mister Barum? Tenilo? What are you doing?"

Tenilo grimaced to himself. "Something very stupid,

Captain. Now please, do as I ask. Go to heading one-five-five and get out of there in... one minute, seven seconds."

He felt the giant ship's massive DEW batteries turn, swivel, and lock onto the five remaining Vindication ships.

"Goodspeed, Richard Morian. Fight the fight," he screamed as he unleashed the energy generated by all ten fusion reactors of energy.

———

AVENGER. REGIS MAGNUM SPACE

"Mr. DeLong, go to one-five-five, flank speed. Now!" Captain Morian shouted.

"But sir, we can't—"

"Do it. All hands. Brace for acceleration," he called over the comm. "All fighters go to one-five-five *now!*"

He felt the ship rock as all of her thrusters went to maximum thrust. Anyone not secured in their seats was thrown backwards before inertia dampeners could mitigate. And Morian watched the screens as *Colossus* fired.

Almost ten terawatts of lasers lanced through space to strike the Vindication ships. As *Avenger* broke off its defense of the station, *Colossus* swept past, raking the Vindication fleet and battering three shredded hulls out of his way.

"That's a really big ship," Morian muttered as he continued watching the two-kilometer-long hull sweep by, blocking out his screens.

When it had passed, he could see that three of the attacking ships had survived, though their wounds were severe. But as *Colossus* cleared his view, the enemy fire continued unabated.

"Helm. Roll to zero-six-five."

Morian, surprised to hear the order, turned to see Commander Jadern was now on deck and was seated in Manda Haal's command chair, his eyes bright, his voice crisp.

"Shields redirect power to the keel," Jadern snapped. "Lower port batteries come to bear on zero-nine-nine. Acquire target lock and fire at will."

One-hundred-twenty 50-megaton Lance missiles streaked away, a veritable sheet of flame as they streaked across the void. Sixty-two were destroyed by point-defense fire; fifty-eight slammed into their targets, blasting hull fragments and railgun emplacements into space.

But still, the enemy persisted.

REGIS MAGNUM SPACE

The battle wasn't going well.

Danis flew as she'd never done before. The space around Magnum was a veritable firestorm of railgun fire, missiles, hundreds of Blue fighters, and ships that belonged to neither the USF nor IMFP.

She banked, she spun, she corkscrewed, she turned and she flipped—all in a fighter less responsive than her own F32A.

"Jennat," she said, "how you doing back there?"

"Doing my best, Domino," she called back, obviously growing queasy. "My stomach... I can barely focus, and I keep having to help you steer."

"Help me steer?" Danis felt a little indignant. *Then again, I hate these cumbersome dead-weight ships.*

"You're making a lot of tight turns," Jennat replied. "Tighter than this ship can handle. I help with some of the tough turns to give you a better shot. But it's getting so hard to focus."

Huh! she thought. *Elio never mentioned having this problem.* But, Danis was quick to realize, Elio was a whole other category of amazing.

"So what do you recommend, Jennat?" she asked.

Jennat snorted. "Besides not getting into a space conflict? I have nothing."

"Attention, 29s," came Axi's voice. "We have just been asked to do a run on one of the big Blue bastards."

"What about that junk fleet?" someone asked. "Can't we ask one or two of them to run interference for us?"

"I had a talk with Avenger," Axi replied. "Junk fleet, as you call it, not responding."

"Why aren't they responding?" Danis asked.

"What matter?" Axi replied. "They still keeping other three USF ships at bay. We peel Blue carrier off their flank, no? Join formation."

"Affirm, Crash-one," Gian shouted.

"Ready when you are, Crash Lady," came Jackknife's insouciant reply.

Danis and her flight settled into the four-flight formation. "Domino Flight ready, Crash-one."

As she looked out at the gathered fighters, her heart sank as she saw that many were missing. Of forty B-29s that had launched, only twenty-four remained. *Good survivability, I suppose; all things considered,* she thought and hated herself for it.

"Joker, you take mast gun," Axi ordered. "I want it gone fast. Multiple angles of attack. Keep them confused. Domino, go for bridge. Jackknife, you and I will take rear. We destroy engines, yes?"

"You got it, Crash," Jackknife replied. "On you, Lady Crash."

Danis had a thought. "What about salvage? Surely they'll want—"

"If they want a piece of this thing, they're welcome to come get it," Axi snarled. "Not my job. I bring back people, not garbage. Ready, squadron?"

"Ready."

"Then we do this!" Axi cried.

The four flights broke as instructed. Danis and her trainees drove straight at what was assumed to be the bridge of the Blue carrier, launching missiles as they went. *Okay, I'll give these barges one credit,* Danis thought. *They don't take as long to reload.* She could hear the automatic loaders working deep inside the fuselage.

Danis could also see Joker-flight making pass after pass at the massive mast turret, forward, atop the ship until suddenly, the massive topside turret exploded in a gigantic ball of blue fire. The enemy carrier began to turn away as Axi and Jackknife's flight began to attack the rear.

Their concentrated barrages began to take their toll on the Blue carrier. Great chunks of its hull began to break away. What once had been the mast turret was now a widening ball of debris and—

Then something extraordinary happened. As they watched in amazement, huge tentacles appeared from ports all around the hull and began pulling the damaged sections back together.

"What? How the hell?" Danis heard several pilots exclaim.

How did they do that? she thought, totally awed by what she was seeing. *How were they able to build entirely new ships, like carriers? How many more do they have like these?*

The blue fighters began circling their mother ship, protecting it from further attack.

As close as they now were, Danis could see that the fighters, too, were different, even from the second-generation version of a year earlier. With the single long body, and the forward-swept fins, they were more heavily armed; their armor was thicker and their weapons larger, much larger.

"I name that model Blue fighter, Ballista," Axi announced. "Squadron. Attack. All fronts. Go!"

And ninety-six railguns opened fire, almost as one, hurling streams of 55-milimeter railgun rounds at the new Blue fighters. The damage was almost instant and immediately devastating, but as the pilots began to cheer, so the Ballistae began to heal themselves.

"Son of a scum-sucking—" Jackknife began to curse.

Only for Axi to preempt his transmission. "Get back in your head. We're out here to fight. We not lose to bunch of nightlights. Squadron, switch to kinetic Harpoons. Domino-flight, attack fighters. Joker-flight, stand by to pick off strays. Knife-flight, follow me. We attack rear. All wait until see whites of eyes." Danis grinned to hear the ancient axiom. "Hit hard and keep hitting. When hull cracks, I want to see precision targeting. GO."

Danis led her pilots in, waiting... waiting... waiting... silently thanking the stars for her clear head and the courage to wait for the right moment.

———

JUSTIFICATION

In Orbit Planet Citrom

Lagu watched Dusina leave. He felt his energy drain away. *How did that just happen?*

"She's lying, you know."

Lagu jumped and turned to find an unfamiliar small woman behind him. "What? How did you—"

"Sneak up on you? I'm very sneaky," she said proudly. "But she lied when she said she slept with other guys. At least, while she was with you."

"How do you know? Wait, are you Hallaba?"

As if in response, she opened her mind a little, and the tingle swept over him.

She was not what he'd expected. Besides being slimmer than most, she had a cap of tight red curls trimmed to the regulation inch. Her eyes were a vibrant green, her nose sharp, and her heart-shaped face was covered with freckles. She wasn't anything like Dusina or any other military woman he'd ever known. She looked… adorable.

"I was a police interrogator before I became Psy-Ops," Hallaba said. "She has a lot of tells."

"So… she really does love me?" Lagu asked, confused.

"Oh stars, no," Hallie replied. "That she was completely honest about. What she liked was being able to control you. As soon as you were promoted, you didn't *have* to listen to her. So she quit. But I'm not going to quit."

"What do you mean?"

"You know why, Lagu," she replied. "We share something different," she said. "That weird fizzy you cause inside in my brain… I want to know what it is as much as you do. And maybe this is a little awkward, me catching you on the rebound like this, but I'm not one to pass up an opportunity. But there's one catch, one thing you need to know before we move on; that is if you want to move on."

"I'm listening," he replied.

"Ooh, confident and patient. I can work with that." She giggled. "You need to know what a real relationship is like. She's twisted that idea in your mind. So—" She stopped smiling. "We aren't going to have sex. At all."

"At all?"

"At all."

He thought about long, cold nights in a lonely bunk. "What about if—"

"Definitely none of that, either." She waggled a finger at him. "Don't even go there. If you do, I'll know."

He almost believed her.

"So, I get an interesting and beautiful girlfriend, and I have to be celibate?"

"What do you mean, beautiful?" she asked seriously. "Do you already have another offer?"

"No. I mean you."

"Oh please," she said, looking away. "I'm not beautiful."

He reached out and touched her mind, and he could tell she really meant it. He could feel the echoes of many past disappointments.

"You know what the hardest part of this... relationship is going to be?" he said.

"What?" she asked.

"Convincing you that you're wrong." He smiled at her. "I really do think you're cute."

"Cute isn't beautiful," she said self-consciously.

"Taken under advisement," he said and reached out with his hand.

"Hey," she snapped. "Last guy who got handsy walked away with two broken fingers."

"I just want to hold your hand," he said as he slipped his hand into hers. "Isn't that what normal, celibate new couples do?"

"You're weird," she said as she clasped his hand. "But I like it."

They started walking down the hall.

"At least until you disappoint me, Sergeant," she said, giving a little smirk. "Then I'll feed you into an exhaust port."

"Again, taken under advisement," he said. "But I'll take the risk."

CHAPTER
TWENTY-SEVEN

REGIS MAGNUM SHIPYARDS

CENTRAL CORE

The Champions

Dagon Jax ran quickly through the hallways of Regis Magnum. The power had been partially restored, but the station rocked from the occasional missile strike, and he had to wonder how many of its systems had failed, how many sections had been breached and were venting atmosphere.

Kasa de Cevoir was close on his heels, not wanting to be left alone.

He rounded the corner to find Commander Haal arguing with Sasha Crowe and several of the *Avenger's* crew. "We need to go. Right now," she snapped.

"Excuse me, Commander. I need to—" Dagon shouted.

But Sasha startled, looked at him, waved a hand at him and said impatiently, "In a minute, kid. Can't you see we're busy?" and turned again to Haal.

"I respect you, Manda, but you're asking us to ignore a critical situation. We need to get someone to Weapons Control and switch the turrets to manual. We have to support *Avenger* and her fighters."

"Support isn't the question now," Haal snapped. "We need to—"

"This is really important" Dagon interrupted again.

"Jax, this is an emergency," Sasha lashed out at him. "Just shut up. We'll get to you in a moment. Now, Manda, we were just about to—"

Haal, beyond frustrated, lost her temper. "No!" she snapped. "You shut up. And don't ever disrespect a member of my crew again. You're not among your pirates here." She turned to Dagon and said, "This had better be good, Mister Jax."

Dagon gulped, took a deep breath and said, "Kasa, here, was in the system trying to restore functions when something took all control away from her. We need to get to the computer core and... um... reboot it or reset it or..." Not knowing what to say next, he looked desperately at Kasa.

Kasa took a half step forward. "Someone, or something, has hacked into the central computer core. We need to find out where in the system the access point was created. "I can... hack in there and cut off their access to all system resources and finish rerouting the..." She hesitated. She'd already said more than she should have. "I can fix it," she finished lamely.

"What she said," Dagon added.

Sasha stared at Kasa, her face pale. *Hyde! The Champions!*

"Everyone," she snapped. "Change of plans. Kasa, or whatever your name is, d'you know the way to the core?"

Kasa nodded.

"Very well," Sasha said. "We'll follow you. Go!"

"Is something wrong, Captain?" Dagon asked after seeing the look of alarm on her face.

"Yes, something's wrong," Sasha snapped. "It's that damn woman, Hyde. She's activated the Champions. Run!"

And Kasa nodded, turned and took off running, Sasha close on her heels, the rest following as best they could.

"What is it, Commander?" Dagon asked as they ran. "What's going on, and what are the Champions?"

"Project Champion," Haal replied. "It's a security force Marshal Hyde created. They're robots."

"Doesn't sound very useful if they don't have access to the... security... feeds." Jax gasped, and the import of what he said sank home.

"You're right, Jax," Haal said, her arms pumping as she ran. "They would indeed be useless... unless they had control of the central core."

———

PLANET CAERUS

Feducere city limits.

Meera, stunned by the extent of her new-found powers, heard Dr. Zettel's words again.

I've never met a TK with this ability, he'd said. *No one else feels the entire world the way you do.*

She concentrated. Her vision expanded. She could feel... everything. She could see the entire city of Som Orsi: the Blues, the humans, the fighters, the fleeing refugees. But she couldn't touch anything. She felt, *etherial?*

Frightened, she pulled back, but not before realizing a terrible truth.

We are losing.

The Blues are everywhere, she thought, almost at the point of panicking. *Thousands of them rising from beneath the city, and they're pushing us back. How did they get here? Where did they come from? From crashed ships from the Slipgate Battle? There were hundreds, no, thousands of them, most of them undetected. Could they have carried cells of Blues? To do what? To hide, to plan, to do... what? It's been more than a year. They've multiplied? Reproduced?*

Replicated? Built new ships? Birthed an army, all underground?

She took a deep breath, closed her eyes, concentrated, and took control of her churning mind.

Help!

Meera spun around. *Where?*

Felt you. Help us. My family... Something here...

She reached out with her newfound TK senses, and she found them. Three kilometers away, close to one of the tunnels where Blues were still swarming out, she could feel *three, no, four souls.*

Show me what you've seen, Meera.

She was startled. Prince Elio had reached out and touched her mind.

My Prince. And she opened her mind to him.

This is really bad, Elio told her, and her heart sank.

We need a plan of some kind, Meera said. *How can we possibly talk about this while we're fighting?*

Great idea, Prince Elio suddenly said, and she felt his touch lessen—only to begin feeling others touch her mind.

Elio, how did you— she felt Andra.

Where did this come from? Proost.

Stars! This is not— Jude.

Listen to me, Prince Elio's commanding presence silenced the others. *Meera has given me a view of the battlefield, and it isn't going well. We've been pushed into a box and we're about to be surrounded. We need a way out. Meera, show them everything you can about the immediate area.*

Meera concentrated, reached out and scanned the area for three kilometers in every direction, pulling in every movement, every tremor, every structural weakness she could sense.

Some of these buildings are already dangerously unstable, Andra transmitted. *We could collapse some atop the Blues.*

How would we—?

Which buildings are you—?

These two, Andra said, *and this one over here... Klaus, if you could accelerate something big directly into this section here.* The view changed to a closeup of the section as Meera manipulated the vision. *Can you do that Klaus?*

I can, Klaus replied.

What about these weak points in the surface, here, here, here, and here? Elio asked. *It looks like there's a huge aquifer down there. Meera, can you shake the surface loose, collapse it so the Blues fall through?*

I... think so, Meera said. *I'll try, but there are civilians trapped to the east; somewhere here. I think they have a Psy with them, and they said there's something... I don't know what it is.*

Understood, Elio replied. The prince sounded grim. *My friends, this is what you were recruited for. I'd hoped to train you more, turn you into a crack unit of civilian soldiers, but time and the enemy wait for no man. Even so, you've exceeded my every expectation. So this is the moment. This is the moment when we live or die.* **I choose to live!** he shouted.

Through Prince Elio's link, Meera could feel a fierce determination rising among her companions. She could feel their powers growing.

Today is the day we will begin to stop this cataclysm, and the next, and the next. And we will never... stop... FIGHTING!

NEVER! NEVER! NEVER! NEVER! they chanted as the Swarm pushed them back into the square to the statue of old King Lorne.

Andra's TK flung Rauf toward the twin buildings they'd pinpointed. He crashed through the first like an orbital strike, then pushed off the foundation to strike the second with shattering force.

Klaus lifted a wrecked gravtruck and sent it flying at a speed approaching two-hundred kilometers an hour to smash into the third building, the corner of the structure exploding in a mass of flying rubble and concrete. The building shook. There was a ground-shaking rumble and the building began to topple onto the massed Swarm troopers. Meera struck the roadways, causing the weakened sections to collapse underneath the Blues, opening up a vast chasm hundreds of feet deep into which more than a hundred Blue troopers fell, the walls of the chasm collapsing in on them, along with several more buildings, their foundations collapsing as the ground fell away beneath them.

Meera took off running past the melee, using her TK to watch the troops ahead and deflect their attack. She was so focused on the enemy in front that she missed the sound of the footsteps following her, nor did she sense the shower of concrete debris that hurtled past her, smashing through the enemy lines.

She turned her head. "Klaus?" she said aloud, her connection with Elio and the rest of the group broken. "What are you doing here? Where's Jude?"

"I told him we should trade partners," he said as he fired a burst from his railgun, tearing the heads of two Blues from their shoulders.

"I think I better for you than Jude, no?" he asked, grinning at her.

"I think... Yes!" she shouted and turned again to face the enemy, Klaus now at her side. His railgun howling as he swept it back and forth, tearing into their ranks, shards of Blue armor flying into the air, glittering in the early afternoon sunlight.

REGIS MAGNUM SHIPYARDS

To the Core

.   .   .

MANDA FOLLOWED the leggy computer tech she now knew to be Kasa de Cevoir as she raced through the labyrinthine hallways. Sasha Crowe, just over a meter tall and a natural athlete, was far ahead of them. The girl seemed to unerringly know where she was going, never pausing, never hesitating.

How does a slip of a technician memorize the layout of a station this vast? Manda wondered as she ran.

There's something strange about that girl. There are too many unknowns. Who is she really? Where did she come from? Not here, that's certain. But there's no time for that.

"We're almost there. It's just ahead," Manda heard Kasa call out, only to see Sasha running back toward them. "Too late," Sasha shouted. "It's too late. Take cover. Now!"

Everyone in the group, all six of them, including Sasha, ducked through an open doorway, the rapid-spattering fire of bullets tikkering off every surface along the passage: walls, floor, ceiling.

Kasa shouted, "That way, through the door, follow me. I can get us there."

"Here, take this," Jax shouted as he handed Manda a DEW pistol.

"Where did you get that?" she asked.

"Picked them up earlier," he said. "I thought they might come in handy."

He peeked out and fired a burst at the advancing Champions, hitting one in the chest. It didn't even scratch it, nor did it stop its advance.

"What the heck, Captain?" he shouted at Crowe. "How are they impervious to laser fire?"

"It's some kind of armored material Hyde developed last year," she yelled back, "heat-disbursing poly-resin, or something. They layer it on, and the top layer sheds heat, but it burns away if it gets too hot. If you—" She pulled back as a burst of railgun fire slammed into the wall close to her head. "If you set your laser to pinpoint and hold it steady, you can burn through it, but who has time for that?"

"Do kinetics work at all?" Manda shouted.

"Only under concentrated precision fire," Sasha replied. "And, well, 55s would probably work, too, but they don't make handguns that big, do they?"

"What's the weak point?" Manda asked.

"There is only one," Sasha shouted. "The AI control functions are located center mass, where the human gut would be, where the armor is heaviest."

"I need marksmen, Mr. Jax," Manda called to him. "Soldiers with rifles. Go to the other hallway and relay that information."

"But, ma'am—" Jax stammered.

"That's an order, Jax," she snapped.

"What about me?" Kasa yelled. "If I can just get to the computer core, I can shut this all down."

"Someone get the tech past the robots," Manda shouted as Lt. Pazon suddenly appeared beside her.

"Need some help, Commander?" he asked as he leaned out and sighted down the corridor. "Holy sh..!" he said and glanced back at her. "They're Blues. How the hell? And they're armed with standard USF weapons."

"They're not Blues," Sasha shouted. "Hyde designed them like that to confuse the enemy."

"And she didn't think they would confuse our own soldiers?" Manda shouted back at her.

Pazon grinned as he fired a stream of 6mm rounds at the leading Champion. "I'm not confused at all," he said, just loud enough for Manda to hear. "One Blue bastard is just like any other," he said as the Champion's armor cracked under the stream of concentrated fire.

"Keep firing, Pazon. And someone get Kasa to the core," Manda shouted.

———

REGIS MAGNUM SHIPYARDS

Central Lab Complex
Corridor P3a

Sasha Crowe joined Lt. Pazon at the door and dropped to one knee. The leading Champion, its chest smoking, was now less than sixty meters away and advancing steadily. Sasha took careful aim and fired her laser at the opening in its armor.

The robot stiffened, then fell forward under its own momentum. By then, Pazon had cracked open three more Champions.

Sasha adjusted her aim, and one by one, she dropped them until the robots were almost on top of them.

She tapped Manda on the shoulder. She was lying prone beside her firing her own laser pistol to little effect, then she grabbed Pazon's arm and shouted, "We can't hold them. Let's get out of here. Come on, Manda. You want to die here?"

"Why are you treating this like a game, Crowe?" Manda shouted as she leapt to her feet.

"All of life is a game. You lose, you die. The point is to win."

"Is that what's gotten you this far?" Manda said as they backed away from the doorway.

"Good thing Hyde isn't here," Sasha said, ignoring her question. "She'd be taking notes on how to improve them."

A bullet pinged off the bulkhead close to Manda's head.

"Careful," Sasha shouted. "I'd hate for you to miss your opportunity."

"What opportunity?" Manda shouted, obviously confused.

"If you make it through this, you'll be a bona fide hero. Probably a promotion in it, maybe even your own ship."

"I'm not doing this to get a reward," Manda snapped.

"And I'm not here to get paid," Sasha shouted, "but you can bet your ass I'll demand extra for this mess. Especially since I'm on record opposing the whole thing."

"Agggh!" Manda shouted and fell to the floor.

Sasha turned and looked at her. The commander was on her back, clutching her bleeding arm.

CHAPTER
TWENTY-EIGHT

LIGHT IN THE TUNNEL

MEERA RAN through street after street with Klaus at her side. Everywhere she looked there were Swarm troopers firing beams of deadly plasma, tearing apart and bringing down buildings, destroying everything in their path.

But the TKs ran on, pushing, pulling, and dodging the enemy.

"Are we almost there, Meera?" he shouted.

"Yes. I can see it," she called back. "There, near that building just ahead. I can see the entrance to the tunnel. It's surrounded by Blues."

"I guess it wouldn't be fun if it was easy," Klaus shouted.

She glanced sideways at him. He looked tired. And for the big tough marine to look tired, she realized he might not be doing so well.

But Meera, with her connection to the... ether, was rejuvenated. She was exquisitely aware of her surroundings. She could *feel* it all. It gave her momentum.

Together they dodged from building to building, from one pile of rubble to another, and always, Meera was aware, in touch. She felt every nook and crevice, every feature of the land and the Blue army that covered the landscape as far as the eye could see.

"Meera," Klaus yelled as he took cover from a hail of enemy fire. "We need a plan."

"I know," she called back. "I'm working on it. See that building—it looks like it was a factory, but now it's in ruins? There's a tunnel in there. That's our objective. We need, somehow, to clear away the Blues."

"I'm on it," Klaus shouted and ran forward, his heavy K-15 firing a stream of 8mm rounds at the more than two-dozen Blues guarding the tunnel entrance.

Then Meera realized something and her heart sank. *They're too close. If any one of them explodes, the blast will kill him.*

"Klaus," she yelled, "come back. You'll be killed."

Klaus stopped running, hesitated for a moment, then ducked as a stream of plasma streaked over his head, then turned, ran toward her, leaped over the pile of rubble behind which Meera had taken cover and slid down in a cloud of dust and debris to land beside her.

"Now what?" he asked breathlessly.

"I don't know," she said. "Let me think for a minute."

"A minute is too long," he snapped. "They'll be on us any second."

"How are you feeling?" she asked.

"I'm good." He frowned. "Why?"

She took a deep breath, looked at him and said, "I need all your strength. There are twenty-seven of them guarding the factory. I need you to push them."

"What, all of them?" He looked astounded at the thought. "I've never done anything like that."

"You must try," she replied. "Together, we can do it. We have to clear the entrance. All you have is that gun. It's not enough."

He hesitated for a moment, nodded, took a huge breath, rose to his feet and said, "Come on, then. Let's do this."

And, together, they climbed to the top of the rubble and peeked over.

"I make it... one hundred fifty meters," Meera said. "Perhaps a little less."

He looked sideways at her. She knew her face had lost its color. He leaned in close and whispered, "On your mark?"

"No," she replied. "Take my hand. As I said, we'll do this together."

She reached out a hand. He looked into her eyes. What he saw must have filled him with confidence because he smiled, took her hand and squeezed it.

She smiled back at him, took a deep breath, and said, "Now!"

And together, they stared across the broken landscape at the Blues.

It took only a moment before the Blues stopped moving forward, then stopped moving at all. They strained and struggled but to no avail. It was as if they were fixed to the ground, unable to lift their weapons.

While Meera held them, Klaus reached out and suddenly, one by one, like rounds fired from a capital railgun, the Blues in the front rank were flung backwards with such force that they struck and shattered those in the ranks behind them.

The link broke. Meera looked at him. He was still staring out over the rubble-strewn gap that separated them from the factory entrance.

She looked again: the enemy had been more than halved, and the remainder, now freed from her grasp, were climbing over the remains of the slain and— "Look," she said. "They're glowing; the dead ones."

And they were.

"Meera, get down!" Klaus shouted. "They're going to explode."

He grabbed her arm and pulled, and together they slid back down the pile of rubble and waited.

The world above her rocked. She tried to sense the battlefield—

Please help!

Meera looked at Klaus, who was looking at the factory. Apparently, he could hear it too. They shared a nod and then upped and ran full tilt for the factory entrance, following the silent voice. The Blues that had blocked their way were decimated, their parts scattered in the explosion.

Together they ran into a world of darkness and shadows. The floors above were gone, collapsed. Holes in the roof and walls let in minimal light. It was hard to see anything in the dim light.

Meera reached out and grasped Klaus' hand.

"We'll wait a moment until our eyes become accustomed to the dim light," she said.

Can you hear? You not speak.

We hear you, Meera said. *We're coming for you.*

She looked at Klaus and said, "There. You'll have to help me."

He nodded. And they concentrated. It took only moments to lift the giant slabs of fallen concrete. And then, under a section of collapsed metal strut braces that had been supporting the concrete slabs, they found an injured man, a young boy, an apparently powerful Psy woman, and *a wild khain?* Meera was at the point of panic when the woman reached out to her.

Not wild. Family pet.

I ain't never heard of a khain as a family pet, Klaus replied.

What can we do to help? Meera asked.

Nothing. We manage. She turned, pointed into the darkness, and continued, *Something down there, below. Something terrible. You must kill it. If not... We all die!*

Can you keep in touch with us? Meera asked.

I will try, the woman replied.

Klaus reached out to Meera. *Amazing what some people can do when they try.* His words were light, but his thoughts were dark. There was a simmering anger deep inside him. And she felt his rage was somehow connected to her.

They stepped into the dim light. The going was surprisingly easy, considering they were surrounded by piles of rubble and debris until—

"That's it," Meera whispered. "There. Look."

"Where?" Klaus said, squeezing her hand. "I can't see anything."

"This way," she whispered and pulled him toward the entrance to a huge tunnel.

"Come on," Meera said, and together, they stepped into the darkness.

They'd gone but a few meters when Meera stopped him, both her hands now on his right hand. "D'you see it?"

"I do," he said. "There's something glowing down there."

Meera sucked her bottom lip into her mouth and held it between her lips. She was shaking. Someone; something was probing her mind.

"Klaus," she whispered. "There's something down there. Something... terrible. We need to—"

"Kill it!" Klaus finished for her. "Come on. Let's do it." And he led the way downward until they stepped out of the tunnel into a vast cavern, at the center of which, surrounded by humans-turned-machines and computers, a giant, semi-gelatinous construct as large as a house sat glowing, pulsing.

Cilia—a membrane-bound organelle found on most types of eukaryotic cells—the size of electrical cables probed, touching, feeling, penetrating the human computers, which hummed and buzzed with a ferocity the likes of which neither Meera nor Klaus had ever seen before.

And Meera could feel them, feel it. The construct was sucking their minds dry of every vestige of vital information, downloading it directly into the Swarm database.

———

PLANET CAERUS

Som Orsi City

ELIO'S DATASCREEN lit up bright red, indicating an urgent communication. He tapped the screen and a holo appeared above his arm.

"—you read us? Prince Elio, do you read?"

"Who is this?" Elio demanded, not recognizing the face. "And how did you get this frequency?"

"Oh, I'm Dr. Alphor, and this is Dr. Bretta. We work for Professor Barum, and we have an urgent warning. You must clear all active battlefield areas and the city immediately. We tried to hack all the communication channels but were unsuccessful, but then—"

"It was my idea," Bretta interrupted.

"Right." Alphor sighed. "She figured that we could just use the emergency code Professor Barum gave us, and when it went to his messages, we extrapolated—"

"Get to the point, please, and quickly," Elio snapped.

"Oh, right," Alphor said. "We've found a way to defeat the invasion."

"You what?" Elio said, stunned.

"We did, but," Alphor continued, "it's kind of non-discriminatory. It could... probably will... cause a great deal of collateral damage. So, we need you to order a general retreat, a withdrawal, an evacuation, if you will, and you need to do it, like, right now."

"Please explain and do it quickly and in terms I can understand," Elio said more calmly. "What exactly is it you're planning to do?"

"Um... an orbital bombardment?" Alphor said hesitantly. "And we're not planning to do it. It's already happening."

Elio looked up at the sky.

The sun was already setting, but the sky was awash with purple, yellow and oranges streaked with thin, gauzy clouds, but above those clouds in the upper stratosphere, he could see thousands of fiery streaks; Alphor's man-made meteor shower.

"But, how in all the blazing stars?" Elio muttered.

"Oh. It was such an interesting idea—" Alphor began, only to be interrupted by his partner.

"Professor Barum gave us the funding right away—" Bretta added.

"We simply reconfigured the gravastatic satellites!" Alphor interrupted. "Well, those and the magnetronic ones. You see, as I said, we work for Professor Barum, and we were supposed to use the gravastatic ones to change the orbits of the space debri—"

"But then there was the attack and I figured—" Bretta cut in.

"And we didn't need the magnetronic ones for it at all," Alphor plowed on. "We just used the gravastats to adjust the orbits of the debris and then slow them until they fell—"

"—into a decaying orbit," Bretta finished for him. "The calculations were the hardest part. Adjusting the orbits of thousands of—"

"Estimated time to impact?" Elio snapped, interrupting him.

"The first will hit in approximately twenty-nine minutes," Alphor replied happily.

Elio cut the call and switched to the Emergency Broadcast channel. "Attention! Attention. Attention! This is Prince Elio Lorne. Evacuate all population centers. I say again, evacuate all population centers immediately. Do it now. You have no time to spare. Head to the mountains and take cover. You have less than thirty minutes, so do it now."

Again, he looked up at the angry sky.

A lot of innocent people are going to die, he thought. *But they were going to die anyway.*

He shook his head, turned and reached out to his own little group. *We have to get out of here, now! Someone has launched an orbital bombardment. The plan is to decimate the Swarm. Unfortunately, it will probably decimate us, too.*

———

"W HAT IS IT ?" Meera asked.

She felt it vibrating the entire structure, and she felt it speak to her, a mental touch.

I am the Will.

"Why... Who... What are you?" she asked, her voice echoing around the cavern.

I am the Will, the voice in her head replied. *I am here to carry out the wishes of the One. I am here to cleanse this reality.*

"Cleanse?" Meera asked. "You mean eradicate? Why? What have we done to you?"

Your people, through your indiscriminate use of what you call the Slipstream, have caused irreparable harm to our reality. You have caused rifts in our time and space. You must be stopped before you collapse not only your own reality but ours as well. Your kind must be eradicated.

"But we didn't know," she screamed. "You can stop this madness. You can teach us."

I am not here to bargain. I exist only to enact the Will of the One upon you.

"You're here to kill us," Klaus shouted. "I don't think so."

You can not harm me, the voice replied. *Your attacks will only destroy you.*

"Is that what you think?" Klaus snarled as he climbed. "Well, prepare to meet your One directly."

A moment later, Klaus placed his hands on the computers

connected to the otherworldly creature. "Because I'm about to shove you directly... up... his—"

The computers flared at Klaus' touch, driving straight through the glowing biological construct. It gave an ethereal scream as it detonated in a column of white fire.

"*Klaus!* Meera screamed and threw everything she had into shielding him from the explosion, even as it engulfed her.

———

Prince Elio and his Guardians, protected by an invisible dome created by their combined TK, could only watch as, for more than thirty minutes, the fiery rain fell from the sky.

Thousands of chunks of debris left from the Battle of the Slipgates burned in the atmosphere until they fell onto the city. The destruction was absolute. The city was leveled to its foundations. More than a million people died during those terrible thirty minutes. But so did the enemy. Thousands of Blues that had emerged from their underground lairs were destroyed in an instant as the fiery metal meteorites—some of them as large as a small house—slammed into the ground among them at speeds in excess of ten-thousand kilometers an hour.

And as much as Elio applauded the destruction of the enemy, his heart sank at the thought of the toll on his people.

But then, some ten minutes after the bombardment had begun, Elio felt a primal shriek reverberate through his mind, a shriek of pain as if from a thousand voices. It lasted but a few seconds, and then it was gone, leaving only its echo reverberating through his brain.

Even after the fiery rain stopped and they emerged from the rubble, the Blues were gone, disappeared. Whether they'd all been destroyed or the survivors had bolted back into their holes, Elio didn't know.

"My prince," a familiar voice said as he gazed out over the devastation. "I'm glad I found you. Are you injured?"

Elio turned to find Major Rosst and a platoon of Conquell guards, most of them in tatters, but they all looked grim, determined.

"Major?" Elio said, surprised. "It's good to see you, my friend. What news do you have?"

"Only that we downed one of their new airborne tanks, my Prince," Rosst replied. "And that the meteor storm seems to have done its job. But where are they now?" he asked.

Elio shrugged. "I don't know. There was a wild scream throughout the Psy, and then they were gone."

"Permission to pursue?" Rosst asked.

"Permission granted, Colonel Rosst."

Rosst frowned. "Colonel? But, sir—"

"Congratulations on your promotion, Colonel," Elio smiled. "That is, unless you'd rather retire?"

Rosst gave him one of his rare smiles in return. "No, my Prince. We still have Blues to kill."

"That we do, Rosst," Elio agreed. "I suggest you take your men and go to it."

"Yes, sir," Rosst replied, then snapped to attention, saluted, turned on his heel, and shouted, "Well, you heard the prince. At the double, Maaarch!"

Elio watched as Rosst and his troop headed out toward the leveled factory.

He stood for a moment staring after them, then he heaved a deep, shuddering breath.

"Andra," he said, "call for a royal evac team, if there's one left, and tell them we have casualties."

Andra looked subdued now that the immediate threat was gone. "Yes, sir."

Elio looked out over what once had been his city, Som Orsi, the capital of Caerus, the seat of the throne of Orso. There was little of it left.

We can't do this anymore, he thought. *We can't keep letting the Swarm target the military by targeting the civilians. But how do we draw their attention away from our planets?*

Andra replied, *We remove the military targets from the populated planets.*

Or, the enemy, by sheer weight of numbers, will eventually win by attrition, he thought, but it was a thought he kept to himself.

CHAPTER
TWENTY-NINE

ASSAULT AND BATTERIES

REGIS MAGNUM SHIPYARDS
Central Computer Core

Kasa de Cevoir, accompanied by three burly soldiers—a sergeant and two marines in full combat gear—was within meters of the Central Computer Core.

"Which way?" the sergeant asked.

"There," she said, pointing at a large metal door standing half-open.

He nodded and ducked through the open door.

"Go!" the second marine snapped and shoved her through.

Room by room they advanced, clearing each one as they went until, "Which one?" the leader asked.

They were in a wide curving corridor faced by doors on either bulkhead.

"That one, I think," Kasa said, pointing.

The sergeant tried the door handle. It was locked. He stepped back and fired a burst from his laser rifle at the lock and then kicked the door open.

"Look out!" Kasa shouted as the blue robot inside fired.

The sergeant fell to the ground, mortally wounded.

One of the marines fired a long burst of heavy rounds into the bot, tearing through its body armor, while the second marine fired a long burst of laser fire into the cavity.

Something inside the bot glowed brightly, then exploded, and it fell forward, inanimate.

Kasa didn't wait. As soon as she thought it was clear, she slipped past the marines, but one of them grabbed her arm and jerked her back just as another robot appeared and fired. The bullets hammered into the dutrinium plates in his body armor. He staggered backward, taking her with him, as the second marine, his teeth bared, fired a long burst of 8mm slugs into the bot's guts, then dropped his rifle, grabbed his laser pistol and fired it into the cavity. The bot stiffened, swayed, then fell over backward.

"Whew," the second marine said as he retrieved his rifle. "That was intense. You all right, brother?"

"Yeah. I feel like my ribs have caved in, but that's better than the alternative, right?"

"Right," the second marine said, then turned to Kasa. "Can you really shut this mess down?"

"Absolutely," she replied, hoping it was true.

"Well, then, let's do it," he snarled, then turned and ran down the hall, screaming and firing his assault rifle.

She followed as closely as she could. *The safest place to be is right behind him,* she thought, feeling guilty. *Why? Why am I feeling guilty? I didn't plan any of this.*

But, deep down, she knew it was all her fault. And people—lots and lots of people—were dying.

She was almost there.

As bullets hurtled past her on both sides, her marine shield, shuddering at the impacts on his body armor, shouted and threw himself on top of the three attacking robots.

She grabbed onto his armor and climbed over him—a childhood spent in the seedy underbelly of the city having honed her reflexes to a knife edge. She didn't have to look at him to know he was dead. *He died to give me a chance to redeem myself.*

Vaulting over the heads of the robots, she landed badly on her ankle, stumbled through the open door into the central core chamber, slammed the door closed behind her, locked it, and then slid into the chair.

She looked around. She was alone.

She flexed her fingers, closed her eyes, and prepared herself to do battle with the implacable force she'd unleashed.

———

DAGON JAX BOLTED BACK through the office and found Commander Haal lying on the ground, groaning in pain. He grabbed her under her arms and pulled her to safety even as she kept repeating, "It's just a flesh wound. It's just a flesh wound."

"Commander, talk to me," he yelled over the commotion. "Are you okay?"

"No, Mister Jax. I am not okay," she said as she winced.

"Fall back, fall back," Jax heard someone from the group of *Avenger* officers at the door shout. And they all turned and ran into the room, scrambling to find whatever cover they could.

Three blue robot Champions marched into the room, their weapons spraying. Jax grabbed a metal desk and tipped it over as cover for his commander. Then he stood, the table in front of him, as the officers opened fire with everything they had. Hundreds of railgun rounds slammed into the three bots.

"Die," he screamed as he fired pulse after pulse of laser fire into the cavities hammered in by the officers. The room turned into an ear-shattering sound box as the railguns on both sides fired almost continuous streams of death across the open space between them.

The three bots were joined by two more, and then another, and the rate of fire increased to a crescendo.

Jax, oblivious of the hailstorm around him, continued to

fire, burning through one bot after another, bullets streaking by on either side.

Something tugged at his left arm, jerking him sideways.

Within a second, something slammed into his right arm. He staggered backwards. *It hurts*, he thought, as he tried to raise the pistol.

———

Tenilo Barum was exhausted almost to the point where he ceased to exist.

His ragtag fleet was almost out of ammunition. As to *Colossus* herself, her shields were down to thirty-four percent, and her hull, though structural integrity was still at ninety-two percent, had been breached more than fifty times. She was out of missiles; railgun ammunition was down to seventeen percent, and twenty-seven of her fifty massive one-terawatt laser cannons had either been disabled or shot away. Nine more were working at reduced power.

On the upside, her ten fusion reactors were running at full capacity, all eight main engines were online, and the remaining fourteen laser cannons were all at one hundred percent.

Tenilo, standing at the battle control console's giant, interactive hologram, was almost at the point of collapse, but still he fought on.

The battlefield was clearing. *Avenger* and her four squadrons of fighters, though also low on ammunition, were still making a heroic stand.

Tenilo, now breathing hard, in concert with Apollo, her Mark C77 AI, concentrated *Colossus'* awesome laser weaponry on one target at a time. And, though the Swarm ships were virtually impervious to laser fire, the concentrated fire from as many as eight one-terawatt cannons—eight trillion watts—burned a hole right through them: a lucky shot might hit the core, causing the ship to explode.

Tenilo was no great tactician; he had no martial training. He simply used every available resource to perform the most basic tricks en masse, and in some cases, that meant using *Colossus* as a battering ram.

And it wasn't long before *Colossus* began to attract attention as he poured concentrated DEW fire into Swarm ships and the fledgling Vindication fleet. Against *Avenger* and the handful of unprepared Sovereign vessels, it would have been an easy victory for the enemy. But Tenilo's fleet of flotsam had tipped the balance of the battle in their favor, and the enemy was on the run. With the firepower at his disposal, it had been nothing short of a rout for the enemy forces. He just wished he knew who he was firing at—had the Blues infiltrated the shipyards? If so, why take the Vindication fleet? If not, who was it and, again, the question was the same: Why take the Vindication fleet?

And then, just as he was able to ease off a little, he noticed something on the Battle Control's hologram, *an anomaly?* He frowned, narrowed his eyes, leaned in closer and peered at it. *What the—?*

Ahead of him, just beyond Caerus' exosphere, his sensors were picking up an odd reading.

He shook his head; *Gravity? A gravity field? No! It's not possible!*

Alarms all across the command deck began to sound. Consoles that hadn't even flickered began to light up. And suddenly, he found himself fighting with Apollo for control of the vessel. *The AI's trying to assert itself? But why?*

He glanced at the Battle Control holo. The anomaly was beginning to swirl, the gravitational lensing growing—

And then Apollo wrested control from him and banked the ship hard to port and dove into—

"What is happening!" he screamed as the ship entered the anomalous Slipgate. A Slipgate that slammed shut as *Colossus* was passing through.

Manda rolled onto her side and tried to get up. Her arm was bleeding profusely. She'd taken a hit to her right arm just above the elbow and another to her left shoulder.

She rolled onto her back, her eyes wide. She could see Jax standing over her, firing a laser pistol, yelling at the top of his voice.

"Die, you bastards," he screamed. "I won't let you hurt her."

She saw his body jerk once, twice, three times. He wavered, lifted the pistol, his left arm hanging useless at his side and as he continued to fire, still shouting that he wouldn't let them get to her.

She closed her eyes, and it began. At first, she willed the vision to disappear, but it didn't.

She saw Lt. Pazon step into the room, firing his heavy rail-gun. The effect was devastating. She saw Jax catch a burst of fire from the doorway and fall on top of her, dead.

The vision changed. Jax fell, as before, but he survived. This time it was Pazon who died, and Jax would... Jax would... the vision wavered. She couldn't see beyond the next few moments.

Why. Why can't I see what happens to Jax?

She opened her eyes. She could just see around the edge of the table. One of the robots took aim. There was a clicking and whirring as the weapon's barrels spun up to high speed.

Everyone was going to die.

No, only one is going to die. Only one.

It took Kasa de Cevoir less than two minutes to hack through the firewalls into the central core, but when she attempted to hack her way through the various firewalls protecting the security and operating systems, she was foiled by the station AI's omnipresence. Everything she needed to recode was under the AI's direct control and protection. Somehow, it had melded itself into every aspect of the station's operations, and she had no idea how to force her way past it.

How did the hack I did six months ago lead to this? And how do I get around it now?

She looked nervously around, making sure she was still secure.

Hmmm? So how do *I...? Got it! The only way to fight this AI was with another AI. But I can't just... I can't just program one out of nowhere. Can I? Hmm! Got it! I know where I can find one.*

Typing furiously, she accessed the Vindication fleet archives. Even though most of the ships were listed as destroyed, there were still AI packages awaiting installation into the ships still under construction. They were housed in separate mainframes to enable compilation without outside interference.

She scanned through a list of the most completed ones. Several were in the final stages of compiling—the ships that were fighting just outside the bulkheads had their AIs installed, but full integration was still not complete. She picked the one that sounded most hopeful to her—*Insightful*—and set it to install inside the station mainframe.

She watched the screen. It was very tense and a little boring, waiting for an AI to start fighting another AI. But...

Insightful gained a foothold and began trying to access station utilities. Regis Magnum saw this as an attack and fought back. *Insightful* pulled system resources away from Regis to expand its own base, and that was when Kasa began her task. Caught in between the two AI juggernauts, Kasa slipped inside the system once again and began searching for the fatal ingress point the Tupeti had used. Once she cut off that point, she was able to target the station's latent defenses. She watched with pride as the shields and missile batteries came online for the first time since the invasion began.

Now we'll see how his rotten little investment paid off, won't we?

———

Captain Richard Morian stood grasping the command rail on the *Avenger* and watched his screens as *Colossus* closed in on the mysterious gravity field. The gravitational lensing caused the image of the massive ship to waver. No, shimmer.

"What in the name of the stars is that?" he shouted. "Where did it come from?" he bellowed, breaking all his personal rules for maintaining a calm demeanor, as he watched *Colossus* heading through the field. "Come on, Mr. Volkov. I need answers, and I need them now."

Volkov didn't answer, but the Sensors officer did.

"We have no idea, sir—"

He was interrupted by a sudden brilliant flash, and then the gravity field disappeared, leaving *Colossus* sheared in two, its halves drifting apart from the sheer force of the... What? Explosion? "What the hell kind of weapon was that?" Morian shouted. "Where did it go? Stars, this can't be happening. How was that done? Ms. Lowery, try to contact the *Colossus*. I want to know if Mr. Barum survived. The rest of you: Answers, now."

But Morian knew he was just venting. Never had his crew let him down, but he knew they knew no more than he did.

"Sir, analysis suggests that it was a Slipgate," Commander Jadern said.

"That's not possible," Morian snapped. "It was within the planet's gravity well; not by much, but it was. How could they generate a Slipgate so close to a planet?" he demanded.

No one answered. No one knew how the Slipgates were generated. As far as anyone knew, they were part of the fabric of the universe. They just... existed.

And yet...

"We're getting energy readings from Regis Magnum," Jadern shouted.

Morian tapped his datapad and the station data began scrolling across the hologram. Regis Magnum was powering up again. He looked at the giant hologram hovering over its generator down on the well deck. Lights all over the gargantuan shipyards came on. The station's shields came up, and its defenses came online.

"Station is at full power," Jadern shouted, and everyone cheered as they watched a missile detonate against the station's shields.

Morian heaved a sigh of relief. *It looks like we're beginning to gain the upper hand,* he thought as he relaxed his grip on the rail.

The station's huge railgun batteries powered up, and warnings flickered across Morian's datapad as its weapons control computers tracked and identified every ship in near space for five thousand kilometers in every direction.

Having gotten a positive response from *Avenger's* transponder and Krista, her AI, the station's weapons tracking moved onto the real threats—the Swarm and the remains of the Vindication fleet.

Maybe it's for the best, he thought. *Those ships weren't the weapons we needed. Too shoddy, too rushed. Maybe the next—*

The station fired the first shots, the powerful cannons holing the *Fearful Symmetry* and the *Absolution*—before moving onto the remains of the *Penumbra*.

"What in the name of..." Morian said. "Why are they firing on our rescuers?"

Again, it was Jadern who answered. "Sir, those friendly ships aren't showing as Sovereign-friendly. AIs are in control. And some of them don't even have transponders."

"Comms, open a line to the station," he ordered.

"Yes, sir... trying, sir," Lowery replied.

Richard watched as the station opened fire on the Swarm

ships, as well as *Breakneck, Periwinkle* and *Fellowship.*

"Lieutenant Lowery," Morian snapped. "I need that channel, now!"

"I'm trying, sir, but they're not responding, and neither is *Colossus.*"

"Open all channels," Morian snapped, then, "Regis Magnum, this is Commodore Richard Morian, captain of the *Avenger.* This is an emergency communication to whoever can hear me. Many of the vessels you're firing on are friendlies. Target only Swarm signatures. Avenger will deal with the rest."

"No response, Captain," Lowery said.

And Morian watched helplessly as *Ironclad, Dauntless,* and *Vassalus* were holed.

And then the guns turned to *Colossus.*

Even battle-damaged, without shields, and split in two, it took the station nearly five minutes to batter the once-magnificent warship into scrap. And Morian could do nothing but watch impotently as the misguided fury destroyed the giant battle wagon.

He stood tall at the command rail, stoically, his hands clasped together behind his back, outwardly; inwardly seething with anger, knowing that everyone who'd come to their rescue had died.

The battle was over, and they'd won, but at what cost?

————

DESPITE THE RAILGUN rounds still flying overhead, Manda forced herself to crawl across the room to where Lieutenant Pazon was lying. His body armor had taken at least a dozen hits and the dutrinium plates had taken the brunt of the attack, but he'd also taken hits to his legs, and one bullet passed between the plates and passed through his left shoulder. He was bleeding profusely, but when she tried to put pressure on it, he screamed and jerked away.

"Don't. You can't. It's..." he said through gritted teeth. "It went straight through, and it hurts back there."

"We'll get help," she said.

"What... did... your vision tell you?" he whispered.

"My vision?" she murmured. She didn't know how to answer him. Her vision had all ended one way or the other. But maybe... maybe this one could end differently?

"My vision was of you surviving this fight, Jason," she said quietly. "You get promoted, lead a battalion. Your battalion sees action in almost every front of the war, and you lead them through shadows and flames, but you survive."

It was a half lie. Her visions had not provided a solution. And, no matter what she said to him, she knew he was fading.

"Thank you," he said weakly and reached out for her hand. "When... I wake up... you can... tell me... more."

He closed his eyes, his grip on her hand relaxed, his head tilted to the side, and... he was gone.

She took her hand from his, looked at it and the blood on it, and... she wept.

———

"MR. JADERN," Morian snapped. "I want emergency crews out to those ships, and I want them out there now! Get whoever you can. I don't care who it is," Richard ordered as he stared at the view screens, at the debris and the remaining forward section of *Colossus* drifting in the gravity shadow of Caerus. "Comms, keep trying to contact the station. Let them know they're firing on friendly ships. Whatever resources we have, we need to get the survivors to safety."

"Captain," the science officer, Henrick Tobbs, called out. "I'm replaying the sensor readings from when those ships joined the fight. Scans show no life forms aboard any of them except *Colossus*, and then there was only one."

Morian frowned, his eyes narrowed. "Belay orders, Mr.

Jadern." Then he turned to the science officer and said, "How can that be, Mr. Tobbs? Were they flying by remote?"

"Analysis of data indicates that may be the case, sir," Hobbs replied. "But, Captain, those ships were already badly damaged."

Morian continued to frown, thinking, then he said, "Didn't I hear something about a salvage operation? Something out near Diminu?"

"News feeds from the palace announced such an operation more than a month ago, Captain," Lowery said.

"Do we know who was assigned to command the operation?" Morian asked, thinking about Tenilo Barum's communications of more than an hour ago.

"No, sir," Lowery answered.

"Mr. Hobbs," Morian said, "go over the scans again. We need to be sure there are no crews aboard those ships." He turned to Jadern and said, "Take an away team and go check the bridge of *Colossus*. I fear what you'll find, and if it's what I think... someone is going to pay, dearly.

"Aye, sir."

"In the meantime, I want all sensor and tactical logs assembled and transmitted to me. You have thirty minutes. I'll be in my ready room."

"Yes, sir! Yes, sir! Aye, sir," the officers replied.

Morian nodded and retreated to his ready room, his mind in a whirl as he sat in his chair thinking. Somehow he knew something was missing, something he should know, something he should do.

He reached out and felt the buzzing of thoughts swirling around the bridge. Not panic, but an earnest, collective of shared determination to work the tasks at hand.

He nodded to himself and reached for his halo, but before he touched it, he realized he was the one person who might be able to find out what he wanted to know quickly.

He reached out through the ether to the dead ships, looking

for signs of Psy or even thoughts, but there was none.

They're all dead, Morian thought. *Unless they weren't there at all. Maybe I don't utilize the power of my Psy as much as I should. I need to do more. I need to be more than just a rank-and-file captain.*

He continued to reach out to one derelict ship after another until, at last, he found *Colossus*. He swept through the corridors, briefing and ready rooms, the hangar bays and the gunnery controls, reaching out for any signs of life, but there were none — until he reached the bridge.

I'm sorry, Mister Barum...

Captain?

Morian could tell that Tenilo was weak, barely alive.

Is that you, Captain Morian?

It is, Richard responded. *And I want you to hang on. A rescue shuttle is on the way. We'll get you out of there, I promise.*

No, Captain, Tenilo replied. *It's already too late. I'm dying. I'm bleeding out. I'll be dead before they get here.*

Dr. Dowd is an amazing doctor, Morian said. *I'm sure she—*

You know, I thought I was dead until I felt you in my mind, Tenilo interrupted him. *I always thought it might end like this, but I decided it was worth the risk. We did win, didn't we?*

Morian bit his lip. He had gotten to know Tenilo on previous missions, and he knew that he was a man of principle and dedicated to Prince Felder, his patron.

Yes, we won, Tenny, Morian replied, *and all thanks to you. You arrived just in time.*

Again, Morian could feel him smile. *So, I don't die in vain... That's good, Captain. That's very good.*

Were there any other souls aboard any of the ships in your fleet? Morian asked.

Hah! No, Captain. Richard could feel the smile. *I did it all... by... myself... I'm... proud to have...* He heaved a huge breath. *Good...bye, Cap...tain...*

And Tenilo's thoughts faded away to... nothing.

CHAPTER
THIRTY

AFTERMATH

Kasa de Cevoir input the final command and wrenched the rest of station control away from the AI and whoever had stolen it. As the station's systems powered and began to come back online under Sovereign control, she frantically tapped the commands to shut down all internal security systems.

She slumped in the tiny chair, exhausted, as she glanced up at the screens and saw the last of the Champions freeze.

And yet she still had troubled systems. She thought for a moment, trying to decide what to do. She knew she had little time left before they found her.

Finally, she nodded, tapped in a string of commands and locked the troubled systems into loops, preventing them from re-engaging. *I don't know if I can do anything about Insightful, though,* she thought. *They may have to accept that their station is now twins,* and at that, she couldn't help but giggle.

But it was done.

She'd righted the damage she'd done, well, most of it, but she knew she was responsible for thousands of deaths... *No, it wasn't me. It was all Hirana Ligarch. I had no choice. Now he'll come for me.*

She could hear yelling and cheering outside. *I need to get out of here now, before they find me, especially that Jax person and his people,* she thought, looking desperately up at the screens for a way out.

Finally, Kasa pulled herself together and got up out of the chair, limped out of the Core chamber and made her way carefully through the celebrating soldiers and officers, trying to stay out of sight of Jax, Sasha Crowe and that infuriating Commander Haal.

The way was strewn with dead bodies and deactivated robots.

If I can just get to an escape pod—

She broke into a limping run, but before she'd gone three steps, something grabbed her sprained ankle, and she fell face-first onto a dead body.

She managed not to scream but looked behind to see what had grabbed her—

It was Marshal Hyde.

"It was you," Hyde snarled. "You did this."

"It wasn't me," Kasa lied. "It wasn't me. Let me go."

"Never," Hyde yelled. "Help, Help. This woman is a traitor. I've caught the traitor. I order someone to come and arrest her."

Kasa tried to struggle free, kicking at the Marshal as she continued to screech like a harpy. But just as she landed the heel of her boot on Hyde's nose and scrambled loose, Sasha Crowe rounded the corner at a run.

Ignoring the pain in her injured ankle, Kasa leapt to her feet and ran.

"After her. She's the traitor that caused all this," Hyde screeched.

Kasa ran as hard as she could, but the pain in her ankle was more than she could bear, and she was no match for the two marines that ran her down and dragged her back.

"Secerna? I was hoping you were dead," Sasha Crowe was saying conversationally to Hyde.

"Hah. No thanks to you I'm still alive and still in charge," Hyde hissed. "If you'd done as I said—"

"You activated an AI-controlled security force in the middle of a cyber-intrusion," Sasha snapped, interrupting her. "Which I told you was a problem in the development process and you wouldn't listen. You overruled me and removed me from the project."

"I did as I saw fit to protect the interests of the USF," Hyde snarled.

"And you failed miserably, and a lot of good men and women died."

"That's enough, Sasha," Commander Haal stepped forward. "I'll take it from here. Secerna Hyde, I am formally declaring you unfit for command. You will be arrested and taken to the infirmary where you be secured until you can be transferred to Som Orsi, what's left of it, for psychiatric evaluation."

"You can't do that," Hyde said, stomping her foot and jutting out her chin. "I hold my rank as marshal by royal appointment."

"You are a civilian Marshal, which means that under Military Code 127.5-3, you are subject to military authority in time of war. Your negligence and refusal to defer to military authority resulted in the deaths of hundreds of people on this station alone, not to mention those who died defending it."

Hyde stared at her, speechless, unbelieving of what she was hearing.

Haal turned to two of the more than a dozen assembled marines and said, "Arrest her."

As the guards seized Hyde and restrained her, she protested, "What about that girl? She's part of the invasion. She was imprisoned, and then she got free?"

"This woman," Commander Haal retorted, pointing at

Kasa, "was nearly killed by the invaders, then aided us in pacifying them and almost single-handedly saved this station by reprogramming the central core. As of this moment..." She paused, narrowed her eyes, and looked at Kasa, then continued, "As of this moment, I trust her a whole lot more than I do you."

The marines dragged Hyde away, still protesting, and after what Commander Haal had said, Kasa had a moment where she thought she might actually escape.

"Arrest her, too," Haal said, nodding at Kasa.

The two marines tightened their grip on her arms. She looked up at Haal with tears in her eyes and said, "But why? You just defended me to Hyde?"

"I defended you because I wanted to put her in her place," Haal said. "Also, because I really did want to thank you for saving the station. But I can't let you go."

"Why not? I'm innocent," Kasa pleaded.

Haal shook her head. "You... What's your name again?"

"It's Kasa," she replied. "Kasa de Cevoir."

"You, Kasa," Haal continued, "are an anomaly. I spoke to Lieutenant Jax about you. You were found wandering around the detention block by yourself, during a blackout. You were attacked by two enemy assassins while the enemy was boarding our starships. You poisoned our prisoner, but fortunately for you, he was already dead. Someone else saw to that. Then, we find out, you have the extraordinary skills to manipulate the central computer. You are, to quote a great, pre-Purge wartime leader, 'a riddle, wrapped in a mystery, inside an enigma,' and I want to get to the bottom of it." Haal sighed. "Who are you, Kasa, and why are you here on this station? No!" She held up her hand as Kasa was about to speak. "I strongly advise you to keep your mouth shut until we can provide you with legal services. Take her away."

Kasa felt the binds slip around her wrists again.

I can't believe I didn't see it, Kasa thought sadly. *How did I manage to create such a perfect trail back to myself?*

But she already knew the answer. *I made snap decisions. I looked at the security vid instead of staying on station. I poisoned Tachier right in front of them, then I let them see what a great hacker I was instead of slipping away to freedom. Why didn't I just escape when I had the chance?*

She already knew that answer, too. And every face she passed on the way back to her cell proved it. They were alive because of her.

But one thought still niggled at her. *How did Tachier so conveniently die just before I poisoned him?*

The answer struck her like a thunderbolt.

There's someone else on station. Someone who knew I'd been captured. Someone communicated off-station. Someone told Tachier and Stakon where I was. There's another spy. I have to tell them. But they'll never believe me.

"Commander Haal. Wait. I want to make a deal."

"I don't make deals," Haal replied.

"Sasha Crowe. Sasha Crowe. I want to make a deal." she shouted. *I have to do something. I have to make them believe me.* "You worked with my team. You know me. You know how smart I am. I promise I will tell you things. Everything. But I need to be protected."

Sasha Crowe said nothing, and Kasa almost stopped struggling. It was hopeless.

"I will admit to any crime you ask, as long as you give me... one minute. One minute, and I will literally let you kill me."

There was no answer.

The two marines hustled her onward, struggling, looking back over her shoulder, pleading.

"Stop," Sasha Crowe ordered.

They stopped, turned her around, and Sasha Crowe walked quickly to her.

"You have one minute."

"Put me in a max security cell with whatever Psy security

you care to use and I'll tell you what I know," Kasa said. "That's my deal."

"Your deal is to be locked in max security?" Sasha looked unconvinced.

"I want to... make amends. And I can't do that if I'm dead, because someone is definitely going to kill me before you do. So I'm willing to tell you everything about what I did... and what I know."

Sasha stood for a moment, staring at her, then looked at Haal, who nodded, then, with a nod to the two marines, said, "Follow me."

They followed Sasha through a maze of hallways until, finally, they arrived in front of a single door at the end of a short, dead-end hallway. Sasha entered her security code, put her eye to the scanner, and the door opened.

"Inside," Sasha ordered.

The room was bigger than Kasa had expected. It was austere, with a white bed constructed from some sort of composite plastic material, a small desk made of the same material, and a polished steel rectangle on the wall that she knew housed a mounted toilet and sink. The walls themselves were lined with a white, textured material she'd not seen before. She reached out and touched it with her fingertips, then looked at Sasha, who was standing in the doorway, the marines just behind her.

"Psy-sheilding resin," Sasha said. "Don't ask me to explain how it works. Just know that it does, and nobody will find you here. We'll talk later. And be sure, we'll know if you're telling the truth or not... Get some rest, Kasa. You look as if you need it."

Sasha took a step back and the door hissed closed.

Kasa sat down on the bed, her hands clasped together in her lap, and she stared at the wall above the desk, wondering what lay in store for her. *Whatever it is, it won't be pleasant.*

She sighed, lay down on the bed, put her hands behind her

head, blinked twice, and activated her nanomod implanted eye, then blinked again and brought up her recordings. And she lay there, tears running from her right eye as she watched Devin die when Hyde refused to step down the temperature inside the containment chamber, and she watched him die again, and again, and again.

She did it to remind herself why she was there. She acknowledged her mistakes, and she'd acknowledge the mistakes of others.

Devin died because incompetent people were trying to win the war for selfish reasons. And she almost died because someone wanted to lose the war for reasons she couldn't begin to imagine.

And now... And now someone was trying to sabotage the war effort again.

If she had any chance to stop them, she would take it.

———

DANIS, almost out of railgun ammunition and down to two missiles, watched as the station defenses came online. She saw her transponder automatically send her B-29's ID to the station's battle control computers, and she heaved a sigh of relief. Her four squadrons had been out in the black fighting not only the Vindication fleet but also the Swarm and what she assumed were their third-generation fighters and now light carriers.

She'd lost nineteen fighter bombers—almost fifty percent of her force had been destroyed by the double enemy. Had it not been for the appearance of... the still unknown supercarrier and its fleet, she had no doubt the entire wing would have been destroyed.

But the carrier had encountered some sort of anomaly and it too had been destroyed, its two halves, hulks, drifting silently.

"Domino," Jackknife called. "On your six. Two bogies. Go starboard. I'm on my way."

"Hold on, Jennat," she called to her TK as she hauled the yoke back as far as it would go and put the B-29 into a tight, twisting, turning loop that made even her own innards knot. And she watched as the two Blue fighters streaked by. Then she snapped the fighter bomber out of the loop, dropped in behind the Blue fighters, her railguns howling. The quadruple streams of 55mm slugs traveling at four times the speed of sound tore into the nearest Blue fighter, ripping through the fuselage, tearing off its port wing before it exploded in a blinding flash of blue fire, but not before her railguns went silent.

"I told you I'd got you," Jackknife yelled as he streaked past, sending a hail of railgun fire into the second Blue. For several seconds, the Blue continued on its trajectory and then it seemed to lurch, then again, and then it too exploded in a fountain of debris.

"Domino to Jackknife," Danis yelled into the comm. "I'm out of ammo. I'm going home to rearm. Escort me—"

She didn't finish. The station's batteries opened fire and she watched as first one Blue carrier exploded, then the huge guns turned to what was left of the Vindications fleet. Their shields and dutrinium armor were no match for the mighty, two-hundred-millimeter guns. The first to die was *Dursana,* her bow section sheared away, then *Expiation, Censorious* and finally *Absolution.*

"Domino to Crash. D'you read?" she called to the squadron.

"I read, loud, clear. Go ahead, Domino."

"Looks like our work is done," Danis replied. "Let's go home. Wait! The station's firing on the friendly fleet. We must stop them."

"Domino to Regis control," she snapped. "Come in, Regis."

She waited. Nothing.

She tried again. "Domino to Regis control. Come in. Come in Regis control. Anybody. Come in," she demanded, but there was no reply.

"Axi," Danis shouted. "I can't get through to control. You try."

"I already try," Axi replied. "Same result as you. No contact. We can do nothing. We go home now, I think."

Danis reached out to Richard, *Richard, are you there? Please. The station is killing the friendly ships. I can't get through to control. You have to stop it.*

I know. I see it, Richard said. *Comms are down. I can't get through either. The fleet is not responding, nor are they attempting to defend themselves. There's nothing we can do. What's your status?*

We've lost nineteen, she replied. *Seven critically damaged. I'm out of ammunition. There's nothing more we can do here. I'm bringing the ducklings home.*

Nineteen? Morian replied. *Stars. That's almost half the wing. There's going to be hell to pay for what's happened here.* She heard him heave a sigh, then he said, *Bring them home, Danis.*

Danis nodded, though she knew he couldn't see her. *Will do, brother. See you soon.*

It was a weary, battle-worn group that landed in the fighter bays. Danis entered first, then sat in the open cockpit watching the rest of her battered wing come limping in. She'd been wrong when she told Richard seven of the twenty-one survivors had been damaged. Eleven of the remaining B-29s had suffered damage of one sort or another.

She sat and watched as they climbed out of their ships. Several of them looked around at them in disgust; one of them actually spit at his.

Danis stood up in the cockpit and commanded, "Fifteen-minute break, then pilots to the briefing room, please."

She heard several groans but knew that she needed to let them have their moment of insubordination. Managing fighter pilots was a tricky process. It took a lot of guts to climb into a fighter, and even more to fly against the Blues. Space, the black, was unwilling to accept mistakes, and of a thousand details, only one stood between a pilot and a quick death. And no one ever knew which detail that might be until they found it and it cost them their life.

Danis was last to enter the briefing, her trio of trainers waiting for her.

"That, my friends," she began, "is what they call a shit show. But it's done. Those of us who survived will mourn our dead. But that's for another day."

She glanced at Axi, smiled at her, then turned again to her pilots and their TKs.

"Shit show or not, you all did well out there. I'm proud of you. Your trainers are proud of you. You've proved yourselves under fire. And, that being so, anyone who wants to be officially inducted into *Avenger* flight— No, don't raise your hand yet. Let me finish. Anyone who wants to join us will be welcome. But again, that's for later.

"Now," she continued, "I understand the desire some of you have to crawl into a hole and hide. It happens to us all, me included, but we have to put the bad times behind us. Today was harrowing; we lost a lot of fine people. But it's the way of things. It's what we do. If you decide to join us, there will be more days like this, perhaps even worse. You're young. You're green, but you will grow into it and you will improve.

"Today... we went into battle riding the lumbering beasts of the field. The next time you go to meet your enemy, you'll be riding some of the fastest, deadliest hunters the USF has ever produced. Next time, you'll fly the F32C. The enemy's nightmares will be the F32C."

She saw some of them nodding and some smiling. Others...

"Think about it," she said. "Don't make a decision before you get some rest and a good hot meal. Debrief is in..." She checked the chron. "In sixteen hours, at 1200 tomorrow. Dismissed."

As the pilots trudged out of the room, she turned to Axi, Gian and Jackknife and said, "Well, that was... horrible."

"I think it was fine," Gian said.

"Yeah, what he said," Jackknife added.

"Commander, I know how it is. I've been in... well, their shoes." She jerked a thumb at Gian and Jackknife. "This was bad battle. Almost as bad as Slipgate. You told them what they wanted to hear. We cannot tell them what they need to hear; they would never get back in cockpit."

"And what would that be?" Danis asked.

"Danis, everything we do is reaction to them, to enemy. There is old saying. Pre-Purge. 'In warfare, there are no constant conditions. He who can modify his tactics in relation to his opponent will succeed and win.' What that means is unless we come up with something to really change the game, we will always be in second place. And, in this war, there will be no second place."

———

Planet Caerus
Som Orsi City Limits

Klaus didn't know where he was. He tried to open his eyes, but he was wracked with pain all over his body, his face, and his ears were ringing. He tried to lift his arms.

"No, no, no," he heard Meera's voice? "Don't move. Klaus, can you talk? I've been so worried."

"Why... worried?" he mumbled as he tried to think what she would be worried about.

And then he remembered. "They tried to kill you," he mumbled. "But I got 'em. And you... you dropped a..."

"I had to," she sobbed. "I had to protect you."

Had to protect you. I like the sound of that... Wait! I'm

supposed to be protecting her? For Sorge. Before our last battle together in the marines, I promised Sorge I'd protect her if something happened to him.

After the battle, Klaus had held the fallen marine, Meera's son, who'd been like a brother to him, and vowed that he'd fulfill his promise. He'd recognized Meera as Sorge's mother at the first Guardians meeting.

"Meera, I want—"

"No. Not now. You need to rest," she said, stifling her tears.

He opened his eyes. *If I'm going to die, I want to see her before I go. Stars, she's as beautiful as in the picture Sorge carried of her.*

"Why are you crying?" he croaked.

"I, I... You're—"

"Not going anywhere," he muttered, then wished he hadn't. "Help me up."

"But—but you—" she stammered, taking hold of his arm.

"I still got both my legs?" he asked.

When she nodded, he said, "Then help me up. We go, yes? We not hangin' around until roof caves in. Get me out of here."

It was a struggle for him to stand, but between them, they made it, and he was surprised. "Why you take all that trouble to pull me?" he asked. "Why you not think me up?"

"I—I'm overwhelmed," she stammered. She shook her head, then said, "Never mind. Let's go."

"I don't feel like walking," he said, only half-joking. "How about we call a gravcab?"

"We can't," she said. "Both our datascreens are dead. So are the comms."

"I joke," he said. "Look around. You think there are still cabs? I think not."

He looked down at her. She was so much smaller than him. And yet, she looked... perfect.

"Meera, I tell you something," he whispered. "I have deep affection for you."

"You... what?" She was visibly stunned.

"I have fall for you. You have feisty determination. You never give up. And you lovely, beautiful." He remembered the picture of her Sorge had shown him. It seemed so long ago. "I love you first time I see you."

"Ha...ha," she replied, not knowing what else to say. "That's not possible."

"No, Meera," he replied. "Truly."

"Then why have you avoided me right from the beginning, when we first joined the Guardians?"

"I younger than you, Meera. Younger than—" He stopped. He couldn't mention anything that would remind her of Sorge. "I think you not take me seriously."

"Well, you're right. What would someone like you want with an older woman like me?"

"Age does not matter," he replied. "Love is love."

"I don't believe it," she said.

He looked at her earnestly and nodded his head. "Is true. How can I make you believe?"

She looked up at him and he could see by the look in her eyes that she wanted to believe him.

"I don't know if I ever could," she replied.

"I am sorry, Meera," he said. "I want to be man who treat you like you deserve, like queen."

She looked away, a small smile at the corners of her lips. "Come on," she said, taking his arm. "We have to get going. You need medical attention and we have a long way to go."

She wants to believe, he thought. *I know she does.*

———

***Avenger's* Bridge**
Planet Magnum, L1 Orbit

. . .

PRINCE TARAK STEPPED DOWN from the shuttle, stood for a moment and glanced around *Avenger's* hangar bay.

"Prince Tarak. Your highness," a voice said. He turned around to find a small party of officers standing at attention.

"Welcome to *Avenger*. I am Lieutenant Commander Jadern. Captain Morian is on the bridge. He's expecting you. If you'll follow me, sir?"

Tarak nodded, dipped his head, and said, "Thank you, Commander. I am at your disposal." And he followed Jadern to the elevator.

After a silent three-minute gravrail ride, Jadern opened the door to the bridge and stepped aside.

"Allo the conn," Tarak said and made the antiquated request. "Permission to board the bridge?"

"Granted," Captain Morian replied. "Prince Tarak. Welcome. It's a pleasure to meet with you in person."

"Mister Jadern, I'll be in my ready room if you need me. You have the conn."

"If you'll follow me, your highness," Morian said, and together they left the bridge.

Tarak followed the captain to his ready room, and as the door slid closed behind them, Morian surprised him when he turned and held out his hand.

Tarak smiled. This was something he wasn't used to. "I've heard much about you, Commodore. Is it all true?"

Morian smiled back at him and said, "Please, sit down. And please, your highness, call me Richard, and no, most of what you've heard is gross exaggeration. But you: you're the infamous Prince Tarak Tudor. Prince Elio thinks highly of you and has been filling me in about your... hobbies."

"I assure you, Richard," Tarak replied, "that, as you say, whatever he told you has been very much exaggerated."

But the look in Richard's eyes told him he wasn't taken in.

"I can assure you, my prince, that if there's one thing Elio is not," he said calmly, "it's hyperbolic."

"Interesting that you call him by name," Tarak said.

"It's an interesting story," Richard said lightly. "Let's just say, for now, that the prince and I are good friends."

Tarak gave a little smile. "As is your sister, perhaps?"

Richard frowned and gave him a level look, to which Tarak replied, "Captain, you believe I'm not dangerous, and I don't believe I'm ignorant, either."

"Oh, I don't believe for one minute that you're ignorant; as to dangerous... that's yet to be seen."

"Touche, Captain," Tarak replied and dipped his head.

"So," Richard said. "Here you are. The question is... why? Why come to me? I'm not royalty. I would have thought Admiral Neboda would serve your needs better than I ever could."

"Ah, but you underestimate yourself, Captain. Your reputation and your connections to the throne of Orso belie your modesty.

"Captain, I need information," Tarak continued. "And who else would I talk to with more experience fighting the Swarm than the Hero of Tor, the Savior of Orso, the Peacemaker of the IMFP?"

"You can stop with those," Richard said dryly, then added, "your highness."

"You amuse me, Richard," Tarak said, smiling. "You are a man after my own heart. We shall get along well together, I think. And I understand completely. Sometimes the titles get in the way of doing business. Two men can't simply discuss terms without weighing all the political angles inherent to the situation. No, Captain Morian, I am a... direct man. And I believe in killing Blues until they're dead and letting whoever lives pick up the pieces. I seek no power for myself."

"Well, that would make you... the third royal I've met who've said that to me," Morian replied. "But, so far, only Elio has actually followed through."

"Very well," Tarak said. "Enough of this idle banter. I need your help, Richard. I've just come from Citrom. The largest criminal organization there, the Dawn Fan, built a monstrosity, a construct of Swarm and human technology that was intended to be a command center for Swarm operations. And when I say human, I mean human beings grafted into the construct. Don't ask me to describe it; I can't. I destroyed it, of course."

"That's not news," Richard replied. "We discovered something similar to what you described here on Caerus, though you've probably already heard that Elio's Guardians destroyed it."

"Yes," Tarak said, nodding. "So I heard, but I've also learned that there is at least one other." He paused, thinking.

Richard reached out and touched his mind.

"Belay that, Captain," Tarak said sternly. "I am a Psy Master. You cannot reach me."

A Psy Master? Richard thought. *Hmm, interesting. I've never heard of such a thing.*

Well, now you have, Captain. Tarak's thought slammed into his mind like a hammer. *Let's move on, shall we?*

Morian was stunned by the intensity of the intrusion, but he smiled at Tarak and said, "As you say, my prince, touche! And where exactly is this new construct?"

"Odin," Tarak replied. "My home world. My mother, Queen Zarah of Odin, now in exile here on Caerus, has charged me with the discovery and destruction of all Swarm artifacts and technology, including live cores. My mandate is simple. Success is imperative, whatever the cost. We tried to enlist guerilla support, but we failed, and now, with the mistrust between Elio and my mother, I doubt we'll see any help there."

"Prince Elio will agree to help," Morian said quickly.

"How so?" Tarak asked. "What do you think you know?"

"Prince Elio is as determined as you to end this war quickly," Morian said. "I know him well. He will help."

"And can I count on such enthusiastic support from you?" Tarak asked slyly as Richard felt a gentle touch to his mind.

"I... I... Yes, of course," Morian hesitatingly agreed. "But I don't see how I can help. I'm involved in rooting out a planet-wide infestation here on Caerus."

This was what Tarak had been waiting for.

I'm not really manipulating him, he thought, trying to convince himself it was true. *It's just the manner of presentation.* But conversational psychology had been drilled into him from such an early age that he could no longer distinguish the line between manipulation and presentation.

"With your permission, Captain?" he asked, raising his arm to reveal his datapad.

Morian nodded and said, "Of course."

Tarak tapped his datascreen and the ready room's holo activated, showing the planet Odin and the Swarm carriers and fighters, an entire fleet, in high orbit above the planet. Another tap and the image zoomed in toward the planet, showing triads of fighters and the newly named ballistas—the carriers—patrolling the mesosphere.

Tarak tapped again and zoomed in on the center of the city of Asgard to show the former governmental seat, the Palace of Odin, bristling with weapons turrets. The palace was now a Swarm fortress.

"Inside that building is the new Imperator of Odin, a red... being, for want of a better description," Tarak said, "and it must die."

"I understand," Morian said, "but I am under Prince Elio's personal command. I do as he tells me. You understand, of course."

"I do indeed," Tarak replied. "And it is to be hoped he will, as you seem to think, comply and offer his help. In which case, I can assure you you will continue to do so," Tarak said. "But I also wanted to give you... an incentive to stump for me, should the occasion arise."

"Are you suggesting that you would try to bribe a USF Knight-Captain?" Morian asked wryly.

"Oh, I very much think I have something you want. In fact, many people want it," Tarak replied, smiling. "No. Not a bribe. Call it a gesture of goodwill."

Tarak handed over a halo taken from the Ligarch research room on Citrom.

"This is one of fifty recovered from the research facility on Citrom," Tarak said. "It blocks Psy transmissions. Wearing it would block almost all Psy communications."

Morian looked at the halo, then stared at it, then smiled.

"As it happens," Richard said, looking at the prince, "I know of several people who will be delighted to know about this, but we already have such halos. They were introduced by your own Queen Zarah several years ago. But thank you for the offer, my Prince."

"It is no consequence," Tarak replied. "But the halo you hold in your hand is unlike any other, as you will no doubt learn. It can block all Psy transmissions from a person of your choosing. Please, keep it and give it a try at your convenience. And now, I would appreciate your advice as to how we might attack a stronghold such as this and kill the Imperator."

"How recent are these vids?" Morian asked.

"About twelve hours," Tarak replied, "but we've been monitoring them for almost a month from a stealth satellite in orbit around the nearby planet Loki. They show very little ingenuity or variation. And with my King and Queen focusing their attention on politics elsewhere..."

Something I advised heavily against. Tarak thought savagely. *Something I warned them would happen. And she still expects me to fix their mistakes.*

"Well," he continued, "be that as it may... Captain, I'd like you to watch something and tell me what you think."

Tarak tapped his screen and the vid changed. He watched Morian's face as a section of space above Odin began to change, shifting the reflected light from the planet, lensing. After a few moments, the readouts indicated a gravitic anomaly. Then a ship, two ships, three—more than a dozen ships exited the anomaly above Odin.

"Is that... a Slipgate?" Morian asked, stunned.

"The enemy has always been able to appear where we least expect them," Tarak said. "And now we know how. The only advantage we have is time. What I just showed you was time-lapsed. That Slipgate took two days to materialize. Why so long? We don't know. The only reason we can think of is to create stability."

Tarak could see Morian's mind working.

"Well, getting close to the planet would be difficult," Morian said. "It would require a large carrier group to overcome —" He shook his head, looked at Tarak and said, "Have you considered orbital bombardment? A few well-placed—"

"Unfortunately, they have hostages." Tarak hated it, but it had to be said.

"The Swarm has been murdering humans wholesale since the war began," Morian said. "There's little we can do about it."

"That is true, Captain," Tarak replied, "which is why this new development is so concerning. Everything is changing, and changing quickly. They're no longer secretive about their ability to generate Slipgates. Why? We don't know. What we do know is that if they learn how highly we value our own, the entire outlook of the war will change. And not for the better." He paused, then said, "I'm sorry, Captain. Sometimes I get a little carried away, but I'm sure you understand."

"I do, my prince," Morian replied, "And I understand, completely. Whatever it takes to eradicate the Blues."

Tarak nodded, pursed his lips, narrowed his eyes, and said, "Thank you, Captain, but for now, I suggest we discuss tactics."

Four hours later, on the shuttle ride back to the *Justification,* he checked a mental box with Richard Morian's name attached.

Done, and done.

CHAPTER
THIRTY-ONE

SHUTTLE 171 GAMMA

Inbound to Planet Caerus
Orso System

Captain Sasha Crowe watched as the shuttle carrying her, her crew, and their important passenger approached *Avenger.*

"Avenger, this is shuttle 171-GC, requesting permission to dock," Lieutenant DeLong transmitted.

Once the dust had settled after the attack on Regis Magnum and the team was cleared to depart, it had taken two weeks to track down Khaila Adstar, the legend herself, the one the Frejyans called Mirabilis, but DeLong had been persistent. Almost as persistent as Dagon Jax would have been, had he been able to go as originally planned.

Docking completed without incident, and Sasha readied herself for action.

A short gravrail ride to the elevators, then a swift walk, took them to the medbay where they found Haltar Sen on a gurney.

"He collapsed again this morning," Dr. Jyra Dowd said as

Sasha helped Khaila get situated. "He's fading fast. If it had been my decision, I'd have started the palliative care much sooner, but he refuses to consider it, and the captain overrode me, so..."

Once again, Sasha found herself impressed by Richard Morian. Her previous meetings with Jyra, back in the Freyjan shipyards, had indicated the strength of the doctor's personality. For Richard to have overridden the doctor's authority spoke volumes about the force of his own personality and the respect he commanded.

"I'll look him over," Khaila said. "But I'm not looking forward to the prognosis."

Khaila sat down next to Haltar and gently touched his arm with both hands. He winced but didn't say anything, and Sasha wondered how much strength he really had left.

Was this all for nothing? she wondered.

———

"WHAT IS IT, KLAUS?" Meera said.

"So... it has been one month since the big battle ," he replied.

"Yes," she said, looking up at him. "A month since we almost died. So?"

"It was not first time for me," he said. "I almost died two times before. Might be closest, though."

"And yet we keep going," Meera said. "I will keep fighting. Someone has to."

"You do not have to fight, Meera."

She almost rolled her eyes. "I know. We're part of the team."

"But we can be team. You and me, no?"

She didn't answer.

"Why not, Meera?" Klaus asked. "Why can we not be partners?"

She turned to him. "Because maybe I'm not ready to risk getting hurt again, that's why. Now, please. Leave it."

"Meera, we almost died, remember?" he said, putting a hand out to touch her arm. "What is little heartache compared to—"

"It's *everything*, Klaus," she snapped, brushing his hand away.

"Okay! So bad wording. You hurt all the time; I see that. I want you to hurt less. I want to be person who helps with that. I not looking for something quick... easy, and I prove it. Mostly."

"How can you prove it *mostly*?" she snapped.

"How many women you think have thrown themselves at me since we become big heroes?"

Meera didn't know, but she had seen him surrounded by young women after the first vidcast about how the Guardians— *Whoops. I guess that's Knights now, since Prince Elio decided to change the name*—helped to save the city.

"What about them, Klaus?" she said, heaving a sigh.

"I could have had any one of them, all of them, but I did not. I want only you, Meera."

Hmm. Maybe he has a point.

"I make you deal," he said earnestly, taking her hand in his. "You let me in and if I let you down... you can kill me."

Meera stared at him, waiting for him to smile, to indicate he was joking, but he didn't.

Stars! He's serious, she thought.

"Klaus," she said. "Don't be ridiculous. Why would I kill you? Stop acting... childish. I'm not a killer."

"Um..." Suddenly he looked oddly nervous. "Meera, you are a killer. You are soldier. You kill hundreds of Blues; maybe even more than Prince Elio or Andra."

And she couldn't help but think back to the fury and rage she'd felt as she'd stormed across the battlefield. And she realized the rage had been boiling inside ever since her son Sorge had died.

She stared up at Klaus, into his huge brown eyes, and something inside her melted.

She sucked in her bottom lip, and she stammered, "Klaus... I don't..." Then she sighed. "Very well... We can see each other. But Klaus, so help me, if I find out you've betrayed my trust, you'll wish you died like Graben did."

"Excellent! Wait... How did he die?" Klaus asked, frowning.

"The *Meritorious* landed on top of him last year," she replied.

"Oof. I served on *Meritorious.* Captain Perrault was good woman. Sad she died."

In that moment, Meera understood something she really hadn't been aware of. Despite his youth, Klaus had already seen more death and destruction than most people would see in a lifetime. If he could endure so much and still be willing to chase a fantasy he hoped might one day come true, then maybe she could too.

"You really do think you love me, don't you?" she asked, remembering all the positive thoughts, the encouragement he'd given her.

"I do," he said.

She stood on tiptoe, reached up, put her hand to the back of his neck and pulled him down toward her. Then she touched her lips to his, gently, and pulled away.

He reached for her to take her into his arms, but before he could, she used her TK to push him gently away.

"No, Klaus," she said, smiling up at him. "Call that a good-faith down payment." And she took two steps back.

"So we're together?"

"Yes, if that's what you really want."

He leapt into the air. "Whoo-hoo!" he shouted, loud enough that she could hear it echo off the nearby buildings.

———

Avenger

Planet Caerus, L1 Orbit
Captain's Ready Room

Danis entered the captain's ready room with trepidation. While she had no reason to think her brother had any reason to reprimand her, she hadn't been able to read his mood, either, at least not since she received a brief flash of happiness earlier.

He knows how to keep his feelings under wraps when he really wants to, but he normally doesn't bother to. Is it me, or something else entirely?

"Ah, Lieutenant Commander Morian," he said as she entered. "Please sit down."

"Why so formal, *Captain?*" Danis asked as she sat down facing him across his desk.

"Well, because I'm about to offer you a promotion," he replied.

"No!" she said, flatly.

"Danis, why not—"

"Because I'm not interested in climbing the chain of command, Richard. I want to be right where I am. I let you promote me to lieutenant commander last time, and that's where it ends."

"Danis, I want to promote you to full commander rank because I want you to have the rank you'll need to restart Ranger Squadron. As a commander, you'd be able to choose your pilots from the cream of the crop, the rank you need to override... well, anyone under my command, except me, in a combat situation. You're the best squadron commander in the entire USF fleet."

"No, Richard." She paused, then continued, "Look, I understand, brother, and I appreciate it, but Ranger Squadron is dead; gone. It is no more."

Morian frowned at her, waiting for her to explain, but she said nothing.

He reached out to her. *Danis, what do you mean?*

"Richard, I'm the only original member of Ranger Squadron still alive," she said out loud. "They're all gone. Dead. I watched them all die. Lucy Chen, Sheva, Wendwood, all of them. There is no one left from my life before the invasion. Don't you understand that? The only close friends I have are Gian and Jackknife. Ranger is gone. I'm no longer a Ranger."

"You'll always be a Ranger," Richard claimed.

"No, Richard," she said gently. "It's over."

"Then what do you want to do?" he asked.

"I'll form a new squadron, Falcon Squadron," she said. "Not to guard, to stand and wait for trouble. Falcon will be a predator squadron. We'll go looking for trouble instead of waiting for it to come to us. We'll strike first."

"What's in a name, Danis?" Richard replied skeptically.

She couldn't explain it to him in words, so she switched to Psy. *Here's a Ranger,* she sent, showing him all the peaceful, protective connotations the word carried in her mind. *And here is Falcon.* The feelings he received now were fierce, angry, aggressive.

That's what we need, what the entire USF needs. I would think the captain of the Avenger would understand. How many ships have we lost? So many of them with peacetime names. Remember Tranquility, Serenity, Safe Harbor? All of them gone.

Danis, I really think you're making a bigger deal of these names than it warrants.

No, brother. I read a lot of reports while you were on Intrepid. I was busy most of the time too, you know?

Hah! Danis, I thought you spent most of that time with Prince Elio.

What? Richard, he's a prince. Even if I did get a little more time with him than most, it doesn't mean I had his undivided attention.

Then why are you blushing, sister?

Why am I— She forced herself not to think about the time she had spent with Elio. The three months since Richard returned had been unbearably difficult, with every thought of Elio, his lips on hers, his hands; *oh, did that man have hands?*

Richard, she reached out again, *you started this meeting out formal. Now you're treating it like a family gossip fest... What are you doing?*

She watched as he took a halo from his desk drawer.

And, so now we're going to talk via halo?

Richard slipped the halo over his brow.

Why can't you just act like the captain you are, and—Richard? Richard?

But Richard had completely disappeared from her mind.

"No, please, go ahead," Richard said, smiling. "Go on thinking about the guy who was handsy with my sister."

She frowned, concentrated, narrowed her eyes, concentrated more, but Richard was no longer there. She searched for his mind with hers, but she couldn't reach him.

So she thought about Elio and watched her brother's eyes.

Richard's face was emotionless.

She thought about Elio's hands doing... Elio things.

Nothing.

She decided to brazen it out and *really* think about what she *really* wanted to do to Elio.

Still no hint of an expression. He didn't even blink.

She even thought about that one outrageous thing that Degus had mentioned once, about five years ago...

He didn't twitch an eyebrow.

She took a deep breath and said, "You really can't hear me, can you?"

"And that may be the sweetest thing I've heard from you all year," Richard said with a smile. "I received a gift today, and I hereby pass it on to you. By which I mean, any time I get a hint of you and Elio, I can slap this thing on my head and cut you out."

Every carefully guarded emotion of the last three months

surged into her reeling mind. She leapt to her feet, saluted and snapped, "Permission to leave, sir?"

Richard took an infuriatingly long time to stand and even longer to return her salute. *If he wasn't wearing that thing, he'd hear—*

"Permission granted, Commander," he said, a lazy smile on his lips.

Danis fled to her quarters, took her halo from the safe—one given to her by Elio, the most advanced model available, and crammed it on her head. "Initiate contact with Elio," she snapped.

The room she chose was one she'd found on the ethernet. It was a bit much for her, but it featured stonework walls, a gorgeous four-poster bed draped in silks, and a balcony with a commanding view over the snow-capped mountains of Olympus, a favored tourist destination on Caerus.

She waited almost five minutes for his avatar to shimmer into existence. "Sorry, Danis," he said, smiling. "I was in a meeting. Why did you call me?"

She grabbed him by the jaw and pulled him into the most passionate kiss she'd ever felt. The halo was incredible. She could feel his avatar's lips on hers. It wasn't as nice as the real thing, but she made certain he understood that she appreciated the nuances of his gift.

When she finally released him, he stammered, "Does... does this mean... that—"

"I don't know where he got it," she whispered, interrupting him, "but Richard has a Psy-blocking halo. And I intend for him to wear it out."

"You mean—"

Again, she interrupted him. "Meet me here at twenty-two-hundred," she ordered playfully. "And don't bother dressing to impress me. I'm already more impressed than you can ever imagine. Now get back to work and think of me."

"Well ...I..." he stuttered. "I'll see you later, then."

She pulled the halo off. *Wow, that was incredible. I could have stayed in there all day. I will stay in there all night.*

But that's all for later. Right now, I need to draw up a duty roster and get ready to inaugurate the Falcons.

Once we get those new fighters, the Blues will know a whole new definition of fear.

You hear me, Richard?

I hear you, sister. Take care what you wish for.

Whatever that means, she thought.

———

LEVEL THETA HOLDING Cells (Classified)
Regis Magnum Shipyards

KASA WAS ALONE in her cell. Again. And had been for almost three months.

True, it was a different cell with fewer distractions. She'd told them about her nanomod implant, but after erasing the confidential information, they had uploaded some educational materials for her to watch. Perhaps they hadn't been much fun after the third or fourth time, but it was a measure of someone's influence that she'd received any mercy at all.

I mean, I'm the traitor that almost destroyed Regis Magnum. The thought lay heavy on her mind. She'd never really imagined the scope of Hirana Ligarch's plans.

I couldn't refuse him. He would have killed my parents. I can only hope they're still alive.

The door hissed open, and Sasha Crowe stepped in. The door sealed behind her.

"Enjoying the vids?" she asked.

"Yes," Kasa said, only half lying. "Did you ask them to do that?"

"No. I don't have the authority to do that," Sasha replied.

"That was Commander Haal. She seems to have a soft spot for you."

"Um, tell her thank you?"

"I will. We've not found this supposed other spy you told us about, but I'll also tell you something positive. The information you gave us about Ligarch checked out. At least, that's what they told me. I don't know much more than that. I've been gone for a month."

"Oh, what for?" Kasa instantly regretted asking the question.

Sasha's eyes narrowed. "Personal business. Anyway, I'm here to inform you that you've attracted some attention, despite being legally dead."

"Who knows I'm alive?" she asked, fearfully.

"Well, Manda, me, maybe the guards who put you in here... Captain Morian, because Manda tells him everything. And of course, Prince Tarak Tudor, who seems to have his eye on you."

"Are we sure he's not the spy?" Kasa asked.

"He's not the spy," Sasha replied. "He's second in line to the throne of Odin and seemingly a law unto himself, but he's loyal."

"So..." Kasa tried to ask politely, "what does a prince want with me?"

"I don't know," Sasha said, frowning, "but I'm sure you'll find out, and soon. In the meantime, I suggest you continue to study the vids. Goodbye, Kasa, and thank you."

She turned and knocked on the door. It opened and shut behind her, and Kasa was alone again with a whole new mishmash of thoughts. She had no idea of how she could interpret them. She also felt something else, something she hadn't felt in a long time—hope.

———

Feducere, Neujaz Apartments

Planet Caerus

FAXIL BREATHED a sigh of relief as they approached the front door of his home. It had been a difficult day, but every moment he'd spent sitting in that court had been worth it.

Kuon bounded in ahead, spinning in circles yipping. To Faxil it was still strange to see her inside the apartment, but he knew he'd get used to it, big as she was.

He turned and looked at Pinari, and for the first time since they'd met, he could see she was scared. She hesitated at the door.

"Come on in," Faxil said.

"You sure, Fax?" she asked skeptically.

He gave her a big smile. "Of course. This is your home now."

She stepped inside and looked at the furniture, touching the pieces one after another. None of it matched, but that didn't matter, not to Faxil, anyway. His family didn't match either, and now, with the addition of Kuon and Pinari, it was an even bigger mismatch. He grinned at the thought.

"So," he said, as he led her through the apartment, "this is the living room, where we play games and stuff sometimes. This is the kitchen and, back here..." He pushed the door open and stepped inside. "Is your bedroom."

He waited for her to follow him in, but she just stood there, her mouth open, looking all around. She looked as if she was about to burst into tears.

"Pinari, what's wrong?" he asked.

"Why are you being so nice to me?" she asked. "I hurt you a lot. I was mean to you."

"I don't... I mean..." He shrugged, looked down at the floor. "I don't know. Maybe you hurt me a little, but I like you, and I want you to be my sister, so I can look after you."

Even though tears sparkled in her eyes, she couldn't help but laugh a little. "A shrimp like you, looking after me?"

"Hey, I'm brave," he said. "You know I am. I found the Blues, didn't I?"

She smiled, nodded and said, "Yes, Fax. You're brave, a little stupid at times, but very brave."

And she stepped forward, wrapped her arms around him and hugged him and whispered in his ear, "I am proud to be your sister." Then she released him and stepped past him into her new room. It was the room where Faxil's mom used to sleep, but he was okay with turning it over to Pinari.

"Faxil, where are you?" his father called.

"In here," he shouted.

He looked at his father and at his other mom. Inoiae was wearing her new uniform. She'd been accepted into the TK Knights as a member of a new combat communications unit. Between that and his father's new job, they would have all the money they needed to take care of a new sister.

"How does she like it?" his father asked.

"I have my own bed again!" Pinari said. Faxil thought she was crying, so he ran into the room, only to hear, "Why did you run into my room like that, Fax? Girls need privacy. Go on, please."

Faxil smiled at her, nodded, stepped back out and closed the door. Then he stood for a moment staring at it.

Kuon nudged him, then sat down and rubbed her head against his thigh.

Faxil couldn't help the huge grin that lit up his face. It felt good to be part of the family again.

CHAPTER
THIRTY-TWO

HEALER'S TOUCH

LEVEL THREE, Corridor B7
Avenger's **Medbay**

IT'S BEEN ALMOST a month since they left. Dagon complained to himself as he ran down to the medbay, where he found Dr. Dowd standing beside Haltar's bed, along with Sasha Crowe and an unknown woman nearly as old as Haltar.

"How bad is it?" he blurted. "Is he going to get well?"

"Who are you? And you; who are you?" the older woman asked as Commander Haal entered the room.

"This is Lieutenant Jax, and I am Commander Haal. Are you the healer? What's the prognosis?"

"Quiet, both of you," Dr. Dowd snapped. "Haltar has gotten past the latest seizure, but they're still coming too fast. I want to sedate him so he can meet his end without pain. But apparently," she said and gave Haltar a mock glare, "my opinion counts little to this one."

"Jyra, you old bat..." Haltar gasped. "You never did give me any news I liked, so why would... you start... now?"

"Dagon, Manda," Sasha said. "This is Khaila Adstar. We've managed to get her here, thanks to Mr. DeLong, but she doesn't—"

"I can speak for myself," Khaila interrupted her, her voice creaky as an old door. "The problem is he has lost too much strength. I am not sure I can help him."

Dagon gasped. Manda choked a little and was about to speak when Khaila said, "Oh, grow a spine, you two. I did not travel ninety lightyears to tell you I cannot do anything. There is something I can try. It is perhaps... stupid and risky, but not to me, so it is your decision." She looked at them.

"Me?" Dagon asked.

Just as Haal said, "*My* decision?"

"He says you two his best friends. Well, and the captain, but he is busy."

Dagon felt an unexpected warmth surge through him. *Haltar said that, but...* The old navigator had been such a constant in his life that he'd never questioned the relationship between a mentor and student, between a junior and senior navigator.

"I can bring one of you in," Khaila said. "You can be... mental life support. Dreamworld to rest in while I do careful fixing. But it will not be pleasant. He will feel less pain, because you will feel it instead. And believe me, I already peeked. Not pretty."

"Well..." Dagon wracked his brain for an answer.

But Commander Haal beat him to it. "Why can't we sedate him? Or at least give him something for the pain?"

Khaila shook her head. "Drugs numb nerves. That covers up damage so I can't find problem. I need him to be fully aware."

"I'll do it," Haal said.

"No, I'll do it," Dagon said.

"Well, which one?" Khaila demanded.

"Take me," Dagon said.

"I said I'll do it," Haal snarled through gritted teeth.

Dagon looked at her.

"I outrank you, Mister Jax, by a lot," she said smugly.

"With all due respect, ma'am," he blurted out, "I haven't spent the last nine months looking after him to stand aside now."

"If you two are done," the healer said, "two of you be just as useful. You can both do it. But—" She raised a finger at Commander Haal. "Will be easiest if the initial focus is on the boy. They share many memories. Create solid connection."

Manda nodded.

Dowd pointed to the two empty beds. "Lie down, both of you. I'm going to give you a light relaxant. I don't want you thrashing off the table."

Dagon was down before Commander Haal. He couldn't help but steal a glance at her long-limbed frame as she settled down. *Careful how you think about Commander Haal in there,* he thought. *There's no telling what will happen in a Psy dreamworld.*

He heard the hiss of an infuser at the next bed, then felt the pressure on his arm, and then... he felt his body relax. He'd expected it to be a pleasant feeling, but he wasn't entirely comfortable.

He felt a light touch on his mind. He opened himself to the touch and found himself in the most comfortable, beautiful place he could have chosen.

And he wondered, *Did I choose it, or did someone else?*

———

Manda Haal felt the touch of the infuser on her skin, but her thoughts were already elsewhere.

Everything she'd been through last month still churned through her mind. She'd experienced thoughts and feelings that had devastated her. She faced the enemy in a firefight to the death. Her more than forty years as a military officer had hardened her. She had little time for weakness and no time at all for fools, but, tough as she was, she felt that another loss, Haltar Sen, would break her, and she would bear any amount of physical pain if it would save his life.

She accepted the touch on her mind and found herself on the bridge of the *Avenger*. But when she stepped up to the command rail, she found it unfamiliar and confusing.

Many of the controls were indistinct, the holos blurred, unfocused, unreadable. She tried to concentrate on them, but they only improved a little.

A dream world to rest in.

She looked ahead and found a familiar head of sandy hair peeking over the secondary navigator's chair. She was flooded with relief and a surprising warmth.

Of course, she thought. *He saved me. He rescued me, and now he's risking his health for his friend and mine.* "Mister Jax, is that you?" she called.

He turned around to look at her, surprised. "Uh, uh, yes, of course, Commander Haal. Lieutenant Dagon Jax, on station."

It looked like him. It sounded like him, but there was a strange slackness to his features. And he seemed somehow smaller.

She pondered the strangeness but started to feel an unpleasant sensation, like the dull tightness that preceded a headache. She winced and tried to ignore it.

She stepped away from the rail and descended the six steps to the well deck, only mildly aware that something else seemed off; what it was, she didn't know. She approached Jax's station. The details became sharper but were still unrecognizable.

An ethereal voice said, *The initial focus will be on the boy.*

The discomfort increased to the point where it became exceedingly painful. She gasped from the severity, and somewhere she heard Jax cry out.

And then the pain began to fade.

As the pain faded, she looked back to Jax. He looked… more boyish.

She lifted her hand to her mouth in surprise, to find she was out of uniform. She was wearing a beautiful, flowing, shimmering sky-blue dress. Her hair, normally bound up in a regulation ponybob, was delicately curled and hung past her eyes and down her back in a Torian twist.

"But… this is my dress," she said to Jax. "How do you know about this dress?"

Jax looked guilty. "I'm sorry, Commander. I saw it at the celebration on Tor after we defeated the Swarm there. You wore it to the senior officers' party."

The focus will be on the boy, huh? the thought intruded. *It appears he's focused on something else.*

"And you dressed me in it instead of my uniform?"

"Again, I apologize, ma'am… Aaaaagh." He screwed his eyes closed, and she gritted her teeth as another wave of pain suddenly burst over her like an ocean wave.

The pain receded. She looked down and saw that the dress fit her just a *little* too well. Every curve of her body was subtly accentuated.

"Mister Jax, I demand that you stop toying with—" She stopped short of saying *my body*, and instead said, "—the dream."

"I'm trying really hard not to think of anything inappropriate, Manda. Uh! I mean, Commander."

"I'll forgive the familiarity if you stop thinking about my clothes. If I had known I'd find this inside your mind…"

He stood up and looked at her, "So you would have left Haltar to die?"

She was startled. Jax had changed. Instead of his usual height, eight centimeters shorter than her, now he was almost as tall as she was. His face was a little more rugged, his features a little more defined. He stared at her with eyes so blue…

"No!" she snapped. "I should have demanded to be the focal point instead of you."

"I can't help the way I feel about you," Jax murmured. He seemed so close to her face. "I can only control what I do. And I have never been anything but respectful toward you, ma'am."

Even the way he said the word "ma'am" seemed so sensual. And the way he looked at her eyes…

Into her eyes…

And what she saw in his eyes was passion. Passion for life, passion to save his friend. And, perhaps, a little of that passion was for her.

"And how *do* you feel about me?" she whispered, as the pain seared through her body.

"If you weren't my superior officer, I would want to… kiss you, very respectfully, of course," he said, the pain obvious on his face. But he didn't take his eyes off hers.

How can he look at me like that?

"Mister Jax, your behavior is out of line." She gasped as the pain peaked.

"No, ma'am. Not me. Only my thoughts." Jax clenched his jaw as the pain started to recede. "You are the woman in my dreams."

He dreams about me?

"But you've never said anything," Manda said, feeling something deep inside her she hadn't felt in more than forty years.

"How could I?" he asked. "You're a commander and I'm a mere lieutenant. Of course I never said anything. You would have thrown me in the brig. I always knew I didn't stand a chance. You're not just out of my league; I don't think we're even playing the same sport."

She felt her breath catch. Her heart was pounding, but before she could say anything, the bridge doors opened.

"Friends," Haltar said. But before he could say anything more, she felt another searing flash of pain. The door slammed shut, and she fell to the floor, hearing the thud as Jax fell too.

When she opened her eyes, she found herself at her command post, peering down at the navigation stations. But now, Jax's sandy hair didn't peek over the back of his seat. He had disappeared.

Haltar stood up from his post at navigation and faced her. "I know that you've always respected me, Manda. And I'm not certain that I'm going to pull through this. Even with your help, I can feel myself growing weaker. So I'm going to tell you something you need to hear."

He pointed at Dagon Jax's empty seat. "That boy there is in love with you, has been since the first day he set eyes on you. He respects you. And I know you respect him. And if you think I haven't noticed how you feel about him, then you should have retired me a long time ago."

"I don't feel... And just how do you think I feel about him?" she asked, outraged but wavering.

He laughed at her. "It's not my place to explain your feelings," he said as another flash of pain seared through her head. Though intense, it was at least brief.

"But by entering his mind like this," Haltar continued, "he might have learned a little more about you than you think."

"Wait—" Manda realized something. "You told that healer to call us both, didn't you? Richard would have come. You know he would. But you insisted on Jax and me. Didn't you?"

Haltar smiled and raised his hands in surrender. "Guilty, my lady."

She felt a twinge of anger. "And you tricked me because—"

"Because I want you to be happy, Manda," Haltar replied. "Ask yourself what you really—"

Then a fresh wave of pain struck, and Haltar disappeared.

She screamed, and screamed, and then... this time when she recovered, she was alone.

———

WHEN DAGON OPENED HIS EYES, he was surprised to find himself at his station instead of on the floor. He looked around, but Commander Haal was gone.

"It's surprising to me," Haltar said from the station next to him, "that even in your own mind, you can't call her by her first name."

"I can't. She's my commanding officer," Jax replied. "Besides, she's not interested in the likes of me. And... she's a Seer."

"You'd be surprised, Dagon." Haltar laughed. "She thinks highly of you, and she wants to be appreciated. Manda Haal is a woman who needs to be appreciated."

Dagon felt a flash of pain, but only for a few seconds before it abated. When he recovered, he found Haltar slumped over his console. Parts of his body were shimmering, as if they were fading away.

"If... you want... to have a chance with that woman," Haltar whispered, "it's important you remember... that she's a woman first... and an officer second. She..."

But Haltar had faded away, and the pain ripped through Jax's body. He felt as if he was on fire, his skin burning, peeling, and he screamed, and screamed and screamed... And then he was alone.

This is all in my mind. I just need to wake up.

He slapped himself, pinched himself, pulled his hair, but nothing worked.

And then he heard a creaky voice. *Wait. This is complicated part.*

He felt himself shoved back down into the dream, only now Commander Haal was there, too.

And she was smiling.

Everything going fine, the cantankerous voice interrupted. *You two find something to talk about. I busy finishing this.*

"So..." he said. "Is there anything you—"

But before he could finish the question, she leaned forward, grabbed his head in both hands and kissed him, and suddenly Dagon Jax had a very good reason to stop talking.

———

Haltar Sen opened his eyes and looked around, something he'd not expected to do.

"Jyra," he rasped. "So I actually made it?"

She smiled at him. "That you did, Haltar. That you did."

And she punched him lightly on the shoulder.

"What was that for, Jyra?" he asked, surprised.

"You called me an old bat, you pruned curmudgeon." she retorted.

"I did?" Then he remembered. "Well, maybe I did, but I was dying. Doesn't one get a little slack when he's dying?"

"I didn't hit you when you were dying, did I?" she said, laughing.

Haltar faked a cough. "Well, how can you be certain I'm not still dying?"

"Because *she* told me you weren't." Jyra pointed at the healer, Khaila. "And I believe her."

And she must have been right because Haltar hadn't felt this good in years.

"So, how did she do it?" he asked. "You said there was nothing to be done, but now... How?"

"I do not do as a doctor does," Khaila snapped. "She uses a machine, looks at the insides, and guesses what is wrong. Many times she is right. But this... it was like your body eating your own nerves. Tearing it apart."

"Yes, you're right, Khaila," Jyra said. "Drath Khor degeneration is an auto-immune disorder caused by—"

"Is not important now," Khaila said dismissively. "I feel damage in nerve, feel them tearing. I feel body attack itself. I teach body new way, not to attack, heal."

Jyra didn't look amused. "That doesn't work. Human nerve

regeneration is one of the oldest myths. Maybe over a few decades the body can recover somewhat, but nothing like what you're claiming."

"Oh? You never learn of Iccod shark? Or growing mantis? What about any lizard growing new leg? Animals do it all time. Humans just need push."

"She's right, Jyra," Haltar said. "It's not just the sharp pains that are gone. I was hurting in ways I can't describe. But now I feel like I could dance."

"Soon you will," Khaila said. "But something else. Something more inside. You find? Make you strong, long, long time. I promise."

"Well?" Haltar asked. "What is it inside me?"

Khaila gave him a strange little smile, got up and left.

He tried to sit up to call after her but couldn't. "Did you strap me down or something, Jyra?"

Jyra said, "No, you old fool. You won't be dancing anytime soon. You almost died, remember?"

"How could I forget?"

"The healer says that as bad as you were, it'll take a week before you can even walk yourself to the head. Even accounting for your miracle, I call it six months before you recover enough to live like a normal person."

Her expression turned serious a moment. "I don't care what she said about your recovery. The chances that you will return to duty are dubious at best, Haltar. Most people who recover from this live the rest of their lives as cripples."

"It's all right," he said. "I did more than most with what I had. If I'd passed here, my mantle was in safe hands." He looked over at the other two beds, where Manda and Dagon still lay. "Thought you only gave them a light relaxant."

"I did," she said with a wry look. "But then, I don't understand all this Psy stuff. I'm just an old-fashioned doctor with a million creds of machinery to help me. So whatever is keeping them asleep, I'm sure I'm not qualified to guess."

Haltar smiled. "I'm sure I don't know anything either," he lied.

———

Dagon sat up on the medbay bed. He was still in his uniform.

He looked at the bed next to him and watched as Manda sat up. She was also in uniform.

He looked at Haltar. He looked to be at peace for the first time in years.

"How is he?"

"He's the same old codger he's been for the past twenty years," Dowd said. "But he's going to make it. Everything I know tells me he could live at least twenty more, so I'd say he's doing fine."

"How long before he's up and around?" Manda asked.

"He'll be in here for at least a couple of weeks," Dowd replied. "After that, there will be months of recovery, and he may never return to duty. His body is exhausted. But the scanner shows no signs of nervous system spikes. I'm sure he'll be happy to see you when he wakes up. How do you feel?"

Manda glanced at Jax and said, "Fine, thank you."

Jax simply smiled and raised his eyebrows at the doctor.

"Please let us know when he wakes up," Manda said. "In the meantime, I'm starving. See you later, Doc." And she slipped off the bed and strode quickly from the room.

Dagon hadn't expected her abrupt exit, so he excused himself less obviously and jogged along the corridor to catch up to Manda. "Um, Commander, ma'am, about what—"

"I'm afraid you have to hold the question, Mister Jax," she said. "I have something I need to do first."

"But what if—"

Manda turned to face him, and he almost ran into her.

"Lieutenant," she snapped. "I believe you need to report to

the bridge for your shift in…" She checked her chron. "Ten minutes."

Her face softened, and she said, "I promise you, I'll answer your questions after your shift." She carded the elevator, the doors opened, and she stepped in, turned, looked at him, and winked just as the door closed, leaving him standing there, both confused and elated.

———

Captain Morian was standing on the bridge when Commander Haal stepped through the door onto the command deck.

"Permission to speak privately, sir?" she asked.

"Of course, Commander," he said. "Let's go to my ready room. I hope you have good news about Lieutenant Haltar."

"Yes, sir. Mostly good news," she replied. "The procedure was successful, and the healer says he should recover well, though Dr. Dowd says his recovery could take several months and that he may never be able to return to duty."

"He'll be sorely missed," Richard said, "but I'm pleased to hear he's doing well. Now, what can I do for you?"

She hesitated, looked him in the eye, opened her mouth to speak, then closed it again.

"Commander?" Morian said, frowning.

"Yes, sir." She took a deep breath and said, "I'm here to ask your opinion on a report of inter-rank fraternization."

The question took him by surprise. "Please explain, Commander."

"Between junior and senior officers in the same chain of command, sir."

Rules and regulations flitted through his mind; he pushed them aside, thinking, *Hmm. What's this about, I wonder? How can I object? I just gave my permission for an officer to consort with a member of the royal family.*

Inwardly he nodded to himself and said, "Commander, we've been at war now for more than four years and there's more to come, much more. Therefore, it's my opinion that we shouldn't begrudge people what happiness they can find. As long as it doesn't interfere with shipboard operations or crew morale, and as long as they don't showcase it needlessly, I don't see a problem." Again, he frowned, then continued, "Do you think they will cause a problem?"

"Well, sir, he's level-headed enough. But she can be a little lightheaded... sometimes."

He sighed. "Well, tell her to keep a lid on it. If she wants to take up with a senior officer, she needs to—"

"I'm sorry for the misunderstanding, sir," she said, interrupting him. "But *she* isn't the junior."

He stared at her, narrowed his eyes, then it clicked, "Oh!" was all he said.

"Permission to leave the ready room, sir?"

He nodded. She rose to her feet, snapped to attention and saluted.

Richard, smirking, returned her salute and said dryly, "Get out of here, Commander, and tell Lieutenant Jax to keep a lid on it."

"Aye, sir," she replied, then turned on her heel and left the room, the door closing softly behind her.

———

NINE HOURS LATER, Dagon Jax's shift ended, and he left the bridge and went to his quarters. He was in a... mixed kind of mood; one of those moods where he didn't know quite how he felt or what the next several hours might bring. So, when he stepped inside, he was totally unprepared for what he saw. And his jaw dropped in surprise.

Commander Haal was waiting for him, and she was wearing the same shimmering blue dress she wore in his dream world.

The one she'd worn that day when he realized just how beautiful she was.

"You seemed to like it," she said as the door whispered shut behind him. "So I thought you might enjoy a closer look."

"So... what happened... I mean, what happened?"

"That's a philosophical question," she replied. "But if you mean, did I choose to kiss you? Absolutely."

"And... the...?" he stammered.

"And all the other things, too," she said with a smile.

"But... but why?" he stuttered. "I'm half your age."

"You know, Dagon," she said. "I spent the hardest years of my life working to get where I am, and I don't regret any of it. Not for a single minute. Oh, I've had my chances, but I've never met a man that interests me the way you do. Dagon, you give and give. You give your loyalty to Richard, and the *Avenger*, and to Haltar, and apparently to me, too. You stood over me and protected me in battle. I've met some very brave men over the years, so I know; I know what you are, and I like it. As to your age... There's an old saying, its origins lost in the mists of time..." She looked him in the eye and said, "Age is just a number, Dagon."

He was struck speechless. All he could do was stare at her in wonder.

"Nothing to say?" she asked. "Very well. If I misread... If I'm not who you want, please, tell me now."

Dagon couldn't believe what he was hearing. "No!" he choked out. "I do want you. I don't want anybody but you, ever!"

"Good," she replied. "Because what happened in the dream doesn't really count. And, from now on, when we're alone, and only when we're alone, you can call me Manda." Then she stepped forward and kissed him again, for the first time.

EPILOGUE

Sovereign Incarceration Institution *Conquell*
Resdon Military Complex
Som Orsi City

Eugma Zettel was in his prison cell, again, seated on his cot, feet on the floor, head bowed, hands clasped together in front of him.

"I don't understand it," he mumbled to himself, the confines already driving him to the brink of... what? *Insanity?* "Everything was going so smoothly, just as I planned. The vision was coming true. I knew exactly what was supposed to happen."

He stopped and looked around. He didn't know if there were listening devices in his cell. How could he know? How could he find them?

"Bissette was the best of them. She always had the clearest visions. She told me everything she saw because she trusted me. She trusted me, and that's why she let me give her the—" He cut off. *Don't want to say anything incriminating, do I? Anyone could be listening.* He giggled at the thought.

Hmm, maybe I should be careful about what I'm thinking, too. This new helmet... I haven't been able to figure out its weaknesses yet, but I will, eventually... I suppose. But what if they have another Psy nearby, in the next cell, perhaps, or outside the door? They could be listening to everything I'm thinking... Oh, this is just too much.

He heard a noise coming from somewhere outside his cell. It sounded like screaming.

The door opened, and a man he'd never seen before stepped inside. He was slender, oh so slender, boyish, yet his facial features were old. He was certainly older than Eugma, and he looked cruel. No, that face spoke of terrible things, horrible things, and... pain.

"Only a month in this tiny cell, and they've already broken you," the man said.

"No, sir, no sir," Eugma said indignantly. "They've not broken me. I'm not broken, not broken at all. I can break out of here any time I choose."

"Then why haven't you done so?"

"Well, sir, if I did that, then they might hit me again and put me back. And I don't like being hit, sir. It hurts, you know?"

"Hah! They've sedated you." The man laughed. "Let me see if I can do something about that."

Suddenly Eugma could sense something happening beyond his helmet... The feeling of sublime euphoria wavered, then... something snapped, and suddenly he could feel again. Sparks flew from devices embedded in his cell wall.

"What did you do?" he demanded of the slender man.

"They have planted weaponized Psy machinery," the man said. "And in such a short time. I am impressed. It suppresses your thoughts, Doctor. Are you beginning to feel like your old self again?"

"Indeed, I do," Eugma said darkly. "Are you going to release me?"

"Of course I am," the man said. "Why would I waste my

time otherwise? Wasn't that the vision you killed people to hide? That you would be captured, freed by your captors, imprisoned again, and then freed once more?"

Eugma didn't ask how the man knew of his secrets; the fact that he knew was itself proof enough.

"But how?" Eugma asked. "If you are a Psy, then you know you can't break out of here. The walls of this cell, and the prison, are forged from dutrinium."

The man looked at the door, and it opened. They stepped into the hallway.

"What about my helmet?" Eugma asked. "Can you remove it? I wish to feel my full power again. It seems like this thing has been on my head for a lifetime."

"Patience, Doctor. In a few moments," the man assured him. "We have some new friends to meet first. Come, follow me. Oh, and by the way, this is Cheon, my associate."

Cheon was a huge burly man who, as far as Eugma could tell, didn't possess the gift of Psy.

And Eugma followed them through the maze of dimly lit catwalks of the ultimate Sovereign prison, as cell door after cell door opened as they walked past. The prisoners followed.

How could these two men overcome all of the prison's security measures? Conquell was, after all, supposed to be impregnable. Nobody, in the more than eighty years of its existence, had ever broken out. Now this?

And, as more and more violent criminals and sociopaths joined their motley pageantry, he began to wonder how this one man was able to control them all.

There were dead guards everywhere. Each of them lay motionless, and, as far as Eugma could see, they'd all died a bloodless death.

Then Eugma realized something. "I heard screaming back in my cell, but these people didn't scream, did they?"

"No," the slender man said with a wry smile. "The screams you heard were in their minds."

They left the prison and walked out in the night air. He looked up at the night sky. All was clear, not a cloud to be seen, just a vast starfield, twinkling, glittering, and for the first time in many a long year, Eugma felt at peace: at peace, but excited. It was happening.

The slender man stopped on top of a small hill, turned and raised his hand.

"Gather round," he said to the criminals who had followed them and then waited until they were still.

"You have all been invited by the One King to join us. We are Disorder, and we will topple this pitiful human government with the powers they parade as the solution to their ills. Those of you who would join us, accept now."

Eugma burned to strike back at the Sovereign Systems that had held him captive for so long. He and dozens more shouted, "We accept."

"And those who would leave? Go their own way? Speak now."

Though it sounded like a series of grumbles, there were perhaps a dozen of the one-time prisoners who refused to join.

"Very well," the slender man said.

And Eugma felt it. It was akin to a solar flare of Psy energy, and suddenly his arm burned. He screamed, and others screamed with him. His skin smoked and blackened, but the slender man just smiled, and those who'd refused to join watched in horror.

The searing pain subsided. Eugma looked down at his arm and saw ⚡⚡ branded into his flesh. It was at that moment Cheon stepped forward, reached down to touch the strap that held Eugma's hated helmet in place and, with a twist of his massive fingers, the strap snapped. On Cheon's arm was a single lightning bolt.

"As for those who refused to join us," the slender man said.

Eugma barely felt the stab of Psy that killed them. In the

blink of an eye, the life force of eleven men was snuffed out, and they fell to the ground, dead.

"I am called Rook," the man said, holding up his arm so that all could see he bore the twin lightning bolts upon his wrist. "I am not the only Rook. One of you may yet receive that honor, or perhaps an even greater honor. But now we must leave. Follow me."

It was but a short walk to the shuttle.

They boarded, settled in, and within minutes, they were in the air, streaking upward through the stratosphere, unfettered by the authorities.

Eugma smiled to himself as he looked out through the port and watched the ground fall away.

It was beginning. He could feel it. Soon he would ascend to heights he never could have imagined.

He would become a god.

Thank you for reading **The Enemy Within** the fourth book in the Sovereign Stars series. I hope you enjoyed it, if you did and would like to read more of the story book five, **Defector: Part 1: Imperator is available now.**

You can stay up to date about this series at www.blairhowardbooks.com.

**Do you enjoy Murder Mysteries?
Get Harry Starke Genesis Book One Free In
Digital Format!
Visit www.BlairHowardBooks.com**

ALSO FROM BLAIR C. HOWARD

Avenger
Gods of War
Armored Fleet
The Enemy Within
Defector: Part 1: Imperator

FROM BLAIR HOWARD

The Harry Starke Genesis Series
The Harry Starke Series
The Lt. Kate Gazzara Murder Files
Randall & Carver Mysteries
The Peacemaker Series
The Civil War Series

ABOUT THE AUTHOR
BLAIR C. HOWARD

Blair C. Howard is a Royal Air Force veteran, a retired journalist, and the best-selling author of more than 50 novels and 23 travel books. Fascinated by the heavens almost from childhood, and a sci SciFi fan for almost as long, he decided to try his hand at writing a military space opera. His first journey into this genre resulted in the Sovereign Stars series. Book 1 in the series, Avenger is followed by Gods of War and Armored Fleet.

Blair lives in East Tennessee with his wife Jo, and Jack Russell Terrier, Sally.

Visit www.blairhowardbooks.com

You can also find Blair Howard on Social Media

FROM BLAIR HOWARD

The Harry Starke Genesis Series

The Harry Starke Series

The Lt. Kate Gazzara Murder Files

Randall & Carver Mysteries

The Peacemaker Series

The Civil War Series

FROM BLAIR C. HOWARD

Avenger

Gods of War

Armored Fleet

The Enemy Within

Defector: Part 1: Imperator

www.ingramcontent.com/pod-product-compliance
Lightning Source LLC
Chambersburg PA
CBHW062105290726
48975CB00001B/119